Ace Collins has tackled just about every genre the book world offers, and now it looks like he's invented a new one. Christian/Action/ Adventure? Whatever it may be called, he's aced it and made it his own.

—Don Reid, author and member of the Statler Brothers

In true Ace Collins hang-onto-your-seat fashion, history and modern times overlap in this fast-paced story about a scroll that may belong to Joseph, Jesus' earthly father. Professor Jefferson Burke finds his life interrupted and turned upside-down when a mysterious historian from the Vatican asks for his help to unravel this secret. Readers will find themselves turning the pages into the wee hours, hooked by Collins' gripping and seamlessly plotted storyline.

—Suzanne Woods Fisher, bestselling author of
the Lancaster County Secrets series

Jefferson Burke and the Secret of the Lost Scroll is a roller-coaster ride of suspense, drama, and intrigue.

—Nora St. Laurent, founder of the Book Club Network
and ACFW Book Club Coordinator

Collins' high-stakes quest will give fans of *The Da Vinci Code* something new to consider.

—J. Alan Sharrer, books editor for Hollywood Jesus

What a wonderful story! Ace Collins gives readers everything they want in a book: high stakes, intriguing characters, nonstop action, and sitting-on-the-edge-of-your-seat suspense. I highly recommend *Jefferson Burke and the Secret of the Lost Scroll*.

—Amanda Cabot, author of *Tomorrow's Garden*

Ace Collins' literary tradition of producing work designed to uplift the human condition and promote justice appears safely carried forward in *Jefferson Burke and the Secret of the Lost Scroll*. Congratulations.

—Bob McGregor, district judge

Ace Collins has written an exciting and ultimately moving story about unexpected adventure and the meaning of life.
—Jeffrey R. Root, dean of the School of Humanities,
Ouachita Baptist University

Surprised me at every twist and turn. I was *so* deeply invested in Burke's challenging quest, at one point I had to walk away from the book for twenty minutes to decompress before continuing. The very divinity of Christ is put to the fiercest of tests as Collins brilliantly weaves in some of the major players and events facing our world today. Someone *must* make a movie out of this heroic adventure!
—Laurie Prange, actress

In *Jefferson Burke and the Secret of the Lost Scroll*, Ace Collins shakes the foundation of Christianity by combining elements of classic radio drama with modern-day events and technology to create an engrossing tale of suspense, action, and intrigue. A true spellbinder venturing far beyond *Raiders of the Lost Ark* and *The Da Vinci Code*.
—John Hillman, managing editor of
Lone Star Christian Sports Network

A fantastic combination of espionage, mystery, suspense, and romance. You'll be hooked from the very first sentence.
—Sierra Scott, news anchor and host of
It's All Good! on KSCW TV

JEFFERSON BURKE
AND THE SECRET OF THE
LOST SCROLL

OTHER BOOKS BY ACE COLLINS

FICTION

Farrady Road (A Lije Evans Mystery)

Swope's Ridge (A Lije Evans Mystery)

NONFICTION

*Turn Your Radio On: The Stories behind
Gospel Music's All-Time Greatest Songs*

The Cathedrals: The Story of America's Best-Loved Gospel Quartet

Stories behind the Best-Loved Songs of Christmas

Stories behind the Hymns That Inspire America

Stories behind the Great Traditions of Christmas

*I Saw Him in Your Eyes: Everyday People
Making Extraordinary Impact*

More Stories behind the Best-Loved Songs of Christmas

Stories behind the Traditions and Songs of Easter

Stories behind Women of Extraordinary Faith

Sticks and Stones: Using Your Words as a Positive Force

Stories behind Men of Faith

25 Days, 26 Ways to Make This Your Best Christmas Ever

Gratitude: Practicing Contagious Optimism for Positive Change

Stories behind the Greatest Hits of Christmas

ACE COLLINS

JEFFERSON BURKE
AND THE SECRET OF THE
LOST SCROLL

ZONDERVAN®

ZONDERVAN.com/
AUTHORTRACKER
follow your favorite authors

We want to hear from you. Please send your comments about this book to us in care of zreview@zondervan.com. Thank you.

ZONDERVAN

Jefferson Burke and the Secret of the Lost Scroll
Copyright © 2011 by Andrew Collins

This title is also available as a Zondervan ebook.
Visit www.zondervan.com/ebooks.

This title is also available in a Zondervan audio edition.
Visit www.zondervan.fm.

Requests for information should be addressed to:
Zondervan, *Grand Rapids, Michigan 49530*

Library of Congress Cataloging-in-Publication Data

Collins, Ace.
    Jefferson Burke and the secret of the lost scroll / Ace Collins.
        p.   cm.
    ISBN 978-0-310-27954-9 (softcover)
    1. History teachers—Fiction 2. Joseph, Saint—Manuscripts—Fiction.
    3. Bible. Manuscripts—Fiction. 4. Jesus Christ—Divinity—Fiction. I. Title.
    PS3553.O47475J44—2011
    813'.54—dc22   2011006398

Cover design: Curt Diepenhorst
Cover illustration: Aleta Rafton
Interior design: Michelle Espinoza

Printed in the United States of America

11 12 13 14 15 16 /DCI/ 23 22 21 20 19 18 17 16 15 14 13 12 11 10 9 8 7 6 5 4 3 2 1

To Carole Lombard,
who brought great joy while she lived
and died serving her country

CONTENTS

DEATH

Baltore the priest had no idea where they had come from. Like ghosts, they seemed to appear out of thin air, but he was well aware that his plight was of his own making. He should have stopped at the inn two miles back. That would have been the logical choice for a man traveling alone. As he dug his heels into his mount, he cursed himself for not being more careful. If he had listened to reason, he'd be safely sharing a meal with a few Roman citizens rather than riding into the face of a cold March wind, fleeing a trio of bandits. Alas, listening to others had never been his strong suit. He always had to do things his way. His mother had told him time and time again that his muleheadedness would lead to his destruction. Now it appeared she was right.

The horse Baltore rode was gentle and trustworthy, but hardly fast. It didn't gallop as much as it lumbered along the dusty trail. He knew that almost anyone pursuing him would be riding steeds faster than his. So, if he had no chance to either outwit or outrun them, why was he urging his horse to go faster? Why didn't he just pull to a stop, dismount, and give up? After all, the chase would not last long, and the culmination of this adventure would be no different if it ended now or five minutes into the future. Yet, as if driven by the hounds of hell, Baltore raced toward the coming night alternately reviling himself for his stupidity and praying for a miracle he knew he didn't deserve.

In the dwindling light, neither Baltore nor the aging horse saw the hole, but the rider felt it. At a full gallop, he had no time to adjust. The gray animal stumbled and tried in vain to regain his footing. Baltore was torn from his saddle and tossed headfirst into a dense thicket. The branches cushioned his fall, but the thorns tore at his skin. Blood oozed from scores of scratches on his arms and cheeks as he awkwardly rolled to his feet. He could hear the bandits. They were still a hundred yards behind him but closing fast. Maybe he had time to remount! Maybe they hadn't seen him fall! Maybe ... then the horrible reality flooded his mind. His horse had collapsed on the far side of the road. The ride was over and so was the chase.

As the specter of death approached, he realized he still had one more holy mission to accomplish. Ignoring the pain, he raced to the dead animal as fast as his short, thick legs could carry him. Pushing aside the flowing sleeves of his clerical robe, the stocky man reached for the leather bag attached to his saddle. But before he could grab it, an arrow pierced his left hand. Time had run out.

In shock, Baltore studied his hand. The arrow had stopped after traveling six inches through his palm. Like him, it was stuck in limbo — not moving. Blood filled his palm. The projectile's tip seemed to mock him, urging him to yell, to scream. Yet though he knew he should be in pain, he wasn't. It was as if he had fallen into a trance with his focal point the arrow. He felt numb, so numb that he barely heard the voices shouting or noted the black-clad trio dismount.

Baltore's world, which just a few seconds before had been consumed by a race down a forest trail, was suddenly void of chaos. There was no mission, no enemy to run from or confront, no yesterday or tomorrow. There was just now. And in the now, nothing mattered except how to deal with this unexpected injury.

A thousand voices spoke to him, and an equal number of questions were tossed his way. Should he pull it out? If he broke it in half, would that make it easier to remove? Would it hurt less just to leave it in? He kept his gaze on his hand until he was grabbed by the shoulder and spun around to face the three marauders. Suddenly he again was a part of the real world. He felt an intense pain.

Like a wounded child looking for compassion, Baltore held his hand out toward the men. The shortest one grinned, grabbed the shaft at the fletching, and yanked the barbed iron tip back through the wounded hand, retracng its path. Baltore's cries filled the woods. Yet no one, except the three men who seemed intent on tormenting him, was there to hear. The injured man's tears rolled down his cheeks and fell to the ground.

"Where is it?" the short one demanded as he stuffed the bloody arrow into his belt.

Baltore feebly shook his head. It wasn't the answer the man wanted. A large fist met the friar's chin, dislodging three teeth and knocking him back into a tree. As he spat, Baltore moaned, "I'm a poor priest. I have nothing of value."

The words had barely cleared his mouth when the final rays of sunlight caught a flash of metal. A second later a sword, obviously handled by a master, sliced off his left earlobe, and the trio laughed. Blood dripped from this new injury.

"We can take you apart piece by piece," the tallest bandit announced in an almost merry tone. "We can make it easy for the birds to dine on a meal of heavenly delight. You see, we know you're a priest. We don't care. Killing a king, a peasant, or a man of the cloth, it's all the same to us. If you value your life, give us what we want."

"But I beg you," Baltore began, his bleeding hand extending forward.

"Don't beg, priest." The leader's words cut the air with the same authority as his sword. "We know what you have. You can give it to us and keep what's left of your fleshy body."

He allowed Baltore to digest that thought before adding, "Or we can simply take it from you after we kill you. It's up to you. How soon do you want to meet your God?"

Baltore glanced back at his dead horse. With that one look, he gave away the only secret he had left. He now had no bargaining chips. No longer was his life worth even a grain of salt.

"Grab the bag," the tall man ordered. The widest of the three, his black hair creeping out from under a metal helmet, waddled toward the horse and cut the rope binding the bag to the saddle, then tossed the pouch to the band's leader.

"Your pope made this far too easy," the tall one said as he glanced into the pouch. "Yes, much too easy for us, but not so easy for you."

"Why do you want that?" Baltore demanded, his voice filled with passion. "It's nothing but an old document written in a language you wouldn't understand."

The tall man produced a grin that cut as sharply as a knife. "My name is Thomas ... Thomas of Myra. I've studied Aramaic, Hebrew, and Greek. I can read seven different languages. I once spent three years in the great library in Alexandria. I've traveled to places you have never heard of and have met men you revere as legends. In fact, I probably know His Holiness as well as you, though the pope doesn't really know me at all. He doesn't know my potential or my ultimate goal. He knows nothing of my methods. I know what this is. I also know why you have it and what you intend to do with it."

The man pulled a scroll from the pouch. He unrolled a bit of the ancient thin leather on which the words had been penned and held it up to catch the last of the fading light. After a few moments of study, he returned it to the bag.

"Baltore," he said. The priest looked up. "Yes, I know your name. I've been following you for months waiting for this moment."

The priest was so amazed by this revelation, he forgot about his pain. Why hadn't he seen these men? How had he not known they were there? He had been so careful. Or at least he thought he had. Maybe one of the monks had given him up. No, that couldn't be.

"Baltore. Wake up!"

The priest looked back at the tall man.

"Have you read what is written here?" the mysterious man asked.

Baltore had been ordered not to, but the temptation had been too great. What good would lying do now? He nodded.

"Did it frighten you?"

"No," Baltore replied.

The tall man grinned. "Why do you suppose these words so frighten the church's leaders?"

Baltore shrugged. His vows ordered him to serve the church, not to question the motives of the men who led it. Hence, they thought and he acted. It had never dawned on him to actually consider their motives.

"It is about power," the tall man, the one whose name was

Thomas, explained. "In this scroll is the power to control not just men but governments. This paper rewrites history, and there are many who don't want it to be rewritten. But I do. Baltore, I will rewrite history, at least my own history. And I can do so with what you have so generously given to me. Sadly, you won't be around to see my rise. As a moral man, I doubt you would enjoy what I will become, but I believe, as a historian, that if this scroll contains what legend says it contains, you would find it fascinating."

The man walked toward his horse and glanced back at his confederates. "Kill him."

If the order shocked them, the men's faces didn't reveal it. The response was swift and sure.

Baltore never saw the sword coming, but he felt it as it sliced into his belly. A second later it slid out of his body as easily as it had entered. The wounded hand no longer bothered him. Nor did the ear. Nothing bothered him. He fell to his knees. As his eyelids closed, the last thing he saw was the blood seeping through his red robe.

The glint of morning sunlight filtering through the naked branches of the trees brought Baltore to his senses. At least that's what he later told his brother. As he lay on the ground peering up at the yellow beams, he wondered where he was. Heaven? Surely not, the air was too cold. But if not heaven, then where? He remembered the flash of the sword, his own murder. He was sure of that. In fact, it had happened right here, on this trail. So if this was death, it was nothing like he expected. What next?

Sucking in a deep breath, Baltore felt air rush into his lungs. He was alive! Everything must have been a dream. That was it, a nightmare. He remembered he had fallen off his horse. He probably had hit his head and imagined it all. Yes, it was a dream, a warning from God.

Suddenly, panic set in. He had wasted too much time. He had an important mission, and he had to move on. He tried to get up off the ground, but the sharp pain proved that what had happened on the trail had been no dream. Moving his hand in front of his face, he saw that a bandage had been carefully wrapped around his wound. He struggled to his knees and looked down, touched where the sword had sliced his belly. That too had been dressed.

"God in heaven!"

Now seized by a sense of fear and confusion, Baltore painfully staggered to his feet. He saw he wasn't alone. Two of the bandits had not left. They were as still as the rocks along the road—dead!

Baltore looked all around. There was no one else. He heard the chirping of birds. A horse was tied to a far tree. It looked like one the bandits had been riding. The priest's leather pouch, the one the bandit had taken, was carefully bound to the saddle.

Baltore made the sign of the cross, then painfully walked to the animal and untied the reins. He pulled himself up into the saddle and headed east. He didn't look back, even once.

As the priest rode away, the lone living member of the trio moved out from the shadows. He stepped over one of the bodies and took a final look around. Then he slipped back into the woods and mounted his horse. He rode off into the west.

History would never reveal who he was or why he chose to spare the priest.

TOO BUSY

Dr. Burke? Dr. Burke?"
More than a bit miffed at having his research interrupted, the thirty-five-year-old man grudgingly pulled his nose from a dusty, century-old book detailing the British assault on Bunker Hill. Ignoring the muffled activities of several students and members of the university library staff, the history professor, who had once run pass patterns on the Illini's football team but whose sprints were now reduced to chasing students who had left their iPads in his classroom, removed his reading glasses, set them on the table, and looked up at a slightly built man at least twice his age. He nodded.

"You are Dr. Burke?" the visitor asked.

Noting the man's laced-up boots, collarless white shirt, and dark suit, Dr. Jefferson Burke said, "You're not from around here, are you?"

"Italy," came the reply.

The words had little more than passed his lips when an elderly woman sorting books about ten feet away from the men put her finger to her lips and shushed the visitor. The stranger meekly smiled before glancing back at Burke, and this time, in almost a whisper, said, "Can we go somewhere to talk?"

"My office hours don't begin until two, and I have a class that meets in twenty minutes. Emma at the front desk can make an appointment for you."

"It can't wait!" The visitor's posture was almost beggar-like, his urgent tone and nervous body language saying even more than his words. "This really is a matter of life and death!"

The man was frantic, and though he despised doing it, Burke gave in. Nodding, he yanked his athletic form from the wooden chair, picked up the book and his glasses, slipping the latter into his brown tweed jacket, and signaled for the visitor to follow him. Throughout the huge room, a dozen pairs of curious eyes watched the men wind through the maze-like wooden bookcases to a large imposing door on the far south side of the room. Etched boldly into the frosted glass were the words "Dr. Jefferson H. Burke, Dean of the School of History." Turning to take a quick inventory of the man who had disturbed him, the professor twisted the brass knob on the ancient door. He flipped on the overhead light, stood aside, and signaled for the man to enter. The professor removed his tweed jacket, tossed it on top of a file cabinet, and moved behind a large walnut desk covered with stacks of books.

"Have a seat, ah ... Mr...."

"The name is Antony Columbo."

"Mr. Columbo," Burke said, his tone as flat as the Illinois landscape barely visible through a far window. "What brings you to Urbana?"

Columbo smiled, removed his hat, and plopped down in the only chair not being used as a platform for books. Burke picked up a stack of files and, after dropping them on the floor, lit on a corner of his desk.

"Dr. Burke—" the little man began before catching himself. "First I need to begin by asking you this question: What do you know about the biblical Joseph, the husband of Mary?"

"Not my department," Burke barked, annoyed that he had stopped his research for a question like this. "You need Briggs in the school of divinity. I'll draw you a map to get you there."

"Actually," Columbo said, his voice again urgent, "I need *you*."

"No, you don't!" came the terse reply. "I'm not a student of the Bible. The little I do know pretty much came from Sunday school lessons a lifetime ago. I teach American history. You've got the wrong man."

"Maybe I need to give you a bit more background on myself."

"Mr. Columbo." Burke's tone revealed the sharp edge of a man who had lost his patience. "I don't care if you're the pope, the ghost of Martin Luther, or even Billy Graham. I'm covered up with work. I simply don't have time to breathe, much less answer questions about things of which I'm only vaguely aware. Dr. Alexander Briggs is your man."

With a wave of a hand, Columbo stopped Burke before the professor could reach over and lift him out of the chair. "I'm not the pope, but I am a historian for the Vatican. I'm here on a matter of the greatest importance. You're the person I need to see, I can assure you of that. Here's my identification."

The professor eased back onto the desk, cocked his head, and studied the papers. "This changes nothing. Briggs is the expert on this stuff. I'll give him a call." He pushed the identification back to Columbo.

Grabbing his ID, now impassioned and a bit panicky, Columbo yelled, "He cannot help me! Only you can get me what I need."

FRUSTRATION

Columbo didn't move. He wouldn't leave.

"So tell me what you need me for," Burke said.

Columbo licked his lips, then said, "What I am going to tell you is one of the world's oldest and best-kept historical facts. It is known by only a handful of men in the Vatican."

Maybe it was because a cloud was crossing in front of the morning sun, but suddenly Columbo seemed to age, the color seemed drained from his face, and his dark eyes lost a bit of their shine. It was almost as if he had seen a ghost. He even trembled a bit. "Very little is written in the Bible about Joseph, the man who raised Jesus. Did you know his death is not even mentioned?"

"Seems to me the New Testament's pretty lean," Burke shot back. "Not much fat in the writing concerning Christ's life. They glossed over the first three decades. It's likely Joseph died during that period, and the writers didn't consider it to be significant."

"Maybe," the little man said, "but what if Joseph didn't die then? What if he was alive when Christ was crucified? What if he was there at Calvary?"

Burke saw this as a tactic students used to throw him off course during lectures — pose questions that had no substantive answers, hoping to kill time and avoid quizzes. That was all right for an eighteen-year-old kid who hadn't done his homework, but the professor expected better of a historian from the Vatican. If that's who he really *was*, and now Burke was beginning to doubt it.

He glanced at the clock on the far wall. "Your time is about up. So if you have a point, make it."

"Do you know how the books we call the Bible were chosen?"

Burke took a deep breath. He had to get rid of the man, get to class. Then, hoping to move things along, he said, "I remember reading about councils that decided what to keep and what to toss out. But what does this have to do with me?"

"It has to do with one of those books," the man from the Vatican said. "Many years ago I was going through ancient papers in the Vatican library. Some papers I uncovered both fascinated and frightened me. In the diaries of four different popes, I found several early references to a reliable firsthand view of Jesus' life, including the time before his ministry—his youth, his time with Mary and Joseph. The document these popes were referring to was not just omitted from the Bible, it was kept secret."

A secret scroll? Burke leaned forward, suddenly curious.

"The diaries each said that the book, or scroll, was written by Joseph. The materials I found were sketchy on details. But something in that document is so explosive that those early church leaders pretended it didn't exist."

"They hid it?"

"Yes. Though it scared them, those early leaders couldn't bear to destroy anything tied to Christ's life, no matter how controversial. In fact, the records I found indicated that a scribe named Simon, on orders from an early church leader, painstakingly created three additional copies of the scroll. By the third century, one had been taken to Constantinople, another was in Rome, and the third was placed in a church vault in Jerusalem. The original was kept in a mountain monastery in what is now Afghanistan."

Burke glanced at his watch again. "Are you about to wrap this up?"

"Only a few more minutes."

Was this story worth the wait? Burke's gut told him no, but his curiosity begged him to hear his visitor out. It was time for his freshman early American history class. Picking up his phone, the professor waited for Emma Street to answer. "Emma, would you go to room 312 and tell my class I'm tied up. Suggest they have a walk."

He looked back at his guest. "Did you ever find a copy of this hushed-up book?"

Columbo shook his head. "The archives were clear as to what happened to them. The copy in Constantinople burned in a fire in 411 BC. In 751, Pope Stephen II decided that the original and the two copies were far too dangerous to keep, and he ordered them to be destroyed as well. He assigned the task to one of his aides, a priest and historian named Baltore of France. While he was highly trusted by Vatican officials, this choice proved to be anything but wise.

"In 752, Baltore removed one copy from its hiding place in Rome and, after burning it, traveled to Jerusalem. With the pope's orders and official seal, he gained entrance to a vault beneath the church and retrieved that copy and destroyed it as well. He then booked passage to the monastery in Afghanistan. It took him four months to convince the monks to give him the original scroll. For reasons known only to him, he didn't burn the original. Sometime in 753 he began his trip back to his office in a church outside of Paris."

Columbo closed his eyes for a few moments, then took a deep breath. The sun again flooded the room, the cloud having moved on, and the visitor's color seemed to return. The old man's eyes once more locked onto his host.

"When it came time to destroy the original document, Baltore could not bring himself to complete his assignment. After all, this was a piece of church history, and he was a historian and a priest. When he died in 791, his brother was given the scroll."

Now fully sucked in, Burke asked, "How did the Vatican know Baltore hadn't destroyed the original along with the copies?"

"Actually, they didn't," Columbo said. "In fact, they assumed he had. It was more than six hundred years before any news of that original scroll surfaced. While returning to England, a knight stopped at the home of a French farmer named Philippe Baltore. After a bit of ale and some food, Philippe told the story of the relic and even showed his guest the scroll. Because neither man could read Aramaic, they could only guess what was written there."

"And this was the actual scroll supposedly written by the father, or the stepfather, of Jesus?" Burke asked.

"Yes. I believe it was. And because of that knight's visit and his later confession to a priest, the Vatican found out about its existence and where it had been kept for the previous six hundred years. Upon hearing of the news years later, Pope Paul II sent a part of his guard to retrieve that document, but before they arrived, Philippe had sold his farm and moved. For more than sixty years, they searched throughout France for the man but never found any trace of him. Hence, the *Book of Joseph* was again lost and would remain out of sight until 1530, when it turned up in England."

"So," Burke said, "Philippe Baltore had moved to the British Isles."

"Yes, and if you know your English history as well as you do your American history, you can put together why it was impossible for the Vatican to obtain it during that period."

Burke did know. In 1530, Henry VIII was in the process of separating the English church from Rome. He never would have allowed an army from the Vatican access to his realm. Thus, there was no way any pope could have recovered the scroll. The Catholics were on the outside looking in. "Did Henry know about the document?" he asked.

Columbo nodded. "He knew that one of his subjects, a blacksmith named John Green, had a scroll that had been passed down for hundreds of years from family member to family member, and that the Vatican wanted it. Essentially King Henry didn't care what was on that document, only that it might bring him a measure of power in his discussions with the pope. Thus, he seized it and tried to use it as a bargaining chip."

Burke smiled. "I'm guessing that even the *Book of Joseph* didn't buy Henry what he wanted."

Columbo shook his head. "It was a temptation almost too strong for even the pope to resist. If he had accepted it, the church would likely not have split. Yet ultimately the pope could not see clear to grant Henry his divorce from Catherine, and thus the Vatican didn't regain control of the *Book of Joseph*. Henry put the scroll in his vault and forgot about it. It was only when Oliver Cromwell overthrew the English crown that the manuscript again came back into play."

To the professor, Cromwell's interest in the document made perfect sense. Cromwell's uncle had once been a trusted adviser to King Henry.

"So his uncle," Burke said, "passed down the story of the scroll."

Columbo shook his head. "Actually Oliver Cromwell learned the information from his mother. She had no idea what was written on the leather scroll, only that it seemed to have some value to the Catholic Church, a group that the noted Puritan had even less use for than Henry did. As leader of England, Cromwell vowed to have it translated, but his short reign offered him little time for such pursuits. When he was tossed out of office, one of his aides, George Temple, took the scroll. Supposedly he crafted a special container to hold the document. He kept it until his death, when it was passed on to his son, and so forth."

"So," Burke said, leaning forward with anticipation, "the Temple clan still has the document?"

"I wish it were that easy. Atkins Temple was a bachelor with no children. In 1774, he was living in Berkshire, England. Evidently an unsavory sort, he was arrested for murdering a local judge at a pub. Temple was hung and his estate was sold at auction. And that's what brings me to you."

CONFUSION

Mr. Columbo, why come to a university history teacher living on the plains of Illinois to find a document sold in England more than two centuries ago?"

"Because," Columbo replied, "in 1940, the Roman Catholic Church got to the house of records in Berkshire a few months too late. The civil and criminal papers of the city, like many important documents in England, had already been transported to the United States for safekeeping until World War II was over. After the war, the official papers were returned to England. One small crate was not returned. It was somehow lost. It was the one with the report of who bought the *Book of Joseph* at auction. I spent a year looking through those old papers and all the records of the transfer of those documents, both to the United States and back to the UK. The papers outlining the auction of Atkins Temple's possessions did not make it back to England after the war. They were in the lost crate."

"And no one noticed?"

"Why should they worry?" Columbo said. "That crate contained old auction documents. To them, the tax and property records were far more important."

"So why come to me?"

"The records were stored at the University of Illinois."

Burke rubbed his chin and leaned in a bit closer. "You think it might still be here at the U of I?"

"That's what I'm hoping," Columbo said. "When I called the administration office, they told me you are the trustee of the facility where the box might have been left. I need to get into that warehouse. I need to discover the whereabouts of the *Book of Joseph*."

Custodian of the records? That was a complete surprise to Burke. When did that happen? Where was this building? He picked up his phone.

"Emma, can you connect me with Dr. Patterson's office?"

The professor glanced back at Columbo as he waited. His story was intriguing, fascinating in a way, but surely the mystery couldn't play into the stability of today's world.

"Pete," Burke said, turning back to the phone, "what's this about my being the trustee of a bunch of stored documents?"

He listened. "I see. Yeah, I'll find the memo, read the rules, and pick up the key later today."

Putting the receiver back in the cradle, Burke crossed his arms and looked back toward his guest. "It looks like I was given those responsibilities two months ago when Dr. Creegle retired. It seems they informed me via inter-office mail. It must be in that batch of unopened stuff sitting in that chair by the wall." He looked at the pile. "Probably two feet down, would be my guess."

"So, you will take me to see the records?"

"No." Burke walked back to the corner of his desk. "The basic rules were just explained to me. It seems, because of the way the insurance is set up, I'm the only one allowed in there. Anyway, why the rush? This thing's been out of sight and mind for hundreds of years. What's a few more?"

Columbo stood up and straightened his black suit coat. "Have you ever heard of Dr. Bruno Krueger?"

He had. Krueger was a South American oil billionaire who kept a dozen ancient history experts on his payroll. He'd found four different tomb sites in Egypt and claimed to know the whereabouts of Noah's ark.

"I met Krueger about ten years ago in New York," Burke said. "The other time was when I arrived late at a South American dig. Didn't much care for his methods or his conclusions. I still have a scar on my leg where an anaconda bit me on that trip."

The snake had done more than that. It had grabbed him as he and his team of interns waded across a stream. It had almost squeezed the life out of him. Burke had finally severed the snake's spine with his grandfather's bowie knife.

"There is a connection to the scroll," the visitor said. "During the early days of World War II, a German spy based in Rome discovered the same information I found on the scroll just weeks before those documents were boxed and shipped here. That spy relayed his findings to Krueger's grandfather, who was a close aide to Hitler. I know that Hitler himself was interested in discovering and translating the document."

"Why?"

"Hitler felt he could use the document to blackmail the Vatican. If he kept it under wraps, then the Vatican would remain neutral during the war. I believe Hitler, who studied the occult, figured the document, if real, might have some special mystical powers as well."

Burke shook his head. "And how does a historian from the Vatican know all this?"

"The Vatican has had a very effective network of espionage agents for a lot longer than either Great Britain or America has had an organized government."

As Burke considered the ramifications of the spying capabilities of the Roman Catholic Church, he also tried to wrap his mind around why the Nazis would have been interested in the ancient scroll.

"Do you know what role faith played in World War II?" Columbo asked.

"What do you mean?"

"I believe," the older man said, "that a large part of the drive to beat the Axis Powers was based on faith. Your leaders and your clergymen, as well as those all across the free world, framed that war as a struggle of good against evil, right versus wrong. How many times have you heard someone say, 'God is on our side'? In World War II, if this was the case, then Hitler must have been in league with the devil. And I believe if you study the book of Revelation and realize that one of the pagan Greek altars was rebuilt in Germany and served as the model for an altar built for Hitler to use in his speeches, that fact rings home to those who believe."

"You mean the Pergamon Altar?" Burke cut in.

Columbo nodded, then, using the index finger of his right hand, waving it like a preacher delivering a sermon, he pushed forward. "It is much easier to get men to fight and die in a war if they believe they are doing God's will. You see, while the Hawaiian Islands might have been attacked, no one in power at the time actually believed the Japanese or Germans would invade this nation. So, unlike in England, where people saw bombs falling on London every night and were fighting a war for the survival of their country, where life, death, and war were so very real and known by all ages, in the United States, war was seen as a faraway crusade. Americans viewed themselves as the noble people out to impose God's will on the world more than protecting their own shores."

Burke considered the theory. It seemed sound. Even during World War II, most Americans actually felt pretty secure. Many had even argued that the war in Europe was one we should have avoided when we declared war on Japan. And there was no doubt the war was sold as one where God was on the side of the red, white, and blue.

"During your research, did you find anything that pointed to this ancient scroll being something other than a tool for blackmail?"

Columbo shook his head. "No. But when I discovered that Hitler was interested, I began to believe that my theory on the power of the scroll was correct."

"What's that?" Burke asked. "Surely Hitler wasn't going to claim that Joseph was the world's founding member of the Aryan race. After all, wasn't Joseph a Jew?"

As if trying to keep his heart from jumping out of his body, the little man folded his arms tightly across his chest. For several minutes, the sole sound in the room was the ticking of the wall clock. It was as if Columbo was struggling with a huge moral decision. When finally he began speaking, it was in tones so hushed Burke had to lean closer to hear the words.

"I hesitate to even speak it out loud," Columbo said just above a whisper. "Up until this moment, I have told only the pope." He paused and took a deep breath. "I hope I'm wrong. There is only one reason I can fathom for the early church not to include this important man's words in the Bible. And for Hitler to spend valuable resources during World War II to get his hands on it, he must have learned that secret."

"What secret can be that powerful?" Burke asked.

"I'm afraid that the scroll might erase the divine element from Jesus' birth. I fear that Joseph may have written that he was ... the actual father of Jesus."

BOMBSHELL

Burke walked over to the window and considered Columbo's words. Was Joseph ... Joseph the carpenter ... really Jesus' father? That news would certainly set off explosions in the worlds of history and religion. And politics. It could change the way the whole course of history is viewed. This was pretty salty stuff.

"Professor Burke." On hearing Columbo's quiet voice, the professor turned his gaze back to his visitor. "If you were to find the scroll and if it was proven to your satisfaction to be authentic, what would you do?"

Burke's answer was simple. "I'd have it translated and published. History would demand it."

Columbo appeared upset.

"Don't you agree?" Burke asked.

"No. I'd burn it."

"But if the divinity of Christ were proven to be a lie—"

Columbo didn't let Burke finish. "Think of what that news would do to the world!"

"But—"

"If Jesus is *not* divine," Columbo said, "then for many, the church is no longer about faith, but philosophy. You see, if Jesus was just a human, then many would not believe there is a heaven. They would not believe in salvation. Millions would likely even cease praying. So much of how we live is based on Jesus as God."

As a historian, Burke knew that no man had affected the course of human history as Jesus Christ had. Jesus was able to impact the world in such a major way only because of his claim to divinity. If there now was a document calling into question the story of his birth, then how many would still believe in his resurrection? Within a few decades, Christianity might become a dying religion.

"It is my belief," Columbo said, "that if Krueger gets his hands on the scroll his grandfather and Hitler wanted so badly, and if it contains the information I fear it contains, then he will use it to threaten the church, to control church leaders, not for anything that is good. Because if he were to make that knowledge public, it would have a profound effect on the world."

"That's a pretty chilling theory," Burke replied.

Columbo shrugged. "If the moral fiber of the world were to be torn asunder, if the very foundation of the world's most compassionate figure were revealed to be a myth, then what is life really about? The meek won't inherit the earth. The mighty will rule. The slave will live and die a slave, and there will be no salvation to break away from those chains in the afterlife. So now you see why I have to find that book and destroy it."

Burke turned back to the window. In the distance, he noted a steeple. In that church, men and women pray for their loved ones. They ask the son of a carpenter to protect them. Jesus gives them hope. It is a scene repeated all over the country, all over the world. What if that hope suddenly was taken away? What if it could be proven that Jesus Christ was merely the son of Joseph the carpenter, not the Son of God? Would those who pray cease to pray? Would they lose their spiritual anchor? Would they no longer believe in God? Would they turn to another religion, another faith, or just walk away from faith altogether?

The professor whirled around. "What if you're wrong? What if the scroll proves that Jesus *is* the Son of God? What if it reveals the words of a man, Joseph, overcome with joy at being chosen to raise the Son of God? Have you ever considered that? Then the scroll would add to the validity of your faith."

Columbo managed a grim smile. "I pray for that, but think for a moment . . . why would the church want to destroy the *Book of Joseph* if the news was not damning? What if I'm right and Krueger gets to it before I do? What if he makes that story public? It would dramatically change the world!"

The little man allowed his words to linger for a few moments. "You are a man who has proven on other historical missions, even in dangerous remote jungles, that you won't give up. You won't back down. Krueger has a head start. He has his grandfather's diaries. I need your help to catch up. Will you let me into that warehouse?"

Burke turned back toward the window. He might well have the key to the story of a lifetime in his hands. Now, what should he do with that key?

"No," the professor replied, "you can't go in, but I'll share with you whatever I find. You have my word on that. Where are you staying?"

"I haven't checked into a motel yet."

Burke opened a desk drawer and pulled out a key. "My place is at 2317 Cedar Street in Urbana. The guest room is to the right off the living room. Get some sleep. You look like you need it. I've got a full day ahead of me, a dinner tonight, but after that, I'll make the trek over to Bruce Hall. If there is something there, I'll find it and bring it back to the house for you to study."

"I couldn't accept your hospitality. I would be taking advantage—"

Pressing the key into the old man's hand, Burke smiled for the first time. "You can and you will. Here's my business card. It has my home address and cell-phone number. Call me if you need anything. I need to go get a key to a building and see what I can find."

CURIOSITY

C uriosity is not a gift so much as it is a curse. Curiosity steals focus. It challenges patience and upsets emotions and plans. Jeff Burke knew this better than most. It was curiosity that drove his life, and it had almost ruined it more times than he could count. Curiosity about what the world looked like from the top of his grandfather's oak tree had given him a broken leg. Curiosity about the nature of wild bears left him with deep scars on his back. Curiosity about why a president had made a certain decision had placed him on an FBI watch list for a while. Try as he could to resist, curiosity drove him to places he simply would have been better off not visiting.

Thus, with Columbo's words still ringing in his ears, it had been almost impossible for Burke to concentrate on a full day of classes or his mandatory appearance at a fundraising dinner. It was well past eight when he finally was able to steal away.

Bruce Hall had once been the home of the history department. Constructed in 1898, it was a two-story rectangular red-brick building fifty feet wide and seventy feet long. Burke knew enough about campus history to remember that the old structure had not hosted a class of any kind since the 1930s. He'd learned today that sometime in the days just before World War II, it had become a warehouse and was filled with old desks, files, and books that had accumulated over time. Because it served no function except as a reservoir for relics of the past, it likely would have been torn down decades ago if it had been on the main part of campus. Instead, time had seen it surrounded by barns from the agricultural department. It was not just out of sight but also out of mind.

Stepping from his SUV, Burke felt as if he had stepped back into another century. Five wide concrete steps led to the large warped double-door entry. Like the windows on the sides of the building, the wooden doors' glass had been boarded over.

There were no security lights around Bruce Hall, and Burke didn't have a flashlight, but luck was shining on him in the form of a full moon that offered enough illumination to make his way up the steps and find the lock. Pushing the key in, he attempted to turn it to the right. The lock didn't budge. Silently cursing himself for coming so unprepared, Burke stepped back and studied the unforgiving entry. Even in the moonlight, he could see the rust and dirt that had invaded the decades-old lock. He'd always been able to find a way around problems in his treks to historical sites; surely he could come up with something in the middle of the Illinois plains.

Glancing back at his SUV, the professor made a quick mental inventory of what was in the Escape. There were at least six empty coffee cups, a dozen empty Coke cans, who knows how many textbooks, and a set of jumper cables. What wasn't there was a flashlight or a can of WD-40.

Frustrated, Burke stepped quickly down the steps, opened the door of the SUV, slid into the seat, and started the car. He had just slammed the transmission into reverse when inspiration hit. Slipping the lever back into park, he pulled the hood release, jumped out of the vehicle, and opened the hood. After twisting the oil cap from the V-6 motor, he returned to the driver's seat and revved the engine for about twenty seconds. Shutting off the ignition, he grabbed an empty coffee cup from the floor and an unused straw from the console. Moving back to the front of the Escape, he used his fingers to push oil that had spewed from the uncapped motor onto the block into the cup. When he had covered the bottom of the cup, he replaced the oil cap, lowered the hood, and returned to the building.

Pulling the key to the door from his pocket, Burke dipped it in the oil. He then sucked a bit of the black liquid into the straw. Putting the straw up to the lock, he blew through the straw, forcing oil into the small opening. Tossing the cup and straw to the side, the professor reinserted the key. This time it gave a little when he twisted it to the right. Keeping constant, steady pressure but being careful not to twist too hard, he felt the latch begin to give. Slowly, millimeter by millimeter, the key made the short journey to the right. When it hit what would have been three on the dial of a clock, the latch clicked.

Burke turned the old brass knob and pulled on the ancient oak door. It groaned as it resisted his efforts, but when it finally surrendered, the night's silence gave way to the screeching of rusty hinges. Dropping the key into his jacket pocket, the professor stepped inside.

Burke was greeted by the overpowering smell of foul air and decay. As the musty odor filled his lungs, he stifled a cough and tried to get a feel for his surroundings. A bit of moonlight sneaked into the chamber through the still-open door. As his vision adjusted, Burke made out several sets of small beady eyes. He was not alone. Feeling along the wall to his right, he found an ancient push-button switch just where it should have been. Pushing the button revealed that the electricity was still connected to the old structure. A single dusty light, its filament almost as thick as a six-penny nail, shed a bit of illumination down a ten-foot-wide hallway and sent a half dozen rats scurrying for the cover of darkness.

Burke watched the rodents push into a hole under a stairwell. Surrounded by forgotten reminders of other eras, he was all but overcome by a sense of history. Reaching down, he retrieved a 1928 college annual from the floor. Blowing the dust off the cover, he flipped through a few pages. Staring back at him were men and women who had once stood in the same spot he was standing. A few of them might have even made history by fighting in a war or developing some kind of advance in science or industry. Now most, if not all, were dead and, like this building where they had once spent so much time, were forgotten.

Carefully placing the yearbook back on the floor, Burke turned his attention to other reminders of the past. To his right, about twelve feet from the entry, was a stack of textbooks on Greek history. Beside them was a vintage kitchen sink. Four twenty-one-inch wire wheels with old bias tires were leaned up against the wall. And the junk seemed to have no end as a hundred more seemingly disjointed and unconnected items, ranging from a horse saddle to a four-foot-high globe, littered the old wooden planks all the way down the hall. Why had the university kept any of this stuff? Who had decided these things would ever be needed again?

He was tempted to take a closer look at the many piles of items from the past, and on any other day, he might have, but on this night another mystery took precedence. After a quick examination of the huge outdated globe of the world, he got back to the task at hand. When he had retrieved the key to the building, he'd been given notebooks filled with information on the inventory to be found in Bruce Hall. There was only a single page that covered the storage of English items during World War II. Pulling from his jacket pocket the copy he'd made of the page, Burke walked over to the dim light and studied the ancient typewritten text. The paper simply stated that twenty-six wooden crates containing official documents from the city of Berkshire, England, had been stored in room 4A on January 20, 1940.

Glancing to his right, he noted room 1A. To the left was room 2A. The sound of his shoes on the ancient wooden floor seemed to awaken the ghosts of the past, and the overhead light inexplicably grew a bit brighter. He walked past seven black metal file cabinets, then came to a door with the number he needed painted on frosted glass. He grabbed the knob, twisted, and a latch released. Hinges squeaked as he entered what appeared to have once been a classroom. He found another push-button light switch, but this time four 200-watt bulbs came on. The bright light revealed what he had feared. Except for one old teacher's desk pushed against the inside wall, a thick coat of dust, five ancient blackboards, and piles of rat droppings, the room was vacant. There was no forgotten crate.

He studied the room for a few seconds, then walked to the room's single piece of furniture. He pulled open the middle drawer to reveal a trove of pre–World War II writing instruments. Burke counted four fountain pens, two small bottles of black ink, six pencils, and a large eraser. A pad in the drawer had scrawls that read "Pick up tickets to the Purdue game" and "Maggie's birthday party on Saturday." Under the tablet was a box of paper clips. After dropping the fountain pens into his coat pocket, Burke continued his inspection.

He discovered the drawers on the right side of the desk were appropriately outfitted with vintage teaching materials, including three 1938 books on European history, some blue books used for testing, and a professor's record book. There was also an August 1939 edition of *Modern Screen* featuring Carole Lombard on the cover and an empty six-ounce embossed Coke bottle from Danville, Illinois. But there appeared to be nothing of English origin.

The desk's one large drawer on the left was stuck. Bracing the old piece of furniture with his right foot, Burke gave a mighty tug. The drawer didn't move. Three more attempts proved equally futile. He needed some kind of tool to force it.

The professor turned and started his trek back into the hall when something out of place caught his eye and stopped his heart. An imposing figure stood in the shadows beside the entry. While there wasn't enough light to identify the intruder, he could see the man's left arm locked straight out in front of him. In his hand was a large and powerful handgun.

FROZEN

The room was almost tomblike. The silence was broken only by occasional sounds of rats scurrying about in the ceiling as the two men faced each other. Burke had never looked into the cold, unforgiving stare of a gun, and he possessed no instincts to deal with this situation. For several moments, he stood unmoving, his eyes focused on an instrument that could end not only his search for a lost biblical text but also life itself. Finally, as seconds passed and a loud greeting from the weapon did not come, the professor's powers of observation gradually kicked in.

The man was dressed in just one color—black. He wore black pants, a turtleneck, and a stocking cap pulled down to just above his eyebrows. Leather gloves covered his hands. The shadows created by the partially opened classroom door so shielded the man's face that Burke could not discern his race, much less any facial features. He was as much a mystery as were the contents of the antique file cabinets he'd passed in the hallway.

"Did you find it?" The voice was gruff, flat, and deep. There was no hint of even a regional accent. He sounded American, but he could have been from anywhere.

"What?" Burke said.

The reply was quick and precise. "Centers told you about the missing crate that belonged to the British. Is it here?"

The professor raised his right hand to his face and rubbed his chin between his forefinger and thumb. Usually this action brought focus and allowed him to probe his mind in a search for answers. Tonight it did nothing other than prove his face was starting to show the signs of stubble.

"I don't know anyone named Centers, and I sure don't know anything about a missing crate."

Even though he couldn't see them, Burke could feel the visitor's eyes studying his face. The silence was uncomfortable and more confining than a straightjacket. Finally, after what seemed like hours, the cold voice spoke again.

"Slowly pull the lapels of your coat open and show me your pockets."

Burke carefully did as he had been told.

"What's that paper?"

"Inventory files for this room."

"Drop it on the floor and slide it over to me."

The professor pulled the page from his inside suitcoat pocket, bent at the knees, placed it on the floor, and pushed the sheet with his fingers across the dusty boards toward the man. It managed to move about five feet.

"Put your hands up and turn around," the man ordered.

Burke nodded, pushed his arms toward the ceiling, and slowly turned on the ball of his left foot. A few seconds later, he heard footsteps, then there was nothing but soft breathing. One minute became two, two became three.

"This is it?" the voice demanded.

Burke looked over his shoulder. "That's all I found."

Finally he heard the click of the light button, and the room was swathed in a blanket of darkness.

The classroom door slammed shut, causing decades of dust and cobwebs to drift down from the walls and ceiling. Burke stood unmoving, still facing the far wall. He was so lost in fear and thought he even continued holding his hands in the air. Finally, dropping his arms, he pushed his hands into his pants pockets and nervously crossed the dark room toward the door. Feeling along the wall, he pushed the button on the ancient light switch, and again the room was bathed in yellow light. Looking down, he saw the inventory list lying on the floor. He stooped to retrieve it and saw the imprint of a shoe. He picked up the list and studied it closely. The print on the paper was red.

Blood!

Stunned, Burke moved back across the room to the desk. Sitting on the corner and holding the paper by the edge, he examined the bloodstain. Glancing back toward the door, Burke noted a few more dark droplets on the dusty floor where the man had been standing. The visitor had been bleeding.

He then noticed something even more threatening — the smell of smoke. Through the door's embossed glass, the hall looked like Dante's Inferno. If he stepped out of the room, he would be immersed in flames. Burke quickly surveyed his surroundings. There were four windows along the far wall. They had been boarded up from the outside for decades. Those offered the only hope of escape. Slipping the inventory back into his suitcoat pocket, the professor yanked a drawer from the old desk and raced across the room.

Burke slammed the drawer into one of the plateglass windows, causing shards of glass to fly in every direction. One five-inch piece lodged in his cheek. Quickly pulling the missile out of his skin, the former college flanker ignored the pain and dripping blood as he used the drawer to break away the rest of the window. He was just beginning to push against the wood that covered the opening when the lights flickered and went out.

The fact that the layer of darkness was not as deep or murky this time was hardly soothing. Burke looked back at the door. The flames were creeping into the room along the base of the old, dry floor. Smoke was rolling in just above those tongues of fire. The clock was ticking, and it was going to take a Hail Mary play to win this game.

With a frantic, terror-fueled rage, the professor slammed the desk drawer into the wood that covered the four-by-eight window. The drawer shattered, but the boards on the window didn't budge. With his next breath, he sucked in a lungful of smoke. Burke fell to his knees, coughing.

Instinct argued that the game was over. He just needed to lie down, wait for the inevitable end, and pray that it came quickly. Yet giving up was not part of his nature. As long as he could move, he would fight to live.

Struggling to his feet, the professor backed up a few steps and again threw his shoulder into the wood. The pain that shot through his arm and neck proved his attempt had once more been futile. The two-inch-thick boards were simply too formidable an opponent. A third attempt fared no better.

For a moment, he found his mind drifting to thoughts of his obituary and memorial service. He wondered if his ex-wife, who had grown tired of vacations spent on Civil War battlefields and in South American jungles, would even show up. He felt the heat starting to bake his skin, and another bit of dark humor hit him. His was most definitely going to be a closed-casket service.

The flames had consumed the doorway and were now marching toward him across the old floor. There was no way out. He shielded his face from the heat. Just then the floor buckled, tossing him onto his back. Rolling over, Burke pulled himself upright and once more put his shoulder into the window. Again the wood didn't budge.

A loud crash drew Burke's attention to the back of the room. The flames had consumed much of the wall. The desk he had sat on just a few minutes before had fallen through the old floor into what was either a basement or a very deep crawl space. He stared at the nine-by-five-foot hole where the desk had slipped from sight. With no thought of what might lie below and no chance to utter a prayer for salvation, Burke launched himself over a four-foot wall of fire and into the black hole.

SMOKE

Smoke filled his nose and mouth and clouded his brain. He was swimming in smoke. No, actually drowning in it. Even running as fast as he could, the strong athletic man couldn't get away from it. It was everywhere, filling his lungs as well as every corner of the blackest night Burke had ever known.

"Mr. Burke."

The voice came from somewhere beyond his view. It was a voice he didn't recognize. Maybe it was a student, perhaps a colleague, but whoever owned it would have to discover their own way out of this flame-filled nightmare. They were on their own. All that mattered to Burke was finding a path to clean, cool night air. There had to be a way. The thick smoke couldn't go on forever.

Hell! What if this was hell? What if he was actually being sucked into the fires of eternal damnation? Did hell really exist? Was he really dead?

"Mr. Burke ... Mr. Burke."

It was a woman's voice. She sounded older, almost motherly. Was she trapped here too? Would someone please just lift the curtain and let him see where he was, if only for a moment? A moment of clear vision was all he needed to come up with a plan.

"Mr. Burke."

He could hear her so clearly. Why couldn't he see her? No time to worry about that; have to find a way out!

"Mr. Burke. Open your eyes. You're going to be okay."

"What?" The sound of his voice shocked him. It was hoarse and ragged.

"He's coming out of it." This time it was a man making the observation.

Staring blankly into the clouds, Burke tried to focus. Taking a deep breath, he shook his head and, after he'd swallowed a bit of sweet, clean air, things began to clear.

There was no smoke. There was no fire. He was in bed, in a hospital room. The woman standing next to the bed was a heavyset nurse. To his left appeared to be a young doctor. The latter stepped forward and offered an explanation.

"The firemen found you. When they got you here, we discovered you had some pretty bad smoke inhalation, a few bruises too. But the worst injury is likely the severe concussion you received when you fell through the floor and into the old basement."

"Didn't fall," Burke mumbled, a piece of the puzzle falling into place. "I jumped."

"Well, whatever happened, it saved your life."

Life. Nice word! His lungs hurt, he had a pretty bad headache, and his vision was a bit out of whack, but being alive was good. It was real good!

"Mr. Burke," the doctor said, "there is someone outside who needs to talk to you. He's been waiting off and on for two days. Do you feel up to it?"

Two days? Had it been that long? It couldn't have been. No, he must have heard the doctor wrong. It was minutes or perhaps an hour or so, but not days.

"Jefferson Burke?" This new voice boasted an air of authority, filling the room like the blast of a foghorn. Burke's head began to throb.

Burke nodded, his eyes attempting to stay focused on the squatty, balding, middle-aged man approaching the foot of his bed.

"Burke. I'm Courtland, Detective Adam Courtland. I'm with the Champaign Police Department. I've got a few questions."

"About the fire?" Burke asked.

The nurse seemed to read the pain etched on his face and handed him a glass of water. He took a few sips and glanced back toward the intimidating figure now standing just six feet away.

"That's the fire marshal's job," came the blunt reply. "I'm interested in something else. Do you know this man?"

Burke pushed himself up in bed and took the eight-by-ten color photo from the cop's meaty outstretched paw. Even though his vision was anything but normal, he recognized the person.

"It's Columbo."

"And who is this Columbo?"

Why was Courtland being so abrupt? Why the questions about Columbo? "He came to see me yesterday," Burke explained. "Excuse me, that would be three days ago. Said he was a historian with the Vatican. Wanted my help tracking down an artifact."

"You have that item?" Courtland asked.

"No. But Columbo thought records that might lead to finding it had been stored in Bruce Hall."

Yeah, Bruce Hall! Burke thought. That's what burned. But how did it start? He could remember nothing beyond arriving at the building. He was going through his mental Rolodex when the cop posed the next question.

"Exactly what was Columbo — I believe that's what you called him — looking for?"

Burke saw no reason not to answer. "A lost biblical manuscript was his ultimate goal. He thought I might be able to help him find some records that would get a bit closer in his quest."

"Would that manuscript be worth a great deal of money?"

"Yeah," Burke replied. "From a historical perspective, it would be priceless."

Courtland nodded, his dark eyes locked on the bedridden man.

"What can you tell me about this?"

With surprising deftness, the policeman turned, pulling from a file folder a piece of paper that had been placed in a plastic sleeve.

Burke studied it briefly. "It's the inventory list for what was in the room. Or what was in that room during World War II."

"And this stain?" Courtland pointed to a brownish spot on the right side of the document.

Suddenly the smoke was gone. Things were clear. The blood! The dark visitor! The man who tried to kill him! He remembered it all.

The fire was no accident. Someone had tried to burn him alive. There had to be something a whole lot deeper than just theology or history behind this. Burke suddenly felt like a pawn in a strange game, and he resented it.

Now fully engaged, the professor spat out the answer to Courtland's question. "That's blood from the guy who set the building on fire."

Courtland looked confused. He looked away for a moment at the far wall, shrugging his shoulders, then continued his line of questions. "You saw who set the fire?"

His head pounding but consumed by the anger of realizing that someone had tried to kill him, Burke said, surprising himself with his passion, "I was followed into the building. A man in black! I didn't see his face, but he held a gun on me and asked for that sheet of paper. He also wanted to know if I had found it."

"It?" the detective asked, trying to regain a bit of footing in a conversation that had gone off the expected path. "I'm guessing you mean the lost Bible book?"

Burke ignored the question. "When I couldn't give him what he wanted, he locked me in the room and set the place on fire. I'd have burned to death if I hadn't jumped through that hole in the floor. I got lucky."

"Could the man in black have been this Columbo?" Courtland asked.

Burke shook his head. "No, this guy was much bigger, much taller."

Courtland smiled, a cat-got-the-canary smile. For a moment, he seemed pleased, almost happy. "So you're saying the guy in black couldn't have been Columbo, the man who visited you."

"Yeah, he was much too large," Burke agreed.

"Do you know why Columbo went to your home?" the cop asked.

"Sure, I gave him a key. Told him to get some rest. Why?"

"The man you identified as Columbo was already dead when you went to Bruce Hall. He'd been beaten to death in your home. I think we are going to find out that the blood on that inventory list you had is his."

Columbo dead? Burke couldn't believe what he had just heard.

Courtland rested both hands on the bed's footboard and leaned toward the patient. "What were you really looking for in that building? Did you and Columbo have a fight before you went there? Things got out of control? Isn't that how the blood got on that inventory list?"

Suddenly being lost in a cloud of smoke seemed almost appealing.

TERROR

The cop's words were still sinking in when the door to the hospital room opened and a young woman with an air of authority came in. For a moment, she stood just out of the light, as if sizing up the two men in the room, then walked past the detective and to the side of Burke's bed.

She was short, athletic, early thirties, with dark brown eyes, black hair, and prominent cheekbones. The shape of her eyes left no doubt of her Asian roots.

"Dr. Burke." Her voice was deeper than he expected, hinting at the kind of low, throaty edge found in someone who had been smoking for decades. But hers was not the complexion of a woman who smoked. It was too smooth. "I'm Lisa Marie Cho. I'm an agent with the FBI. I've been assigned to this case."

"FBI?"

"Dr. Burke, a man was murdered in your home. He was on the terrorist watch list. His name was John Centers. We know Centers had contact with a group helping to finance terrorist missions in the Middle East and in developing nations. You were dealing with a very dangerous individual."

"He told Burke his name was Columbo," Courtland cut in, obviously attempting to appear relevant.

Cho nodded. "Antony Columbo. He likely told Dr. Burke he worked for the Vatican."

"He sure did," Burke replied.

Upstaged, Courtland crossed his arms and frowned, his two chins becoming four as he rested them against his chest. The movement hid the cop's neck, making him look like a before picture in a weight-loss ad.

Cho continued to pull back the curtain on the mystery man who'd somehow died in Burke's home. "Centers was also known as Jose Gomez, Ralph Spencer, Chester Blain, and other aliases." Her eyes never left Courtland as she spoke. "We actually don't know what his birth name was. Each of his many identities had fully developed histories. He was a pro. In fact, he was once an agent for the KGB."

"What?" Courtland's voice sounded like a balloon leaking air. Backing against the wall, he hissed, "You're telling me Burke killed a former Russian agent?"

The woman shook her head. She allowed her brown eyes to remain on the cop for a few seconds, then turned to the silent member of the impromptu party. In carefully measured tones, she snapped off her first question: "Dr. Burke, are you right-handed?"

"I don't see what that has to do with anything," Courtland said.

With a simple wave of the hand, Cho muted the cop. He moved toward a corner like a hurt puppy.

"Yes, I'm right-handed," Burke replied.

Grabbing the professor's right wrist, the FBI agent lifted his hand into the air. "You see anything, detective?"

From a spot by the window, Courtland pushed his fingers through his thinning black hair, the color obviously the product of imprudent use of Just for Men. "What?" he barked. "He's got five fingers?"

Dropping her hold, the agent said, "No scrapes, cuts, or bruises. Check on the left one. You won't see anything there either. If Burke had beat Centers as brutally as he was beaten, the evidence would be right here on his hands. As a righty, he would have led with that hand. It should have been scraped up pretty good."

"But the blood on the list," Courtland replied smugly.

She turned back to Burke. "How did the blood get there?"

The professor was more than eager to explain this point. "It wasn't on the paper when I went to Bruce Hall. I saw it after the man who held me at gunpoint in Bruce Hall had picked it up. But he dropped it when he left. I also saw drops of blood on the floor where he stood when he was questioning me."

"The mysterious man in black." Courtland laughed. "Sure. More like a figment of the professor's imagination. Very creative, Burke. Bet we never find any trace of him."

Cho smiled. "Courtland, you might want to call your office. Two hours ago, they found a body in Bruce Hall. It was burned too badly for us to ID so far, but it was a large male, and the clothing that didn't burn was black. A set of brass knuckles was found in his pocket. Gloves protected his hands, but when we removed the gloves, we discovered lots of bruising, the type usually found after someone has been in a fistfight. Detective, you get an ID on that guy and you'll have Columbo's killer."

Cho turned back to the patient. "Dr. Burke, let me hear all of your story. I need to find out why a man who has been known to support and fund terrorism sought out a professor in the middle of the Corn Belt."

As the agent pulled up a chair next to the bed, a frowning Courtland grabbed his file and headed out the door.

FATE

Bruno Krueger's blue eyes were lit in anger. His right eyebrow twitched as he repeated the same question for the third time: "You didn't listen to me, did you?"

In public Krueger was the model of genteel civility. He was always ready to open a door for a woman, pat a friend on the back, tell a good joke. But he wasn't in public; he was behind the walls of his Chicago penthouse. At six-foot-seven and 210 pounds, Krueger was an intimidating figure. He was built like a swimmer, but with a punch like a professional boxer, he could dispatch a man with just a few well-placed blows. In fact, he had done just that more times than he could remember. He enjoyed violence, relished the pain he inflicted on others. He was likely a psychopath, but as one of the world's richest men, he had no reason to have a shrink tell him that. In fact, everyone around Krueger was a yes-man.

John Fisherman was the man accepting the verbal pounding in Krueger's office. He had served as the billionaire's personal administrator for a decade. He had supervised scores of archaeological digs, paid thousands of business bribes, and settled countless scores. He thought of himself as Krueger's garbageman—doing the dirty work—but he was paid well for it. And he was so good that no hint of scandal had ever visited Krueger International during his tenure. But he'd messed up this time.

"No one can connect us to what happened. In fact, our man is making sure the college professor is on the hook for killing Centers."

Krueger grabbed Fisherman by his silk tie and yanked him around like a puppet, slinging him into an overstuffed leather chair. "And by now the FBI knows who Centers is," Krueger said, his face mere inches from his assistant's. "They have to be wondering why he's in the United States. Why didn't you just get Centers to give us what the professor knew? See that he was pushed to a quiet exit. But no. You couldn't. Now we've got a real mess. It's no longer a local matter run by an incompetent cop we can buy."

Krueger's face had turned a bright crimson. His eyes seemed to bulge. He took a step back. His rock-hard neck was pulsing as he screamed, "What's the name of the man who killed Centers and torched the warehouse?"

"Greg Cones."

"Have you paid him yet?"

"Yes. With his life." The reply was flat, emotionless. "They'll find a body in the warehouse. His prints will prove he has a history with organized crime. He can't be connected to us."

Krueger nodded. He took a couple of deep breaths and became a bit calmer. "At least there's some good news in this mess. Still, it's not enough. You and I both know that."

"This is my fault," Fisherman admitted as he pushed himself from the chair and loosened the tie that was choking him. "I know what that means."

Krueger moved behind his massive wood desk. He sat down in the antique high-back leather swivel chair and turned to gaze out at the Chicago skyline, his interlocked hands positioned behind his neck. For more than five minutes he remained as still as a statue. Finally he got up and slowly moved out from behind the desk. Standing directly in front of Fisherman, Krueger looked directly at his assistant, a look he held as tightly as any noose.

Try as he could, Fisherman could not look away.

"So many others have done even less and suffered the ultimate fate," Krueger noted. "Yet I like you, John. I've come to think of you as a brother. Maybe for once I should toss out the primary directive. I've read that forgiveness defines great strength, though I don't believe it."

Fisherman was stunned. He'd been resigned to his fate — death. But now it seemed as though his decade of perfect work had bought him a reprieve.

Krueger retreated to his desk and pushed a button. An emotion-less middle-aged woman entered the office through a hidden panel beside a bookcase. In her left hand was a small leather pouch that she placed on the desk. She pulled out two syringes and a strip of tan rubber. Without saying a word, she wrapped the band around Fisherman's arm, then stuck the needle in one of the bulging veins in the back of his hand, drawing out enough blood to fill the syringe. Fisherman never moved. The woman then picked up the other syringe and jabbed the needle through Fisherman's pants into the fleshy part of his left thigh. She pushed the plunger all the way in, then withdrew the needle.

"Very good, Victoria," Krueger said as she handed him both syringes.

"John, you once pledged to serve me with your last ounce of blood. There is at least an ounce in this tube." Krueger studied the syringe for a moment. "Thanks to your pledge, I own you and I own this precious red liquid."

Krueger tapped the plastic tube, dislodging an air bubble in the syringe. He tilted the syringe and smiled as the thick liquid slid to the other end.

Krueger's smile was a mix of humor with a large dose of evil. "I can't let you leave without being punished. It would cost me standing with those under your control. Do you understand that?"

Fisherman nodded.

"Good." He looked at the nurse. "Send in Al."

The woman left. Al was a young man built like a heavyweight boxer. Fisherman had seen his work before. He knew what to expect. It would not be a party, but the result would not be a funeral. Standing straight, he braced himself for the series of right and left hooks deliv-ered directly into his midsection. The blows, one after another, were crushing. Fisherman feared Al's fists were going to slam clear through his gut and out his back. The big man stopped his piston-like assault only after Fisherman fell to his knees.

"That's enough, Al," Krueger said. "I'm sure that is all we need to teach this very special lesson."

The enforcer left the room. He'd said nothing.

Fisherman painfully pulled himself upright.

"You took it like I expected, John," Krueger said, a hint of pride in his tone. "Now put your coat on and go back to your apartment while I figure out how to deal with the mess you've created."

MYSTERY

D r. Frank Osterbur had retreated to his cramped office just down
the hall from Cook County Hospital's trauma treatment center. Osterbur was tired. It had been an evening filled with shootings,
domestic assaults, traffic accidents, and one death. His body ached as
though he'd been in one of those car crashes. Another thirty minutes
and he got to knock off work. A shower, a quick meal, and a short
drive to his condo would be a very welcome end to a horrid day.

A nurse stuck her head in the door.

"What do you need?" Osterbur asked.

"The guy who died this afternoon ..." she said, her manner indi-
cating she was about to spring something big on the ER physician.

He wondered if he had messed up. He knew exactly who she was
talking about. He propped his feet up on the desk and leaned back.
"The one who was bleeding out his ears and mouth?"

She nodded. "It wasn't some strange illness or a chemical poison-
ing like you thought."

That was unexpected. Except for the internal bleeding and a
few deep bruises and abrasions on his abdomen, the guy had seemed
healthy. No natural cause of death had even entered the doctor's head.
He had been sure it was some type of exposure to something that
killed him, possibly in a work environment or at home. Sending him
to the morgue for an autopsy had evidently proven him wrong. And
now the nurse, who had messed up on one of his shifts about a year
ago, was here to point out and gloat over his mistake. Might as well
let her pounce. "So, Ms. Manning, what was it?"

"Here, read Doc Ryan's initial findings, then see what you make
of it."

Osterbur took the file and leafed through the four pages. When he came to Ryan's conclusion, he was stunned. It wasn't possible. He looked up at the nurse.

"There were no bites on his body. None. Besides, there is no way Fisherman would have encountered a Komodo dragon anywhere in Chicago or, for that matter, anywhere in the whole country. Ryan's got to be wrong."

"I don't think so," Manning replied. "He has a sample of the stuff in his lab."

Osterbur remembered the case. Two years before, a zoo worker had been attacked and bitten by a Komodo dragon. The bite hadn't been serious, but the poison the five-foot-long reptile had injected into the man's system was. The man died.

"There was a needle mark on Fisherman's right hand and one on his right thigh," the nurse said. "You noted that in the report."

"I remember."

"Ryan believes that venom from the glands of a Komodo dragon was injected into Fisherman's leg using a syringe."

Osterbur didn't need any further explanation. The Komodo dragon's bite is not what kills its victims; the venom, when absorbed into the bloodstream, prevents clotting and lowers blood pressure. That does the trick. So ... this was murder. Premeditated murder. Someone injected the man with the venom and worked him over enough to cause internal bleeding, knowing he'd bleed to death. Once started, there was no chance of stopping the bleeding. By the time he arrived in the ER, there was no way to save his life.

"This was murder," Manning said, her words as chilling as a March snow.

The doctor nodded. "In my twenty years here, I thought I'd seen everything. But this case will likely go down as the strangest. Who would kill this way? You've got to have a sick mind to do that. It's like something out of *CSI* or even a comic book, not life in Chicago."

"Ryan called the police," the nurse said as she left the office.

Still stunned by the autopsy finding, Osterbur mentally reviewed what he had seen—the bruises, the bleeding—what he did, what he ordered. In almost a whisper, he said, "This is one mystery I'm betting they won't solve."

VERSE

It was anything but a happy homecoming. Burke's yard was littered with hundreds of feet of crime tape, his lawn had been trampled by humans and cars, and at least a half dozen neighbors were watching from behind partially closed blinds. And that was the good news. As he and Agent Cho pushed open the front door, the professor saw the real mess the CSI team had left. Shelves had been emptied, furniture was moved. In the kitchen, the sugar, the flour, and even the pancake mix had been emptied from their containers. In the bedroom, his clothes were piled on the floor and his shoes had been moved against a far wall. His mattress and box spring were nowhere near the bed frame. Worse yet, a four-by-six-foot section of carpet had been cut out and removed.

"Why mutilate my carpet?" he asked.

"Bloodstains." The reply was a simple reminder that a man had died in his home. Died a violent death.

"And the rest of this mess was all because of the murder?"

"Yes. I hope you have really good insurance. You own the crime scene and you're the prime suspect."

Burke walked back through what had been organized living space into the main room of the home, retrieved a couple of cushions from the floor, dropped them into place, and collapsed on a living room couch.

"Betty's not going to like this," he noted.

"Who's Betty?"

"My maid. She comes in once a week, and tomorrow is her day."

"She'd better bring some help," Cho said.

Burke walked back through the kitchen, down the hall, and

charged into his home office, Cho right behind him. Like all the other rooms, it was in shambles. Half of what had been on the shelves was gone and the other half was piled on the floor. His computer was gone, as were his notes and personal records.

"I can't even check my email," Burke moaned. "And I need my cell phone."

"I'll see if I can get the cell phone back for you," the agent replied. "Just count your blessings you're not in jail. At least you're free."

"Yeah," he shot back, "with everyone watching every move I make. Especially Courtland." He said the cop's name as if trying to rid his throat of mucus.

Plopping into his desk chair, he picked up a book on Greek history and rifled it at the fireplace. When it not only stayed in one piece but failed to make much noise on impact, he was disappointed.

Shaking her head, Cho walked across the room, retrieved the book, blew off the dust, and placed it on an empty shelf.

"Feel better now?" she asked. When he didn't reply, she picked up a book from the corner of the desk, glanced at the cover, and smiled. "This one must have meant something to you when you were young. At least they didn't take it."

"What are you talking about?" he snapped.

"This Dr. Seuss book."

"What? I don't own a ..." He paused for a moment. "Let me see that."

It was a copy of *The Cat in the Hat*, but it was hardly old. In fact, it looked brand-new. Opening to the title page, he saw an inscription: "To Jeff, from your father, Joseph."

Considering his father's name was Andrew and he'd been dead for two decades, the message being sent through this book was hardly subtle to Burke, but the FBI and the local cops had missed it.

Suddenly fascinated, Burke forgot about the mess in his house. He started to slowly turn the pages. At first glance, nothing seemed out of the ordinary. The book was just as it had been printed. In fact, it appeared as though it had never been opened, much less read. The spine was in good shape. There were no notes, no dog-eared corners or finger smudges. No bookmarks. He was about to set it down when he noticed that the red endpaper on the inside of the back cover appeared to be poorly constructed. He pulled one edge and the paper came loose. Under the endpaper was something that shouldn't have been in the children's classic.

Glancing up, Burke saw that Cho's attention had turned to a book on the history of American crime. She appeared to be engrossed. Burke looked back at the five-by-seven-inch piece of paper that had been hidden in the book's back cover. It was from a local antique dealer—Girton's Collectibles. It simply said, "Sold—one nightstand. Hold for Jefferson Burke."

"You must be amazed by what you found," Cho said, "because I can see your mood has completely turned around."

The agent's echoing of Seuss through rhyme didn't impress him. But what he was studying just out of her sight did grab his interest. Columbo or Centers or whatever his name was must have left this for him. It had to be tied to everything else that had happened since meeting the strange man.

"Cat got your tongue?" Cho prodded in another attempt at Seussian humor.

Burke just smiled and closed the book. Logic told him to show her the invoice. He knew he should let her in on what *The Cat in the Hat* had just given him. But he didn't. Instead he said, "The book was a gift from Dad, and finding it safe makes me so very glad."

DECEPTION

Girton's Collectibles on Vine Street in Urbana was in a small century-old building that had housed a dozen different businesses in the last ten decades. The store had but one large rectangular room. A pressed-tin ceiling still topped the twelve-foot brick walls. There were so many antiques — at least four player pianos, three roll-top desks, and countless bedroom suites — spread out across the floor, it was hard to find a path to walk, much less actually view the merchandise. When Burke walked in, there were no customers. The only employee, a short, thin man with dark eyes, a large Roman nose, and a head of unruly white hair, looked to be in his sixties.

"Can I help you?" The man's voice was strong and deep and seemed at odds with his slight frame.

Burke glanced over his shoulder. Noting no one behind him, he replied, "I have an item that I believe you're holding for me."

Reaching into his pocket, Burke retrieved the invoice and handed it to the man. The clerk glanced at the paper for a moment, then asked, "May I see your identification?"

The professor retrieved his wallet and held out his driver's license.

"Mr. Burke, I've been expecting you. I'm Ralph Girton. I own this little cache of trash and memories."

After shooting him a small grin, the man turned and shuffled toward the back of the store. He stopped about five feet from the back wall and tapped a black wooden trunk about twenty inches high by twenty inches long by fourteen inches wide. "This is it."

Burke moved closer to the trunk, glanced at the antique, and shook his head. "No, the invoice said I was to pick up a table."

Girton nodded. "Yes, sir, that's what I was instructed to write down. And that end table is over there against the side wall." He pointed to a piece that sported a "Sold" tag. "If anyone came in producing the invoice but without the proper identification, I was to give them that table. But if you came in, then you were to get what had really been left for you. Besides the ID you showed me, I recognized you. Sure been a lot of photos that have run in the paper and on the internet the last couple of days." He smiled. "So the trunk is yours."

The professor shrugged. The reputation he'd gained was anything but wanted. But in this case, it had worked in his favor. Girton wasn't treating him like a murderer, so it appeared he had at least one person in his camp.

"Now," the antique dealer continued, "just in case someone is watching you, the little man who brought in the trunk gave further instructions. He told me to load the table into your car so it did look like you picked up the table with his invoice. I am then supposed to sell you the trunk, making out a new invoice so that it appears it was an impulse buy. For some reason, and he didn't tell me, the trunk is what he really wanted you to have."

Burke glanced from the trunk to the table and back. Scratching his head, he asked, "What's in the trunk?"

"I have no idea," the man replied. "It's locked. I don't have the key. Besides, I was paid well to hold it for you, not to open it. Let me add, sometimes what you don't know keeps you healthier than what you do know."

In Girton's case, that might be true, but for Burke it was just the opposite. What he didn't know had gotten him into a whole lot of trouble.

"Mr. Burke, I was also told that you would only be coming to pick up this piece if the little man with the strange accent did not return to pick it up. So, ever since I read the story of Columbo's death, I have been prepared."

Burke nodded, then in almost a whisper asked, "Did you know Columbo?"

"Only met him that once when he brought in the trunk, bought the end table, and gave me the instructions."

"When was that?"

"On Monday, four days ago, just after I opened the store that morning."

So Columbo had come here before going to the campus. He was already preparing a scenario in case he died. He had to have known he was being followed. "How did he act?" Burke asked.

"I would say he was calm. He didn't seem to be in a hurry. He was precise in his directions, paid me well, then left."

"Did he tell you anything about himself?"

The antique dealer smiled. "Only that he too dealt in antiques and was close to tracking down the find of the century. Oh, and there was one other thing. When he walked out, he made a cross sign — you know, like Catholics do when they pray. So I assumed he was a religious man."

If Columbo was Centers and an ex-KGB agent, he didn't lapse into that character while in the store. He appeared the devout Catholic to Girton. Yet maybe his ability to play a role was what made him so good and kept him alive for so many years.

"Mr. Girton, I'm going to take the table now, but could I pay you to deliver the trunk to my home, along with something else?"

"Certainly."

Burke quickly scanned the wall in front of him and asked, "How much is that large piece over there?"

The proprietor followed Burke's eyes to an oak wardrobe off to the right. "That is an older British antique. It's not cheap."

"I figured," Burke replied, "but won't that trunk fit into the large compartment on the left?"

Girton smiled and nodded. "Yes, it will."

"Then deliver it to my home this afternoon. My address is on the check. And make sure the trunk is not seen."

"That can be arranged."

A few minutes later, Burke slipped the table into his Escape. As he slid into the driver's seat, he smiled. For the moment, whoever was watching him — and he knew there had to be someone — would be interested only in a meaningless table.

TRUMPED

Everything Courtland had come up with to collar Burke had been trumped by the FBI, and this was not going down well with his boss. Pulling his cell phone closer to his meaty chin, Courtland said, "Why would he be shopping for antiques? It has to mean something."

As he waited in his car for a response, he fiddled with the LCD light switch on the end of his key chain. He missed the symbolism that he had yet to shed much illumination on the case.

"Agreed," the cop finally responded to the voice on the other end. After tossing the key chain back onto the seat, he added, "I'll get the papers and grab the table. But the judge and DA are not going to overrule the FBI on this one. I'm not going to be able to arrest him."

As he listened to the reply, Courtland frowned. He waited until the tirade concluded before adding, "Got it. But I can't do the impossible! This is well beyond my pay scale."

Hitting the "end call" button on his cell, the cop slid the phone into his suitcoat pocket, eased his rotund body out of his Crown Victoria, and lumbered across the street to Girton's store. He was at the front door reaching for the knob when a raspy voice stopped him.

"Going shopping?"

Whipping around, the veteran detective found himself staring into the eyes of Lisa Marie Cho, whose eyes seemed intent on burning right through him.

"I'm following a lead."

Cho smiled wide enough that a deep dimple appeared on her right cheek. "Who was that you were talking to on your cell?"

"What do you mean?"

"A few minutes ago, right after Burke left, you made a call on your private cell, not the one issued to you by the department."

"A personal matter."

"Doubt it. Personal matters don't keep an impulsive, impatient man like you from your objective." Cho poked her index finger at the man's fleshy face. "You've got an agenda that goes beyond your job, Courtland. You're trying to nail Burke any way you can. Why is that?"

"I don't understand. What do you mean?" Courtland shot back, not bothering to hide his contempt for the woman and the group she worked for.

"Sure you do," the FBI agent replied, "and you know that it will be very easy for me to tap your phone. While I'm at it, might just check your email as well as your financial records."

The words hit home like a .44 slug. The impact was so precise that the blood quickly deserted Courtland's face and beads of sweat popped out on his brow. This was a position he was never in. He was the man who posed threats, not the man who received them. Forcing his hands deep into his pants pockets, he searched for words. He found none that could remotely trump the agent's. Finally he snapped, "You can't do that."

"I can." Cho's tone was calm, her manner almost casual, but the raspy voice was now a growl. "And who is to say I haven't already done it?"

"You little—" but that was all the cop managed before the wave of Cho's hand cut him off.

She smiled, her perfect white teeth flashing in the morning sun as she watched the cop slowly pull his right hand from his pocket and move it toward his belly.

"You have no right."

"And you don't have long to live," Cho replied. Her answer was flat, emotionless. She was stating a fact, one she felt the cop likely knew. "It's the man you just called that you need to fear. You're now a liability to him. You are the direct line that connects him to what happened here. He'll cut that line quickly."

She arched her right eyebrow and looked into the cop's squinty eyes, then pushed past him and walked into Girton's store. From the corner of her eye, she observed Courtland scratch his neck, look nervously over his shoulder, then walk back across the street to his car. He had lost all interest in Burke and the table.

As the cop drove to the corner and turned right, the FBI agent shook her head. Her research had shown that Courtland didn't have a family. That was good, because she doubted she'd ever see the detective again.

ROYAL

Royal, a town twenty miles northeast of Urbana, is a farm community of just over two hundred people. It had been created more than a century before when German immigrants drained off swamps to reveal some of the nation's most fertile black soil. The town had never been large, and its businesses included the bare essentials for an agricultural economy—Busboom's Grain and Hardware, a post office, Vilven Tire Company, a branch of Ogden State Bank, Freeman's Tavern, and Candy's Beauty Parlor. A community building constructed recently beside the Little League baseball field, an elementary school, and an ornate Lutheran church rounded out the other major structures in the tiny hamlet. Off the beaten path, home to little of historic impact, it was one of hundreds of all but forgotten places few visited but that a handful of hardworking people still called home.

Jeff Burke had been introduced to Royal by one of his former students, Nolan Jordan. Halfway through Nolan's junior year, his father died, leaving him the family's two-story home. Jordan was only twenty when he inherited the property. At the time, he needed money for school loans much more than he did a 2,000-square-foot house on the edge of a prairie town. Seeing the property as an investment, but also intrigued by owning a home that had once—before the Jordans—belonged to another professor, Burke purchased it. Initially he'd planned on turning the white house on Main Street into rental property, but five years later, he still hadn't completed the task of updating the plumbing and wiring. He'd moved some furniture to Royal and was using the house as a weekend retreat.

In the 1930s and '40s, Dr. Franklin Cross had lived in the house. Yet there was more of a bond between Burke and Cross than just the house and the elevated degree. Like Burke, Cross had once been the head of the history department at Illinois.

Over the years, Burke had spent many hours researching all the past chairs, including Cross, who was known as a precise, neat man. He had never married, worked at the school for more than a decade. Died in a plane crash while on a trip out west in 1942.

At the estate sale, the Jordan family had purchased the house and all that was in it. The proceeds, according to instructions in Cross's will, had been donated to the University of Illinois scholarship fund. While the Jordan family had often updated the home, the outbuildings had seemingly remained as they were in 1942—filled with junk.

It was just past sundown when the professor drove down the long gravel driveway and pulled his car into a large weathered barn that stood behind the house. His headlights reflected off an old car in the far corner of the building. Long ago, Burke had promised to take a closer look at the pre–World War II auto, but the fact that old boxes covered the path as well as most of the car had always blocked his curiosity. Someday, but not today, he always told himself, he would work his way back to the antique.

Opening the hatch of the Escape, he retrieved a tool kit and made his way across the concrete patio to the back door of the house. He entered, set the tools down just inside the door, and returned to the car to grab the small black trunk. He was halfway across the backyard when a man's deep voice stopped him in his tracks.

"I see you're still trying to fill that place up with furniture."

Burke forced a smile. Milton Meyers, who was standing just inside the ring of light produced by the barn's security lamp, owned the home next door. A retired service station manager, the elderly man had been one of the first to welcome Burke into the community. The professor considered him to be a true friend.

"How you doing, Milt?" Burke asked.

"Better question would be, how're you doing? The papers are full of you being the only suspect in that brutal murder case."

Burke set the trunk on the ground and shrugged. "Hope you don't believe I could do something like that."

Meyers pulled the Marathon Oil cap from his bald head and ran his other hand across his scalp as if smoothing down hair no longer there. "No one here in Royal believes you beat that guy to death. You need any help with that trunk?"

"Naw," Burke answered. "It's light and it's the only thing I brought tonight. I thought it might make a good end table. Got it cheap."

"Sounds good to me. I understand you got dinged up. How you feeling?"

"A little sore and my head still hurts," Burke replied, "but all things considered, pretty good."

"That's great. If you get hungry, come on over to the house. Marge made one of her chocolate pies. Got some soup on too."

"Thanks, Milt, sounds real good. But I'm just going to get this inside, check on a few things, then head back to the city. Maybe next time. And give Marge my best."

The neighbor smiled, replaced his cap, and shuffled out of the light. As soon as the neighbors' back door closed, the professor picked up the trunk and carried it into the kitchen. The antique lock took quite a pounding, stubbornly defying several hard hammer blows before finally springing open.

Burke flipped back the flat hinged top to reveal stacks of papers, a book, and photos. The book appeared to be a journal. The initial entry had been made in 1967. Sitting at the kitchen table he read,

> Operation Joe seems a strange title for a KGB project. Yet today I was introduced to this unique quest. As we feared, Stalin first heard about the lost biblical text from a German intelligence officer captured late in World War II. Though Stalin didn't know what was in the book, he was all but consumed by finding it. It seemed that if Hitler felt it was vital, so did the Soviet leader.

Other entries, penned at irregular times, followed. Some were spaced months apart. Others were separated by years. The final one was written in January 1991, the year the Soviet intelligence agency was officially dissolved.

Each entry dealt with the lost *Book of Joseph*, yet despite the KGB's digging through a trove of Nazi documents and making several expeditions to a monastery in Afghanistan, there were no clues to shed any light on where the document might be or who had it. Time and time again, the quest had run into the same roadblock: the missing box of materials from Berkshire, England. The thousands of hours of research had ultimately proven fruitless.

Burke leafed through a file filled with pictures. Most of the pictures had been taken during a visit to what appeared to be an ancient structure, probably in the mountains of Afghanistan. Except for a few shots of monks and some views of a rather stark sanctuary sparsely furnished with ancient wooden pews, there was simply nothing of interest in the images.

One batch of documents contained maps with locations marked that probably Columbo, in his role as a KGB agent, had visited. The final stack of materials was written in Hebrew and Latin. Since Burke knew little of either language, Dr. Alexander Briggs would have to review these documents. He'd get them to the head of the religion department after things cooled down. Columbo had likely already searched out any threads of information in them.

So everything in the trunk yielded no fruit. Burke had learned nothing. What purpose did the former KGB agent have for leaving these things with him, he wondered. There had to be something he was missing. There had to be something hidden that had cost the man his life. But what?

A creaking floorboard yanked Burke's attention away from the trunk. It sounded like it had come from the large utility room just off the kitchen. Quietly sliding back from the table, he grabbed a hammer and moved toward the back door. It was ajar. He was sure he had closed it. Taking a deep breath, he eased it open and flipped on the light switch in the utility room. It was empty. He glanced behind the wooden entry. No one. Moving past the washer and dryer to a large metal sink, Burke paused. The curtain on the only window in the room was moving slightly. The window was open. The bottom was about a half an inch above the sill and the outside screen was off. He was sure it had been locked the last time he had been out. He knew the window hadn't been open in several years. Someone had been in the house! Someone had gone out the window! A chill raced up his spine.

Burke pushed the window closed, made sure the latch was secure, pulled the shade down, and turned his attention to the floor. He hadn't swept the old linoleum for months. A layer of dust coated the yellow-and-red-speckled surface. In the light, it was easy to see two sets of prints: one created by his size eleven Nike running shoes, the other by a man's dress shoes. Those smaller prints led in a straight line from the kitchen door to the window. He looked outside. Nothing. Whoever had been in the house was gone.

Grabbing an empty packing box marked "Bedroom Stuff," Burke hurried back to the kitchen. Using that box, he packed Columbo's papers and photos into the box, then climbed the stairs to the second floor, walked into the largest of the three bedrooms, and reached for a heavy string hanging from the ceiling. One hard yank and a ladder emerged. He climbed the rungs, pushed the box into the attic, and slid his body past it. He flipped a light switch. A single 200-watt bulb, hanging with no shade from a rafter, illuminated the room. Grabbing the box, Burke took it to a far corner and set it down beside boxes of items that once belonged to previous owners of the old home. Papers Professor Cross hadn't donated to the university had ended up in the attic. The one box Burke had opened contained old clothes and newspaper clippings.

After scrambling down the ladder and closing the attic door, Burke quickly made his way to the kitchen and picked up the black trunk and carried it out the back door. He slid the trunk in the backseat of the Escape, hopped in on the driver's side, and backed out of the barn. As he drove away, he swore he felt someone watching him, yet when he looked into his rearview mirror, he saw no one.

GUMBY

He must have been doing more than a hundred when he lost it." Agent Cho nodded as she walked away from the state trooper and back across a hundred yards of farmland to view the accident scene for the second time. The Crown Victoria had rolled several times, stopping its chaotic final ride on its roof. She'd been one of the first on the scene. She had found the body of the very dead police detective about forty feet from the car. Usually this sort of thing dipped deep into her emotions, tearing at the very fiber of her soul. She'd always experienced a sense of deep mourning at a fatal accident or murder. Not today. As she viewed the carnage, she was ambivalent. She knew enough about the victim to believe he'd sold his soul a long time ago.

The trooper's voice, coming a few steps behind her, startled her. "Some folks just think they can really open it up on Route 150. The road's straight, but the surface is anything but smooth. I'm guessing he must have hit a rough spot and lost control."

Cho didn't reply. Courtland might have been a soulless jerk who was on the take, but he had thirty years of law enforcement experience. He wouldn't have risked his neck driving like a drunken teen for no reason. Besides, there were no skid marks. He'd never hit his brakes. She guessed the vehicle's speed to be more like 140 when it left the road. With the police package under the Ford's hood, she knew that was possible. Unlike the troopers investigating the crash, she was not surprised Courtland hadn't been using his seat belt. The bureau had been watching him for months, and never during that time had he bothered snapping it into place. Maybe it cramped his sizable waist or maybe he was just one who didn't actually believe a large human body could be tossed through a car windshield. No matter, he wouldn't have survived this mess even with a belt.

The chirping of her cell phone took her gaze from the body.

"Cho here."

"Lisa, it's Mason. Just stopped someone up here that you might want to talk to. It's Dr. Burke."

The FBI agent thought for a moment. "Bring him down here. I want to show him something."

Slipping her phone into her jacket, she stepped closer to the body and snapped on her flashlight. Courtland looked like Gumby in an extreme yoga class. His right arm was twisted behind him, his left knee was bent at a 180-degree angle in the wrong direction. His neck had been snapped like a toothpick. He was lying on his back, but his face was twisted into the ground. He must have been alive as he flew through the air. She wondered what he was thinking just before he hit and what drove him to this grand finish. He was slimy, but he was no coward.

"Lisa, here's Dr. Burke."

She studied Courtland a few more seconds before moving her beam toward the voice. Clark Mason was forty, wore his auburn-colored hair short, parted on the right side. His eyes were somewhere between brown and gold. He was five-foot-eleven and a lean 160 pounds. He had a great sense of humor and was not only the best agent Cho had ever worked with but also a man devoted to duty.

"Thanks, Clark. Why don't you get back up there on the road and make sure the locals do their jobs. I don't want anyone down here until our team gets here." As Mason headed back to the highway, she said, "Come over here, Dr. Burke. I think you might want to see this."

She focused the light back on the body. "Don't think you'll have any more problems with Detective Courtland."

The professor winced as he took in the grisly scene. He looked back toward the old US 150 and whispered, "What happened?"

"The locals will write it down as reckless driving, and then the obit will be printed and the department will start looking for a new officer."

Burke continued to look back toward the road. "I take it you don't think it is so open and shut."

"He was running from something or someone," Cho explained, her eyes still on the body. "Might have been the same person who caught up with Centers."

"Why do you think that?"

"Because Courtland was on the take."

"How do you know that?"

"I don't have any proof, but we've been watching him for months. He had too much money for a cop. He simply owned too much property for a man with his income. I think whatever mystery was dropped in your lap is what cost this fat man his life. And I figure he was as in the dark as you are. He was just following orders to hang you."

Walking over to the crumpled Crown Victoria, she picked up a large duffle bag and headed toward the highway, retracing the path Courtland's car had made through eight-foot-high rows of corn. Burke didn't need an invitation to follow. When they got to the highway, now fully lit with flashing squad car lights, she paused and waved at Clark Mason.

"What do you need?" he hollered from across the strip of two-lane concrete.

"Stay there," Cho ordered. "Make sure they don't screw anything up. Only our people have access to the crime scene. I'm going to catch a ride back with Dr. Burke."

She looked at Burke. "Where's your car?"

Burke pointed to a spot about a half mile down the shoulder of the road.

"Let's go," she said.

DRAFTED

It took just over twenty minutes to get to 2317 Cedar Street. Neither driver nor passenger had said a word. Though Burke likely was unaware of it as he drove, Cho was studying him, trying to detect the slightest signs of shock or fear. She saw none. He was naturally apprehensive — that was wise — but not scared. She was impressed as he calmly got out of the car and confidently walked up to his front door. She followed on his heels and, once inside, walked by him through the living room and into the kitchen.

"Turn on the light," she said as she placed the duffle bag on the table.

Burke flipped a switch and moved to a point just off the woman's right shoulder. She sensed him staring at her.

"You're looking at the scar?"

"No," he replied.

"Sure you were," she shot back. "Everyone does. I look at it every time I look in a mirror."

As if he had now been given permission, Burke looked back to the angry, thick raised line on her neck. She could sense that it fascinated him. It likely troubled him too.

"Got anything to eat?" she asked, attempting to ease the discomfort that had invaded the room.

Burke nodded. "Some deli stuff in the fridge. Want a sandwich? I've got ham and turkey."

"Ham, with mayo."

"Sure," he replied. He opened the refrigerator, grabbed the meat and the mayo, and set them on the counter. He pulled out a couple of plates, retrieved a loaf of bread, and placed the stuff on the table.

"Chips?" he asked.

"No. A sandwich is all I need."

"Coke?"

"Do you have a Dr Pepper?"

Burke nodded. As he headed back to the fridge, the agent set the duffle bag on the floor and took a seat at the table.

"What do you want on your sandwich?" she asked.

Returning with the soft drinks, he replied, "Mayo and turkey."

As she slapped the snack together, he opened the cans and took a seat. As they ate, she could sense him looking everywhere but at the scar. Though he tried hard to resist, his eyes constantly flashed back to her neck, his curiosity simply too strong.

"A knife," she said.

"Sure," he answered, mistaking her statement for a question. As he pushed back from the table, he asked, "What kind do you need? Butter or steak?"

"Neither." She pointed to her neck. "It was a large knife that made the scar. You want to hear the rest of the story?"

He nodded, his eyes again fixed on the four-inch gash, long since closed with scar tissue.

"I was an Army Ranger before I joined the FBI, so I thought I knew it all. Figured I had all the answers and didn't need any help. We raided a suspected terrorist cell in New Jersey not long after 9/11. Like a fool, I rushed in, violating all my army and bureau training, and one of the suspects was behind the door. He grabbed me and held a knife to my throat. I tried to get away. It was the wrong thing to do. My movement caused him to react, and the blade dug into my throat. I almost bled to death."

Burke nodded. "Must have hurt."

"Not really," she said, her hand tracing the wound. "It just felt warm. I've talked to guys who've gotten shot. They pretty much say the same thing. It's not pain you feel but the warmth. Guess it's the blood."

The events of that night came back clearly only in nightmares. But now, here in this kitchen, the reality of that evening so long ago was once more fresh. She could smell the musty apartment and feel the blade.

"You know, I did think about dying," she continued. "As the knife went in, it hit me that I could die. I knew it was a real possibility, but it didn't scare me. At least not then. Later on, when I had time to realize what had happened, I was really shaken. But not then. Not at that moment."

She paused again. She had almost died that night. And if she had, she would have had only herself to blame. But she'd caught a break. A bit of luck had saved her from her ignorance. Mason started calling her the "Charmed One" that night. Since that time, she'd never blundered again. She was never again going to be dumb enough to rush toward death. She was intent on living to a very old age, not dying a young hero.

"In truth," Cho said, "I was lucky. We had EMTs on site, and they patched me up enough to get me to the ER. If they hadn't been there, my career would have been over almost before it began. Now the only residual effect is my voice. My grandmother says I sound like an old movie star from the '40s and '50s named Lizabeth Scott. Don't know about that; I've never seen any of her films."

"Sorry," he whispered. "Did you get the terrorists?"

"It was a bad tip." Cho laughed. "There was a lot of panic right after the Twin Towers went down, and we got oodles of tips that were bogus. That suspected terrorist cell turned out to be just high school kids sniffing glue. The guy who grabbed me was high."

Burke nodded, his eyes moving from her throat to her face.

She figured she had gotten him over that hurdle. His questions had been answered. Now he could focus on what she was going to have to ask him to do. But first she needed his trust. "My files said you were once married."

Burke shrugged. "I was. It lasted seven years."

"What happened?"

"I wasn't a very good husband," he replied. "I worked too much, had too many meetings and seminars. I just wasn't ever home. Even when we were together, I was always chasing history, going from one dig to another, one library to another. Vacations were excuses for me to do research."

"Where is she now?"

"Does it matter?"

Cho drained the last bit of Dr Pepper. "Are you better off alone?"

"I don't know." His honesty was almost startling. "Nothing's changed. I still work all the time. I don't have many friends and no hobbies. I'm always looking for the next historical site to discover or explore. Most folks would call what I do pretty boring."

"It's anything but boring now," she said. "But at least having Courtland out of the picture should give you some room to breathe."

"I don't follow," he said, cocking his head to the side.

"The DA is working with us on this. He was more than willing to write you off as a suspect. Courtland wasn't." She studied him for a reaction. It was time for her to take the next step in what she had started at the scene of the wreck. He needed to know what he was really into and that he couldn't get out until they figured out who was behind the killings.

"Jeff," she began, her voice softer, her manner more open, "I am going to tell you something that I probably shouldn't. When Centers, or Columbo, walked into your office, it made you a target. They missed. Courtland was the rogue cop who was supposed to clean up the mess. When you survived, he fingered you to keep everyone's eyes off the real object of the search long enough for those behind the scenes to get what they want. It would have been easy for him. He wouldn't have been taking any chances. But the FBI was called in because Centers was on the watch list. We were already on to Courtland. So when Centers was killed, two different investigations merged."

"You knew Courtland was dirty and still let him work?" Burke cut in.

"Needed to find out who he was working for. Now we need to know how this ties in to that lost book you talked about."

She waited for Burke to finish his sandwich and then delivered her big punch. "You said your life was boring. Well, something you stumbled into has unleashed a scenario where lives have become cheap.

Especially yours. There are only two things that I figure would cause a crime wave like this in rural Illinois. The first might be a tie to some type of gang activity. Yet that sort of thing wouldn't have brought Centers to town. So my gut tells me it's the second."

"The second is?" Burke asked.

"In today's world and with Centers' involvement, I'd guess terrorism. There's a lot the FBI doesn't know, but I can give you these facts. Over the last seven months, Centers, posing as Columbo, was in six different countries, including a trip into Taliban-controlled Afghanistan. Wherever he went, there were several unexplained deaths. The count is well over a dozen. None of these seem to be connected, but each was violent. Someone is trying to make a point in a game that has high stakes. And you are now in the middle of it."

"But I don't—"

"I know," Cho said, "you want no part of this. But your normal life ended when Centers, or Columbo, as you call him, walked onto your campus. If you try to opt out now and go back to your classroom, I can't help you, and I predict that you'll get killed pretty quickly. One of your students might get hurt too. If you work with me, then maybe we can figure out who's behind all this, and you can dodge a few bullets."

Burke paused and licked his lips. "But if I read your tone correctly, you believe eventually one of the bullets will find me."

"Odds are not in favor of your living a long life," she admitted. "But you don't have to be a sitting duck. My dad taught me that ducks in the air are much harder to bring down than those paddling on the pond. Help me solve this thing. As I uncover more pieces to this puzzle, I think you might have a key to translating and putting the pieces together for me."

"And why do you believe that?" he asked.

"Because Centers believed it. He was sure you could answer questions that would lead him to the prize, and finding that prize has to be tied to some kind of terrorist plot."

The professor considered his options.

"What is in the back seat?" Cho asked.

"What?"

"Listen, Dr. Burke, at this point, holding anything out on me is stupid and pointless."

"How did you know about the trunk?"

"Ever since Centers was in your office, I know when you go to the bathroom. I know when you blow your nose. Not only have they been watching you, so have we. I know the trunk is in your car. Besides, I looked over my shoulder as I got in. What was in it?"

"You've been following me?"

"Yes, our people have been."

He paused for a moment, then, with a look of uneasiness, he said, "Nothing really worth noting. Columbo or Centers or whatever his name was wrote a journal about the KGB's attempts at finding the *Book of Joseph*. The trunk contained that journal, some photographs, and some maps. But the bottom line is that during his days with the KGB, they never got any traction. Every trail was a dead end."

He paused and licked his lower lip as if contemplating his fate. "There is one thing that might interest you."

"What's that?" Her tone was demanding. Whatever he was withholding from her, she wanted it now.

"It appears that Columbo was planted in the KGB by the Vatican. His whole mission was to find the book."

She rubbed her forehead. A double agent! It was possible. But that would have meant decades of being undercover. This whole thing didn't smell right.

"Bring the trunk in," she said. "I want to take a look at it."

"It's empty. I took the stuff out and stored it in my place in Royal."

"Fine, but I still want to take a look at it."

Shrugging his shoulders, Burke got up and headed toward the front door. She followed, watching from the entry as he opened the back door and retrieved the wooden box. He'd covered half of the thirty steps to the front door when a shot, fired from a high-powered rifle, rang out and clipped the trunk. He dropped the trunk and fell to the ground.

Cho killed the porch light and exploded out the door, the sound of the shot still echoing. She leaped from the two-foot-high concrete stoop and rolled on the front lawn. Staying in the shadows, she crawled to Burke.

"You okay?" she whispered.

"Yeah."

"Get that trunk inside. Now!"

The professor pulled himself to his feet, grabbed the trunk, and rushed toward the front door. As he made his move, Cho trained her eyes on a spot in the city park across the street where a shooter might be hiding. She held her breath, waiting for a flash of light. None came. Remaining in a crouched position, she spun and ran for the house. Another shot rang out. Cho had just climbed the second step and fell on her face on the porch. She crawled through the door on her belly, kicked the door shut behind her, and rolled onto her back.

Taking a deep breath, her hand went up to the scar on her neck. She traced it with her fingers and smiled.

THE MOLE

Bruno Krueger was in his limo on the way back from the theater when his cell phone rang. Easing back against the leather seat, he checked the caller ID and clicked on the speakerphone.

"What do you have?"

"The agent's dead."

"You're sure?"

"Got the news from our mole in Washington."

Krueger looked out at Lake Michigan and smiled. The woman had been getting too close. Courtland was the last straw. Now there was one less thing to worry about. "What about Burke?"

"We missed him."

Krueger shrugged. "No matter. He can be handled when the heat dies down a bit. Just keep an eye on him. What about Cho's files?"

"They really have nothing on us. Cho knew we had a mole at the bureau, but she couldn't identify him. So she kept much of what she knew in her head until it came time to actually move."

Krueger paused to observe a bevy of college coeds walking down Lake Shore Drive. "Do we know who will take over her spot?"

"Some guy named Mason."

"Keep him in a jar." Krueger laughed. "We need to get back to finding where Columbo hid his information. We need to find that book. With it I can consolidate all my bases and get the control I need to write my ticket with a long list of governments, as well as the Vatican."

Krueger ended the call, slipped the phone back into his pocket, and smiled. *Promises, Promises* had been entertaining, as musicals go, but a promise delivered was far more satisfying.

WAKE

The funeral service was held at First Methodist Church in Galesburg, Illinois. Hundreds turned out to honor the agent, including the vice president and the governor. Joining them was a man who observed the proceedings from the balcony with a covey of FBI agents hovering all around him. Even before the coffin was placed in the hearse, he was whisked away, back to a house on Cedar Street in Urbana. He would then be packed away to Canada, supposedly for a vacation, but it was really for his own protection.

Jeff Burke was more than happy to have an actor playing his role. After only a week in this game, he was tired of being a target. Wearing a fake beard, a body suit that added about sixty pounds, and a janitor's outfit, he had observed the services from the sanctuary's sound booth. Only after everyone had left the church for the cemetery did Burke and FBI agent Clark Mason hop into a church van. For the next two hours, they drove east, past Urbana and Danville on I-74 and into the state of Indiana. Their destination was an FBI safe house.

The farm where Mason deposited Burke had been owned by the agency for years. The FBI even had a couple of agents, posing as husband and wife, who actually farmed the spread. It appeared to be a normal family-run agricultural operation specializing in Angus cattle, but what no one knew was that the back half of one of the old barns had been converted into a very comfortable home. Over the years, a host of informants had stayed there. Burke was the first actually allowed to make the trip without a blindfold. He was the only guest who actually knew where it was and how to get there.

After they drove to the back of barn, Burke waited in the vehicle until Mason checked the perimeter. When the agent signaled it was safe, Burke, still disguised, got out of the van and slipped through a large barn door into a room containing a variety of ropes, hoes, rakes, and an old tractor. A second smaller door appeared to be just part of a wall in the back of a stall. Mason slid a board to the right to reveal a keypad. Punching in a code caused the wall to slide three feet.

"You should be fine here," Mason said before heading back to the van. "Call me if you need anything."

Burke barely had time to watch the entry close before a husky voice posed a strange question. "Well, how was my funeral?"

"You should have been there," he said.

"According to CNN," Cho said, laughing, "I was."

"I'm going to ditch the fat suit," Burke said.

Cho smiled. "With your double going on a fishing trip in Canada and only local agents knowing that I'm not dead and you're not gone, the mole in DC will not have a hint, and neither will the puppet master, whoever he is. You know, my face is everywhere. Kind of fun being a star. According to *Entertainment Tonight*, one of the major studios is planning to do a movie about my life."

Ripping away the beard, Burke said, "Isn't this a bit extreme? I mean, faking your own death and then relishing the publicity?"

"I didn't fake my death. You heard the shot. What an opportunity. They think I'm out of the picture and you are on your way out of the country. Now we can go to work. Besides, I have something to show you."

DATE

Burke, once more looking and feeling like himself, studied the trunk Cho had placed on the kitchen table. Except for the splintering where the slug had entered, it appeared just like it had when he'd first seen it in Girton's. Yet for reasons he didn't understand, the agent was excited.

"I didn't spend the *whole* day watching TV coverage of my death," she explained. "Read the tape measure on the outside from top to bottom."

Burke looked over her shoulder as she measured. "Twenty inches."

"Now watch what happens when I put it on the inside."

Burke observed the agent reposition the tape measure. It now read seventeen inches.

"Fake bottom?" he asked.

"Must be. Columbo, and I think we will stick with that name for the time being, wasn't leaving you the material you found and stored in the attic in Royal. He had pretty much told you that stuff already. He was leaving you whatever is still hidden in the bottom of this trunk. And in a few minutes, we'll know what that is."

Using a hammer and chisel, the agent worked on the side of the trunk just above the bottom. Burke was shocked by the way she attacked the wood. There was none of the careful deconstruction he had seen on *CSI*. Cho didn't seem to care what she destroyed. It took about three minutes to drive the chisel through the side of the trunk.

"I would have used a skill saw," she explained as she examined the one-inch-square opening, "but I was afraid the blade might damage what's under the false floor."

"I'm a bit surprised you aren't being more careful," he noted.

"No reason to," she explained while shining a flashlight into the hole. "This is not going to be evidence in a case. This is just us trying to get to the bottom of why so many people think an old scroll is worth killing for."

Cho set the light down and picked up a small keyhole saw.

"I can use this to make the opening larger. The blade is short, so it won't penetrate deep enough to damage anything."

It took the agent ten minutes to create an opening eight inches wide and one inch high. Her face was shiny with sweat. Setting the saw to one side, she looked inside with the flashlight.

"Okay, Dr. Burke," she said.

"I think it's time you call me Jeff," he replied.

"Fine. Jeff, lift the far end so that whatever is in there slides this way."

Burke grabbed the trunk, raising it up to a sixty-degree angle.

"Tap on the bottom." Her raspy voice was suddenly assertive and businesslike.

Holding the trunk with his left hand, he began to rap with his right.

"Harder!"

His rapping became pounding.

"Anybody home?" he said.

Cho ignored his attempt at humor.

"There we go," she said, "it's loose. I feel it. Okay, it's coming now. You can quit tapping."

After she slipped a single piece of paper from its hiding place, Burke eased the trunk back down on the table.

"That's it?" he asked. "There has to be more."

"Evidently not."

"What is it?"

"I don't know," she admitted. "You're the historian, maybe you can make something out of it."

Burke took the single sheet. In the center of the page was a cross. The sketch had been quickly rendered with little regard for detail.

Other than the four-inch drawing, the page was blank. Flipping it, the professor was presented with a photo of an old car pasted to the back of the sheet of paper. The radiator, styling, and wires dated it back to the 1920s.

"What do you make of it?" she asked.

He shrugged. "The cross could be a symbol for Christ. I can see how that would tie in to Columbo's quest, but I don't see how it tells us anything about the *Book of Joseph*."

"What about the car?"

Burke took a long look at the photograph. It was just an amateur's snapshot. The print measured three and a half by five.

"The car's front plate shows it had been on the road in 1929. The car looks like it was either well taken care of or almost new. I don't know what kind of car it is. Too bad the picture is in black and white. Can't tell the color of the car. There is a man behind the wheel. He's wearing a straw dress hat, a light-colored suit, and is looking directly at the camera. I don't recognize the man as being anyone of historical importance. His face is completely in the shadows."

He placed the paper on the table and looked at Cho. "Surely this can't be all there was in there. I can't see why Columbo would give his life for this!"

"All I felt," she replied. "Why don't you pick up the trunk and shake it with the opening facing the floor. Maybe something else will drop out."

Grabbing the antique in both hands, he went to work. He heard nothing rattling around and, in spite of his aggressive shaking, nothing fell out. They peered in with the flashlight and saw nothing.

Cho picked up the paper. "This meant so much to Columbo that he hid it. Cross ... car? Car ... cross? I don't get it. I was expecting a map or scribbled notes giving us more details on the book. But all we have is this."

She picked at the top corner and carefully peeled the photo away from the yellowing paper. When it was free, she examined the back and shrugged. "Nothing written here either. It's as blank as when it was printed."

Burke took the photo from Cho. Beyond the license plate, the landscape screamed central Illinois. The background showed cornfields spreading across the flat prairie, but there were no buildings to help identify the exact location. And there had never been anything written on the back of the snapshot.

He shook his head. "Maybe Columbo didn't know about this either. Maybe he didn't think of the false bottom."

Picking up the paper, he once again studied the cross. It was a two-dimensional sketch done in pencil. It was almost childlike in style, created with no artistic flair, and except for overlapping lines, not much detail. It was only when he flipped the page over that he saw something new.

"Look, Lisa." He paused, realizing it was the first time he had used the agent's first name.

"You can call me Lisa," she assured him as his eyes caught hers. "What is it?"

"There's something faintly written on the page. It had been hidden by the picture."

"Let me see."

Moving to a lamp, she studied the faint scribbling. He looked over her shoulder. "Do you think it's what we need?"

"Could be. Can you make it out?" she replied. "My close vision is not very good. What do you see?

Burke took the sheet, pulled glasses he used for reading out of his pocket, and placed the paper directly over the top of the lampshade. Even with the light shining through it, he could barely see the light pencil marks.

"The lab could easily get the information for us," Cho noted.

"And if I had a scanner, so could I," Burke replied. "I could scan it, import it into Photoshop, and adjust the contrast. It would pop right out."

"There's a scanner in the communication room here." Cho grinned. "Follow me!"

Cho led Burke to a small back room filled with surveillance monitors. She flipped a switch and the scanner came on. Glad we got your laptop back."

"Let me plug the MacBook in. We'll put that sucker on the scanning bed and go to work."

Five minutes later, the hidden message was clear. Even though they could both see it on the screen, it was Burke who whispered, "January 16, 1942."

LACUNA

Jumping online, Cho typed the date and did a search. She spent five minutes studying several dozen entries. Clearly exasperated, she moaned, "It makes no sense."

Reading over her shoulder, Burke noted three newsworthy events that happened on January 16, 1942. "The Japanese advanced on Burma, William Knudsen was appointed a general in the army, and a plane crash took the life of movie star Carole Lombard."

"How could any of those be the link?" Cho asked.

"We're focusing only on American history," Burke noted. "Let's expand the search to examine world events."

This new search revealed nothing additional.

He looked at Cho. "Is the date a code? Could it be a location or a name?"

"I have no idea," she admitted.

"Okay," Burke said, "let me at the keyboard. Maybe we're missing something on the car."

"I can help you with that," she said. "Give me the picture again." She studied it for a moment and then turned back to Burke. "Do a search for images of 1926 to 1929 Franklins."

"How did you know—"

She cut him off before he finished his question. "My father has two hobbies. One is car restoration. I went to a lot of shows as a kid and nothing looks like a Franklin."

Burke went to work again, with Cho leaning over his shoulder. Three minutes later she announced, "The car in the photo is a 1928 Franklin."

"And that means what?" he asked.

"Nothing I know of. Here is what I can tell you. The company was founded in the early 1900s in Syracuse, not surprisingly by a man named Franklin. The car was revolutionary, expensive, and the engine was air cooled. The car company went under in the Depression, though the company continued to manufacture motors for the aircraft industry for years."

"So it's not the make of the car that was important?" he asked.

"I don't think so," she replied. "Maybe it's the man in the picture. But since I'm dead and there's a mole in Washington, we can't scan the photo and send it off to the FBI lab. If we could, they could do a facial recognition search and see if anything pops up."

"So," he sighed, "we're at a dead end."

"For the time being. Let me see the picture again."

Cho's eyes were locked on the image when Burke asked what he knew would be an unexpected question. "Why did you go into the Rangers?"

Cho smiled. "My dad was a Navy pilot. My older brother went into Special Forces, but he chose the Army. Mom had been an Army nurse. She and Dad met in Korea in the 1970s, when they both were stationed there. So I come from a military family. It was a natural and expected move."

"So your mom was Korean?" Burke asked.

"Wake up, man." Cho laughed. "If that were the case, my name wouldn't be Cho. No, she was born in Arkansas. My dad was born in San Francisco. His people emigrated from Korea more than a century ago. He is a third-generation UCLA grad. Bet you didn't expect that."

Burke laughed. For the first time, he felt an almost human side to the agent. Maybe there was a heart there and a sense of humor too. At least for a moment, she wasn't all business.

"Why did you leave the Rangers?"

She shook her head. "Wasn't cut out for it."

"You mean too small?"

"Hey," Cho shot back, "I know about a dozen ways to kill you with my bare hands. And I can do it too. I passed every physical test with the top scores. It wasn't that."

"So, what?" Burke asked.

"Someone I loved got killed." Her voice was now softer, as if she was swallowing something other than her words. "I lost my zeal after that. Then when my brother almost died, I opted to not re-up. But I still wanted challenges, and the FBI needed a female agent with my skills."

Burke was about to ask an even more probing question when Cho's cell phone rang. "Yeah." She paused. "Got it. Thanks."

She slid the phone back into her pocket. "That was Mason. You are on your way to Canada to go fishing."

"I hope I have a good time." Burke laughed and his green eyes locked onto her brown eyes. For a second they lingered there, but the gaze he got back made him strangely uncomfortable and completely intimidated.

"Back to what we found," he said in an effort to escape what seemed to a hypnotic trap. "We have a date, a car, a man in a suit, and a cross. Columbo or someone else hid this information for a reason. Is everything on the paper valuable, or is there just one thing we need to know?"

"Who knows?" she replied. "Time to think like an agent or historian. Let's go back and look at what we do know and start there."

She tapped the desk. "Evidently the book's worth killing for. The Vatican has been searching for it for centuries. It was then seen about the time of Henry VIII and was supposedly sold at an auction about 240 years ago. No one has turned up any record of it since."

"And," Burke said, picking up the trail, "the clue Columbo wanted might have been in a building that burned on campus last week."

"Then, since we can't make heads or tails of this, it would seem our only choice is to try to figure out what the South American is up to."

"Krueger."

"Mason and I think he is tied in to this because of the book, though I don't know why he would want something this rare. Mason has a tag on him, so we can do no more until Krueger makes a move. I need to get some sleep. I'm going to my room. You need to get some sleep too."

Burke nodded, but instead of heading to his room, he picked up the photo in one hand and the paper in the other and carefully studied them again. A cross, a car, and a date. The latter two drew only blanks, but what about the cross? The drawing was crude, but it had to mean something.

He put the page back on the scanner, hit the button, studied the menu, and set the scan to 800 percent at 300 dpi. He then waited for the image to pop up on the screen.

After hitting the magnification button until it rendered the document at the full 800 percent size, he slowly went over each random line on the sketch. And there it was! Adjusting the contrast, the tiny, once barely visible marks became clear. He saw the words "Filius Baltore."

A quick Google search revealed the meaning of Filius. It meant "son." Yet son of Baltore made no sense. Baltore was a priest. He shouldn't have had children. So who or what was the son of Baltore?

Driven by curiosity, he turned back to the screen. There had to be more words hidden somewhere. Slowly he continued to study the cross in extreme detail. There was nothing on the upper portion of the paper. The middle drew a blank as well. But at the very bottom, something popped out. It was faint, but it was there. After adjusting the contrast, it became clearer. "Custodis Joseph Lacuna."

Another Google search revealed the meaning: "Keeper of Joseph's words."

Was Baltore's son the keeper of the *Book of Joseph*? What did that mean? Burke had assumed that Columbo had drawn the cross. Maybe he didn't draw the cross. Maybe this was something he found. Maybe he realized it was important but had yet to figure out why. If so, this sheet of paper wasn't an answer; this sheet of paper was a question.

Turning back to his MacBook, Burke typed in "Keeper of Joseph's words." He hit the search button and waited. Twenty-two websites came up, but none offered any answers. Yet going to a blog search did give him something to chew on. In an entry about secret organizations and societies, "The Keepers of Joseph's Words" was listed. The entry under the name was short.

Supposedly founded in England in the late 1700s, The Keepers of Joseph's Words (KJW) was a group whose sole purpose was to possess and protect a mysterious spiritual artifact. Members supposedly included historians and theologians. One legend suggests Thomas Jefferson was a leader in the society. The last mention of the KJW in England was in 1822. There were a few reports of the society operating in the United States as late as the 1930s.

If it ever really existed, the KJW was likely nothing more than a social club—a way for husbands to spend a night a month away from home. Some believe that the item the club protected was nothing more than a jug of hard cider.

Another hour of searching provided no more information on the KJW, but unlike the experts, thanks to one piece of paper, Burke was now sure this society had been very real. Turning his attention back to the drawing and the photo, a thought hit him. Was the man in the car a member of the society? If so, maybe Columbo hid it because he couldn't figure out who the man was.

FOUND

We've got it!" Mitzi Fogleman exclaimed.

Krueger looked up and smiled. Normally anyone who entered his office without being announced met his wrath. But not Fogleman. She had orders to interrupt him anytime day or night if she had news on the lost scroll. So with a beaming face, he welcomed the middle-aged scholar and pointed her toward a chair beside a massive aquarium.

Krueger knew every facet of Fogleman's life. She was an only child, the product of a late marriage. She was born when her mother was forty-five. Her father, a minister, had sheltered the child, even homeschooling her to keep her from any negative influences. With few friends and no siblings, she turned to books to fill her long days. Fogleman had read the encyclopedia from A to Z by the age of eight. When she was twelve, she was taking high school courses. She graduated from Columbia at sixteen and earned her doctorate in ancient studies from Harvard before her twenty-first birthday. She worked for the Smithsonian for a decade before being recruited by Krueger International. With her parents both in the grave and no close friends, she had nothing else to live for but her work. She was therefore the perfect employee. Sensing her abilities and dogged determination, Krueger put her to work finding the *Book of Joseph*. She'd given every moment of the last twelve years to that quest.

"So," he asked, "have you found the book?"

Fogleman, clad in a dark blue suit, her graying hair placed carefully in a no-nonsense bun, adjusted herself in the large leather chair and answered, "The news is not *that* good. But an important missing puzzle piece is now in our hands. In fact it was so interesting I chose to fly back to the States. I hope my use of company funds was not inappropriate?"

Pulling up a chair beside hers, Krueger smiled. "No, you were right to come in person. I take it you found this new clue in London?"

"Yes." She smiled. "What a quest it was! It took me six months in the British Archives until I finally uncovered a document linked to the auction of Atkins Temple's possessions. It is not the original document we have been searching for, but rather a paper from the auction company working with the city of Berkshire during the 1780s."

Krueger leaned closer to his guest. "A paper you say?"

She smiled, placed the fingertips of her hands together, and explained, "The key was finding that the Niles Auction House was in charge of selling the goods."

"So," Krueger cut in, "the document was listed in their records?"

"No," she said, shaking her head and moving her hands slightly forward to emphasize the point. "Not specifically. But logic tells me that is not a problem. You see, the items were not auctioned individually. Everything Temple owned—his home, clothing, papers, and even his horse—were sold in one lot. And thanks to the Niles records, we have the name of who purchased it. With that information, we can begin the process of tracing the buyer's descendants. In other words— the trail, which has been dead for so long, is fresh."

Krueger grinned. He got up and walked over to the window. Twenty years of work was about to be realized. He could sense it. Finally everything he needed to gain power over the Vatican and, in time, shift the philosophy and beliefs of much of the Western world was in his hands. And it was a woman who had never been kissed who'd broken it open for him—a woman as pure as a nun! What a hire and what an irony!

Without turning back to Fogleman, he posed the obvious question: "The name?"

"The document listed the buyer as Joseph Lacuna of London."

Joseph Lacuna! He silently chanted it several times. It had a flow to it. It rolled off the tongue in a musical fashion. Joseph Lacuna. A very unusual name, but that fit, as this was a very unusual quest. He spun back to face his guest.

"Must have been an Italian," Krueger noted.

"Could be," the researcher replied. "I don't know much about him yet. I only discovered an address for him. There was a bookstore in London, and Lacuna was listed as the owner until 1807. I'm going to dig deeper when I get back to the UK to find out where he went from there. I do know there is no listing of his dying in reports through 1840. So I have a lot more papers to dig through. I'll make reservations today. I can catch the late-night flight and be at the archives when they open in the morning."

"Good," Krueger replied, "but don't bother with the reservations. We'll take one of the company planes. I'll go with you and hole up at the estate outside of London. You can stay at the suite downtown. My driver will pick you up at five this afternoon. Make sure you pack enough clothing to remain in England until we get the answers we need."

"That only gives me three hours," she replied. "I'll get started now."

"And, remember, no one is to know about this but you and me."

"That's why I flew in to tell you," she explained. "You told me to keep this a complete secret, and I have never shared a word about this with anyone. And you have always told me phones could be tapped and emails hacked."

"Very wise," he assured her. "I deeply appreciate not just your work but your loyalty. Now, run along!"

"I will see you very soon, sir."

"Yes." He smiled.

Krueger watched Fogleman exit before returning to his desk chair. The mess at the University of Illinois didn't matter now. Cho was dead, Burke was in Canada being protected by the FBI, and there was no one else in the picture. If it took a day, a month, or even a year, there was now no rush. Finding the heirs of Joseph Lacuna and uncovering what he did with Temple's possessions was doable.

Yet there was one tragic element. When Fogleman gave him the location of the book, her usefulness would be over. She couldn't be trusted; she was too idealistic. And she couldn't be bought off; she was too honest. So he'd treat the woman to a night out on the town, give her the very first kiss of her life, and arrange an accident. She'd never suspect a thing, and at least she'd die happy and unaware that her life's work and discovery would be used for something she would hate. It would really be an act of compassion to keep her from realizing how many would be crushed due to her discipline and skills. Killing her would not be an act of cruelty, but one of mercy.

LORD BALTORE

Born in Atlanta in the years before Martin Luther King was organizing his civil rights movement, Dr. Alexander Briggs grew up in a poor, segregated section of the city. His father was a street worker and his mother was a teacher. While other young boys in his neighborhood were pushed toward athletics, Alexander's parents emphasized academic achievement. This mentoring and focus, along with a chance meeting with Dr. King as an eight-year-old, shaped his vision, direction, and determination. Surprising no one, he earned a full scholarship to Harvard, where he graduated with honors in 1972. His master's came from New York University. He then earned a PhD from Southern Methodist University in Dallas. He continued his studies in Rome and Jerusalem before landing at the University of Illinois in 1984. Patient, wise, and modest, Briggs was the image of what a college professor should be. No doubt these traits led to his being named dean of the Religious Studies Department in 1990. Within a few more years, he was also one of the area's best-known citizens.

Tall and thin, his ebony skin accented by a full head of gray hair, he was viewed as the most distinguished man on campus in 2000 and the most respected professor in the Faculty Senate. His strong voice, great command of the English language, and unique storytelling abilities — learned at his grandfather's knee — made him a student favorite as well. In the classroom, his charm and wit were combined with his vast knowledge. It was a formula that worked so well that half of those who took his courses did so as an elective.

Briggs had a light schedule on Wednesdays, finishing his final class just before noon, and had planned to leave his office early to spend a bit of time with his granddaughter. Though still in elementary school, Monique was an accomplished pianist and had a recital scheduled for five. He'd promised to be there and was determined to make good on that promise. Yet just as he was shutting down his computer and readying for his departure, an unexpected guest walked in.

This was the last thing Briggs needed. His initial reaction was to simply to tell the man he would have to come back tomorrow. But being rude was not in his nature. The professor sized up the visitor for a moment, then, his southern accent dripping from his words, said, "Yes. What can I do for you?"

"Dr. Briggs, my name is Clark Mason. I'm with the FBI. I'm sorry to bother you without an appointment, but I can assure you it is very important. It's actually a matter of national security."

Briggs almost laughed. "Those are words I never expected anyone to say to me. I've heard all about an emergency with a stopped-up toilet or an assignment, but never one that centered on the welfare of the entire country. Surely you are overstating the issue."

"I think not," the agent replied.

The professor smiled. "Then you have my interest. And, if you are working locally, then you must have been a friend of the young FBI agent who was shot last week. So you have my sympathy as well."

"I am," Mason answered. Then, correcting himself, he said, "Rather, I was. In fact, that is why I am here. I need your help with the case involving Lisa Marie Cho."

"My help?" Briggs pointed to his chest. His deep voice reflected his disbelief. "That's a bit hard to understand. I might know a great deal concerning the case of Cain and Abel, and I could give you enough material to convict David of a wide variety of crimes, but my knowledge of modern forensic science is limited to the programs my wife watches on TV. And, besides, I didn't know Miss Cho."

Mason nodded. "Your friend Dr. Jefferson Burke believes you might have knowledge that could provide a motive for the shooting as well as for the brutal murder at his home on Cedar Street and for the burning of Bruce Hall."

Briggs shook his head and, after glancing at his watch, replied, "I doubt it, but feel free to probe my rather feeble mind. And, as the chairs in here are rather hard, I think we'll be more comfortable if we sit at the conference table in the next room. No one is using it right now, so we'll have privacy. Follow me."

The conference room was next door to the professor's office and resembled a small library. Except for the two windows on the outside wall, the room was covered by floor to ceiling bookshelves. The books that filled those shelves looked to be as old as the school, and it had been founded in 1867. Briggs noted Mason's eyes taking in the overwhelming amount of dusty reading material.

"These volumes are here because the university has no other place for them. In other words, no one has any use for them. Their purpose is largely decorative and environmental. By the latter, I mean they serve as great insulation against the outside heat and cold. And there are times when I come in and pick one out to read. I've found some good information here and a lot of trivia for my classes."

"Interesting," Mason replied.

Briggs fingered several books on a center shelf as he spoke. "Probably not that interesting. Just think, when these books were written, they were important enough for the university to purchase and place in the main library. But now they are like clothing from the eighties, hopelessly out of style. By the way, I have a few leisure suits for sale if you need one." Briggs smiled as he turned toward his guest and posed a question: "Books on religion are constantly being written. Do you have any idea why?"

"No, sir," Mason answered, his eyes glued to his host.

"Because with each new generation, new views on faith surface. We are constantly filtering religion through the light of modern experiences. It is amazing how differently the theologians of 1750 viewed Christ as compared to the way today's writers view him. The same goes for Muslims' views of Muhammad. Views are always changing, and they are tempered by the present, not the past."

Briggs cocked his head, his brown eyes somehow mirroring a genuine smile that displayed his perfect teeth. "Pick any of the chairs you like."

Mason chose a padded green leather model nearest a corner of the fifteen-foot-long table.

Briggs took a matching one opposite the agent. "I often wondered," he said, "if so many books with so many different views on our spiritual mentors are written to more deeply explain faith or to serve as a platform for personal agendas. As I grow older, I am becoming convinced it might be more the latter. Here I am, a man who has penned more than two dozen books on religion, and I am telling you that you might be better served just to read the Bible than the stuff written by experts like me."

"Thanks for the insight," Mason replied, "but I think I might just pick up one of your books anyway."

"My publisher and my banker would appreciate that," the professor admitted.

"Now, Dr. Briggs," the agent began, "Dr. Burke told me that you had studied the religious practices of American presidents and how their faith influenced decisions made while in office. In fact, he said you are the authority."

"It is a passion of mine," Briggs admitted, pacing his words as carefully as an African American minister speaking before his flock, "and I have presented many seminars and written dozens of papers on the subject. Let me ask, are we speaking generally or do you need to focus on something specific? I hope it is the latter, or we will be here for months."

"Thomas Jefferson."

The professor smiled. "There is a great deal to know about that man. It would be a lot easier to give you information on William Henry Harrison. He only served thirty days."

Mason laughed. "True. But what I'm looking for deals with only one religious matter. Specifically, a secret society he might have been a part of."

Briggs folded his hands together while resting his elbows on the table. As he spoke, he raised his eyebrows. "You *do* know that Jefferson was a Deist, not a Christian? The same was true of many of our founding fathers. They believed in a supreme being but thought God walked away from the world after he created it. Today we tend to reframe Jefferson and others in the way faith is viewed now. We like to think of him as being an evangelical Christian. In his time, religious leaders respected him but viewed him as being a bit 'New Age' and not Christian at all. Pardon my using a term from current language to put old history into perspective. But if you were to ask most preachers back then, they would have told you Jefferson was a good man but was going to hell when he died. Imagine that kind of message being given today from a pulpit or the halls of Congress about one of our founding fathers!"

"What he was or believed is not what concerns this case," Mason assured him. "I need to know if in your studies you discovered his association with Custodis Joseph Lacuna."

Briggs smiled. "Keepers of the Book."

"You've heard of it then."

Briggs nodded. "You have to understand that during that period of time, there were a great number of so-called secret societies. Many were much to do about nothing. Supposedly Jefferson was a part of several of them. There are hundreds of books in this room dealing with secret societies. Most highlight everything from Knights Templar to the Masons. But I only know of one that even mentions Custodis Joseph Lacuna. Some believe it to be a spoof of all the others."

"But it was real?" the FBI agent asked.

"It is my belief it was a minor player. So yes, it was real."

"Any theories on why it existed?"

"My guess," the professor continued, his tone suddenly a bit more scholarly, "has always been that it was there to protect and preserve some historical relic that either was created or owned by a man named Joseph. I had a teacher at Harvard who once told me he felt it was the coat of many colors. And while a coat is not a book, I guess that guess is as good as any, though I tend to lean toward a lost sea scroll or something. Who knows?"

Mason nodded. "Do you believe Jefferson kept whatever it was in the White House?"

Briggs raised his hands. "Sounds as good a theory as anything else, that is, if there really was something to the legend. But if you're wondering if it remained there, I doubt it. It's likely that the next president wouldn't have been a member of the society, so Jefferson would have taken the object with him when he left."

"Any idea on who would have gotten it next, after Jefferson?" Mason asked.

"Since we don't know the members of the society," Briggs explained, "and as we don't know what they were protecting, I can't hazard a guess on that."

Suddenly Briggs turned the tables and became the polite inquisitor. "Mr. Mason, I am beginning to feel like one of my students facing an oral examination. So, if you don't mind, let me reassume my position of authority by posing this question: What in the world does this have to do with Miss Cho's death?"

"Maybe a great deal," Mason replied. "Dr. Burke is guessing that the object that the Keepers of the Book was formed to protect is very real and might well be the key to rewriting one of the most vital elements of the Christian faith. Lisa was getting too close to finding the person who was looking for it. If she had found that person, then she would have known why it was worth killing for."

"The divinity of Christ?" Briggs cut in.

Mason didn't respond. His head never moved. His eyes gave away nothing, but Briggs sensed he'd guessed right. So that was what this was all about, he thought. The divinity of Christ was still a hot-button topic. And without proof, it had always been more a matter of faith than logic. But if there was a document that could be proven authentic, and if that document could turn the Christian concept of Jesus Christ upside down, then nothing would ever be the same again. That kind of document would definitely be worth killing for. Given time, it might even change the course of history and the balance of world power. A world without a divine Christ would be a very different world indeed.

Slowly pulling himself out of his chair, Briggs walked around the table to a far wall. In the middle of the fifth shelf, he pulled down a book with a green canvas cover. It was one of the few books in this room he had studied often. He flipped through about a third of the manuscript before pausing to scan the text. He turned an additional half a dozen pages before finding the passage he wanted. Walking back to the table, he placed the book in front of Mason.

"I told you I had been through many of the pages in this room. Read the third paragraph."

> Though there is little known about Custodis Joseph Lacuna, it was said the society never numbered more than twenty at any given time. One man was chosen to protect the artifact. That man was given the honorary title Lord Baltore. What the society possessed has never been revealed.

"Does that help?" Briggs asked. "In the thousands of volumes in this room, that is the only mention I know of Custodis Joseph Lacuna."

"I don't know if it contains an answer," Mason replied, "but can I take this book to Dr. Burke? He might know."

"Sure. When he's ready to bring it back, Jeff can find me. Now, as I don't have anything else I can add, I need to bid you adieu. There's a concert I can't miss that begins in less than an hour."

The agent rose and presented his hand. "Thank you, Dr. Briggs."

The two shook hands, then the professor said, "Good luck. Oh, and Mr. Mason, remind Jeff he still has one of the props I use for my class on New Testament history. I need it back before next semester."

"I will, sir."

Briggs watched Mason leave, then sat down again at the table. A single question would hound him for the remainder of the night, and for many nights after that: What if my entire life has been based on a lie?

PLANS

L ord Baltore," Burke whispered as he reviewed the passage for the fifth time. "That seals it for me. The society was real and was formed to protect the *Book of Joseph.*"

"Well," Cho replied, "what difference does that make if we don't know where the book is? To get on the road to solving a mystery, you have to have a starting point. Not only do we not know where we are going, we don't even know where to begin."

"Maybe we do," Burke replied. "Did Mason find Krueger?"

"The world thinks of Krueger as a businessman, so he doesn't hide his moves. He's in London. The company press release says he's there to investigate purchasing some oil leases in the North Sea. Oh, by the way, his chief researcher of historical documents is with him."

"Then there is no reason for us to be there."

"Why not?" Cho asked. "Since we don't have a place to start, shouldn't we assume that he is one step ahead of us and we need to be where he is in order to catch up?"

Burke smiled. "Let me take you back to when you were a student at UCLA," he said. "Do you remember when you were placed in a group and given a group project?"

"Sure. I hated it."

"Of course you did," he replied. "But remember this, usually there was one person who did almost all the work and the other students just waited for that one person to finish before actually getting involved in preparing the final presentation. So who was the wisest student? Was it the one who spent days on research or the five or six who waited for that ambitious student to finish their work for them?"

"Is this a trick question?" Cho asked.

"No." He laughed. "I want you to answer it honestly."

"Okay, the smart ones were the people who let the other guy do all the work. That must make me the dumb kid because I was always the one who did all the work."

"You get an A, Miss Cho," Burke replied. "Now take this same concept forward to our problem. When it comes to Krueger, we just need to wait until they are finished with their research. We borrow what they find. So just have someone in London keep an eye on them. If and when they find something, we can move in."

"So we stay here at the safe house and wait?" an exasperated Cho asked. "I've been here four days, and I don't know how much more I can stand. I have to do something!"

"No, Lisa," he assured her. "I don't want to wait either. History and discovery might come together in one place, but there are many different roads to take to get to that point. Do we have the information on Columbo's travels?"

Picking up a legal pad, she scrolled through her notes. "In the last six months, he was in Rome, London, back to Rome, to Santiago in Chile, Rome again, and then he tried to get into Afghanistan, but was turned back. In fact, he tried three times to enter Afghanistan and never made it. He was in Pakistan before he came to visit you."

Burke absorbed the information, mentally tracing each move in Columbo's trek. Afghanistan and Rome were the constants. The man was repeatedly drawn to those two places. The Vatican was obvious, but why the other? The answer might be only an hour away. "We need to get the papers from my house in Royal. Let's go on a road trip."

Cho looked at him as if he'd gone mad. "Anywhere that people will easily recognize you is off-limits. And I'm officially dead."

She was right. A dozen folks would spot him the minute he drove into the small town. A minute later, thanks to cell phones, everyone would know he was there. Within five minutes, Marge would be inviting him over for chocolate pie, and the world would know he wasn't in Canada. Then he would be a target again.

"Lisa, initially I didn't think what was in the trunk was important. But with the latest bit of evidence we found, I've changed my mind. But I'm going to need help. I can decipher the maps, but there are papers I can't translate in that trunk. And it will take knowing what is in those papers to figure out where Columbo wanted to go in Afghanistan."

"Okay," she said, "Mason could bring the stuff back here. After all, the FBI has an interest in your home and your welfare."

She grinned and then posed an odd question: "So, do you have any fishing equipment there?"

"What?"

"Rods, reels, that sort of thing."

"Sure, but what does that have to do with anything?"

"You're supposedly in Canada fishing, remember? Mason could pick up some stuff and tell folks he's sending it to you. It's a plausible story that would create less suspicion than searching for evidence."

Made sense, but Burke hated not getting to go. Still, for the moment, he had no choice. "Okay, just get Mason there as soon as you can and have him bring the stuff back here. I'm betting Columbo was trying to get back to the monastery he'd visited with the KGB. Since he tried to go there before he came to visit me, he likely believed that whatever was there was a vital link in the information chain."

The agent shrugged. "Sounds good to me. We should be able to get the materials here within a few hours. Mason's still in Urbana."

That was all good, but it wasn't enough. The materials alone wouldn't do it. Burke had to have one more piece to fully understand this part of the puzzle. "We need something else too."

"Yeah, some burgers and chili from Steak 'n Shake." She laughed.

"Well, that too, but I need Dr. Briggs here. He can translate materials I couldn't read the other day."

"We can make that happen. Anything else?"

Burke nodded. "Yeah, can you get us into Afghanistan?"

Cho shook her head. "That's a place that holds some really strange memories for my family."

"What?"

"Nothing, Jeff. Nothing. Forget I said anything. But getting in there will not be easy. I might just have to rise from the dead to pull off that kind of miracle."

THE SHIPMENT

It would have been far better to send Fogleman back to London by herself. Then, when she found what he needed, Krueger could make the trip. But impatience had won out over logic. He just had to be there when it happened. This kind of behavior was so childlike and so beneath him, and now he was paying for it.

It really wasn't the waiting that bothered Krueger as much as the fact he hated England. He didn't like the climate, the food, or the people. For him, it was hell on earth. He wouldn't have mourned if the entire UK just suddenly blew up, the company holdings included, as long as he was either back on his South American estate or in his Chicago penthouse.

It was almost the middle of the afternoon. He was pacing back and forth in a huge drawing room. All over England, people were stopping for tea. Krueger had long wondered how they could drink that vile concoction. It's bitter and the aftertaste lingers like a nightmare. The only way to make it passable was by mixing it with scotch, and that seemed like such a terrible waste of spirits.

While his private mental debate gave him no answers for British tradition, it did create a yearning for a real drink. Strolling across the drawing room to the bar, he grabbed a bottle of whiskey and poured four fingers into a crystal goblet. He studied the liquid for a moment, watching as the afternoon light showing through French doors caused the drink to shimmer and sparkle. Surely even the most staid Englishman would admit that a cup of tea never looked so sweet and certainly didn't carry the punch that his choice of tonic did.

"Can I get you anything, sir?"

Krueger didn't bother to look at Jenkins. He just shooed the butler away with a casual wave. He'd been trapped on the estate for four interminably long days, and having Jenkins and the other employees constantly checking on his desires was another thing that was driving him mad. What was it with English servants? Why were they constantly hovering about?

He drained his whiskey in one gulp. Licking his lips, he put the empty glass back on the bar's marble top and moved out to the patio. The fall air was crisp and, in spite of the sunlight, there was a dampness that made it seem much cooler than it was. Why would anyone who had money choose to live in England?

Pulling the collar of his sports jacket tight around his neck, he sat down in a wrought-iron deck chair. Geese were congregating around a pond in the garden area. Beyond that one of the gardeners was trimming some bushes. Another was tending one of the scores of flower gardens. How many employees did it take to maintain this place? He vowed to find out.

"Mr. Krueger."

Once more the billionaire did not acknowledge the butler, instead maintaining his gaze in the direction of the pond.

"There is a Miss Fogleman in the library."

Pulling himself to his feet, Krueger turned toward Jenkins. Krueger had inherited him when he purchased the estate in 2004.

Jenkins was a short, delicate man with thinning white hair whose appearance completely disproved the theory of intelligent design. He had been blessed with huge pale blue eyes but no chin. His fingers were too long and his legs too short. And he never smiled or frowned. It seemed his face was frozen. Maybe this was caused by a prodigious snout so heavy that it was all but impossible for the man to muster anything but his droll expression. The old man had been serving on this piece of property for more than four decades. What a waste of good time.

"Should I bring Miss Fogleman out here, sir?"

That was Jenkins, always trying to make life easier for everyone but himself. How could anyone respect a man who bent so low to do his job? Doormats were walked on less than the butler. And how could he speak so precisely when his lips barely moved?

"Jenkins."

"Yes, sir?" As he spoke the servant's eyes never made contact with Krueger's.

"Have you ever seen the movie *Gone with the Wind*?"

"I've heard of it, sir. American, I believe. But I have never seen it."

"You should," Krueger explained. "There's a woman they call Mammy in that movie who serves the O'Hara household. Study Mammy for a while and try to emulate the way she does business. She has backbone and grit."

"I will do that, sir. Now about Miss Fogleman?"

"I'll meet her in the library," Krueger replied. "And see that we are not disturbed."

Krueger waited for the little man to shuffle off before leaving the patio, then walked through the drawing room and entered the estate's library. He found his researcher studying the room's lone bookcase.

"Kind of strange it is called a library," he noted, catching his guest off guard. He waited until she had turned around before continuing. "After all, this room is more than a thousand square feet and there are only ninety-six books in the entire library. And that includes the dictionary in the desk's top right drawer. I know this obscure fact because I counted them all yesterday and the day before and the day before that. In fact, there are more cigars in this room than books."

"Nevertheless it is a beautiful room," she replied. "I think the tapestry above the fireplace once hung in Henry VIII's castle. I saw it in the background of a painting of Henry. The desk looks like a Louis XIV."

"Right on both counts," Krueger replied. "After we finish with our meeting, feel free to wander throughout all sixty-four rooms. By the way, there are supposed to be ten baths. I have only found eight, so if you come up with two more, draw a map so I can find them."

He waited to see if his less than subtle stab at humor elicited any reaction. When Fogleman failed to smile, he knew she had taken him seriously. Before the night was over, he was sure he would possess a detailed map, drawn to scale, pointing out all the washrooms in the three-hundred-year-old palace. The woman was even less human than Jenkins.

"Let's sit by the fireplace," he suggested.

She nodded, picked up her briefcase from the desk, and marched over to the green leather overstuffed chair.

Fogleman was wearing a gray suit. He'd never seen her in anything but navy blue. In this woman's world, such a move would be considered a radical shift in style. What had possessed her to change her uniform?

After the mild shock of seeing her dressed differently wore off, he took the chair across from his researcher and asked the question that had been haunting him for four long days. "Have you found anything?"

"Yes and no." The answer was quick if not precise. "Lacuna sold the bookstore about a decade after the auction. His name is not listed on any other piece of property or legal documents after that time. The only place I found it was on an obscure shipping manifest from 1799."

"So he left the country?" Krueger asked.

"I don't know if he did or not," she explained, "but I can tell you that on June 7, 1799, he placed something on a ship bound for the Far East."

"What was it?"

"Supposedly a crate of Bibles and various theological books. But there was no specific listing of the inventory or the size of the container."

"You sure it was the Far East?"

Fogleman nodded. Opening her briefcase, she pulled out a legal pad filled with handwritten notes. She flipped through a dozen pages. "Here it is. The ship was named the *Prodigal Son*. Its destination was Singapore. It made stops in New York, Rio de Janeiro, San Diego, and Manila before arriving in China. Another ship, *The Merry Star*, picked up cargo there in early 1800 and continued on to Bombay. That is where the crate was unloaded."

India. That made no sense. Why would Lacuna send the book there? Or perhaps the book was not a part of the shipment. Maybe this was another wild goose chase. Sadly, this was the only lead they had.

"So," Krueger noted, "we've hit another dead end. There is no way to track something like that in a city that size after all these years."

"The crate didn't stay in Bombay," she assured him. "That's just where the sea voyage stopped. I have records that show the crate was unloaded at that point and placed in a caravan. The ultimate destination point was a monastery in the Hindu Kush mountains of Afghanistan. The shipment was intended for a monk named Andre. According to my records, and they are far from complete, he received that package in May of 1800."

Krueger nodded. Maybe this tied in with his grandfather's diaries. It made a kind of perverted sense to have the document returned to the country where it had been stored before Baltore retrieved it in 753. It also would have been much easier to hide and protect there than in England or Europe. And who would make that kind of trip just to get a piece of paper? "Mitzi, precisely where are these mountains?"

"On the far eastern part of the country along the border with Pakistan. Supposedly it is in the area where Osama bin Laden often hides from United Nations and Pakistani forces. It is currently controlled by warlords and the Taliban."

No traffic agency could book that kind of trip, so for a normal person, the simple location of the monastery would have ended the quest. But Krueger had men who would be more than willing to go into the mouth of hell if the pay was right. And in this case, money would be no problem, and he was sure he could also arrange protection while on the ground.

"Mitzi, what do you know about this monk?" Krueger reached out and touched her left hand.

"Father Andre?"

"Yes. What can you tell me about him? Did he ever leave the monastery?"

"We have no way of knowing what happened to him without actually having access to the monastery's records."

Her explanation, while not unexpected, was hardly satisfying. "Is the monastery still there?"

"Mr. Krueger, the buildings were still there the last time anyone visited, but it is likely the Taliban executed the few remaining monks. They have not been heard from since the 1980s."

"What do you know about the order? What would they have done with the monastery's records?"

"I can only guess," she replied, "but historically, monks carefully hid all documents if they sensed they were going to be taken captive or killed. The Taliban warriors wouldn't have cared about the records, so if they were hidden, they are likely still there."

"At least that works in our favor. By the way, does the monastery have a name?"

"Yes, Domum Lignarii. Translated, it means 'home of the carpenter.'"

Krueger smiled. The named sealed it. Somewhere, buried under rocks or hidden in a wall, it was there, the greatest biblical discovery in history, and it was waiting for him. The trip to England had been worth it after all.

"Mitzi," he said as he jumped up from this chair, "take a few days off—enjoy some time exploring the city's many wonderful sites. And don't worry about expenses—the company will take care of everything. I will get a team assembled and you and I will go explore a monastery."

If the thought of visiting a place in one of the most volatile spots in the world frightened her, she didn't show it. In fact, there was a fire in her eyes he'd never seen. For a moment, she seemed somewhat attractive. Could there actually be a real woman buried behind those thick glasses?

Suddenly a thought hit Krueger. As the image grew clearer, he began to chuckle. The chuckle quickly grew into a laugh. With a confused Fogleman looking on, tears began to roll down the billionaire's face. Wouldn't it be ironic, he thought, if Osama himself is hiding in the same place where the monks hid the *Book of Joseph*. And all this time, the old terrorist doesn't know he's sitting on something that could do far more damage than all the suicide bombers in the world!

"Sir?"

"Yes, Mitzi?"

"Why is this so important to you?

"Knowledge is power," Krueger whispered. "Knowledge is power."

ON THE EDGE

The band of adventurers was made up of university professors Burke and Briggs, agents Cho and Mason, an Army Ranger, and a local guide. They had been traveling on foot through the Hindu Kush mountains for more than six hours. The temperature was well below freezing, and the strong winds made it seem closer to zero. Only the native Afghan and the soldier had ever experienced anything like it. And if Burke had his way, he never would again.

But they all were prepared. The FBI had outfitted the Americans in special heated clothing. They were also custom fitted with the latest mountain boots. Not only did this footwear grip in both dirt and on rocks but was designed with a heel that actually reduced pressure on the foot and bounced with movement. So a person could walk longer with less stress because of the spring the boot added to each step. The local guide had turned down the offer of the state-of-the-art survival wear, preferring to layer his clothing as his ancestors had been doing for hundreds of years. As he led them across the mountain pass, he didn't seem to fit with the rest of the team.

The Hindu Kush mountains are rugged and unforgiving, a barren landscape. The weather was brutal. It took a very special kind of person to live in this region. They had seen no one in more than five hours.

"This has to be the most godforsaken place on the whole planet," Cho grumbled, drawing her heavy coat tighter around her athletic frame and turning up the clothing's thermostat a notch. "My brother *told* me it was like this, and he was right."

"Your brother was here?" Burke hollered so she could hear him over the thirty-mile-an-hour north wind.

"Yeah!" Cho shouted. "He took a bullet and almost died in this area. He would not be happy if he knew I was here."

Looking up the trail, Burke watched his colleague Briggs carefully make his way along the rocky path more suitable for mountain goats than humans. This had to be one of the more unusual ways for a professor to spend the university's fall break. Though a full generation older than any of the other five taking part in this trek, he was doing remarkably well. During the hike through the rugged terrain, he'd never once asked to stop and rest. In fact, the three times they had paused, it was Briggs who had bounced up first when the call came to move forward. Whatever he was doing to stay in shape was working. Everyone ought to be following the same routine.

Yet the trip almost didn't happen for the two professors. It had taken a half dozen phone calls to Washington to clear the way for Burke and Briggs to be a part of the mission. Only when they had signed a dozen disclaimers and taken an oath of secrecy did the FBI allow their participation. And to make sure the two had a chance at surviving, a special operations officer had been assigned to protect them. Before they left the United States, this adventure had seemed like a great idea. The two professors had demanded that they be allowed to go. Now Burke wondered if they should have waited at home instead.

Along the edge of the steep mountain trails were sharp dropoffs, some falling more than a thousand feet. The narrow paths were sometimes no more than six inches wide. The Americans were linked together with a rope for security. If one slipped, then the other four would provide the anchor to keep that person from plunging to their death. Burke thought it more likely that the whole group would be pulled to their deaths. He hadn't mentioned his fear and hoped his theory wasn't put to a test.

For the last two hours, snow had been spitting at the small troop. The sky was warning that the flurries would soon intensify. Slick snow on the trail increased the danger. Reaching their destination quickly was now more than a goal; it was a major concern.

"Raymond," Cho called out, "will the snow be a problem?"

The Afghan shook his head. "It matters not. The place you search for is just over that ridge."

The guide turned back to pat the mule packed with supplies, then continued his steady walk along the edge of a sheer cliff. The slick conditions, the wind, and the freezing temperature seemed to have no effect on him or on the four-footed friend he was leading.

Stopping to take in the steep drop, Burke looked at Cho. "How does an Afghan get a name like Raymond?"

The agent grinned. "That's not his real name. He doesn't want anyone to know he's working with Americans. If the word got out, his family would be picking out funeral clothes. So he gave us the name Raymond."

"How did we find him?" Burke asked.

"He guided UN forces a few times. He was raised in the area. Even showed me a Bible he'd been given as a child by one of the monastery's monks. Said they carved toys for him too. So he knows how to get to Domum Lignarii."

"And what about the captain?" Burke asked, his eyes still looking down into the barren valley far below.

"Captain Casteel?" Cho asked.

"Yeah."

"Lou Casteel is a member of Army Special Forces," Cho explained. "He's trained in survival, is an expert shot, and you don't ever want to challenge him in hand-to-hand combat. The only one in this group who might have a chance against him is me."

Burke glanced at the man walking at the end of the line. Casteel couldn't be more than five-foot-nine and maybe weighed 160 pounds. Ghosts made more noise than he did. His footsteps fell silently; Burke's echoed up and down the mountains. In fact, Casteel was more a shadow than a living, breathing person. He'd only spoken once, when they were introduced before getting on the helicopter that brought them to the staging point. Then all he'd said was, "Nice to meet you, sir." Since then he had remained silent.

"You're holding everything up," Mason yelled back.

Turning, Burke faced the wind, leaned into the rock wall, and moved forward. Surely Cho knew what she was doing when she accepted Casteel as their protector. And even if she didn't, maybe because of the weather and the lack of recent violence in this remote area, they wouldn't run into any problems that required an Army Ranger's skills.

"There it is!" Raymond shouted from near the top of the 8,000-foot peak. "There is your monastery!"

"Yes" was the only word Briggs said before a rock gave way beneath his left foot. The older man quickly adjusted his balance to the right side of his body. The move postponed the inevitable, but it was too little, too late. He slid off the trail and out of sight. The rope linking the group jerked taut.

Burke, Casteel, and Cho had time to lean to their right and dig in. Mason, who was first in line after Raymond and unaware of what had happened, did not. When the rope jerked tight, he was yanked backward. Only his shoulders hit the four-foot-wide rocky trail before he plunged off into the void.

Burke had grabbed on to a rock jutting out of the edge of the cliff. The professor withstood the initial hit, but when Mason hit the end of the rope, the new force brought Burke to his knees. Only the special shoes gave him the traction he needed to be able to hold on to the rocky ledge. He glanced back. Casteel had a grip on the same jutting rock. Cho was braced. For the moment, they were safe. But how long could they hold the weight?

Turning his head, he could see only the blue cord going over the edge. He figured Briggs was about twenty feet beyond his view and Mason must have been swinging forty feet below. With snow now flying in his face, he wondered just how much time they had before he lost his grip.

"Don't let go!" Cho screamed.

The loud ping of a hammer hitting a metal object was muffled by his coat's thick hood. "I can't hold on much longer!" he yelled.

"Yes, you can!" the agent hollered as she kept her hammer going.

"We can do it!" Casteel yelled to Burke.

Then, just as he believed he could hold on no longer, the hammering stopped. He felt someone crawl over his kneeling form, felt hands on his waist. Suddenly the pull on the rope was gone. Nothing was pulling him toward his death.

With shaking legs he stood, hugging the rock wall, afraid to look to either side. He and Casteel were tied only to Cho, who had hammered a steel rod into the cliff face and tied the blue rope holding Briggs and Mason to the rod. As long as it held, they were safe.

"In my backpack," Cho shouted to Burke, "there's a small sack. Red. Inside is a cranking mechanism with a ratchet. Get it out."

Burke opened the backpack and carefully removed the red bag.

"Do you have it?" she asked.

"Yes."

"Take my place," she ordered, her words quick and loud. "Dig in. Get your feet locked and hold on to this line. Grab behind me, not in front. Hold on to a section between me and Casteel."

Burke dug in, grabbed the blue line, and leaned back against the rock wall.

"Good," Cho said. "I need some slack. We'll pull them up at least two feet. Go one hand over the other on my count."

Burke dug in harder.

"Now!" Cho screamed as she pulled with all her strength. Burke and Casteel felt the weight tearing at their muscles. Hand over hand, they pulled the dead weight toward them. Three inches. Six. A foot.

"How much slack do you have behind you, Casteel?" Cho yelled.

"A couple feet."

"Good! I'm going to let go!" Cho shouted. "Get ready!"

She gradually released her grip on the rope. With the device secured, she carefully crawled along the edge of the trail. Only the front half of her feet was on the path. She knocked a few small pebbles off the trail, and they tumbled down into the valley below.

Burke heard more hammering but didn't turn his head.

"Okay, let go of the rope very, very slowly!" Cho shouted.

Burke's eyes found Casteel's. The Ranger nodded. Together they released their grip on the line.

"Dr. Burke," Cho said, "get on your knees, lean over, and check the status of Briggs and Mason. Casteel, come here and take my spot. You won't need to pull; you're just a safety anchor in case one of the two spikes starts to come loose. And they won't."

Burke crawled to the edge of the trail. He looked over the edge. Briggs and Mason had their hands and arms wrapped tightly around the blue rope. Briggs' eyes were closed. Mason was looking up. They were swinging slowly back and forth, brushing up against the side of the cliff as they twisted on their tether.

"How are they doing?" Cho yelled.

"They're okay!" Burke shouted.

"Tell them we're about to bring them up."

"Alexander! Clark!" Burke yelled. "We're going to pull you up! Just hang on!"

Briggs didn't move, but Mason looked up and grinned.

"Dr. Burke," Cho barked, "stay where you are and let me know if the rope gets hung up on anything. I'm going to start cranking."

That's when the professor saw it. "Lisa!" he screamed. "The cord's frayed right where it hangs over the trail! I don't know if it'll hold much longer. Looks like it's cut halfway through!"

Cho nodded. "It'll have to hold."

Cho turned the handle on the ratchet. An inch at a time, the rope moved upward. The frayed section passed by Burke and wormed its way slowly toward the pulley. He finally allowed himself to breathe when it passed Cho and was resting, no longer needed, on the ground behind her.

"How much until Briggs is up?" she asked.

"About three feet," Burke said.

"Don't try to help him," she yelled as she continued to crank. "Let him get completely up over the edge first. Then you and Casteel grab him under his arms and steady him as I continue to crank. Don't pull! Let the crank do the work."

Those three feet took three minutes. Burke knew because he counted every second. Briggs' gloved hands appeared first, then his arms, and finally his face. When the older man's eyes met Burke's, he smiled. Burke and Casteel finally held on to Briggs as the rope slowly dragged him the rest of the way up over the edge.

Briggs laid down on the trail, held in place by the rope, the other end still tied to Mason as he swung on the end of the security line. Cho quit cranking and locked the device. The spikes in the rock wall held.

"Okay, I can't remove the cord from Dr. Briggs yet. I'm going to tie us to the spikes, and we are going to pull Clark up. I have another rope in my pack."

Burke crawled to the edge and looked down. "Clark, we have to get a couple of things locked down. Then you're coming up."

"No hurry. The view's incredible."

The wind picked up, swirling the snow as Cho tied the men to the rock wall face. Briggs stayed stretched out on the trail.

"On three!" she yelled. "And let's try to move it about six inches with each hand-over-hand motion. Now! One ... two ... three!"

The first six inches was easy.

"Again!"

They pulled and fell backward. The rope was slack.

No one moved. Then Cho and Burke peered over the edge of the cliff. In the swirling snow, they could see only the limp rope tossed by the wind. Clark was gone.

THE SPOT

FBI Agent Clark Mason had vanished without a sound into the unknown at the bottom of the cliff. Everyone just sat on the trail, shocked by the sudden loss of one of their own. It was Cho, the one who had been closest to Mason, who decided the rest period was over. She began to store her gear in her backpack. As she was putting her tools back, she studied the spikes, picking up each one and examining the place it had been anchored. Lucky! Again she had been lucky. The "Charmed One" had lived again.

After carefully repacking her equipment — rolling up and stowing the blue cord — she pulled on her backpack. Unnoticed by the others, she also reached inside her coat and retrieved a pistol. She then pushed up the trail and disappeared over the crest.

Even through the now steadily falling snow, she could see the objective. About five hundred feet below, as a crow would fly, built along the bottom of a rocky cliff, was the monastery with a half dozen buildings. The buildings were the same gray color as the mountains and would have been almost impossible to see from the air. Constructed from stone that had been quarried in the area, they had survived for hundreds of years in one of the most inhospitable places on earth. Yet though the buildings looked ready to use, they were empty. The monks who had called this place home were gone. She'd known that fact long before they began the mission.

Cho carefully studied the landscape, her dark eyes examining the trail, the monastery, the sides of the mountains, looking for any movement. She saw none. Where did he go? she thought.

She took off her backpack and pulled out a set of goggles. Slipping them on, she flipped a switch and again studied the area. The glasses were heat seeking and revealed the presence of any warm-blooded creatures. She noted a couple of forms of what were likely rodents or rabbits. Scanning the old monastery revealed nothing.

Then she saw it. Up on a mountain to the left was something. It looked like a figure standing in the entrance to what was likely a cave. It couldn't be Raymond. No one could have made it from where she was standing to that point in even two hours, and he had been gone less than thirty minutes. Yet there was someone or something there. The figure didn't move.

She slipped her goggles into the pack and slid the gun back inside her coat. After dusting the snow off a boulder, she sat down. This moment, being so close to where her brother had almost died, didn't feel like she thought it would. In fact, she felt little emotion. The irony of her brother having almost died in a monastery, a place of peace and tranquility, had not been lost on the brother she so admired. In fact, he often had said that the only reason he'd lived was because he'd been shot at Domum Lignarii, a place of miracles.

"There it is," Briggs exclaimed as he joined Cho. "I recognize it from the photographs Jeff had."

The man's words swept away the bittersweet memories for the moment. "Yes, there it is," she said. "But where is Raymond?"

UNEXPECTED GUEST

In their mad fight for survival, the Americans seemed to have forgotten about their Afghan guide. Only Cho had noticed that when Briggs and Mason tumbled over the cliff, their guide had already disappeared.

"Still no sign of him?" Burke asked, shielding his eyes from the snow and staring across the valley.

"None," Cho replied.

"What do we do?" Burke asked. "Is he on our side or working for someone else?"

Casteel joined them. "He doesn't have a gun. I searched him back at the camp. So he can't pick us off from a distance. But that doesn't give us much security. Odd that he would guide us this far, then just walk away."

"More like evaporate," Cho said. "It wouldn't surprise me if he had weapons hidden somewhere around here. After all, he knows this area. And he does have our supplies on that mule, so he can eat for a while."

"Are you sure this is the right place?" Casteel asked.

"Yes, it's the right monastery," Cho said. "Even though I didn't know how to get here, I have known about this place for several years. An Army Ranger told me about it. He was here for four days. So at least Raymond didn't mislead us."

Burke agreed. "It looks like the pictures Columbo had in his files." He yanked an iPad from his backpack, fired it up, and clicked to open iPhoto, shielding the device from the snow. "See, the buildings might have eroded a little since the 1970s, but this is the place."

Briggs also knew a great deal about the monastery. "The largest building, the one toward the back of the complex, would have been the residence, kitchen, and dining area. The one to the right was the chapel. The other smaller buildings were likely used to store tools and supplies and house farm animals. The open area to the right was a pen for the livestock. The area to the left would have been where they raised whatever meager crops they could produce. I can't imagine how tough life would have been here. Those monks were a different breed."

Cho picked up her pack. "We need to get moving. With this storm, the light won't last much longer."

Cho led the way. Though it appeared they could almost reach out and touch the monastery, it took an hour to make their way down the mountain to the monastery's outer walls. At the entry, a ten-by-ten-foot wooden gate had long ago been knocked off its hinges. It was lying on the ground just outside the twelve-foot-high walls.

"Quite a fort," Cho noted.

"It wasn't for protection," Briggs explained. "These men didn't fear being attacked by anyone. They just wanted to keep the outside world out of their lives. The walls were not for defense; these walls were more of a spiritual barrier."

Cho nodded. She pulled out her gun and led the way inside. Maybe more than the others, she understood the power and peace of solitude. But she also was well aware of the irony of the monks who lived here being either captured or killed by an outside band who also claimed to have been motivated by religion.

"It's deserted," Burke noted as he passed through the gate. "Appears to have been empty for a long time."

"Do you think the Taliban killed them?" Briggs asked no one in particular.

"No one knows," Cho replied. "CIA reports said the few locals who would talk heard that the monks were rounded up and imprisoned during the Soviet-Afghan war. So they might have been killed, or they might still be rotting in a jail somewhere. Maybe a few escaped to the higher mountains and then made their way to civilization."

"What do you think?" Burke asked the man with more knowledge about monks and monasteries than anyone else.

"Until we look around," Briggs replied, "we won't know what is left. My guess is this will be an interesting trip, one that I will always remember, but I fear I won't be taking anything back with me but my skin and the memory of Clark Mason plunging off the cliff."

Cho put her gun away, then pointed to the large building toward the back. "It'll be dark soon. Let's move into the old living area. We can explore tomorrow. We can unpack and get some rest."

They all followed the agent. She had moved about a dozen steps when she suddenly yanked the gun from her coat and whirled around.

"Get down!" she barked.

Burke and Briggs hit the ground. Cho and Casteel were on their knees, their eyes glued to the area outside the gate where Cho thought she'd heard a noise.

Her face quickly turned to a broad smile. The cause of the disturbance casually walked in as if he owned the place. Their pack mule was alone.

Why hadn't the mule shown up on her glasses? she wondered. How had its heat signature escaped her? Where had it been hidden?

She glanced back toward the mountain where she had seen the one large heat signature. Who was he? What was he waiting for?

THE PEW

Fatigue was the potion they needed to go to sleep. No one had any problem embracing deep slumber. But the rock floor, cushioned only by the lightweight sleeping bags, left them stiff when dawn finally chased away darkness.

Casteel made a breakfast of powdered eggs and canned bacon. As he cooked the meat, he couldn't help wondering what the locals would think of them beginning the morning with pork. Maybe it was just as well that Raymond had disappeared.

Briggs and Burke were still working out the kinks in stiff joints as they ate breakfast.

"Let's search each building as a unit," Cho suggested. "The complex is not that large, and I'd feel better about protection if I could see each of you at all times."

The snow had stopped during the night, and the winds were relatively calm as the four went through each building. If someone had been offering Domum Lignarii as a rental, it would have been listed as unfurnished. It seemed that what the Taliban hadn't destroyed, scavengers had taken.

After eating an MRE lunch, provided by the United States military catering department, they wandered back to the chapel. It was a little after two. Briggs took a seat on the one pew that had remained upright and pointed out the obvious: "Have you noticed there are absolutely no religious symbols in the entire complex?"

Burke nodded and took a seat beside the older man.

Casteel and Cho continued their search of the building, hoping to find hidden compartments in the floor and walls.

"What do you suppose these two holes in the wall are for?" Burke asked.

Briggs looked over at the two gaps cut into the front wall. "They're shelves. I've seen them in other ancient houses of worship. They were likely formed in the wall when the room was built."

"What do you think they held?" Cho asked from across the room.

Briggs shrugged. "My guess would be some kind of relic used in communion, or maybe they placed prayer candles there."

"Well," Casteel said, "if they aren't that important, I'm going to cover this one up, lean this broken table top against the wall. I'm tired of tripping over all this stuff on the floor."

Cho studied the religion professor as he scanned the rest of the room. His next words continued the theme he had started a few minutes before. "It seems the Taliban destroyed everything related to the monks' faith. There are no crucifixes or paintings depicting biblical history. The few books we found also contain no references to Christianity. The very inspiration for this place being built in such a desolate corner of the earth has been erased."

To Cho, it seemed somehow appropriate that there were no religious symbols left. After all, she had never been to such a godforsaken place.

Casteel chimed in from across the room. "Why should that be surprising? I've been in this country a lot over the last five years and learned enough to know the Taliban despises all things connected to Christian faith and practices. They've even executed their own people who converted to Christianity."

Briggs added a bit of perspective. "In the United States we tend to focus on what they've done to Christians and Christian symbols, but the Taliban is an equal-opportunity persecutor. They've also destroyed countless items associated with other faiths, including Buddhist and Hindu temples and shrines and anything relating to the Jewish religion. Tens of thousands have been killed for being something other than practitioners of Islam. The Taliban have also destroyed some priceless artifacts. In 2001, on a mountain cliff northwest of Kabul, they blew up the Buddhas of Bamiyan. Those carvings dated back fifteen centuries and measured between a hundred and two hundred feet in height. They are considered one of the great man-made marvels of another time."

"So," Cho said, "you're saying what they did here is minor league stuff."

"One out-of-the-way monastery," Briggs said, "probably wouldn't even rate a footnote on their long list of hostile acts against other religions."

Cho walked over to a window that had long ago lost its glass. A quick glance was enough to assure her that they were still alone. When she turned around, Briggs and Burke were both staring ahead as if lost in thought. Their worn expressions indicated both fatigue and disappointment. She understood how they felt. They had almost lost their lives, and for nothing. There were no clues here. In fact, there was nothing here. Like so much of war, this was a long and dangerous mission where the objective—the monastery—was now worthless. And Clark was gone!

Resting her shoulders against the cold stone wall, she considered an unspoken irony. Though she hadn't shared the information, she was the only one here who had gained any personal understanding and satisfaction from this trek. She'd seen where her brother had been. She had walked in his steps. The next time he spoke of the events that happened in Domum Lignarii, she would be able to feel the wind, smell the mountains, and visualize the landscape. They would have a bond that they never had in the past. Perhaps it would help her begin to understand the quiet man who was thirteen years her senior. The brother she barely knew. The man her family seemed to put on a pedestal much too high for her to reach.

Turning her attention from the professors to Casteel, Cho noted the Ranger's frustration. He was examining spots they had already covered several times. He was hoping they had missed something. Yet she was sure they hadn't. They had seen what was here, and essentially it totaled absolutely nothing. Like the rest of the buildings, the only thing in the chapel, except for a broken table and the overturned pews, was dirt. It would take a lot of holy water and elbow grease to get the room clean. As far as the group's mission, it evidently would be marked down as a complete loss. Worst of all, she'd lost a good friend and colleague. For nothing! Mason's senseless death would haunt her for the rest of her life.

Taking a deep breath, she glanced up at the ceiling and closed her eyes. It was seeing nothing that gave her the vision she needed to finally see what she should have noticed four hours ago. Her eyes popped open and she confirmed the image that had just invaded her mind.

"Excuse me!" Cho's voice placed the attention of the others squarely on her. "I have a stupid question. Did one of you pick up that pew Dr. Burke and Dr. Briggs are sitting on?"

"No," Briggs replied, "it was this way when we came in."

Cho shook her head. "Why do you suppose that only *that* pew was still upright?"

"Maybe those who destroyed this place left one pew up for a resting spot," Casteel chimed in. "They trashed everything in the residence area except the table and chairs we found around the table. They probably used those too."

Cho turned her attention to the closest overturned pew. Stooping, she saw something unusual on the stone floor—a large wooden peg. She picked it up and began a search for where it might have fallen from the pew. There didn't seem to be any place where it would fit. Then she noted the construction of the pew's feet. There were four large holes carved into each of the supports, two on each side. She slid the peg into a hole. It fit perfectly with the large, carefully carved head overlapping the top of the hole like a washer to keep it from sliding through.

Falling to her knees, she noted about a half dozen other pegs—many were broken. With her gloved hand she swept away layers of dirt and trash and found places where these pegs had once been driven into the stone floor.

Yes!

Pushing herself to her feet but keeping her eyes on the floor, she discovered where each pew had been placed originally. Every one of them had at one time been secured in the same method. It was likely they had been affixed to the floor for centuries by the pegs.

"Dr. Briggs," Cho said as she rose to her feet, "it took a great deal of effort to knock these pews over. They were held in place on the floor by long wooden pegs. I'm no expert in this field, but I think it would've been a tremendous task to remove the pegs and flip the pews. Why not just take a sledgehammer and smash them to pieces? That would have been far easier. But you see, none of these has been broken. They could all be set up today and reused."

On one hand her revelation hardly seemed important, but at least it gave the team one more mystery to try to understand. In that way the agent had injected some life back into the adventure. For the first time in hours, there was a sense of real excitement. As four sets of eyes searched the floor, hope returned to Domum Lignarii.

"You're right," Burke all but shouted. "There are tool marks on the pews, floor, and the pegs. This wasn't done quickly! The pews were carefully removed. Why?"

"I doubt a rogue Taliban group would have done it that way," Briggs added. "If the pews were attached to the floor, like Miss Cho suggested, they would have just smashed them."

"And look at the one pew that was left upright," Cho added. "It wasn't set upright. It was never knocked over. The pegs are still in place. Why do all the work to remove the others and leave this one?"

Burke and Briggs stood up and turned around slowly. In short order Casteel and Cho were beside them. Each was staring at the undisturbed pew. It was Briggs who finally broke the silence.

"Why didn't I see it before? It is so obvious. Now that I look at the evidence and consider what we haven't found, I don't think the Taliban destroyed the monastery. If they had, we would have seen at least bits and pieces of artifacts. There are no broken crucifixes or smashed statues of the Virgin Mary here. There is no evidence that those items, so important to Catholic worship, were ever in this chapel. I was a fool for not noticing this when we walked in."

As he stooped to examine more closely the one standing pew, Burke asked his friend, "Do you think it was the monks who trashed their own monastery?"

"It's a possibility," Briggs replied, "one I should have considered earlier. If they knew the Taliban was planning on demolishing this place and taking them prisoners, they might have staged this whole thing."

"For what purpose?" Casteel asked.

"Throughout history," Burke explained, "many groups have given the appearance of destroying valuable items in order to save them. Crooks have often used arson to cover up thefts. Ships have been sunk after treasure was removed. Art museums have been burned to the ground after the valuable art was removed. The trick is an old one, but one that still can work."

"I get it," Cho cut in. "And as they had been good to the locals, the monks no doubt had friends who gave them the advance warning they needed to accomplish that. Given that time, the monks destroyed everything that had no ties to their faith and then took the items they treasured and deserted before anyone arrived."

"And," Briggs added, "when the Taliban got here and saw the damage, they assumed another Islamic group had beaten them to the punch. So they wouldn't have stuck around for too long or even searched for the missing monks."

"What's this?" Burke asked, pointing to a dark spot on the upright pew. "Could it be what we are looking for?"

Casteel swept away some dust and carefully examined the five-inch stain. He voiced what everyone was thinking. "It might be blood."

Pulling a kit from her backpack, Cho went to work. Less than a minute later, a luminal spray confirmed the theory. "It's blood, all right," she said. "But I think it got on this pew much more recently than thirty years ago."

As the others bent to examine the stain, the agent just watched. She knew whose blood it was, and she also knew when it had fallen on the ancient pew. In fact, if she did a DNA test, the markers found on that pew would be a strong match to her own.

WRITTEN IN RED

Even as the others hovered over the stain, Cho confidently declared, "I doubt the blood is important."

"But you said it was from a fairly recent event," Burke argued. "Consider the implications."

"You are thinking as if this were a crime scene." Cho's voice was assertive, her posture echoing her tone. "We are not in the States and we have to get beyond FBI-like thinking. You need to look at this in the context of war. Maybe someone was shot here in the last few years. But what does that tell us? It means that blood doesn't have anything to do with our mission. We are looking for clues that are much older than that. Think like a member of the military. What have we seen that has something to do with our objective?"

The diminutive former Army Ranger let her words sink in.

"We have to stay focused. We can't be here forever without being spotted," she said. "And I don't want to deal with any local warlords. Let's find what we need and move out."

Once she was sure she had their full attention, Cho put the focus back on what she saw as their only significant find, a find that was even more significant to her. "If Dr. Briggs is correct about the monks staging the destruction of the monastery, then why didn't they remove this pew?"

"The obvious answer seems to be, they ran out of time," Burke said.

"No," Briggs said, "for them to have taken every important relic out of this place and so convincingly trash it, they would have had plenty of warning. This was left in place for a reason. But no one was supposed to notice it. It was to be seen as just a random item."

Cho smiled. The group was now considering what they had. She could see that each of them was thinking. With the team's combined knowledge and experience working on the only clue they had, perhaps they'd come up with something. Perhaps this wouldn't be a worthless excursion to the gates of hell. Maybe she could find something that would bring some value to Mason's death.

It was Burke who discovered the first clue. He got down on the floor, rolled onto his back, and tucked his head under the ancient pew. After his eyes focused, he smiled. He tapped the underside of the bench with the knuckles of his right hand.

"There are more red stains here, but there's a big difference. These are some form of writing. Must be a message. I can't make out anything, but my esteemed colleague, with his language skills, just might."

Like football players trying to recover a fumble, Cho, Briggs, and Casteel quickly dove for the floor under the bench. In a matter of seconds, four heads were pressed together and four sets of eyes were studying the bottom of the pew.

"Let me get a flashlight," Cho said. "A spray in my kit will make that drawing pop. I guarantee I can bring out the detail."

As they waited for Cho and her forensic magic, Burke posed a question: "Why, of all the things they could've used, did the monks leave a message on the bottom of a pew?"

Not pulling his focus from the letters just a foot above his eyes, Briggs said, "Without knowing the men and how they thought, I can only guess. But I do have an idea."

"Well," Burke replied, "your guess is probably better than mine. So guess."

"This is pretty wild," Briggs said, "but my theory goes back to the way early leaders in the church spoke of understanding their faith. There was a term that was used: 'the seat of knowledge.' In a religious sense, it meant sitting and learning from those who were wiser. The monks would have meditated and prayed in this room while sitting on these pews. This was where God spoke to them, directed their lives, brought them wisdom. It would be the place to hide a message for someone who thought and believed as they did. That someone would have come back to this place to look for answers, even answers as to what happened here in the last days."

"So this is the seat of knowledge," Casteel said, with a tinge of sarcasm.

"We almost didn't have the wisdom to find it," Briggs said. "Now the question becomes, are we wise enough to figure out what that message is and what it means."

"And if it will lead us to the *Book of Joseph*," Burke added.

Cho was back in her former rule as a special ops officer, using her investigative skills on the pew. After she finished with the spray, it was obvious she was more than pleased.

"Okay, it's much clearer now. And, in case you were wondering, this was written with ink or paint, not blood."

The message was a series of seven lines. Each line was made up of a series of numbers and letters. Written with no punctuation, they appeared nothing like the codes the agent had studied in school.

"This has to be some kind of key," Cho noted. "If it is code, it's one I never saw before. We may just have to shoot some digital images and take them back with us. Let the agency decode it."

"No way," Burke argued. "What if we got all the way back and then, after unlocking the code, had to return to this place? We've got to figure it out now. This might be our only chance."

Seeing no use in continuing to stare at something she couldn't comprehend, Cho slid out from under the pew. She watched the other three. Burke and Casteel were looking up at their discovery with blank expressions, but Briggs was much more engaged. He had retrieved a pen and piece of paper from his pocket and was writing. When he finished, he quietly slid out from under the pew and stood up. Cho had seen this look before, watching her father work through a mechanical problem with one of his planes. Briggs had figured it out.

The professor said nothing as he walked out the chapel doors and onto the grounds. Once he had a clear view of the stark, rugged landscape, the old professor's brown eyes looked beyond the walls at the snow-streaked mountain to the south. As he studied the scene, he appeared to be counting. From time to time he would look at his notes, then return his gaze to the mountains. Briggs seemed oblivious to everything, including the bitter cold.

"You know the code?" Cho whispered. She stood a few feet to his right.

"It's not really a code," he explained, keeping his focus on the mountain. "It's a once-common language. The numbers represent measure and distance. No one has used those units in centuries. The letters, which are often seen on fraternity shirts, are directions. Do you see this one?" He pointed to a word on the paper he had carefully scribbled onto the back of a scrap of paper retrieved from his pocket: Στάδιον.

She saw it, but it meant nothing to her. "It's Greek to me."

"It's *ancient* Greek," Briggs said.

"What does it mean?"

"It stands for about six hundred feet," he said. "The other numbers represent distances too. So even if the Taliban had found it, they likely wouldn't have figured it out. Yet any member of the order who returned to the monastery could read these letters and numbers and know exactly how to find what had been hidden."

"And you know where it leads?" Cho asked, her eyes following his about halfway up a mountain.

"Pretty much," he replied, pointing to a barely perceivable opening in the wall of stone. "I think the message left under the seat of knowledge will lead us up there."

That cave was where Cho had seen the human form in her heat-seeking goggles the day before. She pulled off her right glove and reached deep into her pocket. She fingered an ancient gold coin, rolling it between her fingers. It had been her good luck charm for almost five years. It was now time to return it to its rightful owner.

THE ROOF

So what did you find?" Cho asked.

Before answering, Casteel dusted a bit of snow from his shoulders and sat down in the chapel. "The climb's not bad. Not as tricky as the trail we came up on. In truth, it's more of a hike than a climb. I went about halfway and didn't run into any real trouble. We can all make it. It'll take about two hours."

An excited Briggs jumped into the conversation. "Guess we need to get started."

"Actually no," Casteel replied, his manner firm, "we don't. We don't have enough daylight to get to the cave, much less get there and get down."

"So we wait until tomorrow?" Briggs said, his disappointment obvious.

"Yeah," Casteel said. "If there is anything up there, it has been up there for a while. It'll keep. I was assigned to this group to make sure you stay alive. I don't want to lose anyone else. For me to do my job, we wait. I don't want another repeat of the cliff-diving episode."

Cho nodded. "We have other fish to fry anyway. Dr. Briggs, can you make an English translation of the writing on the pew so we have a record and convert the information into a map?"

"Sure," he replied, "if that will help."

The agent nodded. "It will, thanks. I do better with something visual. Casteel, you cut away that section of the pew. I want the board the writing is on and the bloodstain. We'll take them back with us when we leave. Jeff, can you write a log of what has happened so far on this little junket. I'll use it for my report."

"What are you going to do?" Burke asked.

"I'll spend the rest of this day as a lookout. While we may be alone for the moment, that could change. There's a place on the roof of the residence hall that will give me a pretty good vantage point of the whole area."

Burke watched Cho leave. She was a different woman here. Maybe it was the old Ranger training coming back or perhaps the pain and guilt in losing Mason, but she seemed colder, more distant than she had in the safe house. His curiosity kicked in.

Ignoring Cho's order to produce a log, Burke walked outside. Initially he strolled away from the compound and out the front gate. He stared at the gray skies before retracing his steps to the chapel. He considered going in, but there was something much stronger than penning a report tugging at his mind. He headed toward the residence building. With each step his stride grew longer and faster. At the building's eastern wall, he jumped up to a window ledge, grabbed the lip of the eve, and pulled up to the roof. Once there he stood and carefully followed Cho's path. As a cold wind picked up speed and whipped around him like a cowboy's lasso, he approached the woman and gave a slight nod.

"Thought I told you to write a report."

He smiled. "I have all night. Can I join you for a few minutes?"

"I would say it's a free country, but where we are, it is anything but free. But sure, sit down."

Cho was resting her back against an old stone chimney. There was room for Burke too, but only if their shoulders met. It was a strange sensation. In the few days that he'd known her, they had never touched each other except on the trail when they'd rescued Briggs.

"Anything out there?" he asked.

"No. Don't mind me. Get as comfortable as you want."

No clever comebacks came to him. So he just stared off into the distance. All he saw in the late afternoon haze were the mountains. It was the mountains that got him thinking about two of his grandfather's favorite singers, Roy Rogers and Gene Autry. "Wonder if the Afghans write songs about this area."

Cho gave Burke a "what are you thinking" smirk.

He picked up on what must have been going through her mind and felt a need to prove he wasn't completely off the wall. "In the old West," he explained, "the cowboys wrote songs about the lonesome country they called home. I was just wondering if those who live here do the same thing."

He looked at her profile, hoping to see some sign of understanding. Instead all he got was that same belittling smirk. Logic told him to let it be, but like a high school nerd trying to impress a cheerleader, he dug deeper. "You know, maybe there are some goat herders who sit out under the evening skies and compose ballads about lost loves or even a wayward goat."

As he pictured a man in Afghan robes and a girl in a burka, the guitar didn't fit in and he saw his argument falling apart. Who writes songs about goats?

As he sank into the hole he'd dug and began to bury himself in self-pity, a slight grin spread across the woman's face and she looked at him. Her brown eyes suddenly sparkled.

"Something humorous?" he asked.

Cho grinned. "I just got a picture of Osama and his gang sitting around a campfire, strumming guitars and singing the Afghan version of 'Home on the Range.'" She smiled for a few more seconds, then grew solemn once more.

"Mason's death hit you hard," Burke said.

"Is that why you came up here," she replied, "to see if I needed a shoulder to cry on? Let me assure you, I don't."

"Everyone needs to mourn," he said. "It's a part of—"

"Of what? Is this your attempt at teaching me how to deal with death? I've dealt with it more than you know. I dealt with it as a soldier and as an agent. I see it all the time. It is a fact of life. You get close to people, they die."

"So you are pushing me away now? Is that why suddenly you keep me and everyone else here at arm's length? Are you afraid if you—"

"I am not afraid. But you should be. Death follows me. It doesn't get me, but it follows me and gets those around me."

"So you play the tough guy to keep from letting others see a woman."

"No, I'm not playing a part. Female or not, this is who I am. It's who my father is. It's who my brother is. It is in my blood."

"A natural-born hero."

She shook her head. "No, just a person with a calling. I believe I am where I am because of a specific reason. Being here in this place is part of that."

He considered her strong, almost stoic, but well thought out reponse. "So your calling is to find the scroll?"

Continuing to stare at the horizon, she shook her head. "What I'm looking for might be right here, but it's not the scroll. It's justification."

"Justification?"

"I don't know," she admitted. "I can't really define it. When you've killed people, it's not easy to deal with. When you watch a friend die, it eats at you."

"But you didn't kill because you wanted to," he argued, "it was because you had to. And Mason's death was an accident you couldn't have foreseen. Besides, you almost saved him."

Even though it was cold, Cho pulled off her cap. The fading sun became a spotlight as its yellow rays fell on her face. Except for the scar on her neck, her skin was flawless, her brown almond-shaped eyes were set atop high, slightly rounded cheekbones. Her slightly parted lips revealed perfectly straight and brilliantly white teeth. She was beautiful. Yes, he had noticed it in the hospital room. And he had been aware of it when they were together at his home and in the safe house. But now he wanted to know who this woman was. What motivated her.

"Did you grow up wanting to be a soldier?" he asked.

Turning until their eyes met, she replied, "I once wanted to be a dancer. Surprised?"

"No. I've noticed you move gracefully."

Cho grinned. "I was joking, Jeff. Do you give the third degree to your students too?"

Suddenly he wondered why he had followed her to the roof. The silence that encircled them was more than a bit unsettling for him.

"Don't worry about it," she said.

"Worry about what?"

"You're wanting to know who I am. It's natural."

"You mean because I'm a teacher?"

"No, because we are part of a small unit, and we've found ourselves in a dangerous situation. Whenever I was in this position in the past, whenever I was out in the field with my comrades, we opened doors into our lives and shared secrets. Those were good moments. Bonds developed. But then when a person you shared a part of your life with gets killed, it hurts. It makes you pull into a shell. You even vow never to get close to anyone again. I had almost forgotten that feeling until Mason died."

She let those words hang in the cold air. "Here's the short scoop. I'm three years younger than you. My college degree is in psychology. I was an officer the moment I graduated, thanks to ROTC. My skills in firearms are so good I was the designated sniper on specific missions. I have a brother, my parents are both still alive, and I love to fly planes. It's a passion I share with my father. I've already told you about restoring cars."

"You didn't mention marriage."

"My career and special skills keep me on the move. It would be very, very hard to put up with that kind of lifestyle and maintain a relationship. In fact, it's hard to hold on to friends. As I mentioned, friends die on me."

She paused and looked directly at him. "My files on you say that you are a good teacher, one of the best at the university."

"And that may be where my talents start and stop," he said. He took a deep breath, then offered a confession. "I've been in over my head for the last two weeks. And it all started when I was forced to step away from my natural environment. All the stuff I did in fieldwork in the Amazon and Central America didn't prepare me for this. For most of my adult life, I have lived in a world where I plan my semester and classes months before the term begins. I teach the same courses over and over again, year after year. I walk the same halls, park my car in the same space, and even eat at the same place day after day and week after week and month after month. Structure is a part of every facet of my life. Even my expeditions were planned in detail. Now look at me. A week ago I'd never heard of this place, and now

I'm halfway around the world trying to uncover something that isn't in a textbook and isn't part of fieldwork. I don't know how you do it."

"I like not knowing," she replied. "I like having to always be ready. I like having to adapt on the fly. But if you think I came into this mission blind, you're wrong. In the case of Domum Lignarii, I have been planning this trip for almost five years."

Burke was shocked. "What? How can that be? Did you know about the scroll?"

Darkness comes quickly in a valley between mountains, and it was the darkness of night that now hid Cho's features. Even though he was close enough to hear her breathing, he could not actually see her. The words that came out of the blackness sounded even more dramatic. But even at noon, under a full sun, they would have been chilling.

"I came here because of my brother's blood."

It suddenly made a degree of sense. Her talk of a calling, the way she framed the mission. She wanted answers, and she was seeking them about something beyond this world.

"So," he whispered, "is this about a search for faith? Protecting the blood shed by Christ and his mission is why you wanted to be a part of this exercise?"

"Jeff, you're really a teacher. I can tell you're always looking for symbolism even when there isn't any."

"How so? It seems pretty straightforward to me."

"This isn't about God," she explained. "I'm not talking about 'brother' in a Christian sense. For me a part of this is about my brother. He was right here. He should have died here. But something happened, something he calls a miracle, and it changed him in ways that I can't begin to understand. You're here to find clues that you hope will lead you to a lost biblical text. I'm here to meet an angel. I'm betting the odds of me accomplishing my mission are better than yours. But end of discussion. My mute button is once again engaged."

Burke looked out into the darkness. Lisa Marie Cho was full of surprises.

THE ALTAR

Just as Casteel had promised, the journey up the mountain was more a hike than a climb. Only a half dozen times did the group need to use ropes to scale a rock wall, and those ascents were never more than a dozen feet. Still, it was far from a walk in Central Park, and the cold combined with the thin atmosphere took a toll on the team. It was just past ten, and they were all breathing hard when they rounded a corner and got their first clear view of the opening that was about two-thirds of the way up the stony nine-thousand-foot peak.

If an alien had landed a spaceship in the Hindu Kush mountains, he would have likely assumed earth to be a completely inhospitable environment. The gray rocky peaks streaked with snow, often hidden by clouds, might have been beautiful in a stark sort of way, but if you were having to navigate through them, you sensed that they were a magnet for pain and suffering. The few who called this place home didn't so much live here as they did survive. And, as he worked his way up the rocky path to the cave, all that was on Burke's mind was surviving. It wasn't the mountain trek that he feared. It was easy. His fear was the thought that Raymond and his friends would be around the next corner and blow them down the mountain far more quickly than they had come up.

As they stopped to study the path between themselves and their objective, Cho looked across to the mountains on the north. Her face clearly showed worry.

Concern was also evident in Casteel's voice when he asked, "You see something?"

"It's the clouds," Cho answered. "Another snowstorm is coming. We're not going to be able spend a lot of time up here."

"Well, in ten minutes we'll be at the cave," Casteel assured her. "We'll look around, grab what we can find, then head back down."

As the Army Ranger finished his sentence, a lone snowflake drifted down from the gray clouds. A sober-faced Cho must have sensed her job was about to get much more difficult. As if responding to a cue, a few more flakes swirled around the small band of explorers.

"If you ever leave the FBI," Burke quipped, "you've got a career in meteorology."

Grabbing his arm, Cho leaned close, whispering so only he could here. "It's not funny. The snows here are vicious. When it opens up, we will be stuck wherever we are standing at that moment. So make sure Briggs doesn't drag his feet."

The group covered the last three hundred yards in less than five minutes. It was no surprise that Briggs broke out into a jog as the trail leveled out and widened. He was that anxious to view a discovery that was rightfully his. After all, he had deciphered the writing. The man was only ten feet ahead when Casteel hollered, "No one goes in before I do."

The assertive directive stopped Briggs. He turned to look back, and his face was awash with disappointment.

"Sorry, professor," Casteel said. "We don't know what or who is in there. It could be booby-trapped. Let me take a look and make sure it's safe. Then you can have your fun."

Briggs waited while Casteel went on alone. The soldier studied the entrance for a few moments, touching the edges and the ground carefully with his hands. The opening was about seven feet high and four feet wide. He reached into his pack and pulled out some kind of small handheld instrument.

Briggs looked to Burke, who simply shrugged his shoulders.

"Searching for explosives," Cho explained as Casteel disappeared into the cave. A minute became two and then three.

"What's keeping him?" Burke asked, not realizing he had actually given voice to his fears.

"Let him do his job," Cho said. "This is why he's here. It is his skill set."

Though the temperature was below freezing, Burke was hot. His face was red and his mouth was dry. While the others took seats on the large boulders that lined both sides of the path, he paced — ten feet one way, ten feet back, over and over again.

Finally Casteel emerged from the cave. With no fanfare, he nodded and waved them forward.

They didn't need a second invitation. With no hesitation, the two professors led the way.

"Get the lanterns from your backpacks and turn them on," Casteel ordered. "It's dark in there. You're not going to see anything for the first fifteen feet except a large boulder on the right. There's a three-foot opening in the wall behind that rock. If what we need is in this cave, we will find it in that chamber because there is no other place to look. Follow me."

Walking back and showing them the opening, Casteel dropped to his knees and crawled in. A few seconds later, Cho pushed through the hole. Briggs went next. Getting on his knees, an anxious Burke peered ahead, looking at where the others had disappeared. The tunnel was about three feet wide and three feet high. It was fairly uniform. It appeared to be natural, not man-made. The rock floor was relatively smooth. The small passage led to a larger room.

Burke crawled through the short tunnel and was greeted by three lanterns illuminating an oblong chamber running about fifteen yards into the mountain. At the entry point, the room was six feet wide. At the back the width grew to more than twenty feet. The roof sloped from little more than five feet at the entrance to at least twelve feet at the far wall.

The room was furnished with a small table and chairs, a few shelves holding canned foods, and three buckets filled with water. Near the entry point, stacks of books lined the right-hand wall, and to the back were several metal and wooden crosses and at least a half dozen religious statues.

Casteel was standing near the left-hand side of the entrance, his eyes following Briggs and Cho. They were peering at a black box sitting on a table at the back of the room.

"Jeff," Cho called out, her words echoing off the room's walls and ceiling, "you've got to see this. It looks just like the trunk Columbo left for you."

Pulling to his feet, Burke moved quickly forward, the sound of his steps echoing off the walls. Cho was right. The small black trunk could have been a twin to the one that was sitting at the safe house in Indiana.

"Have you opened it?" he asked.

"Not yet," Cho replied.

"And you won't until I take a look at it," Casteel announced.

The three stepped back as the Army Ranger carefully examined the outside of the black box. The man ran his bare fingers across every edge. He even used a small blade to search the area under the lid. Finally, with everyone holding their collective breath, he carefully released one latch at a time and gently opened the chest.

"Guess it's safe," Casteel noted. "I mean we're still here."

Joining him, the curious quartet peered in. What they didn't see was a book, parchment, or scroll. What they did find were hundreds of gold coins and a wide array of jewelry.

"Look what is carved in the top of the box," Briggs pointed out.

Moving his gaze from the treasure to the lid, Burke saw it too. Carefully engraved into the wood was writing. As could be expected, it wasn't English, but he was sure that Briggs would be able to translate the marks. A second later he was proven correct.

"The Treasure of Baltore," the older man explained.

"Well," an obviously disappointed Cho sighed, "it's not the treasure we're looking for."

"Yeah," Burke replied as he picked up a few of the coins, "but many of these coins go back to the seventh century and some are even older. They could have belonged to Baltore. And the fact that the other trunk matches this one means that both were likely his."

As Burke carefully examined the money he had lifted from the box, Cho retrieved a small tape measure from her pack and set about measuring it. The look on her face answered Burke's question even better than her words.

"Is there is a false bottom on this one?" he asked anyway.

Cho shook her head. "No. What you see is what you get. Normally finding a treasure would excite me, but not today. Why don't you take a look through those stacks of books."

As Briggs studied the old volumes, Cho reached in and removed one of the gold coins. Holding it in the light, she studied it and smiled.

"Probably worth quite a bit," Burke noted from the other side of the chamber.

Dropping the coin back into the box, Cho mysteriously added, "More than you could know."

After scanning through a half dozen books, Briggs looked up and announced, "These are basically Bibles and theological texts. They're old, but not ancient. Nothing that likely dates back before 1750, and certainly nothing from the era before the printing press. In fact I've seen almost all of these volumes in various libraries. I even have a few of them in my office."

"It does prove a theory," Burke said as he placed an old Bible on one of the room's primitive benches. "It seems likely the monks were responsible for trashing their own monastery. What they wanted to save, they brought here. Someday, when it was safe, they likely vowed to reopen Domum Lignarii and return these volumes and the religious artifacts so carefully placed in that corner to the monastery."

Tossing a can of beans to Burke, Casteel noted, "Maybe a few of them never left."

Catching the tin, the professor asked, "What do you mean?"

"That can of beans has an offer of a free coupon for another can if the purchaser cuts off the label and sends it to a post office box in New York."

Burke said, "So what? That kind of deal has been going on for decades."

"But that coupon was good for a limited time only," a smiling Casteel explained, "and it doesn't expire until next month. And there's very little dust here. The candles seem fresh, the bedding on this old cot looks pretty clean. Someone either lives here or has lived here until very recently."

Burke looked across the chamber to the table. There was a candle-holder and a crucifix. Matches were set beside the cross. He was just about to point out his discovery when Briggs said, "It's an altar."

"Yeah," Burke agreed. "So the monastery we know as Domum Lignarii still exists. It has simply been moved up the mountain."

Casteel shook his head. "If this is the monastery, then where are the monks?

"Right behind you," Cho said.

ARE YOU ABEL?

Burke, Briggs, and Casteel turned toward the chamber's entrance. Standing before them was a small balding man wearing a long robe. His blue eyes twinkled, his thin lips hinted at a slight smile, his gray eyebrows hung over deep-set sockets. He couldn't have been much over five feet and he was rail thin. He stood straight, his hands clasped together in front of him.

"She is right," he announced in an English accent that reflected more London than Chicago. "Domum Lignarii still exists. It has just ... how do you Americans say it ... ah, yes, gone undercover."

As a trio of shocked faces studied the man, Cho pushed her right hand his way. He nodded as he took it in his. Gently holding it, his eyes staring deeply into hers, he whispered, "Bless you, my child."

Evidently deeply shocked by the visit from their unexpected host, Burke, the color drained from his face, finally found his voice. "How many of there are you?"

The little man smiled. "There are many. But I am the only one here."

"The others?" Briggs asked.

"They are all dead," he explained.

"But you said there are many," Casteel argued.

"Oh, they are here, but their souls are no longer of this earth. I buried each of them."

The little man released Cho's hand and once more clasped his together. "Would you share a meal with me?"

Burke shook his head in disbelief. The bizarre world that had collided with his two weeks before had just taken an even stranger turn. But this time that bend in the road was not wrapped in fear. Here was a man who had practically nothing and was offering to share what little he had with strangers who had just invaded his home.

"We are sorry if we frightened you," Burke said.

"My son, I was not frightened nor was I shocked. I have watched you. I have waited to see if the Lord revealed to you the way to find me."

"The writing on the pew?" Burke asked.

"Yes. You are the first to find it. But you not only found it, you were given the gift of tongues to understand its message. So you are not strangers. Rather, you have accepted my invitation. That makes you brothers and sisters. What is mine is yours."

Burke moved forward and extended his hand. "I'm Jeff Burke, a history professor at the University of Illinois in the United States. It is an honor to meet you."

"Bless the Illini," he replied with a smile. "You may call me Abel."

The monk knew a great deal more about the world than Burke would have assumed. As he stepped away, the older professor eased forward.

"I'm Alexander Briggs. Like Jeff, I am a professor at the University of Illinois. I teach in the school of religion."

"Ah," their host said while reaching to take Briggs' right hand. "A man of my own heart. I'm sure that there is much you could teach me."

"I doubt that," Briggs replied.

"And you?" Abel asked.

"Casteel. Special Forces. Hardly a man of the cloth."

Abel gently waved his thin fingers in the air. "The Lord guided you to this place, and that is all I need to know."

Cho glanced toward Casteel, "Why don't you check on the weather."

"No reason to send him," Abel said. "The snow is coming. It will be here soon."

With the clock ticking, Cho once more took charge. "Casteel, get out there and keep an eye on things. I'll wrap this up as quickly as I can."

As Casteel crawled out of the chamber, Cho posed the question everyone wanted to ask: "What can you tell us about the *Book of Joseph*?"

His eyes smiling almost as much as his lips, Abel nodded. "I can tell you *The Words of the Father* were once at Domum Lignarii. If fact, they were here twice. Once when our order was very young. That would have been in the fifth century, long before the monastery you visited was carved from this mountain."

Burke nodded. "It stayed here for almost three centuries. Is that correct?"

"You are a student of history," the monk said. "A priest named Baltore presented the brothers with a letter from the pope in 752. Though they did not want to give it up, he left with it nonetheless."

"You said two times," Briggs cut in.

"Yes, the book, as you call it, returned to this place in 1800. One of our order, a brother named Andre, was given the responsibility of caring for it. He was a part of a very small sect of men known as the Custodis Joseph Lacuna."

"The keeper of the book," Briggs whispered.

"That is right," Abel replied in a cheerful tone.

"So where is it now?" Burke asked. "Is it here, in this cave?"

"Oh, no." Abel smiled. "It is not here, though in the trunk we have money and jewelry that once belonged to the House of Baltore."

Burke glanced back at the chest. The tie between the two trunks now seemed proven. But if it wasn't here, where was it? Did the monk know?

"Brother Abel," Burke said, "what was in the text of that book?"

"I have no idea," he said. "No one did. Legend has it that not even Brother Andre read it. Imagine the temptation he must have experienced. In the false bottom of a black trunk just like that one, he had the words written by Joseph, the father of our Lord. Wouldn't it be amazing to know the thoughts of that simple but blessed carpenter? What would you give for that opportunity? And yet because of orders that went back centuries from a pope he knew almost nothing about, he was not allowed to read it. I assume that he kept that directive."

"But," Burke asked, "wouldn't that same directive have commanded him to destroy the book?"

"Ah." Abel smiled. "You have an understanding of the complexity of the quandary facing Andre. It was what consumed Baltore and all the lords of Baltore that followed. Would you destroy something that had been touched by Joseph?"

"Of course not," Burke replied.

"You and Brother Andre share a common line of thought. And remember this, it was Baltore who was given the order to destroy the book. Thus Brother Andre was under no such directive. His calling would have been to protect it in much the same way the ancient monks who founded this mission did."

Briggs jumped in. "When you consider what might be in the document, at least the rumors, the theological significance of the artifact demands it be made public. Don't you think?"

"As you can see," Abel replied, "I am not a public person. I am also one who spends little time concerning myself with rumors. But if you are asking if I would destroy it because reading it might destroy my faith, then I would tell you my faith would be worth nothing anyway. You see, my faith is not based on words, but rather it is based on my experiences with God. He is very real to me. I feel his presence here each and every day. My faith has grown even stronger with your visit today."

"If the book is not here," Cho cut in, "then where is it?"

Abel shook his head ever so slightly. Once more folding his hands and allowing the robe's sleeves to cover them, he closed his eyes as if in prayer. He remained in that state for what seemed minutes. It was only after he finally opened his eyes that he spoke. "Brother Andre was given orders to leave here in 1805. At that time, he had been here more than twenty years."

"You said orders," Burke cut in. "Do you mean from the pope?"

"I have the old records. I have saved them. And I know from those records that the orders did not come from Rome. In fact, he left with a visitor. The man was an American."

"Did he take the document with him?" Cho asked.

"He was the keeper of the word. He would have died before leaving the trunk here. And it was good he left. Less than a year later, the monastery was invaded by a consortium of warlords intent on ridding this place of the Christian faith. They burned and destroyed everything. The monks hid in the mountains, and after the raiders left, they rebuilt and restocked. Someday in the future, we will do the same. It is my job to live until that time."

"Do your records give a name for the American?" Cho asked.

"His name was Breckinridge. He must have received a message from God to come here. Just think, if he hadn't given the word for Brother Andre to leave, then the words of Joseph would have been lost forever."

Cho, now locked into full investigative mode, said, "Breckinridge, you said. What was his first name?"

"Just Mr. Breckinridge. That is all that was recorded in our books. So if your quest was to find the *Words of the Father*, it seems your time was not well spent. But I have nevertheless enjoyed my moments with you. And I do believe God brought you here and gave you the keys to finding me."

He gently waved his hand and pointed toward the small entrance. "Now the snow will move in quickly. I have witnessed more of these storms than I can count. You need to hurry if you are going to make it down the mountain safely."

Ignoring the man's warning, Burke asked, "Do you believe that Andre went to the United States?"

"Let me ask you a question," the monk replied. "If you received orders from a German to leave this place with him, where do you think you would go? If a Frenchman came and took you with him, where do you think he would take you?"

"I see your logic," Burke replied.

Briggs added, "Breckinridge was likely a member of Custodis Joseph Lacuna."

Burke snapped his fingers. "Of course. It fits! John Breckinridge was a senator from Kentucky. In 1805 he resigned his office in order to become US attorney general under Thomas Jefferson. He and Jefferson were close friends. Breckinridge even wrote many of the bills passed during the time Jefferson was president."

"Then," Abel said, "you have found your reason for coming. You have the information the Lord intended for you to have. Now, before you go, take Baltore's trunk."

"But you could use it for so many things," Briggs argued.

"I have what I need. The things I don't have are brought to me by the locals. They keep my hiding place a secret. They watch out for me. I have no need for the trunk. Besides, it has been here since Baltore visited. It was our payment for giving up the scroll."

Seeing no purpose in arguing, Burke quickly walked to the table. He closed the lid and fastened the latches, picked up the chest, and walked back to the monk's side. "Are you sure?"

"I think you will need this," came the simple reply. "I feel you can use it somehow. Maybe it will buy your safety. Or maybe it will keep the devil away. I don't know, but you will find out. Now go. The mountain is dangerous enough without snow."

"Thank you, sir," Burke said.

"Won't you go with us?" Briggs asked.

"You have your place," Abel said. "And I have mine. Go in peace."

Briggs went to the opening, got down on his hands and knees, and left the chamber. As Cho and Abel watched, Burke set the trunk on the ground and shoved it through the opening. He was about to follow when he heard the monk ask the lone remaining member of the team a very simple question. "Lisa Marie, how is your brother? I hope he is well."

Turning back, Burke looked across the room at Cho's face. Tears were rolling down her cheeks. She suddenly seemed very human.

"He is well," she said. "And he is much different than before you saved him."

"His change had little to do with me."

Cho reached into her pocket. "He would want you to have this back."

"I just gave you a trunk full of them." Abel laughed. "You should keep it."

"No, this one is yours. Josh wants you to give it to the next lost soul you touch."

"Then I will. Now, go in peace, my daughter."

She caught the monk off guard as she wrapped him in her arms. The embrace lasted long enough for Brother Abel to lightly place his arms around her as well.

This was a private moment—one Burke suddenly felt very uncomfortable witnessing. Turning, he hurriedly pushed through the opening, picked up the trunk, and waited at the mouth of the cave for the woman he now felt compelled to get to know much better.

AMBUSHED

The team made it off the mountain and back to the monastery. Though coming down had been much easier than going up, it still took more than an hour to cover the slick, rough, barely evident trail. When they finally arrived at the gate, the skies opened up with snow so thick the nearby mountains could no longer be seen.

Having carried the heavy trunk all the way down, Burke was bone tired. Others had offered to relieve him, but he felt a need to do this job on his own. Now, less than fifty feet from the shelter offered by the residence building, he could go no farther. Dropping down on the chapel steps, he lifted the trunk off his shoulder and set it on the ancient stones.

Briggs and Casteel walked past him, trudging through the quickly accumulating snow. Only Cho stopped.

"You should've let me help you," she said.

"I needed to do it on my own. I think you would understand. This was my mission or maybe even my calling."

She nodded. She did understand.

"We got here just in time," she noted, sounding more like a concerned friend than a government agent. "Fifteen minutes later and someone might have gotten hurt. We could have been stranded up on the mountain. The upper part of the route is probably impassable now."

"So you and Casteel covered your responsibilities as well," Burke said, weariness evident in his voice.

"It's too cold to sit out here," Cho pointed out. "Let's go in with the others."

Burke shook his head. "No, I need to go to the chapel first. I have a theory I want to test."

Pulling himself to his feet, he picked up the trunk, grunting as he lifted it to his right shoulder. He then walked slowly into the old house of worship. There was still enough daylight coming through the windows to see. Moving around the broken pews, he walked past where the altar once stood to a far wall. He stopped in front of one of the deep holes cut into the stone. It looked right, but there was only one way to find out.

Burke lowered the trunk and held it in front of one of the openings. He set it on the ledge and eased it into the hole. When the back of the trunk touched the wall, he stepped back.

There was no more than a quarter of an inch clearance on the sides and top of the trunk. The outside end of the chest was flush with the opening. A perfect fit.

Cho joined him. She ran her fingers along the edges of the shelves. "The two holes in the walls were made for the two trunks."

As he studied the chest, now positioned where it likely sat for many years, maybe centuries, he was struck by a now obvious bit of remodeling.

"We missed something," Burke said. "This is far too new."

A piece of wood had been placed on the bottom of each shelf. The professor grabbed the plank and gave it a strong pull. It didn't budge.

"You're right," Cho said. "This looks like it came from the broken bed frames we found in the residence hall. The marks made by the saw are rough. This wasn't sanded before it was placed here. It appears to be a quick job. Dollars to donuts, these were put here when the monks trashed the monastery."

"Dollars to donuts?" Burke asked. "What does that mean?"

"Just something my grandfather used to say when he was sure he was right. I've got a small pry bar in my pack."

The agent dropped her pack to the floor, opened the zipper, and retrieved the tool. She then placed the edge of the blade between the edge of the stone wall and the wood. As she gained leverage, the board groaned, but stubbornly held fast. Then, with no warning, it fell to the floor with a loud crash.

"That likely woke the dead," Burke cracked.

"Some echo in here," Cho added. "Must have been great for choral singing."

Where the board had been, there was indeed a message. The writing didn't jump out in the dim light, but it was there.

"Can you read it?" Cho asked.

"No, but I'm sure Dr. Briggs can. I'm betting it translates into something like 'Baltore's treasure.'"

"I'll bet you're close."

Startled by the strange voice, Burke and Cho whirled toward the door. A tall, solidly built man filled the space. A grin framed his face. Burke knew the devil himself had just stepped into the chapel. And he was well acquainted with this version of Satan.

"Bruno Krueger," Burke hissed.

"It's been a long time, Jeff. Strange I should find you at the Domum Lignarii. I thought you were more into North and South American history. And weren't you supposed to be on a fishing trip to Canada?"

From the corner of his eye, Burke saw Cho slowly reach inside her coat.

"Stop right there, young woman," Krueger ordered.

His words were still bouncing off the walls when a half dozen men, rifles raised, rushed into the chapel and fanned out on either side of him. "You'd never get the gun out of your belt before bullets would pass through you and into the wall. Now let me see both hands."

Cho shrugged and raised her arms. Krueger took one step toward her. "You're supposed to be dead."

Cho shook her head. "If he was your man, you should think about moving him to a different position in your organization."

"I will," Krueger replied. "But before I do that, you will be needing a new funeral." Turning his head toward the door, he hollered, "Dr. Fogleman, I need you."

The woman walked through the chapel's entryway and stopped beside the billionaire. She seemed shocked. Was it the presence of the two Americans or the guns pointed at them?

Burke smiled. "Mitzi, didn't imagine you ever left the library."

"What are you doing here, Jeff?" the woman asked, a frown creasing her forehead.

"You know her?" Cho asked without taking her eyes off Krueger.

"She and I have crossed paths several times," Burke explained. "I had no idea who her employer was or I wouldn't have been nearly as accommodating."

"So much for reunions," Krueger broke in. "Mitzi, I need you to translate what is written on that shelf over there, the one next to that black chest."

She studied the chiseled text, then announced, "The Words of the Father."

"Jeff," Krueger said, his smile growing even wider, "you and your friend will need to move over to the far wall."

"Do as he says. We don't have much choice," Cho whispered.

After the professor and agent were in their new location, Krueger walked confidently over to the shelf.

"So this is it."

Pulling the trunk from its resting place, he set it on the floor and popped the lid. Crouching, he ran his hands through the coins and jewels.

"Impressive. Mitzi, what do you make of this?"

The researcher examined the contents. "Sixth or seventh century. Beyond the money and trinkets, there appears to be nothing else. There's no book or scroll in here."

Krueger turned to Burke. "Where is it?"

"I honestly don't know," he replied. "I've taken nothing out of the trunk. It's just as I found it."

"You will pardon me if I don't believe you. Gentlemen, would you carefully, but not too gently, search those two?"

Two large men, both Middle Eastern, roughly went over every square inch of Burke and Cho. They included every bit of their bodies in the groping. The only thing they found of any interest was the woman's nine millimeter.

Krueger smiled. "Well, this is interesting. Your friends on the inside didn't have anything either. What do you think, Mitzi?"

The woman once more turned her attention to the trunk. "I doubt if the book was ever in here. No one would have placed a valuable scroll or document with something that could have damaged it, like these coins. But, now, as we know this item was shipped here and we know who shipped it, and we can clearly see the writing on the wall, I think the answer to where the book is might be hidden in the trunk itself. We would need to get it back to our research center and disassemble it. I have a feeling we'll find a map or a code that will lead us to the scroll."

Burke chuckled.

"What's that for?" Krueger demanded, his look as cruel as his tone.

"That's a ridiculous assumption," Burke quipped. "Pure amateur. Fogleman's conclusion has no basis in reality. She's relying on a wish, not facts in evidence. Bruno, you can surely afford better help than this!"

Krueger smiled. "You protest too strongly that the trunk has no value. You're a lousy poker player, Jeff. You overplayed your hand. You didn't run a convincing bluff. Now, if you had assured me that all I needed was in the trunk, then I would have known it was worthless. One of you men, pick up that chest and take it out to the rendezvous point. Jeff, you and the agent are going back to the other building to join the others. I have a surprise planned."

At gunpoint, Burke and Cho were marched across the grounds. The snow, which had been so heavy just a few minutes before, had all but stopped and the wind had died down as well. It was as quiet as a wake. Burke feared it was about to become one, and he was going to be one of the honorees.

Opening the door, Burke walked in, with Cho directly behind him. Sitting at the table were their two companions, and neither was in a partying mood. Along a far wall, a trio of mercenaries stood with guns ready.

"Take a chair," Krueger ordered.

"What now?" Cho asked.

"Well, the weather has cleared," the billionaire explained, "and my ride will be coming in shortly. After I leave, and I'm far enough away that I can't be connected to the events, you will join those who used to call this place home."

"You're going to kill them?" a shocked Fogleman asked.

"I'm not," Krueger replied. "I don't get my hands dirty. These men will take care of their needs."

"But we can't do that," the researcher whispered.

Krueger considered the woman's words. "I'm sorry you feel that way, Mitzi. And if you choose to not align with me, then you will join them. I can find someone else who can unravel the code hidden in that chest. I have four other top researchers on speed dial. The choice is yours."

The door opened and a small man clad in local mountain garb walked in. He whispered something to Krueger, then left as quickly as he had appeared.

"The helicopter will be here in a few moments," the billionaire said. "So it is time for me to say goodbye." He paused and smiled. "Actually, it's more of a final farewell. I love the irony of a group from the plains of Illinois dying within a few miles of one of bin Ladin's hideouts. No one who cares will ever find your bodies."

"You flew in?" Casteel asked. "Funny we didn't hear you."

"We must have been in the cave," Cho said. "Should have had a lookout."

"Goodbye, my friends." Krueger laughed as he moved toward the door.

"I've alerted a UN force where we are," Cho shot back. She forced a smile before adding, "They're picking us up tonight, and they'll be here" — she glanced down at her watch — "in a few minutes."

"Nice try," Krueger said, "but Raymond told me they didn't allow you to bring any type of communication equipment. You have no GPS, no radio, not even a satellite phone. You had to remain silent. Otherwise the terrorist operations in this area would have found you. And if you'd been discovered or captured, US authorities were going to claim they had no idea who you were or what you were doing here. You were on your own. In fact, I know you don't even have any official identification on you. You took a big risk. It almost worked. But almost doesn't count for much. But I will say this for you, Miss Cho, you run a better bluff than the professor."

"What about the Taliban and al-Qaeda cells all through this

area?" Cho asked. "And you know I'm not bluffing now. Your chopper will alert all of them that you're here. They'll blow you out of the sky before you get two hundred feet in the air."

Krueger smiled. "Ah, Miss Cho. You don't shoot the goose that lays the golden egg. I fund them. They are my friends. I can come and go as I please. I hold all the trump cards."

Krueger pushed Fogleman toward the door. Just before he left, he turned back to his men. "Wait until we've been gone for a while. Make sure you create obvious signs that this was a Taliban operation."

The trio remained against the far wall, automatic weapons ready to carry out their task. The others followed Krueger outside.

"Anyone got a deck of cards?" Casteel asked.

"Better yet," Burke said, "since none of us is evidently any good at poker, anyone got a plan?"

THE EXECUTION

It seemed like only seconds after the helicopter took off that the three henchmen stepped out of the shadows and walked toward the table. Burke figured their only chance was to make a move just after he heard them lock their weapons. Maybe he could move fast enough to whirl a chair at them as a diversion and then ... but what then? The henchmen had automatic weapons, and what did they have?

Burke's eyes turned from the men's ugly but stoic faces to Cho. She smiled. If that was the last thing he saw on earth, then things could have been worse. Yet he sure regretted not getting to know her better.

In an unfamiliar language, one of the brutes barked an order. From the corner of his eye, Burke saw the automatics slide up to the men's shoulders. This was a firing squad! There would be no call from the governor granting a reprieve. Lifespan was now measured in seconds. He prepared for a quick roll off the chair to his right, but someone else moved first.

In a last ditch but not unexpected effort, Cho shot upright and reached for a bowl on the table. Her fingers had just touched it when a cold chill filled the room. It was like someone had opened the door of a walk-in freezer. Four or five shots rang out in rapid order. The weapons' repercussions bounced off the walls, and the smell of smoke filled the air. Then time slowed to a crawl.

Resisting the urge to stare death in the face, Burke's eyes never went to the assailants or the sound of the gunfire. Instead they remained affixed on Cho. Her image filled his senses and masked his fears. The pain had to be coming. But when? What was keeping it? Where was that warm feeling he'd heard about?

He was not the only one stuck in time—hovering somewhere between life and death. Cho did not move either. Her face was set. Her eyes were unblinking.

Burke had read theories on death, the notion that even as your body dies you continue to see yourself as being alive. Your brain's way of coping with shock. Was that what was happening? Was this the afterlife?

He heard the bodies fall to the floor. He heard the thuds. Was it Briggs or Casteel or both?

"Mason!" Casteel cried out.

"Yes," came the quick reply.

Mason?

Cho moved.

"Clark!" she screamed as she ran toward him. "I saw you go over the cliff! The rope went slack; we lost you."

"Almost," Mason replied with a grin as he wrapped his arms around her. "I fell about fifty feet to an outcropping in the rock. Must have knocked me out. Guess the snow was so thick you couldn't see me. You're not the only charmed one now." He looked down at her and winked. "Once I came to, I worked my way down the side of the cliff to the valley below. Had a heck of a time finding my way back to you. Looks like I got here just in time."

As the two walked back toward the others, Mason asked, "Who was in the helicopter?"

"Bruno Krueger," Cho said.

"So, you were right," Mason said. "He was the force behind all this. Who was the woman with him?"

Burke said, "Dr. Mitzi Fogleman. She's a historian, and I figure she must have been duped into working for him. I doubt she had any idea of his true nature."

"Shame," Mason said. "I watched as she was pushed out of the chopper. The body's on the rocks just behind the compound."

"They killed her?" Briggs whispered.

"That's the way Krueger operates," Cho said. "When someone doesn't do their job or questions his motives, they pay for it with their life."

"We need to get out of here," Mason said.

Cho agreed. "We can't go back the way we came, at least not at night. Way too dangerous."

"We can't stay here either," Mason added. "With the noise we've made, this place will be crawling with locals within an hour. You might not have seen them, but there are people living in these hills. I observed them with their sheep and goats as I worked my way back to you. Few if any will be on our side."

"Any of them have a guitar and sing songs?" Burke quipped.

"What?" Mason asked.

"Never mind," Cho said. "Put on your gear and grab your packs. We need to at least make it past the base of those mountains."

"Grab their guns," Mason added. "We need all the firepower we can collect."

For the first time, Burke looked over at the three dead men. The fact that they had once been his potential executioners didn't prevent him from seeing them as human beings. As they lay in pools of their own blood, parts of their faces blown apart, he was sickened. What a waste! The fact they died for a paycheck rather than a cause made that waste even more pronounced.

"Let's get moving!"

Cho's voice pulled Burke away from the mercenaries. He suddenly felt the urge to not just leave this place but run from it. Pushing through the door, he joined a crew that once more numbered five as they hurried through the snow and out the gate of the monastery.

THE GOAT BARN

It was almost dark. For the moment, no one seemed to be near except for Fogleman. They spied her crumpled body sprawled on rocks to the right of their path.

Briggs was the only one who verbally acknowledged the ghastly sight. "My Lord," he sighed.

No one responded. Maybe it was because there were no words to say.

"Which way?" Cho asked.

"I came through a valley just behind that ridge," Mason said. "Can't be more than a mile. There was some vegetation and some old buildings. We might hole up there until morning."

"You lead the way," Cho replied.

Moving over the rocky, snow-covered ground at a steady pace, the team made it to the ridge in twenty minutes. As they stopped to catch their breath, Burke turned to study the monastery. Two sets of lights, likely from all-terrain vehicles, were approaching from the west.

"They're on their way," Mason noted. "Our trail won't be hard to follow through the snow. If we can get some cover, we have enough firepower to hold off a small band. But not for long."

"Let's get moving," Casteel urged. "We have to get dug in."

Now the horror of what they had been through was heightened by the fear of what would likely be next. The fact they were exhausted was quickly forgotten as they picked up their packs and their pace.

On the far side of the ridge, the landscape changed. The ground in the valley was flat. There was soil rather than rocks beneath the snow. Small trees hugged the cliffs and a few goats could be heard.

Pulling a flashlight from her pack, Cho shined it down the middle of a field that looked to be more than a mile long.

"Look up there."

"It's the buildings I saw," Mason replied. "One is a lot bigger than I thought."

"Let's get our bearings," Cho suggested, "then I'm turning the light off. I don't want to make us an easy target."

With Mason leading the way, the troop managed a slow, steady jog, driven by fear and Casteel's urging. Cho signaled for them to stop about fifty yards from the collection of buildings. Just beyond the largest of the four structures were lights.

"It's a house," Burke whispered. "Someone must live here."

"Yeah," Cho replied, "and odds are they don't want our kind of company."

"Let's move quietly to that barn-looking thing," Casteel suggested.

"That would sure hold a lot of goats," Briggs noted.

"That very well might be what we find in there," Mason said.

The five carefully picked their way through the barren field to the metal building that had to be 120 feet long and 90 feet wide. It stood out not just because of its size but because it was covered with pressed metal. It looked like something that should have been in the Midwest.

"Why build something like that out here?" Casteel asked.

"Let's go inside and find out. There's a small door on the side."

With Cho leading the way, they hurried to the door. She listened for a moment, then nodded to the others. She turned the knob, pulled the door open, and disappeared inside while the others waited.

She stuck her head out and whispered, "There's no one here. Not even livestock. Everybody in! Let's snap it up!"

Mason went in first, followed by Briggs, with Casteel on his heels. Burke was the last one in. Cho silently closed the door. There were no windows. It was pitch black.

"Do you smell that?" Cho asked from the darkness.

"Gas," Mason replied.

"Oil too," Cho added. "There's machinery in here."

The mystery of what was in the well-built structure held only until Cho flipped on her flashlight. "My Lord," the agent whispered. "An airplane!"

The beam from the flashlight followed the contours of the plane. It was not state of the art. Far from it. It was an antique painted an ugly brown. But even with the bad paint job, it looked almost brand-new.

"Why would a plane be hidden here?" Burke asked.

"Opium," Mason offered. "This was likely used for running drugs. Might still be."

Cho jumped in. "Dollars to donuts, it's now used to deliver weapons and ammunition to the Taliban or al-Qaeda."

"Dollars to donuts?" Casteel asked. "What's that mean?"

"Don't ask," Mason said. "She says it all the time."

They walked over to the plane. "I don't know much about aviation," Mason said, "but I do know this isn't just an antique piece. It's being used. You can smell that the engines have been fired recently."

Cho studied the vintage bird, paying particular attention to the two motors.

"This is a Douglas DC-2," Cho said. "Wish Dad could see this. He made me read all about these when I was a kid. The DC-2 was manufactured for only a couple years back in the mid-1930s before it was replaced by the DC-3. I've actually flown one of those. This model is powered by two radial engines, each generating over six hundred horsepower. It can go over two hundred miles per hour and, with a full fuel tank, stay in the air for over five hours. The only ones left on the planet are in museums. Guess no one in the civilized world knows about this DC-2 because *this* is no museum."

"Think the pilot lives in that house?" Burke asked.

"Maybe," Cho replied.

"Then we will just have to charter this baby." Mason grinned. "Might have to force the old boy to take us out of here.

"The charter service makes sense," Cho agreed. "But we don't need him. I can fly it. It flies just like a DC-3. If there's enough fuel, we can be out of here in an hour."

Now Burke grinned. "You can fly this sucker?"

"And about anything else you throw at me," Cho replied. "Besides, the DC-2s almost fly themselves."

"And we can take off across that field?" Briggs asked.

"They've been doing it," Cho said. "And here's the really good part. If this bird has been used for what I think it has, no one is going to try to shoot us down. They're going to assume we are on a mission for them."

"You really believe you can do this?" Casteel asked.

"It's better than walking," Cho replied. "But when I fire up these motors, it's going to make a lot of racket. Those folks in that house are going to be raising the hounds of hell to get here."

"Colorful analogy," Burke chimed in. "I'll bet dollars to donuts, she's right."

Cho glared at him.

He smiled and shrugged.

"I don't get this dollars to donuts thing," Casteel said.

"Don't worry about it," Mason said. "How long will it take you to get ready?"

"I'll have to check on the fuel situation," Cho explained. "Has to be a supply in here. I'll find out how much is in the plane. We really only need about a half a tank to get to where we need to go. These things were known to leak oil, so I'll check the the oil levels too. I can teach someone how to crank the engines and get them started. I really believe we can be in the air in an hour. If we have fuel."

"Can you do what you need to do with just Dr. Briggs and Burke?" Mason asked.

"Sure."

"Okay," Mason said. "You get this ship ready to jump into the air. The captain and I are going to pay a visit to the neighbors. Don't want them spoiling our going-away party."

BAGS OF MONEY

I see three of them," Casteel whispered. "They're sitting around a table playing some kind of game."

"Weapons?" Mason asked.

"Automatics resting against the far wall. They won't be able to get to them."

"Okay," Mason said. "Let me sneak in through the window on the other side. Give me one minute and then burst in the front door. If they go for the weapons, I'll plug them from the back."

"What about the gunfire?" Casteel cut in. "We fire guns, then our location will be given away. The folks now at the monastery will be up here before we can sneeze. Shouldn't we simply use hand to hand?"

Mason pointed to his pistol. "Silencer. An assassin's favorite fashion accessory." The man then issued a blunt warning to Casteel. "But you can't shoot, my friend. You are the decoy. I'll be pulling the trigger if it is needed."

"Sounds good," Casteel said. He glanced at his watch. "Sixty seconds from now. Be ready."

As Mason hustled around the side of the home, the Army Ranger counted time down. Right at the sixty-second mark, Casteel's size tens shattered the door's latch. It swung open like a chute at the rodeo. The two Americans rushed in like mad bulls after the same bullfighter.

Mason didn't understand the words being screamed as the trio spotted the Americans, but he sensed, by the tone, they might have been laced with profanity. One man upset the table, knocking his chair on its side as he stood up. The other two reacted a second later, rising and twirling toward the wall where they'd left their guns. Before they could take even a single step, Casteel hollered out something in what Mason guessed was a dialect or language common to the region. He knew enough Farsi to know it wasn't that. But whatever Casteel said, it caused the trio to freeze. Mason grabbed the guns and did a quick and cursory search of the house.

"Lots of money, both euros and dollars," Mason said. "There are banks in the States that aren't as well capitalized as this house."

He reached into a satchel and pulled out a wad of bills. Then, for no apparent reason, he tossed the money into the air and watched it rain down. "Always wanted to do that."

After the last bill had found its way to the floor, Mason turned to Casteel, "You know their language?"

"Like a native. My mother was from Afghanistan."

"Then ask them who they work for."

"Ourselves," the one closest to Mason replied in English.

Without missing a beat, the agent barked, "Doing what?"

"We fly in weapons. We sell them. That is all we do."

Mason looked to Casteel. He shrugged.

"You speak excellent English," Mason said, taking two threatening steps toward the man, his gun aimed at his large crooked nose. He'd evidently been in a few fights and lost most of them.

"I have a degree from the University of Illinois."

That was unexpected. "What's your name," he demanded.

"Does it matter?" he replied, his voice as cool as a fall breeze.

"Not really," Mason admitted.

His dark face was calm — his black eyes showed no shock, surprise, or fear. His beard was neatly trimmed, and he was dressed in a blue Nike warm-up suit. His two companions looked more like shepherds.

"And your friends?" Mason asked. "Who are they?"

"They're locals. They work with me. They unload the goods. I can guarantee none of us has ever raised a gun against anyone. We are not warriors, we are businessmen. In fact, my degree is in business."

"Yeah," Mason replied, "but by flying in the weapons, you are responsible for a lot of deaths. Businessmen who play this game are just as guilty as those who pull the trigger."

"The Crusaders caused a lot of death too," he answered. "And someone supplied the weapons for them as well. In war there is business. Someone makes and sells the weapons your troops use to kill Afghans. This is business. That is all it is."

"The business of death," Mason said.

"When you're holding the gun," he replied, "the weapon is the business of life."

"What do we do with them?" Casteel asked.

Mason considered the situation. In a real sense, these men were at best privateers and at worst in league with the likes of Osama bin Ladin. Yet he wasn't a judge or executioner. He wasn't comfortable making that call.

"What do you have to offer that is worth your lives?" Casteel demanded.

That was a question Mason hadn't even considered. Yet it cut right to the quick.

"Who are you?" the man replied.

"FBI," Mason said.

"I figured CIA," the man shot back. "You're out of your territory."

"Special assignment," Mason countered. "Terror knows no borders."

The arms dealer stared at the agent. His expression was emotionless. "You don't want money. So that's one bargaining chip that I could offer but would be refused. I assume you don't need my old plane either. But I do have a condo in Aspen. We could start with that."

He was cool. Mason had to hand him that.

Casteel, now fully into his role as the "bad cop," spit. "You have nothing."

"No," he replied, "as long as you have the guns, anything I have you can take. That is the way the game is played in this part of the world."

Casteel looked at Mason. "The smart thing to do is kill them. Dead men can't talk."

"But without a plane," Mason countered, "they can't deliver their goods either. Let's tie them up and make them very uncomfortable."

"No one comes here," the dealer said. This time there was real passion in his voice. "We might starve before anyone finds us."

"Life comes with risks," Casteel said. "Sit back down in your chairs."

The command was simple, but the response was not. The smallest of the three drew a knife from his belt and lunged at Mason. Thanks to the silencer, a bullet quietly found his head and he fell to the floor. His intended victim looked calmly at the other two. "Anyone else? I have plenty of bullets."

The man who had not spoken shook his head. The dealer pulled his chair upright, placed his posterior in it, and pushed his hands behind his back. He seemed to believe his chances of getting loose before starving were much better than taking on the two Americans.

"Tie us up and take what you will."

Casteel went to work while Mason searched the remainder of the small home. It was amazingly modern. A generator supplied power. There was satellite TV, high-speed internet, even a microwave. He also found five dufflebags stuffed with money.

"We should take the money," Casteel suggested. "If we leave it here, he'll just use it to get back in business."

"Be best if we break the generator too," Mason added. "I believe my knife should be able to accomplish that."

By the time Mason finished that chore and returned to the central room, the two privateers were tightly bound and widely separated from each other. It would take them a long time to get loose — unless help arrived.

"Captain," Mason announced in an official tone, "we have five dufflebags that will be going back with us. Are you all finished here?"

"I am," Casteel assured him.

"Good. I figure Cho is ready as well. The bags are beside the front door. Let's pick them up and head for home."

The pair took a final look at the two captives in the now dark room and stepped back out into the cold night, into a blinding swirl of snow whipped by a north wind.

FIRE UP

Cho was waiting for them just outside the door. "Mission successful?" she asked.

"One dead, two tied up," Mason reported. "What about here?"

"Been waiting for you. Done all we can do. It's gassed and greased. Appears to be perfectly maintained. But won't know until we fire it up. Let's roll those doors open and find out. What's in the bags?"

"Money," Mason said. "Lots of money. We might just take an extended vacation after this is all over."

Cho glanced over to see if the agent was serious. She couldn't tell. What she did see was impatience. The agent wanted out, and it couldn't come soon enough.

The first step in accomplishing that mission was easy. The barn doors were well lubricated and opened effortlessly. Next was the hard part.

The cold night air and snow rushed in. "Get in the plane. Leave the copilot's seat open for Jeff. There aren't any other seats. Use the cargo netting to secure yourselves. I already have Dr. Briggs belted in."

Mason nodded as Cho pulled herself up into the plane. She waited in the pilot's seat while Mason and Casteel got on board. Satisfied that all was ready, she slid the window open and yelled, "Let her go!"

Burke slid a crank into a slot and began to turn the crank. When the spring was tight, he backed off with the crank in hand, pulled a flashlight from his pocket, and gave a signal.

Cho hit the switch, adjusted the choke, and fed the old engine a bit of juice. It stuttered, coughed, and died.

"Crank it again!" she shouted to Burke. "I think I may have starved it."

When he was done, he again backed off to a position under the almost forty-foot wing and flashed his light.

Cho repeated the starting procedure. This time, after the cough, the motor caught. "That's right, baby," she whispered. "Talk to me."

The roar rattled the barn and rumbled across the valley. In the close quarters, it was almost deafening. Yet Cho didn't mind. In fact, she relished the sound. It might well have been the most beautiful purring she'd ever heard.

"Thanks, Dad," she whispered as she ran her hand over the throttle.

As the motor smoothed out, she watched Burke's flashlight pass in front of the plane to the other side. She glanced over as he cranked the left engine. His light again waved as he backed away. Pulling back on the choke, she eased into the throttle and said a prayer. It wasn't answered. This motor didn't surge to life on the first try, or the second, or the third. It simply wheezed and gasped.

"What's wrong?" Mason hollered from the cargo area.

Cho glanced at the man who had now moved into the cockpit. "They're not like modern engines," she explained. "You just don't flip a switch and it starts. Each motor has its own personality. You might choke one all the way, but the other will just need a smidge. They react differently to the throttle. If I flew this plane all the time, I'd know what each one liked—I'd understand the motors' personalities. But we are not close friends yet. In fact we have barely been introduced. This is our first date."

"You will be able to start it?" her partner asked.

"Clark," Cho replied, "don't you trust me? Of course! Now go sit down."

She was not nearly as confident as her voice sounded. Glancing out the window, she saw Jeff waving his light. He was ready again. She repeated the process a fourth time, this time barely tugging on the choke. She finally had uncovered the way the baby wanted to be fed. The old Pratt and Whitney engine fired off like a new one. As it smoothed out, Cho had more than 1,300 horsepower at her beck and call. Now all Jeff had to do was yank out the wheel chocks and they'd see if the machine could fly.

The agent was adjusting the air-gas mixture and studying the lighted dials when Burke climbed into the plane, pulled the door closed, and plopped down in the seat beside her. After latching his seatbelt, he looked at Cho.

"Got your list?" she asked.

"Yep."

"How's it look?"

He glanced down through the sheet she'd scribbled out for him. "Everything appears good."

She grinned. "Oil pressure is great, more than three-quarters of a tank of fuel, and lots of power. I like this old bird. If we get it home, I'm going to see if Dad can buy it. It'd be great to fly it to the big air show in Oshkosh."

Burke nodded. Cho's confidence seemed to convince him that their problems were behind them. Yet that bravado hadn't fully woven its magic around her. She was nervous. Would the DC-2 get in the air and make it over the ridges? Logic said it would. After all, it had been taking off from here for a while now — maybe years. But at night, with so little light, a crosswind, and now blowing snow? Would she be able to do it? There was so little room for error, and she and the plane didn't know each other yet. It was, after all, their first time to the ball.

"Please be good, first date," she whispered.

As Cho eased into the throttle, the motors roared and the DC-2 rolled out of the barn and into the night air. Giving the right motor a bit more gas, the plane made a bending turn.

"Holy smoke!" Cho pulled back on the throttle and the engines eased to an idle.

Burke, who'd been studying the gauges, looked up. "Where did they come from?"

"Don't know," Cho replied, "but they've got guns and they have us blocked with their truck. Get Mason up here."

All this horsepower and it was being held in check by a few guys and an old Chevy. She looked down at a man waving a lantern with a gun pointed right at her. Burke scrambled back to the cabin section.

"What do we have?" Mason asked as he moved between the two seats in the cockpit.

"Company," Cho said. "Their truck has us blocked. Judging by the way he's waving the light, I'm guessing they want to talk."

"They won't like the looks of us," Mason replied.

Cho continued to stare out the windshield. If they were going to fire on the plane, she figured they would have had already done it. So they likely wanted something, or perhaps they knew the man who owned the DC-2.

As she considered her options, she heard the plane's door open. Then she saw Casteel, his form illuminated by the glow of the truck's lights.

"What's he doing?" Cho asked.

"I didn't send him," Mason replied, "but he knows the local language. My guess is he's working on instinct. Let's give him a chance."

Cho watched the scene play out in front of her. As the Ranger approached the truck, the man set the lantern down but aimed his gun at Casteel. The two began talking. Soon the man lowered the weapon.

So far so good. The group didn't seem agitated.

A few minutes into the conversation, things appeared to get even better as Casteel and the one who was evidently the leader looked toward the cockpit. They both waved.

"What was that about?" Burke asked.

"Whatever it was," Cho replied, "it looked friendly. If he can bluff his way through this one and get that truck to move, I'm buying him the biggest steak in Chicago."

The wave was followed by several nods and more talk by the band's leader. Then Casteel slowly walked out of the light. The man didn't follow. Instead, he looked toward the plane. The other members of the troop continued to lean casually against the truck.

Cho kept her eyes on the men even as she heard the captain return to the plane. A minute later, Mason was again beside her.

"Casteel convinced him he was an American defector and a new member of the crew. They think Nassar is the pilot. That's the guy who owns the plane. Casteel informed him that Nassar couldn't come out because of some engine problems. In other words, he had to keep them running."

"So," Cho asked, "what do they want?"

"Guns. Specific types of anti-aircraft weapons."

"Okay," the agent replied, "and what did Casteel tell them we could do?"

"Get them for them. He even guaranteed they could pick them up right here in forty-eight hours."

"That sounds good. But why aren't they leaving?"

"Because," Mason explained, "the man in charge wants to go with us. He wants to inspect the merchandise before he forks over the money. Casteel said he'd have to clear it with Nassar."

"I don't think that's a good idea," Cho replied. "I don't think I'm what he's expecting."

"The truck's not moving until we allow him to board." Mason paused, then added, "I know of a really good reason to extend the invitation."

"What's that?" Cho asked.

"The man with the lantern is al-Rahim Barot. Does that name sound familiar?"

Cho smiled. He was on the CIA's and FBI's terrorist list. The man was one of the new wave of al-Qaeda leaders. He might even be in line to replace bin Laden. Turning back to Mason she said, "I hope you have the welcoming committee ready."

Mason patted Cho on the shoulder and headed for the door. Moments later, Casteel strolled back to the truck's lights. The Ranger smiled, said something, opened his arms and hugged Barot. After the two patted each other on the back, the terrorist passed the lantern to one of his associates. A few words were exchanged, and the others got back into the truck. They pulled forward far enough for the plane to pass by easily. As Casteel and his guest turned, Barot slung his automatic over his shoulder and laughed.

"Stay here," Cho ordered Burke.

Sliding from her seat, she eased back to the plane's cargo area. Mason was on one side of the open door, Cho took a position on the other. There were no lights on, so their guest could not see in. Casteel's flashlight beam led Barot behind the wing and to the plane's door. As there were no steps, the middle-aged visitor took the weapon from around his shoulder and pushed it onto the floor of the DC-2.

Grabbing the side of the door, he pulled himself up on his stomach. He was about to turn over when Mason's hand closed around his mouth. A second later, Cho placed her knee in his back and yanked Barot's arms behind him. As she did, Casteel jumped into the plane and shut the door.

Even in the dim light, Cho could see the man's eyes. They were on fire! The Arab struggled, trying to break free, but when Casteel delivered a swift hard kick to his head, his struggle stopped.

"Gag him," Cho ordered.

Thirty seconds later, Mason lifted his hand just enough for Casteel to apply a piece of duct tape. At the same time, Cho tied up his hands and rolled Barot over.

Satisfied she wasn't needed, Cho moved back to the pilot's seat. Pushing on the throttles, she eased the plane forward. It bounced along through the swirling snow until she reached the end of the valley. Slowly spinning the plane in a 180-degree arc, she looked into the now thick frozen precipitation. At the end of the runway was a ridge and mountains beyond. Earlier she could see them. Now she couldn't. So she had no way of gauging just how long the runway was. Could she get the plane off the ground and gain enough altitude to avoid spreading pieces of the DC-2 all over this part of Afghanistan? She gunned the engines. She was flying blind, and there was only one way to find out if she could get the plane off the ground in time. It was either going to work or they were all going to die.

GROUNDED

If only she could see! The snow was now so thick that to her eyes, there were no mountains. In fact, there was very little but the huge flakes of puffy frozen moisture.

Five large gauges were positioned in front of her. Speed was to the left, but even though they were still on the ground, it was the altitude gauge on the right that drew all of her attention. She had to get off the ground and over the ridges. Then came the mountains. The snow — the blinding snow — was the problem. Because of it, she simply couldn't see what she had to avoid.

If they waited long enough, perhaps the storm would pass. Yet if there was too much snow on the field then they wouldn't be able to take off anyway. Darned if she did and darned if she didn't and likely dead either way.

Mason had come up from the back and was looking over Cho's shoulder. "What's the holdup?"

"Can't see," Cho answered. Her tone was flat, showing none of the nervousness that was rocking her body.

"Can we wait it out?" the agent asked, his tone reflecting his complete confidence in his partner.

"What about those guys down at the monastery?" Cho asked. "You thought they'd be coming up here as soon as they heard the engines."

"With this heavy snow," Mason said, "I doubt if they'll be moving."

Maybe sitting it out was the right thing to do. Maybe they did have the time to wait. Maybe the snow wouldn't pile up so much they'd get stuck. Maybe in this case he who hesitates would not be lost.

"Look over there," Burke said, pointing toward the house. His voice sounded concerned.

Barot's men had gotten out of the truck and were walking up to the front door of the house. Waiting out the storm was no longer an option.

"They're looking to use Nassar's place to get away from the storm," Mason said. "Won't take them long to realize they've been duped."

The terrorists would no doubt come out of that house with guns a-blazing. Cho knew they had one shot to fly out and this was it. Though she couldn't see much beyond the house, the time for departure was now.

After checking the gauges, she glanced at the windows to once more study the engines. They were purring and ready to go. Grabbing the throttles in her right hand and holding the wheel in her left, Cho started the plane rolling. Just as the old bird got moving, she saw a series of flashes. They'd been made. Even though she couldn't hear them over the engine noise, guns had fired.

"Hang on!" she shouted as the DC-2 picked up speed and bounced across the field.

"They're in the truck!" Mason hollered. "I know you know what you're doing, but can't you pick things up a bit?"

"We're plowing through drifts," Cho explained, "and the crosswind's not helping."

Just as Cho finished her explanation, a round pierced the plane's body less than three inches above her head. She was sure more would follow.

"They're trying to cut us off!" Mason yelled.

"They'd be smarter shooting at the engines," Cho replied. "I'm doing my best to get our speed up."

Two more rounds tore through the plane's skin.

On an ideal day on a good runway, a DC-3, which she had flown a few times, could lift off in less than a thousand feet. But tonight was different and maybe a DC-2 was too. Maybe it took a longer runway. How long before the ridge? She wished she knew. She was going to have to guess on the minimum speed for takeoff. One wrong guess and there would be no others.

The plane was finally picking up speed. It felt almost ready, but she wasn't sure, so she pushed it harder. With the conditions, she figured she needed more speed to fight through the wind and snow.

She squinted as she tried to see through the blinding sheets of white. She could see nothing.

"The truck's falling back!" Even as Mason spoke, another series of rounds tore into the plane. If this continued, the old DC-2 was going to look more like Swiss cheese than a hunk of American engineering. But so far the motors hadn't been hit. Neither had the fuel tanks.

"Are you going to lift her off the ground before you see the ridge?" Burke asked.

Cho ignored him. Between the rough ground and the layer of snow, the plane wasn't responding like she'd hoped. She glanced down at the speed. Was it enough for liftoff?

Though she still couldn't see the ridge, she sensed it was looming ahead. There would be no second chance. Gunning the engine, the ship picked up a little more speed. She adjusted the flaps.

The old bird lifted for a moment and then came down hard on the ground. Even as the DC-2 shook, Cho gave the old gal even more gas. Suddenly there was no vibration. They were only a few feet off the ground, but they were in the air!

Cho's heart was racing. She had to climb, but she couldn't push the bird too hard or it would stall. As she pulled back on the wheel, the instruments told her they were now two hundred feet above the ground and climbing. She stared out the windshield. Where was the ridge?

"Wheels up!" she barked.

Burke hit the switch to raise the landing gear. He felt the thud of the wheels locking in place just as Cho jerked the nose toward the heavens. Burke never saw the ridge fill the windshield, but Cho did. She guessed they cleared it by no more than a dozen feet.

One hurdle out of the way. Another loomed just ahead. There was a pass between two mountains. She'd absentmindedly studied it two days before when they had hiked in. She now wished she'd paid a lot more attention to the region's geography. There was no time to gain enough altitude to go over the mountains. She had to fly the plane through that pass. But how far to the right would be enough?

After banking the plane, Cho continued to peer through the snow as the DC-2 climbed into the teeth of the storm. Strong storm winds buffeted them. With no warning, the plane would fall twenty feet and then shoot up forty. It was the kind of ride barf bags were made for. It was a life-and-death struggle just to hang on to the wheel.

"Are we in the clear?" Burke hollered. "And are we supposed to be bouncing around this way?"

Cho didn't reply. Somewhere out there was the pass. Was it to the left or the right, or did she have the plane headed right where it needed to be? If she was wrong, she would be dead wrong!

The old bird was now at 7,000 feet. Speed was 150 miles per hour, and Cho was still flying blind. She didn't really know why, but she felt an urge to push the plane toward the right. Adjusting course, she continued to stare out into the blinding snow.

"Are we in the clear?" Burke asked again.

He seemed just like a child demanding to know if they were there yet. It was irritating, but understandable. Yet *there* was not the problem for Cho, it was *where*! Where were the mountains? Where was the pass?

Other than her seeing it just before the explosion, there would be no warning if they struck a cliff. The others would likely die before they knew what hit them. If she'd guessed right and they were shooting through the pass, it wouldn't happen. It was that simple. There was that thin line between life and death.

"My Lord!" Burke screamed.

There was nothing in front of her, but when Cho glanced to her right, she saw the wall right next to the wingtip. They were in the pass, but too close to the cliff.

Banking slightly to the left, she pulled the bird away from the mountain. If her memory was correct, she needed to climb a few more thousand feet, then stay on a straight-line course for twenty miles. She wondered if she had overcorrected. Were they gradually moving closer to the peak on the left? Should she bank the plane a bit back?

Suddenly, with no warning, light filled the cockpit. The snow was gone and the moon lit up the night sky. They had flown out of the storm. She could see! She was no longer flying blind.

More than a half mile to her right was the mountain they'd almost scraped. The other was less than a hundred yards to her left. Ahead was smooth sailing. She'd guessed right.

"We're in the clear," Burke said.

For an instant Cho felt safe. Then she glanced over at the left engine. It was running well now, but it wouldn't for long. The moonlight revealed it was hemorrhaging oil. The black liquid was staining the wing and dripping down into the valley below. They would soon be through the pass, but they were hardly out of danger.

REMARKABLE

In his past expeditions, Burke had always been in charge. How odd to have no control now. For days, his life had depended on others. Mason had saved him. So had Casteel. Now it was Cho's turn. He looked down, as helpless as a man on an amusement park ride.

"How far is the nearest base?" Mason asked. He was crouching between them again, so close to Burke their shoulders were touching.

"Ours or theirs?" Cho asked.

The man didn't seem to appreciate the humor. "Just tell me."

"About an hour at our current speed."

"So we can get there on one engine?"

"On distance we're fine," Cho replied. "The plane can fly just fine with only one motor. But I don't know if I can climb enough with one to get over the last peaks. And there's no place to set her down between here and there."

"How much height do you need?" Mason asked as casually as he would have requested a piece of gum. He either had nerves of steel or complete faith in Cho. Maybe both.

"About 12,000. If that engine holds, I think we can do it."

In his classes, whenever broaching the subject of wars, Burke had tried to convey the thin line between life and death. He had attempted to get his students to understand the price of war and the fragility of life. Now he realized that in all of his years of teaching, he hadn't known how thin that line really was until now. In actual war, every moment is a struggle. The reality of death is never more than a heartbeat away. Nothing is assured. And there is no way to begin to describe it. No wonder his classes hadn't gotten it. He hadn't gotten it—until now.

Consumed by a sense of helplessness, Burke studied the rugged terrain below. This place looked more like the moon than earth. Why would anyone choose to live here? Why had so many wars been waged over this inhospitable piece of terrain? It made no sense. After getting a very small firsthand taste of war, he decided that war fought over anything made no sense.

"You all right?" Cho asked.

"Yeah," he answered. "For a man who should be dead, I'm fine."

Cho kept her eyes on the space in front of them. "Lots of us should be dead. Mason should be dead, but he managed to survive and save us. Without that ledge that broke his fall, we'd all be dead. We've all managed to dodge the bullets with our names on them."

She was right. But it didn't bring any feeling of relief or sense of purpose. The enemies they'd killed — the men Mason had gunned down to save them — the images of their bodies would remain with him forever. And then there was poor, misguided Mitzi Fogleman. She had no idea who she was working for and when she found out, she couldn't get out. All this death over a religious artifact!

Cho interrupted his thoughts. "Five years ago, not far from where we took off last night, my brother was badly injured in an ambush by local Taliban-supported warlords. The five men who were with him thought he was dead. Still taking fire, they placed his body on a pew in the chapel at Domum Lignarii and evacuated without him."

Burke turned toward the woman flying the plane that was almost eighty years old. Her stoic expression masked the pain she surely felt. As he considered her words, he began to understand her need to go to the monastery. She had told the monk that her brother had changed, and she had to find out why. He sensed that she had a new perspective as well.

"The blood on the bench was your brother's."

She nodded. "Brother Abel found him there."

"The monk saved his life?"

"I guess," Cho said. "I know something did. With no medical supplies or equipment, he really should have died, but somehow he didn't."

Burke shook his head. "That's the miracle you spoke of."

She nodded. "It took a month. Four days in the monastery, another three weeks in the cave for Josh to recover enough to leave. Before local friends of Brother Abel escorted him to safety, my brother asked the monk why he had done what he had done. Abel's answer was very simple, 'I am my brother's keeper.'"

Cho allowed the words to sink in. "Then Josh asked him why he didn't die. The answer was this, 'Good men never die at Domum Lignarii.' So I wasn't worried about you dying even when the guns were aimed at our backs. You're a good man, Jeff Burke."

Burke felt nothing like "a good man," but he was sure that Lisa Marie Cho was a remarkable woman. And he was convinced that she was also her brother's keeper. He was more than glad to be considered her "brother" at this moment, and maybe he wasn't out of place after all. Maybe he needed to lose control in order to really find it.

THE MOUNTAIN

There it was, all 11,742 feet of it! Seven years ago, while with an FBI group working in support roles in Afghanistan, she'd seen it a dozen different times from the other side. She had even given it a name, "Yul," because the top was rounded like a bald man's head. With two engines, getting over Mt. Yul would have been just like jumping a puddle, but with just one motor, it loomed ahead like an executioner waiting for the judge's order. The left engine had died not long after she'd seen the oil streaming from it. Getting over the mountain peak would be hard enough in the daylight. At night, with one engine, Cho could only pray that they'd make it. How many rpms could the motor take? How high could the old Pratt and Whitney lift them? These were answers she would soon receive.

Easing the nose skyward, Cho began to nurse more power from the engine. Like a faithful dog, it enthusiastically responded. Nine thousand feet became 9,500. But she needed more, a great deal more. At 10,500 the motor was howling so loudly that Burke frowned. Cho didn't blame him, yet as much as she hated the noise, it was the slight shaking that caused her more discomfort. The plane was reaching its limit. Much more and it might just start falling apart at its old riveted seams.

As she stared at the spinning propeller, she was reminded of the old TV series *Star Trek*. Her dad loved that show. He'd always laugh when Kirk begged Scotty to give him more speed. When asked for the impossible, the engineer always replied, "She's giving us all she's got, Captain." Well, that was where Cho was now. The old DC-2 was giving her all she had.

Glancing down at the gauge at the top right, she noted 11,000. She needed another thousand feet. Could the old gal climb that high? Was that asking too much? The needle moved up as she watched.

Though it was still a few miles ahead, the moonlit mountain seemed to be filling the space of the windshield.

"Come on, sweetheart," she whispered, gently patting the throttle. "You can do it. I don't want our first date to be our last. Dad needs to hear about me and you teaming up."

The plane must have liked sweet nothings whispered into its ear because it quickly climbed another five hundred feet, but then it seemed to give up. Its desire was strong, but it might well have reached the its limit.

"Get Mason," Cho barked. "Hurry."

Burke quickly got up and headed toward the back of the plane. A few seconds later, the other FBI agent was in the cockpit.

"Didn't I see an old piece of equipment lashed in the back of the cabin?"

"Yeah," Mason replied. "It's one of those pneumatic hand-operated forklifts for moving pallets. Probably used for arranging weapons and ammo. It must weigh a ton."

"Open the door and push it out," Cho said. "And be quick."

"But why—"

"Do it!" Cho screamed.

Oblivious to the frantic action behind her, Cho's eyes flashed between the gauges and the windshield.

The sounds of rushing air were quickly accompanied by a lowering of the temperature. The door was open. A few seconds later, metal wheels rolled across the cabin floor. Then nothing but the rush of air!

As if it had been kicked in the rear, the DC-2 jumped upward three hundred feet. The mountain was now almost below their altitude. But almost was not enough!

"How we doing?" Mason yelled from the back.

"Close the door!" Cho screamed. "It's causing drag!"

Burke jumped up to help Mason. Seconds later, the sound of rushing air was gone, replaced by the droning of the single motor.

Now, with a lighter load, Cho asked the DC-2 for a few more feet, and the old girl responded. The mountain slid beneath her and clear skies filled the windshield.

Just as she thought the mission had been accomplished, she felt a sharp bump. A strange scraping noise echoed through the cabin. A moment later, it was gone.

"What was that?" Burke asked as he returned to his seat.

"The mountain saying hello," she replied. "We just scraped the top of Yul's head. Guess we should have thrown out Barot too. Glad this thing is built like a truck."

Cho smiled, but the sense of relief did not last long. They were less than a half a mile beyond the mountain when the right motor coughed, sputtered, and went silent. She'd asked it to do too much. Now the only noise was the wind on the wings.

"You said these things could almost land themselves," Burke reminded the pilot.

"We're about to find out if I'm correct. The base is just ahead. I can see the runway lights. Hit the gear."

He did, but nothing happened. He looked at her for advice.

The bullets fired as they had taken off had likely found the hydraulics. The wheels could be cranked down, but she didn't have time to tell anyone how to do it. Like it or not, this was going to be a belly landing, and she didn't like it.

"Hang on!" Cho yelled.

As she fought the bird, trying to keep the plane level, she looked down at the base. There had to be a debate going on in the control tower. She could hear them now, "Friend or foe?" If they decided the latter, everyone on the antique plane would be dead before they found the ground.

She glanced back at the instruments. Did the radio work? Why hadn't she thought of that? Grabbing the mike, she flipped a switch and adjusted the frequency.

"This is Lisa Cho with the FBI. I've commandeered this aircraft in order to evacuate my team. Both engines are dead and I have no landing gear."

She flipped to receive and waited. At first there was nothing.

Then she heard static. Of course, the tubes had to warm up. She jumped back on the mike.

"This is Agent Lisa Cho with the Federal Bureau of Investigation. I've commandeered this aircraft in order to evacuate my team. Both engines are dead. I have no landing gear."

"Say again. Who are you?" the voice that came over the ancient speaker demanded.

"Lisa Cho, FBI."

"Need more," the voice shot back. "FBI doesn't operate out of here. You keep coming, we will shoot you down."

Casteel grabbed the mic. "This is Captain Louis Casteel, Army Special Forces. Blow off the protocol and let me get my butt on solid ground. I wasn't made for this air jockey stuff."

The radio was silent. They waited.

"Come on. Let us land. We're running out of air here."

More silence. Finally the voice said, "You've got clearance, but I need to talk to the pilot."

Casteel handed the mic back to Cho.

"Agent Cho here. I may need some help. I've got five passengers, including one high-level member of al-Qaeda. No one is hurt, but we might get thrown around on landing. Can't get the wheels down. No way to dump the fuel that's left, so have fire equipment ready. And say a few prayers."

A second later the fuzzy sound of the man's voice returned. "Will do. Come in on that dirt strip on the outside of the base. You have a better chance there than on concrete."

"Thanks."

"Cho, I can't wait to find out where you found that old bird."

"It's a long story," she shot back.

Cho checked the speed and altitude one more time. Now it would all be on instinct. She had to keep the nose up, hope the plane had enough speed not to drop like a rock, and pray she could put it on the ground so it didn't cartwheel across the landscape. As the plane continued its descent, she whispered, "I should have paid more attention to you, Dad."

In the silence of their glide, the ground rushed toward them. She could see several fire trucks heading toward the dirt strip. Other vehicles were right behind them, lights whirling, beacons everywhere. She prayed none of the emergency equipment had to be used.

Burke began calling off the altitude. She hadn't expected that, but it was strangely comforting.

"Three hundred."

He had a nice voice.

"Two hundred."

"One hundred. Almost down."

A second later the belly hit, hugging the ground as if it were a long-lost relative. The clamor of metal scraping ground was loud, but it also was the sweetest sound in the world. Surprisingly, the old bird didn't wander left or right, it just kept going straight down the dirt strip, friction slowing it down much more quickly than Cho had expected. The DC-2 came to rest halfway down the runway. The dust created by the belly landing was swirling around the plane as trucks surrounded it. As she had expected, the soldiers approached the old crate with lights blazing and weapons ready.

Getting out of her seat, Cho moved back to the cabin. Mason was unlatching the door.

"You go first, Captain," she said to Casteel with a weary tone. "When they drop their guns, we will follow."

As soon as the door slid open, the Ranger leaped down to the ground. Soon the weapons were lowered and Cho slid out the door. She walked to the plane's nose, studied the badly scarred aircraft, then gently patted the brown metal skin. Leaning close, she whispered, "Good girl. You were a great first date." Then she kissed the DC-2, her lips lingering just long enough to assure the old bird there would be more outings in the future.

YOUTUBE

What do you mean?" Krueger shouted. Pounding his fist on the table he screamed, "You're missing it! You have to be. It has to be there!"

Spread in front of the billionaire were the carefully deconstructed pieces of the old chest. For the last four days, a team made up of some of the top historians in the world had gone over the pieces of the chest again and again and found nothing.

"It was just a wooden trunk," Franz Schulter explained. "Except for the writing on the lid that declared it to be Baltore's, there is nothing else. I can give you a complete breakdown of the contents. They are interesting, of great value, and tied to the era you thought they would be from."

"I'm the richest man on the planet!" Krueger barked. "What do I care about a few thousand dollars' worth of stuff? No hidden compartments?"

"None."

So Burke wasn't running a bluff, Krueger thought. Burke knew the trunk wasn't the key. Who'd have thought the history professor could beat him in a game of poker.

As he glanced back at the tall, thin man he'd assigned to head up the team, Krueger experienced a sudden sinking sensation in his gut. He'd gotten rid of Fogleman too soon. Maybe she could have told him something. He had been so sure the quest was over and he had all he needed. He had been so sure he didn't need her anymore.

"Get out!" he yelled at Schulter. The German historian hurried out. Krueger poured a glass of scotch and collapsed in a chair. Loathing the silence, he grabbed the remote and flipped on the TV. Even though he was in Rome, it was tuned to an English-language cable news network. The channel was covering something that had transpired in the Middle East.

In this video, taken with a Flip video camera by a soldier stationed in a remote area of Afghanistan, you will see something remarkable. An eighty-year-old plane, its motors dead, making a belly landing. Where did the DC-2 come from and why did it suddenly appear in a war zone? No one is talking. But this video, placed on YouTube, seems to show one of al-Qaeda's top leaders being led away in handcuffs. The man in the video appears to be Abd al-Rahim Barot. Barot is supposedly one of those closest to Osama bin Ladin.

This video was taken down from the web almost as quickly as it was placed there. And government officials will not comment on anything concerning this incident. In fact the remote base has been locked down.

It wasn't Barot that caught the billionaire's eye. There was something else on the report that made this homemade digital recording much more interesting. Rewinding it to the beginning of the report, Krueger again watched until he came to the point that showed the plane's passengers jumping to the ground. Hitting pause, he studied the moment frozen in time.

Burke! Cho! They're alive! How? Those two have more lives than a cat! How many more times would his men screw up before these two were dead? Who had saved them this time?

Krueger tossed down a lot more of his drink. A bad day had just gotten worse. He hurled the glass into the fireplace, and the shards came flying back into the room. Krueger cussed, first in German and then in English. Then he smiled.

This was not bad luck at all. Actually, fortune had been kind. Though he didn't know where to look for the book, Burke did. If that video was taken four days ago, then all he needed to do was get his organization moving to find out where Burke was now. Knowing that, he could be back in the hunt. No, this wasn't bad news; it was great news! Burke being alive was the greatest gift the world could give him.

Grabbing his cell, he made a call. His main orders were simple: find Burke, stay with him. He knew it might take some time to carry them out. He sat there, phone in hand.

Then Krueger made one more call.

LAST WORDS

Is this the fourth?"

Burke and Cho looked at each other and then back to Milton West III. West was the national authority on Thomas Jefferson. He'd written scores of books on the man's life. If anyone would know the last utterances of this founding father, it would be this scholar. But those four words, "Is this the fourth?" were not what they wanted to hear.

"Nothing else?" Burke asked.

"Those words, in three slightly different forms," West explained, "were recorded by Robley Dunglison, the doctor attending Jefferson during his final days; Thomas Jefferson Randolph, the president's grandson; and Nicholas Trist. The latter was married to Jefferson's granddaughter Virginia. Each was very specific about Jefferson's remarks on the evening of July 3, 1826. He wanted to know if it was the fourth."

"But he died on the fourth," Burke argued. "That is one of the great ironies of history. That was hours later. Surely he said something else."

The short gray-headed scholar adjusted his tie, as if he needed time to think. "He did speak on the fourth, but he said nothing historic. He asked to have his servants come to his bedside. Those words are not recorded. I assumed he was thanking them for their service."

A disappointed Burke walked over to the window. The house West called home in Bethesda, Maryland, had to be more than a century old. It was colonial in style, which matched the man's chosen career path. But as beautiful as it was, it was not the land of Oz, and West was not the wonderful wizard who had all the answers. The trip appeared to be a royal waste of time.

Jefferson, if he really was a Lord Baltore and had the scroll for safekeeping, must have passed it on to someone else. Who was that next keeper of the book, and how would they find him? Burke had a theory, but that was all it was. Would it simply lead him down another blind trail? Could West give him the lead he needed?

Turning to once more face his host, Burke posed a question he knew West could easily answer. "Did Breckinridge visit during those final days?"

"John Breckinridge?" West was incredulous. "Surely, as a professor of history, you know he died two decades before Jefferson."

"Not John," Burke replied. "Was there any member of the Breckinridge family who visited Jefferson in those final days?"

"No," West replied confidently. "Over the years Jefferson wrote a few letters to John's son Robert. That was natural as John had named the boy after the president. His full name was Robert Jefferson Breckinridge. But in 1826, Robert was twenty-six years old. He was a politician in Kentucky. So he had no real direct contact with the president."

"How about the will?" Burke asked. "Did Jefferson leave anything to Robert?"

"I don't understand the importance of this," West replied. "I was led to believe you needed information on Thomas Jefferson."

Cho jumped in. "Is there any way to check if a Breckinridge was listed in the will?"

"There's a copy of the will in the research center at Monticello. I'm sure you could pull some strings and see the real thing. You could also probably find it online. Yet I've read it several times and don't remember anything about a Breckinridge. I doubt I'd have missed that either."

Burke nodded. "Thank you, Mr. West. We appreciate your time and your insight."

Their host nodded, seemingly more than a bit relieved his guests were leaving. As the trio stepped off the small brick porch and into the crisp afternoon air, Cho popped the question Burke knew was coming.

"Dead end?"

"Maybe not," the professor answered. "Robert was a wild man, a pioneer version of a party animal until just a few years after Jefferson's death. Then he suddenly became a very devout Christian. He even went so far as to become a Presbyterian minister. History states that this dramatic change of life was due to the death of a child. Maybe his son's death did have that kind of effect on him. But what if it was something else? Sometimes men change when they are given dramatic responsibilities."

"The scroll?" Cho asked.

"If he was made Lord Baltore, if he was given the *Book of Joseph*, it might have sobered him up and helped him chart a new course. After all, if Jefferson put that much faith in him, it could well be a life-changing moment."

"Did the older Breckinridge, the one who was Jefferson's friend, have any other children?" Mason asked.

"Another son, also a preacher, named John. But it was Robert who became the president of Jefferson College. He was also a backer of Lincoln and, even though a slave owner, came around to feeling a need to free the slaves. He had the kind of mind Jefferson would have been drawn to."

Cho shook her head. "Jefferson knew hundreds of people in positions of power. Any of those people could have gotten the scroll. And that's assuming Jefferson had it."

They made their way back to the car. With Mason at the wheel and Cho taking the shotgun position, Burke slid into the back seat.

"My gut tells me it's Robert," he said as he snapped his seat belt. "Think about this. When Jefferson died, Robert was anything but a devout Christian. Jefferson wasn't either. In fact, though he often worked with Christian groups, especially the Baptists who were strong believers in separation of church and state, as he was, most of his writings show great contempt for denominations and especially for men of the cloth. He goes so far as to blame the Christian faith for most of the world's great wars."

"So," Cho said, "he chooses Robert because of his lack of faith. Yet when the man became a preacher, that kind of blew up in his face."

Burke smiled. "Not even Jefferson could predict the future of the country or the paths taken by individual men."

"There's something that makes no sense to me," Mason said.

"What's that?" Burke asked.

"If Jefferson was so against the church and so distrusted the Christian denominations of his time, then why not just release the *Book of Joseph*? Wouldn't those words essentially end the church's power in the country?"

"That is a question that has been troubling me as well," Burke admitted.

"Do you have a theory?" Cho asked.

Leaning back in the seat, Burke gazed out at the fall colors. Why indeed? Logic told him that Jefferson would have made the document public. After all, the president had even rewritten the Bible and published papers, attempting to disprove the divinity of Christ. Why not use the book against the very body he distrusted most—the Church of England?

"Why did he hate the organized church?" Mason asked.

Burke turned to once again face those in the front seat. "Well, the Revolution was waged against King George. George was the head of the Church of England. Thus, in Jefferson's mind and for many others, that war for independence was not just a battle to separate from the crown but from the church that the king led. Remember, the colonists were paying taxes not just to support King George but also the Anglican Church. Jefferson saw the church as a tyrannical force."

"Yet he believed in God?" Cho asked.

"Yes," Burke replied. "He was a Deist. He saw God or, as he often called him, Providence, as having made the world but then walking away from it. Jefferson probably didn't see Christ as being the Son of God because Jefferson wouldn't have believed God would have cared enough to send someone to check up on us, much less save our souls."

"Then," Mason cut in, "I don't understand why he didn't release the document."

"Because," Burke continued, "and this is only a guess, it would be against his nature. If he swore to Breckinridge to keep the code of the society that was protecting the book, the Custodis Joseph Lacuna, if he was his generation's Lord Baltore, he would not have gone back on his word. For all his faults, and I feel he had fewer than most men, he was a person of great integrity."

"Could there be any other reason?" Cho asked.

"Yes," Burke replied, "several. One was his close alliance with the Baptists. He might not have believed as they did, but he found their independent attitudes appealing. He likely saw them as an important element in making sure the Anglican Church never gained power in this country. He likely realized that what was in the book might hurt the Baptists as much as it would damage the Church of England. So why cut off your nose to spite your face?"

Burke shrugged before adding, "But until we actually see what is in the book, if we ever do, it is all just a theory. After all, like Columbo, we are thinking the worst-case scenario."

"Where to?" Mason asked. "Are we going to Monticello? I've actually never been there and would love to tour Jefferson's home. With my badge, we can pretty much get the full Cook's tour."

Burke said, "Been there, done that, have the T-shirt."

"So, if not there, where?" the agent shot back.

"To Danville, Kentucky."

"Why?" Cho asked. "Is it close to Louisville? Are we making a run for the roses?"

"In a way," he admitted. "I'm playing a hunch and putting my money on a long shot. We're going to Centre College. We might just find a few answers in their archives."

THE DIARY

The plane ride was uneventful and uncomfortable. The Delta flight ran into turbulence, and the jet rocked almost all the way from DC to Lexington. Still, riding coach in a storm sure beat crossing the mountains of Afghanistan in the DC-2.

A rental car was ready for the trio to take to Centre College, where an enthusiastic history major was assigned to show them around the campus of the almost 200-year-old school. From the moment the Ohio native opened her mouth, Burke knew Hillary DuBose had given the speech many times. Though she tried to sound excited, her tone belied the truth. She was bored, simply following a script.

"From US vice presidents and Supreme Court justices, to the founder of the Hard Rock Cafe and the inventor of plastic Baggies, our alumni have a tradition of extraordinary success. It all begins with our first-rate academics. We are rated as one of the top fifty schools of higher education in the country. Did you know that Centre hosted the 2000 vice presidential debates? This in spite of the fact that fewer than 1,500 students are enrolled at the school at any given time!"

"Thank you, Miss DuBose," Burke said when the fast-talking nineteen-year-old finally paused to take a breath. "We're not here for a tour."

"You're not?" Her voice indicated a touch of relief.

"We are actually here," Burke explained, "to do a bit of research in the archive section of your library. The dean of the history department cleared our getting into the reserved room. He said you are familiar with it."

Her blue eyes sparkly, she nodded. "My first job as a student was there. I know it like the back of my hand. Well, actually better than that."

Mason grinned, Cho shook her head, and Burke smiled. If nothing else, Hillary was cute! And she appeared to have the connections they needed.

"Good," Burke replied while stifling a laugh. "Do you happen to know if there are any papers from a former president of the school? His name was Robert Breckinridge."

"Sure," she replied. "Nobody ever looks at them though. I pulled the stuff out and inventoried it last year. I'd bet that was the last time those files have seen daylight."

"Can you take us to the papers?"

"Of course."

A short walk across campus led to them to Grace Doherty Library. Cho was shocked when Burke didn't inquire as to who Grace was and how the woman had earned the right to have a building named after her. She vowed later to compliment the man on keeping his curiosity in check.

Breckinridge's papers where in a small locked research area toward the back of the second floor. Once Miss DuBose retrieved the two file-sized boxes for the guests and showed them to a table, she left and the team went to work.

It took Burke only a few minutes to find the will. He was impressed with the man's detailed explanation of who got what. Unfortunately there was no mention of an ancient book or scroll or a trunk.

Mason busied himself skimming through pages and pages of handwritten letters. After about an hour he said, "Nothing here."

Cho contented herself with reading diaries. Ninety minutes after they had entered the room, she finally came up with something.

"This is interesting. The day Jefferson died, Breckinridge was in Kentucky celebrating the holiday with some locals. On July 4, 1826, our hero drank himself into a stupor. He noted the local brewer outdid himself."

"I'm not getting much here either," Burke admitted.

Cho scanned a few more pages until she came to a passage written on November 23, 1826, concerning the fate of a man named Jonah.

"Listen to this," she said as she began reading from the man's journal:

> I received a letter today from a Constable in Tennessee. He is holding a Negro in a jail outside of Nashville. He claims the man is my property. While I do own five slaves, I have never heard of this Jonah. The letter claims he is a big buck with broad shoulders. He also supposedly knows how to read and write. I have penned a reply sending money to the Constable to pay to keep the man in jail. I assured him I will travel to Nashville sometime next year and pick up my property.

"Sad commentary on our history," Burke noted. "Let me know if you find anything that actually has something to do with Jefferson or the book."

Almost an hour later, Cho snapped her fingers. "Got something. This time it might just tie in. It's a second reference to the slave. Let me read this entry.

> April 5, 1827
> Just visited the jail where they have been keeping the slave they claim is mine. The Constable has obviously been feeding him very little. He is weak and sick. He has also been beaten. After I told the Negro who I was, Jonah retrieved some papers from the back of the cell. It appeared I did own this man. I had owned him since July 4th of the preceding year. I had not bought him but rather he'd been given to me.
> As I glanced through the papers, Jonah explained that he was supposed to present me with a small trunk. When I received that trunk I was to provide him with papers of freedom. What was in the trunk Thomas left me?

Cho tapped on the table as she pointed to the entry. "What do you think?"

Burke quickly reviewed the passage and turned to the next page. "We've got something!" He then read the following day's entry out loud.

April 6, 1827

I was charged $20 to obtain Jonah. Only after we were a safe distance from the jail did I ask him about the trunk. He told me he'd hid it in a cave in the woods along the Cumberland River. I followed him to the spot where he produced the trunk. Upon opening it, the only thing I found was a metal tube. I lifted the top off the object and pulled out a scroll of some sort. The writing was in a language I had never seen. I put the scroll back in the tube and tossed it in the trunk. I demanded to know what had happened to the rest of the contents, but Jonah assured me there had never been anything else in the trunk. I sensed he was being truthful. Needless to say I was very disappointed. Fortunately I found some local ale that eased my pain.

"He had the *Book of Joseph* in his hands," Mason whispered.
"Yeah," Cho replied, "but he didn't know it."
Leaning over the journal, Cho read the next passage.

April 7, 1827

I went to the courthouse with Jonah and, with the papers he had given me was able to prove my ownership of the man. I then paid the costs and signed documents freeing the slave. I suggested he go to Ohio and then even further north. As he had no money or clothing, I gave him a gold piece and bought him new clothes. So that he would have a way to carry them, I also gave him the black trunk. I certainly had no use for it. That was the last I ever saw of the slave I owned but never used.

"Was it like the trunk Brother Abel gave us?" Mason asked.
"Could be," Burke replied. "But there were only two shelves in the monastery for trunks. We took one apart to find the secret compartment. Krueger got the other. So, how does this one tie in?"
As Burke and Mason puzzled over the diary's entry, Cho began to leaf through a second diary. This had been written during the Civil War. As soon as she snapped her fingers, both men were at her side.

June 19, 1863

I was invited to the White House today. This marked the third time I have visited with the president. He asked me the strangest question. He wanted to know what happened to Jefferson's trunk. At first I remembered nothing, but then I thought back to the slave and the meeting in Nashville. So I told the president my story. For reasons I did not understand, a sad look came over his face. It was as if the trunk actually had some value to him. He didn't offer to explain and I didn't ask.

Since that meeting all I have thought about is that trunk and that scroll. Was it connected to the founding of the United States? Was that why Jonah had been sent to give it to me? Surely not, it was not written in English.

"Look at these drawings," Cho said as she pointed to the page.

They all studied a series of three ink drawings. The first two showed the trunk. The second the metal tube.

"How do you find a former slave?" Mason asked. "One who only has a first name and who vanished to parts unknown almost two centuries ago?"

"You probably don't," Burke admitted. "But that is not an option. Let's hope the city of Nashville has a file with documents covering the granting of freedom to ex-slaves."

"But that doesn't tell us where he went," Mason argued.

"Freed slaves were given last names," Burke explained. "If we have a last name, we might be able to track his movements and find out if he had heirs."

TRACKING

Well?"

Bruno Krueger's one word was not a question, it was a demand, and Ernest Duncan knew it. If he couldn't deliver, then he'd be out on the streets or worse. Just thinking of the latter made him sick to his stomach.

Duncan was thirty-five and had a background that included a six-year stint with the CIA. He was a self-described tech-nerd and proud of it. But at six-foot-four and boasting a chiseled 224 pounds, he didn't fit that image. He looked more like a middle linebacker. Yet he'd never even been to a football game.

Duncan's parents were researchers for Dow Chemical, so he came by his intellect and curiosity naturally. It was in his genes. He figured he would spend his life working cases for the CIA, and he would have, if not for a chance meeting with Krueger. The billionaire offered complete freedom to develop new software meant for industrial use as well as a chance to own a piece of each platform he created. That was a deal the CIA couldn't match. The only catch was Duncan would be on call for special jobs at Krueger International. So without warning, he was sometimes called to a secret meeting with the company's head man. That order had come last week, and since that time his life had been devoted to finding the whereabouts of Jefferson Burke. Now it was time to give his report. As he stood in front of the boss's huge desk, he hoped the information he had was enough.

Feeling like a child in trouble standing before the school principal, he began, "Mr. Krueger, once Burke was debriefed and returned from Afghanistan, he camped out at a hotel in DC. Our mole at the FBI informed us that after two days of rest, he went to see a writer named Milton West III in Maryland. That meeting lasted less than an hour. Burke then traveled to Kentucky, where he spent time in the archives at Centre College."

"Is he alone?"

Duncan didn't have to check his notes. "No, FBI agents Mason and Cho are with him."

Staring directly at Duncan, his expression stern and unforgiving, the billionaire noted, "Probably added a second agent for added protection."

"Anything else?"

Krueger nodded. "You've been briefed on what I'm looking for."

"Yes, sir."

"You've gone over Fogleman's notes?"

"Yes, sir."

"Then you know why we have to keep a tail on Burke at all times."

"Yes, sir."

"Every detail is important," Krueger added. "Nothing can be overlooked. Now why did he go to see Mr. West in Maryland and then travel to this college ... what did you say the name of it was?"

"Centre College," Duncan replied. "A top-notch school."

"So, what's the story?"

"As far as the visit to Milton West III," Duncan explained, "we don't know what Burke wanted. We could likely push Mr. West some and get that information, but I feel it would be taking too big a risk with Cho and Burke knowing you are an active player in this."

"I'll accept that judgment," Krueger said. "But do you have any idea as to what West would have that Burke might want?"

"Not really," Duncan explained, "but I can tell you that West is the country's most noted expert on the founding fathers. He has penned a number of detailed books on Jefferson, Adams, and Franklin."

"Doesn't fit," the billionaire growled. "I hope you have more on the Centre visit."

"Yes," Duncan said. "A Centre College student confirmed Burke studied the papers of a pastor named Robert Breckinridge. We also have access to those papers. I have a team scanning them. I'll use my latest software to find any connections to our objective. I'm confident we'll soon know more than Burke's team."

Duncan watched Krueger's reaction. The man was cold and cruel and had a sadistic streak a mile wild, but no one could say that he wasn't sharp. In fact, Duncan believed his boss to be the intellectual equal of any man he'd ever met.

"I don't see how Breckinridge is a player," Krueger mused. "But Burke has a puzzle piece I don't have. So I've got to assume he's on to something. Any idea where he's going next?"

"Burke's in a rental driving south on I-65 with his two traveling partners."

"Wonder where he will stop."

Duncan knew the question was simply Krueger thinking out loud, but his silence made the computer tech even more uncomfortable than he'd been, so he decided to volunteer a few words. And those words were meant to appear valuable as well.

"Wherever it is, I'll know within minutes of his arrival. We have a GPS tracking device on the car. We installed it during the group's stop at Centre College."

"Keep me informed," Krueger replied. "And get back to me the minute your team finds anything in this Breckinridge material."

"Yes, sir."

Duncan had another question he needed to ask, but he wondered if he should. He was about to leave when his boss looked at him and opened a door. "Is there anything you need?"

"About Dr. Fogleman," Duncan said in almost a whisper. "Do you know when she will be coming back?"

"Why's that?"

"I enjoy her company," Duncan replied. "We play chess. She's the one person who offers me a real challenge."

"I see." Krueger smiled. "You will need to find a new partner."

"She took another job?"

"No," Krueger explained. "But I was forced to terminate her. She's overseas at the moment."

"I understand. Thank you, sir."

"Mr. Duncan," Krueger said while raising his eyebrows and crossing his arms. "Don't let me down. I'd hate to have to terminate you."

"I won't."

Duncan quickly exited the Chicago penthouse and took the elevator six floors down to his lab. Sitting in front of a large bank of computer monitors, he considered his boss's last words.

Clicking on his mail program, he composed a short email.

Mitzi,

Missing you. Hope you come back to Chicago soon. So sorry you were fired.

Ernie

FREEDMAN

The trek to Nashville through an incredible thunderstorm was a walk in the park compared to trying to find papers for a slave freed in 1827. The few documents that existed had once been housed in the courthouse before being given to the city library. The library stored them in the basement for five decades before presenting the still-boxed documents to the Nashville Museum of History. The museum director, a very sweet retired schoolteacher named Beatrice Lane, explained they had had the collection until about four months ago, when it was loaned to a Milton J. Freedman. A genealogy expert, he was cataloging the facts and putting the information online for African American genealogy. Freedman, a retired lawyer, worked from his home in Ashland City.

Lane also added one other disturbing bit of news. Her voice echoed her sadness when she said, "Many of those documents were damaged during the flood of 2010. It was sad. We lost so much during that time. Of course, so did lots of other organizations and individuals. I'm sure you saw on the news what happened to the Grand Ole Opry."

As they left the museum, Cho placed the call asking if the team could visit with Freedman and study records from the 1820s. He was so excited by the prospects of the FBI and a scholar from the University of Illinois being interested in records of freed slaves, he was standing outside the door when they arrived.

"I'm happy to be of service to you," he announced when they got out of the car. "So few people ask to see the history of slavery. You must be Agent Cho."

"Please call me Lisa. And this is Dr. Jeff Burke and Clark Mason."

"Nice meeting each of you," Freedman replied while waving toward the front door. "Please come into my home. I have things set up on the dining room table."

Freedman was a small, lean man. Burke couldn't ascertain his age, but he had grown through his hair. He was bald, clean-shaven, and wore glasses as thick as the bottom of an old Coke bottle. But he moved very, very well.

His home was a typical ranch-style brick structure containing about 2,000 square feet. The interior was understated, painted in earth tones, and the walls and shelves were lined with what Burke guessed were family photographs. Many went back more than a hundred years.

After leading them through an entry and the living room area, Freedman pointed to an open dining area. There, on an antique table held up by what some called a cannonball pedestal, was a small cardboard container. As the guests chose their chairs, Freedman picked up the box, which was six by eight by twelve inches in size.

"This is what I have," he said. "I had no problem finding the years you asked for because I was about to enter the information from the 1820s onto my site."

"There are no more?" Burke asked.

"Not from that decade," Freedman replied. "You see, there simply weren't that many slaves given papers of freedom at that time. And remember, the cotton industry didn't really explode in the South until the 1830s and 1840s, so the huge growth in the black population came during those decades. That means the African American population in general was not large either."

Those facts might have been new to Cho and Mason, but Burke was aware of them. In fact, this was within his sphere of expertise. He didn't need to be told that only 20 percent of the African American population during that time was made up of free men and women. Not every black person was a slave then, but none should have been. The mere fact that they were looking through records that contained documents proving that people had been owned as property pointed out that the history of the United States was not as neat, clean, and honorable as many believe.

Freedman removed the top from the box as if he were handling a delicate piece of antique lace. He smiled as he peered into the box and asked, "Do you know who the owner of the slave was and the year he was supposedly freed?"

Burke set his laptop on the table, turned it on, and went to his notes. He scrolled through the information gathered at Centre College. Looking up from the screen he said, "The date we found is April 7, 1827. The owner was a Robert Breckinridge."

Freedman's small, thin fingers began to search through the ancient papers. His touch was gentle as he slowly went through the box from front to back. After studying the final paper, he shook his head. "I probably just missed it," he explained. "I really haven't fully organized this material yet."

He looked again. This time he began at the back and moved forward. His pace was slower. It took him ten minutes to reach the first paper in the box. Glancing up, he shrugged. "I am sorry. There was no slave freed whose owner's name was Breckinridge. Are you sure about the name?"

"Yes," Cho explained, a sense of urgency in her tone, "the information was carefully recorded in Robert Breckinridge's diary. The slave's name was Jonah."

As he stretched his arms and leaned back his chair, Freedman nodded. "Very common name for a male at that time. My studies indicate that there were two routes for naming slaves. One was much like picking a name for a pet. Thus there were a lot of men named Mush, Rex, Spot, and the like. The other method was to choose a name from the Bible. Jonah, Josh, Moses are typical examples. So there were likely thousands of slaves with that name."

"What about the date?" Burke asked. "Is there a Jonah with that date?"

"I have discovered that when papers were filed and when they were dated was often different. Thus, while the slave might have gotten his papers proving him to be free one day, a clerk might not have filed those papers for days, weeks, a month, or ever. A freed slave was not as important in Southern society as one who was still a piece of property."

Burke glanced over to Cho. Her expression said it all—another dead end.

"Mr. Freedman," Cho asked, "what names do you have after that date in 1827?"

Freedman again leafed through the box. "Okay, on April 24 we have a Rachel. Two days later we have Jacob. Jig was the next one. I have a Jonus, Minnie, Patch, Andrew, and Buck next." He looked to his guests and added, "I am sorry, but there is no Jonah."

"You said Jonus?" Cho asked.

"Yes. Jonus. On May 2, a forty-two-year-old slave named Jonus was given his papers as a free man as witnessed by Judge John H. Carpenter."

With an urgent tone, Burke leaped back into the conversation. "Do you have any more information? Such as who owned this man?"

As Freedman's eyes returned to the box, Burke considered his own last words. Here they were, sitting around a table, talking about owning another human as if it were a normal fact of life.

"Dr. Burke," Freedman said, "I can sense your discomfort with the idea of slavery. I'm sure, when confronted with this type of thing, the real weight of it hits you. You were not there. You did not participate."

"I know that," Burke said, "but I just can't fathom it being an accepted part of our culture—even in 1827."

"Right now, Dr. Burke," Freedman continued, "there are tens of millions of slaves on this planet. The shirt you are wearing might have been made by one of them. It is not just in places like the Far East or Africa. Now, what was your question again?"

"Who owned Jonus?" Burke replied.

The small man glanced back at the document and smiled. "The owner was from Virginia, and his name was Thomas Jefferson. I wonder if that is the same Thomas Jefferson who wrote the Declaration of Independence."

Burke's eyes went to Cho's and then Mason's.

"I think it is," Burke assured his host. "Mr. Freedman, could a slave be left to another person in a will?"

"Yes, it happened."

"And," Burke asked, "was there an exchange of ownership noted on papers at that time?"

"Usually," Freedman said. "But, just like some people purchase a used car and never change the title, it happened that way with humans too. If the new owner didn't want the slave, then he might free him rather than accepting ownership. Most places allowed that to happen, though, as a lawyer, I question the legality of this type of transaction."

Burke smiled. This had to be their man. The clerk just wrote the name down wrong. He heard Jonus rather than Jonah. But there was another question he had to ask. One that might be the key to continuing the search for the *Book of Joseph*.

"Did they give the freed slave a last name?"

"Actually, in most cases, the slave would have chosen that name. Forms for this purpose varied from county to county and state to state. Some listed that name at the top, others put it in the body of the filing, and others toward the end. It should be listed here somewhere. This text is very faded. This was one of the boxes damaged in the flood of 2010. We're lucky it survived. If it had been on the first or second shelf rather than the third, we wouldn't be looking through it now."

Freedman adjusted his glasses, put the paper on the table, and, using his right index finger as a guide, carefully scanned the document.

"Ah, here it is."

The small man had the group in the palm of his hand as they waited for him to provide the information they needed. Yet, it wasn't forthcoming. Freedman took off his glasses, set them on the table beside the paper, and rubbed his eyes. They were moist. A suddenly forlorn expression accompanied a few tears. The only sound was the ticking of an antique wall clock.

"Are you all right?" Cho whispered.

The small man nodded. He cleared his throat and put his glasses back on. Then he looked at his guests.

"I have been looking for this man for decades," he explained. "You see, Jonus chose 'Freedman' as his last name."

"Did you know—" Cho's question was cut off by the wave of their host's hand.

"No," he replied. "I didn't know there was anyone by that name in this box. But it makes sense now. My grandmother told me that my great-great-great-great-grandfather had once been employed in the White House. There were no records of his having worked there, so I assumed it was just a legend. It was that legend that put me in search of my roots. But until this moment, I had never been able to take it back any further than 1882. Through your visit, you have introduced me to my past. I can't begin to tell you how much this means."

The gravity of the statement plunged the room into silence. No one looked at each other or said a word. Burke finally broke the silence.

"Mr. Freedman, is there perhaps an old text or a scroll that is a part of your family legacy?"

"No," the man replied, "nothing like that. Until my generation, we didn't own enough to hand anything down except for a few photographs and marriage certificates. The family Bible wasn't bought until 1922."

"Was there possibly a small black trunk?" a hopeful Cho asked. "It would be about half the size of the trunks you normally see, and the top is squared off, not rounded."

"Or maybe a metal tube," Burke cut in, "that could hold a rolled-up document?"

Freedman shook his head. "Sorry, no metal tube. I'd have remembered that. On the trunk, I can't recall ever seeing anything like that."

"Too much to hope for," Burke replied. Looking over to Cho he added, "We have a name and a time frame. And, since Mr. Freedman is with us in this room, we know that Jonah or Jonus lived long enough to produce a family."

"I don't suppose you could tell me what this is all about," Freedman asked. For the first time he seemed deeply curious about the group's motives.

"No," Cho replied. "Not at this time we can't. But you said you traced the family tree back to the 1880s. That might help us get closer to Jonus."

"That information is in my desk in the den," Freedman replied. "I'll make you a copy. Would you like something to drink while you wait?"

Burke and Mason shook their heads. Cho was the only one who verbally begged off. "No thanks."

When Freedman left the room, Cho walked back to the entry. Burke watched her through an archway as she examined Freedman's framed family photographs. At first she appeared to be like a child at an art museum, showing only a vague degree of interest. Then something seemed to catch her attention. It was a small picture in the middle of an arrangement of five larger ones. She carefully pulled it from a bookshelf and returned to the dining room.

"Look at this!"

Burke took the postcard-size framed tintype. It was a picture of a young couple and their three small children. Behind them, a quilt had been strung as a backdrop. The man and woman were seated in two ladder-back chairs. A boy, perhaps five, stood beside his father, while the woman held a small baby in her arms. The other child, a girl, perhaps three, was seated on a black box.

Cho pointed to the picture. "Doesn't that look like the trunk Brother Abel gave us and the one Columbo gave you?" Just as she finished, their host returned.

"Could I ask about this family?" Burke inquired.

Freedman picked up the photo and shook his head. "That poor woman was cursed. In this shot, it looks like she has the world by a string. And, according to the standards of the time, I guess she did."

Their host set the framed image back on the table. He smiled, tapping the glass that protected the tintype. "Her name was Sarah — Sarah Meadows. That picture had to be taken around 1895. Her maiden name was Freedman. She was the sister to my grandfather. She represents the generation that signaled the end of my own quest to find my roots. That is until today when you gave me another name that took me back to 1827. And, with Jonus being owned by Thomas Jefferson, more doors will likely open up for me soon."

"You said she was cursed," Burke cut in. "How?"

"Her husband, Josh, was well educated. He was probably smarter and better read than any man in the region of eastern Tennessee — white or black. Yet he was frustrated. He was relegated to jobs requiring hard labor. He couldn't use his brain to make a living. But that didn't keep him from trying. In fact, it was his desire for improvement that led to his being murdered. One night, as he walked home from a job sawing wood, he bumped into a young white woman. Newspaper accounts of the time stated that he raped her. I doubt it. The end result was that he was lynched by a group of Klansmen."

"If he didn't assault the woman," Cho inquired, "why hang him?"

"Because he had been organizing the blacks in the area and was petitioning for better schools. He also made speeches in churches calling for equality. He was demanding things black men were not allowed to demand back then. In time, folks got scared he might stir up a riot or worse—a rebellion."

"So killing him was a way to silence a movement," Burke suggested. "It was also a warning to anyone who might try to pick up that mantle."

Freedman's response was short and direct. "Yes."

"What happened to his wife? To Sarah?" Cho asked.

"The Klan burned her barn. She was working in their garden at the time. I would hope that those who set the blaze didn't realize her children were playing inside that old structure. All three died in the fire. Sarah found their bodies."

Burke's eyes were drawn back to the photo. Prejudice and violence had robbed her of her entire family. How could anyone survive after enduring that kind of hate?

"What did she do?" Burke asked.

"Sarah's brother came down from Pennsylvania, packed up her belongings, and moved her to Philadelphia to live with him. She stayed there for a few years, then a pastor in the community, Charles Albert Tindley, found her a job as a maid and cook for one of the area's families. She worked for them for a decade or so before, the story goes, she took her life."

"So," Cho cut in, "she never did get over her loss?"

"No, I guess she didn't," their host replied.

"Mr. Freedman," Burke asked, "do you know the name of the family she worked for?"

"No," he replied. "No one talked about Sarah. What little I know, my grandmother told me as a child when I found this picture in an old album. I was told no one talked about Sarah because she was daft."

"Daft?" Cho asked.

"Crazy," Burke explained. "And who, subjected to what she'd been through, wouldn't be?"

"My grandmother explained she'd been dead for weeks before my great-great-grandfather was told she had shot herself."

"Who told your family?" Burke asked.

"Charles Tindley. He tried so hard to help Sarah. He sure could put the right words to music. He wrote powerful gospel songs such as 'Stand by Me' and 'Leave It There.' But he couldn't get through to her. She simply couldn't overcome the trials she'd endured in her life."

"Any idea what happened to her belongings?" Burke asked.

"She likely had very little," he replied. "I was told that everything she had was given to Tindley by my great-great-grandfather. You see people then were superstitious. They believed emotions and bad luck often were connected to objects. So naturally, my ancestors would not have wanted anything from her in their home."

"Well," Cho said as she looked to Burke, "any other questions?"

He shook his head.

The agent turned to their host. "Thank you so much. We will go now."

"Here is my family tree," Freedman said. "If you find out anything else about my family, especially on Jonah or Jonus, I would appreciate it very much if you would send that information to me."

"We will," Burke said.

Burke liked Freedman. He would have loved to have stayed longer and gotten to know the man better. But it was time to go to church, and for that visit, someone else needed to rejoin their team.

IN CHURCH

Burke smiled as he watched his friend and associate step out of a cab in front of the Tindley Temple United Methodist Church. "Thanks for meeting us in Philly, Alex."

"Wouldn't miss this," Briggs replied. "I have a teaching assistant filling in for me for the rest of the week. You know, Tindley was the greatest preacher of his time and perhaps one of the most forward-thinking men of his era."

"So we've heard," Burke said.

As his brown eyes scanned the huge brick and stone church on Philadelphia's South Broad Street, the older professor shook his head. "Imagine a church with 30,000 members in the 1920s. That's what Tindley had back then. Each time the doors were open, thousands came to hear him preach and listen to his new compositions. His gospel music is still sung today."

Burke, Cho, and Mason followed Briggs as he reverently walked up to the entrance. As if he were about to meet the president of the United States or the queen of England, he stopped and adjusted his tie and smoothed his suit before opening the door. From there he marched directly to the sanctuary and took a deep breath. In front of him, behind the altar, a massive pipe organ filled an entire wall. On all sides were balconies. Wood, stained glass, and a sense of majesty hovered around him like London fog.

"Think of it," Briggs said, his voice low, respectful. "Dr. Tindley standing in front of that organ, delivering a sermon to a packed house. And then consider this, both races were here. Imagine a man who could somehow reverse the rules and bring whites and blacks together in the early part of the last century. We are standing in the presence of something powerful and inspiring. In this place, a man born to a slave really began a movement that would lead to what Martin Luther King and others continued to build on in the 1950s and '60s."

Burke studied Briggs' worshipful expression before turning his eyes to take in the large room with its white pillars and red carpet and rich wood. It was impressive. And even though he was not a religious man, he could feel something very different here. Maybe the ghost of Albert Tindley still walked these floors and stood behind that pulpit. With those powerful images in mind, Burke noted the obvious: "Must have been quite a speaker."

Briggs turned and looked at his friend as if he were out of his mind. "Jeff, he was so much more than that. Yes, his sermons are still studied to this day, but that is just the beginning. He was a social reformer. He opened a soup kitchen right at the church. He started educational programs, banks. He convinced businesses to open up to black customers. He worked with white people at a time when races didn't mix. He might have been the most influential man in Philadelphia. Not black man — any man! When he wrote the song that we know as 'We Shall Overcome,' he believed it and lived it."

Briggs pointed to an old photo hanging on a wall. "Look at him. He was six-foot-four. He had shoulders as wide as an axe handle. His voice was deep, powerful!"

Briggs' eyes lingered on the photo, then shifted back to the three. "Do you know where it all started?"

As if they were students in one of the professor's lectures, Burke, Cho, and Mason shook their heads.

"He was a teenager, son of a slave. It was just after the Civil War. He found an auction sheet and wanted to know what it said. No one he knew could read. Think of that, no one around him could even read! That drove that young man. For the next year, he would walk eight miles every night after work just to go to school. From wanting to know what was on that scrap of paper to building what you see here and starting a movement that would touch tens of millions. This was a giant of a man!"

Burke had never heard Briggs speak with so much passion. It was now obvious why he jumped at the chance to meet them here. This trip was a pilgrimage.

Briggs was about to continue his discourse on the life of Tindley when Cho cleared her throat, reminding them of their purpose. "We have an appointment with Mrs. Jennings. She's the historian here. We're supposed to meet her in the church library. I think it's down this way."

The FBI agents left the sanctuary and began a trek down a hall. Briggs didn't follow. Instead he continued to stare at the church's very simple pulpit.

"Alex," Burke said softly as he placed his hand on the man's shoulder, "we need to get to this meeting. You can spend some time in here a bit later."

Briggs smiled and nodded. "Of course."

Gloria Jennings was a big woman with an even bigger smile. She greeted them as they walked in, her voice almost as loud as her bright blue dress. "Come in, children!"

"Ms. Jennings."

The woman shook her head and waved a finger at Cho. "It's Sister Glory. That's what everyone calls me. You call me that too!"

"Sister Glory," Cho began again, "I'm Lisa Marie Cho, from the FBI. This is my partner Clark Mason. And Dr. Jefferson Burke and Dr. Alexander Briggs are from the University of Illinois."

"So wonderful to be in such great company," Sister Glory said. "Dr. Briggs, I've read several of your books. Have used them in some of my studies. Lawdy, I love the way you write."

"Thank you," Briggs replied.

"Having this caliber of folks enter my little world is a rare thing indeedy. I can hardly wait to hear what you need from a humble soul like me. Now, you all have a seat around this old table, and we'll get to the heart of this matter."

The library was modest. Many of the books were obviously old. All around them were photographs of the men and women who had served the church. Burke imagined the walls must have been kind of a hall of fame. There were ten filing cabinets. That was pretty much it. Yet it somehow seemed complete. What was needed by the church members was here, and what was not needed was not. If only life were that simple.

Burke was staring at an image he assumed was Tindley when he felt Cho gently nudge him. "Sister Glory," Burke began, "we deeply appreciate your time and your meeting us here. I hope you can help us in our search for the story of a woman who went to church here a century ago."

"Goodness gracious, Dr. Burke," she replied, a concerned look in those large brown eyes, "I couldn't tell you the story of very many of the folks who go here now. Just too many of them. For me to go back to the time when my great-great-grandfather was a deacon would be nearly impossible. But maybe we have something in our church records that would help. You've got my curiosity ablaze, so tell me about her."

Burke smiled. "There's not much to tell. All we know is there was once a woman Reverend Tindley found work for named Sarah Freedman Meadows. According to information we have uncovered, she died in 1911."

The woman nodded, clasped her hands to her large bosom, and sighed, "Of all the women, you chose this poor soul. Yes, I know the story of Sarah. I know it well."

"What?" Cho's surprise was evident in her tone. "How?"

"I've read all of Reverend Tindley's sermons many times," she explained. "He pulled the inspiration for his messages from what he saw in his life." Sister Glory leaned back and looked toward the ceiling. "There were many messages he taught that moved me, but this one was the only one that haunted me. I felt so sorry for this woman who was such a victim of the racist world of her time."

"Do you have the sermon?" Briggs cut in.

"Of course," she replied, pulling herself up from the chair. She walked over to a series of wooden file cabinets, opened a door, searched for a few moments, then returned to the table with several pages. "This isn't the real thing. We have that securely stored, but this copy is easier to read than the original."

As Briggs scanned the text, Glory continued, "Do you know her story?"

"Yes," Burke assured her. "We know about the loss of her husband and children and her coming to stay with her brother. We know that Reverend Tindley found her work with a well-to-do family."

"The Cagles," Glory said. "Sarah became their housekeeper and cook. It's there in the sermon too. And she would come to this church every Sunday and Wednesday. According to the words in that message, she had turned her life around. Praise be, her spirit had been restored! She was singing with the choir and teaching Sunday school. Then she snapped."

Briggs looked up from the message he'd been scanning. "What happened?"

"Oh, Lord," Glory said, "if only we knew. According to that sermon, she just changed one day. After that she was always scared. It was like the devil himself was waiting for her just around the next corner. Reverend Tindley never could get her to talk about it. In April she died. The police said she shot herself."

A hush fell over the room. It was almost too horrifying to fathom — a woman whose life had been so hellish driven she simply gave up.

"It says in the text," Briggs noted, "that Dr. Tindley tried to get the police to investigate the death."

Burke noted Briggs' use of the title of doctor for the preacher. When he said it, there was a touch of awe in his tone.

Glory sighed. "Yes, but they didn't see the use in investigating. Her life didn't matter to them. She was just a black servant, and the pastor hadn't gained much influence in the city at that time. Most in the white community viewed him as an ex-slave who could read. Reverend Tindley was a novelty in 1911. So nothing came of it. He didn't give up easily. He kept a file on the case."

"He did?" Cho said. "Where is it?"

Glory got up from the chair and walked back over to another series of cabinets. She pulled a drawer out, found the file she needed, and brought it back to the table. "Here you go. I found this a few years ago, but didn't read it. I felt it would be far too sad. And I've seen enough misery in the world without inviting more into my heart."

Cho eagerly opened the file. Burke leaned closer to see what was in it. Inside were only a few newspaper clippings and some brief notes. The agent studied the reports. Then, looking up at the others, she said, "There was no gun."

"What?" Mason said.

"There was no gun found at the scene," Cho explained. "She was murdered! If she'd killed herself, there would've been a gun. This changes everything."

As the others watched, the lead agent scanned through Tindley's handwritten notes. "Her room had been ransacked. Someone was looking for something."

"The scroll?" Burke asked.

Cho, reading from the notes, said, "Tindley believed that whoever was responsible must have been interrupted. It seems Tindley himself arrived on the scene while Sarah was still breathing. He wrote that a man ran out just before he entered. He thought he heard another gunshot, but there was a band concert just beginning in the park, and the music drowned out any other noise. When he looked outside, he saw hundreds of people, and there was no way of telling if any of them had been in Sarah's room."

"Why didn't they pursue a murder investigation?" Burke asked. "This seems way too obvious to pass off as a suicide."

A controlled but excited Cho explained. Her words spewed from her mouth at lightning speed. "The notes indicate the police claimed Tindley had hidden the weapon and staged the scene to save the family the pain of a suicide. And there is more. Tindley writes that Sarah kept saying the name Dean over and over again. He searched for a man whose name was Dean, but never found anyone with that name connected to the woman."

"I wonder what happened to her belongings?" Briggs asked as he looked back to Glory.

"I only know of one thing that we have that belonged to her," Glory chimed in.

"Jeff," Cho said as she continued to study Tindley's notes, "listen to this. The few things Sarah had were placed in her small black trunk. When the Freedman family told the pastor they didn't want them, he sold the trunk and the items at a church sale to raise money for the building fund. He was shocked when a tall, thin, well-dressed blond-headed white man, driving a motorcar, came to the sale and bought all of Sarah's belongings as a lot. He paid a hundred dollars. It says here Tindley was overwhelmed as the items were worth only about ten dollars."

Cho pulled something else from the folder. "Now look at this. It's a photograph of what appears to be Tindley beside a big car. He's posing. The trunk is sitting in the passenger seat. I wonder why he had his picture taken beside the car?"

Burke offered his best guess. "Cars were still pretty rare. If you had a chance to pose beside one, especially one this fancy, you did. So that's not that unusual."

"Maybe," Cho replied, "but the fact that it's in this file must mean it was tied to the case."

"So," Briggs cut in, "you don't think it was Dr. Tindley and one of his cars."

Burke looked back to Cho. "Anything else in that file that's not related to Sarah's death?"

The agent shook her head.

Burke's next question was the one the agent was waiting for someone to ask, and she was more than ready to answer. "Is there a name listed as to who bought the stuff?"

"Cross," Cho exclaimed. "Joseph Cross. It's a shame he's not pictured here."

GLORY BE

Joseph Cross.

Who was he and why, a century ago, did he suddenly appear at a black church to pay far too much for the belongings of a troubled maid? It was a question that begged them to find the answer.

"Sister Glory."

"Yes, Dr. Burke."

"You said there was something here that belonged to Sarah?"

"Yes," the woman replied. "Dr. Tindley kept her ashes for years in this church."

"That makes sense," Briggs cut in. "Dr. Tindley called his sermon 'Ashes to Ashes.' I was trying to figure out why. And there's one part in his message where he says, 'I hold her in my hands.' He must have been holding up an urn with her ashes."

Glory smiled. "That's one of the reasons the sermon was so remembered. He vowed to find justice for Sarah. Thus, her ashes sat on his desk until his death in 1933. It seems he held up the ashes to every police officer who came to visit him. He'd point to those ashes and demand justice."

"What happened to them after he died?" Cho asked.

"They had a service," Glory explained, "and spread her ashes at Freedom Park."

"But you said they were here!" Burke argued.

"No," the woman replied, "I said we had something. What we have is the container that once held the ashes. I found it in a box some years back. The only reason I knew what it'd been used for was the name 'Sarah Meadows' was etched on the side. Would you like to see it?"

"Yes," Burke replied.

"It's down the hall buried in the back of a closet."

After the door had closed, Briggs sighed. "Ironic, we keep coming to churches to try to find a document that might well undermine the reason for worship. If we find this scroll, then this grand old building might well become just a historical reference point. It might serve no other purpose. We will have destroyed its spiritual message. Christ will be nothing more than a Jewish Confucius."

Cho waved her hand toward Burke. "I know why I want to see it—it's a part of an unsolved crime. But why do you want to look at the urn?"

"Just a hunch," he replied. "By the way, where do we go from here?"

"Well," Cho replied, "we need to find out more about the man who bought the trunk. If he paid that much money, then he likely had some idea as to what was in it."

"The secret society?" Briggs interjected.

"They'd likely kill to get it back in their possession," Cho noted. "So it is a possibility."

"Yes, especially if they were just killing a black servant," Briggs added. "The life of a Negro, especially a Negro woman, was not worth much back then."

Those words created an uneasy silence in the room. None of them really wanted to once more confront a past where inequality was so obvious and painful. The group was saved from those somber reflections when Sister Glory opened the door.

"Here it is," she proclaimed, setting it on the table in front of Burke.

"My Lord," Briggs whispered.

"Could it be?" Cho asked.

The object the woman had retrieved was a metal tube, almost a foot long. It was old. Its finish was dull. Picking it up, Burke tapped the side. He noted Sarah's name etched in the ancient metal. He turned the object so the others could see.

Cho whispered, "Do you think it's the tube we're looking for?"

"Could be," Burke replied.

"You're looking for this?" Glory asked. "That's why you came here? Is this some kind of cold case thing?"

"Colder than you could guess," Mason said. He looked at Burke. "Anything in it?"

Burke put his hand on the end of the tube and pulled. It took a few moments for the cap to release its hold. He glanced in. "Nothing here."

"So maybe it's not the tube," Briggs said.

Burke smiled. "No, it's what we're looking for."

"How can you be sure?" the religion professor asked.

"Because the name 'Lord Baltore' is etched on the inside of this cap. That was surely done by the Custodis Joseph Lacuna. This tube once held the scroll. I believe we can confidently say this tube was once in the White House. But where are the contents now?"

Handing the cap to Cho, Burke turned to Glory. "Is there an ancient scroll written in a foreign language in Reverend Tindley's papers?"

She shook her head. "No, nothing like that. Lots of handwritten papers. Some are hard to read, but they're all in English. Now there are books Dr. Tindley collected that were written in Greek and Latin."

"Bound books?" Burke inquired.

"Are there any other kind?" Glory asked.

"So," Cho cut in, "what do you think? Did Reverend Tindley destroy it?"

"No," Briggs assured her, "he would've carefully studied it and stored it if he had found it. He was a scholar. He wouldn't have destroyed it. So it couldn't have been in the tube when he gained possession."

Burke drummed his fingers on the table. So where is it? The document was in the tube when Jonah or Jonus Freedman took it north. If it wasn't in the tube in 1911 ... Logical thinking would indicate that the person who murdered Sarah Meadows found it and took it with him. But if that were the case, then why buy the trunk?

Burke looked at Cho. "That's evidence in an unsolved murder case. You will need to take it with you."

Cho looked momentarily puzzled but then smiled. "Definitely."

"As long as we get it back sometime," Glory said. "I'd love for Miss Sarah to rest in peace, and that can only happen if we track down who killed her."

"Thank you," Burke said. "Now, if you want to help in the matter of Sister Sarah, I have a favor to ask you, Sister Glory."

"Anything, hon."

"Here is my cell number. I want you to go through the files, all of them, and see if you can find any reference to something called the *Book of Joseph*."

"It will take quite a while," she replied, "but if it's important, I can get my Bible study class to help me."

"Call me if you find anything," Burke replied. "Now, we need to take the files on the murder and a copy of the sermon. Can we do that?"

"Sure," she said. "I can make another copy from the original sermon."

"Thank you so much," Burke said as he picked up the files and stood up to go.

"You're welcome," Glory answered. "And Dr. Briggs, what an honor to meet you. You must come back and speak to my class sometime."

"I will," he assured her as they hugged.

CROSSWISE

It should have been easy. All they had to do was a bit of digging. Yet the problem was with the name. If it had been Armitage Duncastle, there would have been no problem. Yet Joseph Cross was a totally different matter. There were five men named Joseph Cross living in Philadelphia in 1911. There were dozens more within a five-state area around the city. Which one was the Joseph Cross who bought the trunk from Dr. Albert Tindley?

Three days of tracking leads provided them with nothing. None of the men fit the description, and none of those they found had money to burn. Sister Glory's search proved fruitless as well. She called and gave Burke the bad but expected news that there was no mention of a *Book of Joseph* in any of Tindley's papers.

It was eleven o'clock on the third night when the team met in Burke's room at a Day's Inn just a few blocks from downtown Philly. The eighteen-hour days combined with no rewards had left them all exhausted.

"Where do we go from here?" Briggs asked.

"I'm already there," Mason explained as he stared at his computer screen. "I'm starting to look for men whose name was Cross and had J as a middle initial."

"I'm not sure that'll do any good," Burke replied. "The more I think about it, the more I'm convinced the man gave a false name."

"Why?" Briggs asked.

"We are looking for words written by the father of Jesus," a weary Burke explained. "His name was Joseph, and Jesus died on a cross. You put it together."

"If that's the case," Cho noted, "then we have no hope at all."

"That's not entirely true," Mason explained. "Maybe Jeff is right. Maybe it is a false name. But if we were to solve the crime ..."

"You mean find out who killed Sarah?" Briggs asked.

"Exactly," Mason said. "The murderer is likely the person who bought the trunk. What other motive would there have been for killing a simple maid?"

"So," Burke quipped, "you're going to solve a hundred-year-old case in order to find a two-thousand-year-old scrap of paper?"

"Well, Jeff, can you think of a better way?"

"Whatever," he replied. "I haven't eaten all day. There's a Waffle Hut down the road. Anyone want to come with me?"

"I'll go," Cho replied.

The pair didn't speak to each other during their four-block walk or even as they ordered. Burke was tired and numb. He had no clue why Cho was mute. Maybe she felt the same way. As they waited for their food, she finally broke the silence.

"My assignments are never like this." She sighed.

"So you miss the action?"

"No. Just don't like the frustration. I've had enough action for a lifetime."

He nodded and offered his take on the roadblock they were facing. "In historical research, there are always a lot of detours and many dead ends. There are also things you never really uncover. Countless men searched for the tomb of King Tut. The ones that didn't find it are forgotten, but everyone remembers Howard Carter, who did discover it."

"So," she asked, "why keep digging for this scroll? Just so you can be the Howard Carter of the *Book of Joseph*?"

Burke looked through the window at the dark, cool night. Indeed, why was he so caught up in this quest? Why had he so eagerly gone into Afghanistan? Why risk his life? Was having his name connected to a discovery of an ancient artifact that important?

"Krueger."

"Krueger?" Cho asked.

Burke didn't even realize he had actually voiced the name until she repeated it. Yet more than the historic significance of finding the document, this was about beating someone else to a find. That was what was driving him. For once in his life, he wanted to beat Krueger. He wanted to prove that good can win out over bad.

"Yes, Lisa," he admitted, "it is all about Krueger. I've gone up against him four times, and he won each time. He had the money and strings to get there ahead of me. He took the artifacts and hid them away. They are not being studied. They are not where scholars can even view them. They are at his home in Colombia or have been sold to other private collectors. I just want to win one time."

"So, it's not about the book; it's about vengeance? Competition? Seems like kind of a selfish reason when you're dealing with the faith of millions of people."

Cho's intellect and courage were at times intimidating. She never got tired, never looked haggard, and she seemed to always see clues where others missed them. Most times she was like a machine. Tonight, at this moment, she seemed ... more human.

"You want any more coffee?" the waitress asked.

The mood was broken. Burke pointed to the cups. "Yes. Top them off."

After the waitress left, he turned back to Cho. "It is about the book and not my need to win. If it exists, then it could be one of the most important unfound historic pieces in the world. We could learn a great deal from it. And I don't want Krueger to get it. Ever. It's not just because I can't take losing to him again, but because he might use it to accomplish something I don't want to even think about."

"Like what?" she asked. "I mean, other than killing us."

"We don't have what he wants," Burke said, "so we are safe for the moment. But if Krueger gets his hands on that scroll, on the *Book of Joseph,* and if it contains what I think it does, he'd use it to destroy the Christian faith. He wants power, and I think what's in the scroll would give him a tool he could use. And Krueger believes that."

Jeff thought about the hate that drove Krueger. "He would use the book to erode American and European support for the nation of Israel. Think of what it would mean if Jesus *was* just another Jew and not the Son of God. America might have no more interest in Israel than it does in any other Middle Eastern country. It might have even less, since those other countries have oil this country needs. The balance of power in the world could shift. At least that's my theory, and I figure Krueger might even have grander plans."

"What do you know about Krueger's background?" Cho asked.

"Krueger's grandfather was a member of Hitler's inner circle. He was one of those behind the 'final solution.' He escaped at the end of the war and lived the next twenty-five years in various secret locations in South America. I once wrote a paper on the man for part of my master's thesis. He remained safe because of a couple of well-executed plans. As early as 1943, he was taking large sums of money and converting it into gold and silver. He smuggled it all to his brother in Colombia. Thus, he had millions waiting for him when he escaped. Bribes will take you a long way."

"He lived under his own name?" Cho asked.

"No," Burke said. "He adopted the name of John Doch. When he died in 1970, his family released the information and allowed the press to come see his body. He looked just like any old dried-up man then. With his death verified, they buried him under his real name. At that point his son, Bruno II, went back to using Krueger and, using his father's wealth—all of it stolen from concentration camp victims and taken from treasures all over Europe—built an empire, run by the Bruno Krueger we know."

Cho took a sip from her cup, tilted her head, and posed another question. "But why would this Krueger so hate Israel?"

Burke took a gulp of his coffee before continuing. "One summer I opted to devote all my time learning everything I could about Krueger. It is my belief he hates all Jews. You see, after the war, his grandfather was hounded by Israeli intelligence every day for the rest of his life. He was always looking over his shoulder. Using their economic might, the son and grandson are trying to even that score."

Cho shook her head. "We have long known a shadowy figure with great wealth was funding many terrorist operations. Most in the CIA and FBI believe the source of that money to be the Middle East, connected to the oil industry."

"And you?" Burke asked.

"I am one of the few who believe the cash, especially for certain groups bent on attacking Israel, the United States, and certain European nations, came from a source within the United States."

"So what caused you to look at Krueger?" Burke asked, taking another swallow of coffee.

"Two reasons. The first was information that he was funneling funds to congressional figures to lobby for bills that favored Arab nations over Israel. That made no sense. It seemed that Krueger International would not benefit from the passage of certain bills that Krueger himself was pushing."

"So his illogical moves made him the logical choice?"

"Yes," Cho admitted, "but only in my mind. Those on the task force investigating the funding of terrorist groups didn't see it. Didn't agree with me. I was about to give up when I noticed something else."

"And that was?" Burke asked, suddenly caught by the woman's deep passion to bring down their common enemy.

"Well, as I looked into the money trail, I happened upon the man you knew as Columbo. He was paying out modest amounts to individuals, some associated with certain Middle Eastern groups. Wherever he went, I noted that an employee tied to one of the many shadow companies of Krueger International was there as well. At first I thought they were working together, but then I became convinced that Krueger International was watching Columbo."

"Interesting," Burke said, leaning forward to better hear Cho's hushed explanations.

"There was something else too." Her voice was now barely audible. "The information we were collecting was leaking out. Krueger seemed to know what we were doing and was always one step ahead in getting to a place where I might have some evidence against him. That stopped when I quit sharing what I collected with others at the FBI. Krueger has a mole in the FBI. I think the reason he tried to kill me was because they guessed I had figured it out."

Burke said, "And he bragged that he was funding terrorist groups when he thought we were going to be executed in Afghanistan."

"Our word against his," she said as she leaned back into her seat. "And we were officially never there. So without the paper trail, we still have nothing. But there is one good thing."

"What's that?"

"Krueger brought us together. We might be able to actually bring him down because of his obsession to get his hands on an ancient scroll. So, if you find the scroll, what will do with it?"

Those words sealed his dilemma. Cho had posed a question he simply couldn't answer. What if he did find the book? Wasn't he morally obligated to make the information in those pages known?

But if he did that, even in the name of education, wouldn't he be guilty of the same kind of act he was ready to hang on Krueger? Were they really that different?

That was a thought Burke didn't want to consider.

THE PACKARD

The north wind was blowing directly into their faces as they walked back to the motel. It was past midnight, and the streets were all but deserted. Cho leaned into Burke as they walked. When she did, he put his arm around her.

She glanced up into his face. Earlier she'd sensed something. Or at least she thought she had. Was this adventure creating a bond? If so, what kind of bond was it? She now wished she hadn't been so open in Afghanistan. Her words on that rooftop might have convinced him she had no real interest in ever having a relationship with anyone. And at that time she didn't. She'd seen too many die she thought she could have loved. And at any moment, Burke could die too. Every nerve in her body was pushing her to get close to him, but the timing was all wrong. And maybe he was too much of a machine devoted to his quest to even have the desire to ever give himself to anything but his work. To anyone.

"Lisa."

"Yes?"

"What was the name that Sarah Meadows kept saying as she died?"

The professor was once more thinking about the case. Yes, he was a machine. "Dean." Her tone hinted at her disappointment.

"Yes!" Burke said. "That was it. I might have an angle, one I should have thought of earlier. Hope Mason is still awake."

Burke grabbed her by the hand and almost dragged her down the street. This was not the way she wanted him to hold her. Too impatient for the elevator, he pulled her up the stairs to the second floor, hurriedly inserted the pass card, and pushed the door open. Briggs had evidently retired to his own room, but Mason was plugging away at the computer. He looked up, and Burke shot out a question he knew the agent couldn't answer.

"How many cars do you suppose were registered in Philadelphia in 1911?"

"I don't know."

Cho could hear the excitement in Burke's voice as the energy returned to his body. It was almost as if the history machine had been reborn and the man had disappeared.

"Don't you see?" he continued. "That's the key. We need to find records for car ownership. Where's the picture?"

"In the file in my briefcase," Cho said, pointing across the room.

Burke grabbed the file and tossed it on the table. He hurriedly went through it. When he found the photo, he took it over to the lamp. "We have to find out what kind of car this is, then search for who registered it. Look, we can even see the license number."

By the standards of the time, the automobile was huge. It looked to be over six feet in height, with a rounded brass radiator and large lights mounted just inside the fenders. The tires were thin, the wheels had wood spokes, and lanterns were set just in front of the cab. The steering wheel was on the right side. The body had a lot of wood around the windshield and the windows. There was no bumper. It had a hand crank. And hanging below the crank was a license plate. The license number — 114 — was from the state of New York.

Cho had been so busy thinking about the name and the man in the photo that she had missed the key. She suddenly felt stupid. The mistake had cost them valuable time. She now knew she'd seen this car or one exactly like it. Without saying a word, Cho hurried down the hall to her room. She fired up her iPad and was still online when she rejoined the others.

"It's a Packard," she announced. "It was probably made some-where around 1910. This was a big, heavy, and very expensive car."

Mason grinned. "Lisa, you're full of surprises. How did you know?"

"My father not only loves old airplanes; he restores classic cars. He has a couple of brass era Packards. They have a unique look."

"What about the license plate?" Burke asked.

"Those records were likely destroyed decades ago," Mason said.

"This was a custom-bodied car," Cho said. "They all were. A coach builder put his stamp on this one. A historian in the Packard club will probably be able to tell us who owned this car."

"Wow." Burke grinned.

"Thanks," she replied. "And thank Dad for his classic cars."

THE KEY

Jim Cho was a short, sturdy man who looked every bit a military officer. His hair was cropped close to his scalp. There wasn't an ounce of fat on his body, and his bearing was ramrod straight.

Burke was impressed with Jim Cho. He might have only stood five-foot-six, but he tossed a giant shadow. He was straightforward and no nonsense.

"Nice to meet you, Burke," he said as the professor entered the man's home. "My daughter has told me a few things about you."

Cho was a man Burke hoped to never make angry. So he wondered if whatever had been said was positive.

"Where is Lisa Marie?" the major asked.

"She's working on another angle to this case."

"She doesn't visit much," he said. "But she did call and tell me she got to fly a DC-2. In fact, she kind of bragged about it. First time in her life she's beaten me to something. She wouldn't tell me where she found the plane or where she flew it. Can you?"

"No, sir."

"Too bad. Wish I could have gotten my hands on those controls." He paused for a moment, licked his lower lip. "I think Lisa said you were from Illinois."

"Yes, sir," Burke replied. The small talk was making him feel like a teenager having to visit parents while his date was getting ready. He hadn't been in this position for two decades, and it placed him on the defensive as time seemed to slow to a crawl.

"You look a little beat down," Cho noted as he pointed to Burke's posture. "You might want to consider joining a gym. Get yourself in shape."

Cho was blunt. That made Burke a little uncomfortable. "I will, sir." Before Cho suggested they go for a run and do some push-ups, Burke plunged into the reason he had come to upstate New York. "The car?"

"Right," Cho replied. "I'm like you, I don't like to waste time either. Come with me."

Lisa's father led the way into a small den. There were a few childhood pictures of Lisa and her brother along with scores of photos of planes and classic cars. One wall was lined with trophies from classic car shows. The room had a small couch, two wooden chairs, an end table, a lamp, and a coffee table. Unlike his daughter, who embraced the iPad for everything from notes to reading books, the retired major apparently was a pen-and-paper person. On the table were notes and a few photographs. Cho sat down and began delivering his information like bursts of fire from an automatic weapon.

"My daughter was correct. It is a 1910 Packard. It was called a Model 30 Deacon. Weighed almost 4,000 pounds and was powered by a huge four-cylinder motor. It is easy to trace these cars because of the custom bodywork. This car stands out in that it had the original body removed and replaced by one designed by a coach builder. It is called the Deacon because the man who created this body was Fred Deacon. The car still exists and has been owned since 1974 by Lillian Hubert of Colorado Springs. I actually saw this same vehicle two years ago at the club's national show."

Burke picked up a recent photograph of the car. It looked almost like it did when Tindley had been photographed beside it a century before.

"Major Cho," Burke said while placing the photo back on the table, "do you know who bought the car back in 1910?"

"Ah, so you're not interested in the car, but the owner. That's a pity. Cars are usually much more interesting than people. But maybe not in this case."

He glanced back down at his notes and picked up a small piece of paper. "The club records indicate the car was originally purchased by Jasper Cross. A quick Google search — and don't look so surprised, I do own a computer — shows that Cross was a wealthy textile merchant who had an office in the New York garment district. He also was deeply invested in mining in the states of Nevada, Colorado, and California."

"The name and the initial fit what we are looking for," Burke said.

"Here's a photo of him I printed off the web," Cho said.

Burke took it and shook his head. "You sure? This man is short and balding. That's not the way he was described to us."

"From what I found out today," Cho said, "he was about my height and had been bald since his twenties. He would've been fifty when he bought this car."

"Doesn't add up," Burke said. "It doesn't add up at all. There's something wrong here."

"I think I know the problem," Cho replied. "Cross had three sons. Two were much taller and thinner than Jasper. That's probably why he ordered not just this Packard but two more at the same time. At least that's what our Packard club records indicate."

"Do you know the name of the son who drove this one?" Burke asked.

"It's not on the web yet, but the Packard club has been researching the ownership of custom-bodied cars for generations. The man who had the actual title for this car was named Joseph."

"There's the Joseph we need!" Burke said.

"I'm glad I could help. I do have a bit more on him."

"Anything you can give me would be deeply appreciated."

Once more Cho leafed through his notes. When he had his information assembled, he spit out the facts in a no-nonsense manner.

"The man who now owns this car spent about twenty years running down all the facts on the family. I called him this morning and he emailed me this overview. The oldest son, William, headed up the family interests in silver and gold. He was often out West running the mining operations. A second son, John, took over the family textile business. Joseph, who was born in 1880, spent his life in the field of education. He was loyal too. Records show he continued to drive Packards until he died."

Burke shook his head. This didn't match at all. Something was wrong.

"What's wrong, Dr. Burke?"

"The man we're looking for murdered a woman."

"Joseph's probably not your man," Cho said. "According to what little I could dig up, he had the reputation of being one of the most generous and gracious people in Pittsburgh. But it is well known in the car club that his brother John was a rogue. A liar and an immoral SOB. He ran one of the family businesses into the ground and died in the 1920s. He was shot. The murder was never solved, though there were rumors."

Burke's jaw dropped. A black sheep and a white sheep! Happens in so many families. Maybe Joseph bought the trunk, paying too much for it, to help his bad brother cover up a crime. Maybe something in that trunk was incriminating. Cho's information might solve Sarah's murder and explain why Joseph Cross paid such a generous amount for the trunk, but Burke didn't see any tie to the *Book of Joseph* or to Custodis Joseph Lacuna. "You said there were rumors about the man's death? His murder?"

"We have talked about it at club meetings. It's always the rogues that are the most interesting. Don't know much about Joseph, but know a lot about John."

"But why would a car club keep talking about John Cross?"

Cho smiled. "John's car still exists."

"What are the odds?" Burke whispered.

"Not as long as you think. Custom-body cars have a much better survival rate than everyday drivers. There's a guy in Arkansas named Collins who owns the Packard that John Cross was driving when he was killed. The car still has three bullet holes in it."

As any good storyteller does, Cho let the information settle in before picking up the tale. "Collins seems to think that a powerful man in Philadelphia had John rubbed out. A hit. Evidently that man had a son who was in his early teens, and he found out the boy he thought was his son was actually fathered by another man. By John."

"Do you know the name of the man who ordered the hit on John?"

"Gringle, Capell, something like that. I can't remember exactly. I could call Collins. I have his number."

Burke nodded. "If you could, please do that. It might help us. A lot."

The host walked into the hall, hit a few buttons, and waited. Burke heard a few mumblings before Cho marched back into the room and announced: "Cagle."

That tied things together. Sarah worked for the Cagles. She must have known about the affair. Somebody knew she knew and was afraid she would talk. She was silenced. The man who killed her was eliminating all evidence of an affair. But why did Cross buy the trunk? The only logical answer was that Joseph Cross was simply taking care of family business, a trail of scandal that might lead to John and the Cross family.

"What is this all about?" Cho asked.

"Don't know yet," Burke replied, "but I can assure you, you've helped us a great deal. We can now tell what might be the main road out of a blind alley."

Burke got up. Cho stood and smiled.

"I take it it's time for you to go."

"I need to check out a few things. Something very obvious just hit me, something I should have realized days ago."

"What's that?" Cho asked.

"Major Cho, Cross is a very common name, isn't it?"

"Yes, I would think so."

"Do you happen to have a middle initial for Joseph Cross?"

"Yes, I believe that it's in the notes here. Let me see ..." He scanned one of the papers. "It was F."

"Now I know why the crate was never returned to England."

"Excuse me?" Cho said.

"Let me make a quick call, and if the information is right, I'll tell you the story."

Burke pulled his cell from his pocket. Within seconds, he was connected. "Emma, get into the history department records and tell me if there was a Joseph Cross who taught at Illinois in the 1930s.... Yeah, I'll wait."

Burke got the news he expected. "Thanks, Emma. I'll see you soon."

Burke slipped the phone back into his pocket and smiled. "There were two professors at Illinois named Joseph Cross."

"It was a common name," Cho said.

"One of those men, probably to make it less confusing, went by his middle name — Franklin."

PEACE

Though she'd been all over the globe, seen all the major cities and most of the natural wonders, Lisa Marie Cho noticed something very different, something she'd never felt before, in the tiny hamlet of Royal, Illinois. There was something about the flat prairie, the well-kept cornfields, and the slow pace of life that sucked her in. Or maybe it was the smiles. It seemed that everyone she saw smiled. And they asked her how she was even though they had no idea who she was. And then there was Madge Meyers, who kept offering her a choice of homemade banana bread or a piece of chocolate pie. She didn't find out how the bread was, but the pie, with its six-inch-high cream topping, was incredible!

No, there were no awesome views like on the east rim of the Grand Canyon. No breathtaking grandeur as found at the Taj Mahal. There wasn't the bustle and excitement of Paris, Los Angeles, or DC. This wasn't a place that begged her to take out her camera or buy a postcard. But it was special because it silently screamed "home." And home had such a good sound to a woman who'd been on the move her whole life.

As she soaked in the local flavor, as the taste of the pie lingered, it was hard to believe there was any trouble anywhere in the whole world. Yet it was there, lurking just out of sight, watching her moves and checking for her weaknesses. She could never fully forget that fact. Even as she stood in Royal, she was in a war.

"What are you looking at?"

Cho's large brown eyes moved from the corn picker harvesting this year's crop in a field across from the white house on Main Street back to her host. For the last ten hours, Jeff had been going through the papers of Joseph Franklin Cross. She'd been with him when he'd pried open the missing Berkshire crate they'd found in a corner of the attic, up against a wall. She'd seen his disappointment when the contents seemed to be nothing but 1941 newspapers—hundreds of pages. She was with him going through each of those pages, looking for some clue. She'd left the attic after hopefulness turned to hopelessness. She'd retreated to the large concrete porch. After sucking in a few deep breaths of fall air, the machine driving her life of duty and service turned off. Now the *Book of Joseph*, Krueger, even her job didn't seem nearly as important as embracing this single wonderful peaceful moment.

"I'm thinking about getting off the bus," she announced. Though this thought, expressed verbally, was not really meant to be heard, he heard it.

"What?" Burke asked.

"The bus," Cho explained, "the rat race, the drive to change the world, to find new things, to somehow control my destiny, to root out all the bad guys. I think I'm tired of all that. No, I *know* I'm tired of all that. The important stuff is not somewhere else; it is here. It is right here!"

"I don't get what you're saying," Burke admitted, confusion etched on his face.

"My life is filled with noise," Cho explained. "When I was in special ops, there was the noise in battle, noise getting ready for battle, noise in the barracks, noise on the planes—there is always noise. My life with the FBI has been pretty much the same. There is the noise of the office, the noise in the cities, the noise in training. Even when things are quiet, you know the noise will be back soon. I don't want any more noise. I want to hear sounds. That's what I'm doing out here. Hearing sounds. I hadn't heard the wind in the trees in years. And the bird songs! The sound of a squirrel racing up a tree, chattering at another squirrel. Even the sound of a mother calling for her child to come in for dinner. I love those sounds. The world where I've spent my adult life is full of noise, but here there are sounds. And taste."

"Ah, the chocolate pie." Burke smiled.

"It was sinfully good." She laughed. "I can still taste it. I'd forgotten what it was like to eat something prepared by someone who loves to cook. There's a difference between that and the finest food in the world's best cafés."

"I guess," he replied, "though no one has ever said that about my cooking."

Did he get what she meant? Did he understand? If he did, his face didn't show it. His eyes might have been staring out at the field, but they were seeing something else.

"We are not singing from the same hymnbook," she said.

"What?"

"Nothing important," she assured him. At least not important to him. Not now anyway. Maybe someday. Maybe someday they'd both be ready to share a special moment. But not today. The trail was too hot, the scent too strong, and Jeff was again the bloodhound who couldn't resist.

Cho took a deep breath and let the cool, crisp air fill her. She cocked an ear to hear a robin chirp, then closed the book on this new world she'd just discovered. She knew he wanted her to ask a question, so she did. "Find anything?"

"Yeah." He smiled. "I found the auction document. It was in the bottom of the crate. I think Cross just repacked everything else in the other crates and kept the one thing he didn't want others to see. The newspapers were a history teacher's way of hiding the obvious. After all, who was going to actually dig through all those newspapers and then actually read anything in the one next to the bottom to find the document?"

"Who indeed?" she said. It was an observation on personality more than a comment on his triumph. After all, until today she'd had the same drive to know that he still had. Her drive had simply, for the moment, taken a vacation.

"I figure," Burke explained, "he probably should've destroyed it, but as a historian, he couldn't. I understand that."

Cho shook her head. "That's just a guess. You can't know what was on his mind."

"In this case maybe I do," Burke replied. "You see, one of the newspaper stories dealt with a break-in at the university in early 1941. Nothing valuable was taken, but several of the crates were opened."

246 / ACE COLLINS

"Who would have gone to the trouble?" she asked, while still looking at the farmer harvesting corn in the field. "Were they searching for the scroll? Didn't find it? But wait, didn't Columbo tell you the elder Krueger knew about the auction, that the Germans had already searched the files before they were shipped out of England?"

Burke shrugged. "Maybe Columbo was right, maybe he was wrong. Or maybe they just wanted to make sure no one else got their hands on the scroll because they didn't have it." Burke's cell ring interrupted his string of thoughts.

"Burke here."

Cho watched as the man listened to words she couldn't hear. His focus was only on the quest. She couldn't expect him to see what was around him. Not now, maybe not ever. Perhaps he would always be chasing something. Maybe he'd never sense the peace that was his if he would just open his eyes to it.

"That nails it," Burke said, his voice again filled with excitement after the phone call. "The reason the papers of Berkshire were sent to the University of Illinois is that Cross went after them. He sent several letters to Berkshire, begging them to designate U of I as the caretaker. The agents who've been looking through all university documents of that period found copies. It appears this was the only English city he contacted. He knew that auction document was in those papers even before they arrived."

"But how?" Cho asked.

"He was a researcher," Burke answered. "There's no other answer. There are boxes of papers I still haven't gone through. I need to get back to work. You want to help me?"

Cho looked back toward the cornfield and the open prairie beyond. No, she wanted to stay right here, to relish doing nothing, to forget the mission and let the quiet countryside assure her there was a life beyond war zones. Yet she was still part machine. She wasn't completely human yet. When there was a job to be done, she had to do it. She would likely always surrender to the mission. Like Burke, she realized she'd probably always be chasing something or someone.

THE SHOE BOX

Joseph Franklin Cross was a stickler for records. The boxes in the attic contained every student grade going back to his first world history class at the University of Pittsburgh. Those reports ended with the fall semester of 1941. He died after that fall semester ended.

But more important than his need to collect stuff was the fact that he was also an organizer. Except for the crate containing the auction information, each of the files was placed in date order in the boxes. Along with them were photographs, personal letters, and notes—all of them carefully placed with items from the same time period. In a 1937 box, Burke found a picture of the teacher and photos of every one of the cars he'd owned, along with several original titles and registration forms. There was even a photo of the 1910 model. Rather than toss those items back in the box, he handed them to Cho to give to her father. Though the material was at times interesting, Burke realized that everything in the boxes was worthless.

"Well," he sighed looking into that last box, "we struck out."

Cho glanced over his shoulder.

"Clothes," he said, "nothing but clothes."

Pulling himself off the attic floor, Burke walked over to where he could stand up straight. He had struck out. The chill air of the attic reminded him that winter was coming. He could sense it. Winter had always been a hopeless time for him. His parents had died in winter. His divorce had become final in winter. He was convinced nothing good ever happened when snow was on the ground.

Allowing his shoulders to rest against a support board, he turned back to watch Cho. She was still working, pulling out Cross's clothes from the final box, carefully unfolding and studying each garment.

She refused to give up. Maybe it went with her job or maybe it was just a part of her fiber. He doubted he would ever really know.

As if feeling his gaze, Cho posed the question he'd been expecting for several days. "What did you think of my dad?"

Burke had been trying to come up with an answer since he had left her dad's upstate New York home. He still wasn't sure what to say. "He's a nice man."

"Really," she replied with a grin. "Are you sure you went to my father's home?"

"Okay," Burke admitted, "he was no-nonsense."

"Yep, now that's my dad." Cho smiled, then quickly changed the subject. "Did you know Cross even kept his old shoes in the boxes they came in? Who does that?"

"It doesn't make sense," Burke said. "At least not to me."

"What, the shoe boxes?" she asked.

"No, that a man like Cross could be involved in the cover-up of a murder. Everything I've read in the last two days — his private letters and notes — paints him as a person of incredible integrity. There didn't seem to be a violent bone in his body. If he had one fault, it is one I share with him — curiosity. He was simply too curious."

"Everybody slips at least once," Cho said. "Probably even Mother Teresa."

Burke nodded. The agent was right. Besides, Cross was likely acting to cover up the sins of one of his own family. That could almost be forgiven. But it still didn't fit with the man's character.

Burke glanced back at Cho. Here was a tough, gritty, battle-tested soldier, a member of the Special Forces and now an FBI agent who'd killed people and survived in the harshest surroundings, yet she was taking great care with items no one wanted. Cross's clothes would either be thrown away or given to a secondhand store. She was handling them as if they were cherished family heirlooms. She was even opening each shoe box, running her hands over the old wingtips inside, treating them as if they were her grandfather's shoes, before carefully placing each pair back in the box. A strange mix of contrasts. Maybe that was why she was so fascinating.

"Nothing." She sighed. "Absolutely nothing."

Cho got up, stretched, and headed down the attic ladder. Having nothing better to do, Burke followed her down the ladder and out of the house. They walked into the back yard and headed toward the barn, Cho still in the lead. She was pushing open one of the old building's large swinging doors when he finally caught up.

"What are you doing?"

Without turning around, she pointed to the old car almost buried by clutter in the ancient wood structure. "I need a break. I need to work on something I know I can figure out."

"And what's that?" he asked as she began tossing old buckets and farm tools out of her way.

"The old Packard," she said. "I grew up with those. I helped my dad work on them. It was one of the few things we could actually do together without getting on each other's nerves. The tag says it hasn't been on the road since 1942. I want to see if the motor is still free. If it is, then I'm going to spend a day or two and get it running."

"Why?" Burke asked as he started to help her uncover the old relic.

"Just because," she shot back. "Is this heap yours?"

"It came with the property."

"Do you have the keys?"

"I don't know. I've never paid any attention to anything in this old place."

She stopped, an incredulous expression etched on her face. "You're a history teacher. This barn is full of history. You trek all over the world on expeditions to uncover ruins, and you don't even have the sense to take a look at a barn-find car? Do you know how rare these are? What kind of man are you?"

"Well …"

"You claim you're curious, yet you don't care to save a 1937 Packard and put it back on the road. This is a classic!"

Burke plopped down on an ancient milk can. Was she right? Had he missed something special? Or was she caving to the pressure and going crazy?

THE SEAT

It took over an hour to uncover the Packard. Sweat pouring from her brow, Cho stepped back to get a better view of the relic from the Art Deco age.

"Beautiful," she said. Then, as if giving a lecture at a museum, she added, "Look at that stately grill, the fender-mounted lights, even the dark green paint. This might have been a simple four-door sedan, but it was magnificent and can be again."

Burke sighed, his arms folded across his chest. "The interior is moth eaten, the tires are cracked, and—"

"Zip it," Cho said. "Think of it as history. There was a time when this was one of the finest cars on the road. Its straight-eight engine was something men talked about at parties. If you drove one of these, you had real class. This car tells us a lot about Dr. Joseph Franklin Cross."

"If you say so."

Cho walked over to the driver's side and twisted the handle. The door opened and she smiled. Sliding in, she sat behind the wheel. For the moment she was a little girl again. Grabbing the huge steering wheel in her hands, she rocked it back and forth. Burke smiled as she slid her fingers over the instruments as if running her hands over fine china. This was pretty much the same way she had treated the DC-2. He figured, given time, she would start talking to the car too.

"Hey, look!" she cried. "The key is in the ignition. We have the key!"

Holding the newfound treasure in her hand, Cho slid across to the passenger side and opened the glove box. She leafed through a couple of maps, then studied some receipts.

"Cross had it serviced right here in Royal on January 5, 1942.

How do you like that?" She glanced into the rearview mirror. "Look, there is a U of I decal in the back window. Amazing!"

Cho pulled the handle and pushed the passenger door open. Stepping out, she looked back lovingly at the old vehicle. A bored Burke glanced inside the old car. "This is stealing focus," he said.

"What do you mean?" she asked, patting dust from her shirt.

"We need to be working on figuring out where the scroll is."

"That's a dead end for the moment." She leaned in and studied the old felt headliner. "You know, I can transform this car into a show winner."

She patted the seat. "Need to call Dad and have him give me the rundown on how many of these were built. Let's pull the seat cushion out."

"What?"

"One of the most interesting things about old cars is what you find under the seats. You know, coins, old magazines, pocketknives, the stuff that slides between the cushions when passengers are sitting in the car. Come on! Go on the other side and grab the bottom of the cushion and lift."

Burke grudgingly moved to the driver's side of the vehicle. He pushed his hands under the sides of the old cushion.

"When we have it, I'll hand it to you," she said. "Just lean it up against the wall."

The seat lifted up easily. When it was completely free, Burke pulled it out the driver's door and leaned it against the wall. He had just turned around to retrace his steps when Cho, her head tilted looking down where the seat had been, whispered, "What's this?"

Burke spied it as well—a manila envelope on the car's carpet halfway between the two doors. Cho gingerly reached down and picked it up.

"This has stamps on it," she informed him, "but it was never mailed."

She walked over to an old wooden bench against the north wall and eased herself down. Burke joined her.

It was a simple six-by-nine-inch envelope addressed to Dr. Jacob Sonnenberg in San Francisco. The return address was a post office box in Royal. The FBI agent flipped it over. On the back flap, three words had been written in longhand—Custodis Joseph Lacuna.

"My Lord," Burke whispered. "Cross was a member!"

Cho nodded as she traced the writing with her index finger. "Maybe he was."

"You know, Lisa, he might have been his generation's Lord Baltore." He took the envelope and turned it over a couple of times. "If so, then the answer to where to go next might well be in this envelope. It even could be at this address in Frisco."

Cho smiled. "See, my passion for cars and planes seems to always pay off. But you're jumping way too far here. Remember your training as a researcher. You can't judge a book by its cover. I'm sure you nag your students with stuff like that all the time. So don't jump to conclusions. What's inside might be something far different."

"At the very least, we have beaten Krueger."

"Let's see what we've beaten him to," Cho said, her tone flat and businesslike. "Let's go inside. Got something in my kit that will loosen that flap with very little damage."

Burke led the way as they hurried from the barn, back in the house through the back door, and to the kitchen table. Cho laid the item on the oak surface and retrieved her kit. After drawing on gloves, she picked up the envelope, sprayed the flap, and inserted a small blade under the sealed area. Starting on the left, she pushed less than an inch before it released.

"That was easy," she said while laying the blade to one side. "Guess the glue was so old it was ready to let go. Now let's empty the contents and see what Dr. Cross didn't mail."

The first thing that fell out was a hand-drawn map showing a location, but the sketch had no names or even landmarks.

"Any guess as to where this is?" she asked.

Burke shook his head.

Moving the map to one side, Cho slipped out another sheet of paper. On it was a list of names.

"Jackpot," Burke whispered.

"Let me hear your take," Cho said while taking a seat at the table.

He pulled a chair over next to her. For the first time since the night in Afghanistan, they were again shoulder to shoulder.

Burke studied the document for a few more seconds and smiled. "You're the investigator. Look at who's listed here. See any names that pop out?"

"Sure," Cho said. "John Breckinridge, Thomas Jefferson, Robert Breckinridge, Jonah Freedman. We've talked about those men enough recently, but the names before them don't mean anything to me."

"One might," Burke explained. "Note the Andre Prevot listed before the first Breckinridge."

"The monk!"

"Could be. The rest of the names must belong to the men who cared for it after the auction. A Google or Bing search would likely turn up some kind of profile on at least a few of them."

"But it ends with Freedman," Cho pointed out. "And what about Robert Todd Lincoln? We haven't run across him in our search."

Burke rubbed his chin and shook his head. "Of course. Look, there's a line through Robert Breckinridge's name, and Freedman's was written in above it. Then Lincoln's name was also crossed out. Probably at a later time. The ink is a different shade of blue. Cross somehow knew Robert Breckinridge was supposed to have the book, but when he found he didn't, he marked through his name. It makes sense. Remember Breckinridge's journal? That's why Abraham Lincoln asked Breckinridge about the scroll. It likely was supposed to go next to Robert Todd Lincoln, the president's son. That means that Abe himself might have been a member of Custodis Joseph Lacuna. With Breckinridge getting up in years, the group might have chosen young Robert Todd as the next Lord Baltore. The president must have called Breckinridge to the Oval Office to urge him to pass on the scroll."

"The problem was," Cho cut it, "Breckinridge had unwittingly already given the document away."

"Thus the chain had been broken," Burke added, "because Jefferson hadn't explained things. Or maybe the president figured Breckinridge's father had given the son that information. Either way, a huge problem suddenly revealed itself."

"It makes sense," Cho interjected. "There are several references in papers I've read of a Robert Lincoln speaking to Cross's students."

"What a cover!" Burke replied, his words now shooting out of his mouth with the force of a Canadian cold front. "They worked together to find the book. When they had it, Cross became the next Lord Baltore."

"Why not Lincoln?' Cho asked.

"Because by 1911, Robert Lincoln was an old man. The group would have wanted someone younger and in perfect health to be the keeper of the word."

"Well," Cho said, "if Cross was that man, then where's the book?"

"That map must have something to do with it," Burke suggested as he pointed to the paper Cho had placed on the table. "Anything else in there?"

Setting the list to one side, Cho looked inside the envelope and pulled out a smaller envelope. On it was a handwritten address to the district attorney in Philadelphia. The bold, flowing script matched the writing on the San Francisco address. On the back, the writer had printed in bold letters, "Please mail after my death."

Cho, dismissing FBI procedure, hurriedly tore the envelope flap and pulled out the letter. Two sets of eyes scanned the document.

July 7, 1931

Dear Sir:

I could not come forward during my life for reasons that can't be explained even years after my death. But there is something I need to confess so a wrong can be made right.

In 1911 I was involved in a crime in Philadelphia. A Negro woman named Sarah Freedman Meadows was murdered. My brother John was the killer. I arrived just after the events, discovered my brother standing over the body and holding the weapon. Though it was wrong, I spirited him away from the scene.

John had acted in this manner because he felt he had to protect me from scandal. He became aware of my relationship with Victoria Cagle, who was a married woman and

Mrs. Meadows' employer. Sadly, John was mistaken. I was not having an affair with a married woman. I had only gotten to know Mrs. Cagle to get close to her maid. Mrs. Meadows had something that had an important historic significance to a society that I headed.

John was unaware of the reasons I had endeared myself to the woman. He was afraid that if word got out, it would cost me my position at the university. I arrived right after he shot the one person whom he believed had knowledge of my supposed indiscretions. Yet, by not staying at the scene, I am as guilty as he was. But, because of historical matters that had much larger consequences than a single life, I could not afford to have the reasons for my actions revealed nor did I want to see my brother spend years in prison.

John was later murdered in New York City. Essentially he paid for his actions. Hopefully this letter will allow you to change the cause of Sarah Freedman Meadows' death to murder and not suicide.

Sincerely,
Joseph Franklin Cross

"So the child wasn't John's," Cho noted.

"Evidently not," Burke replied. "Just a rumor. There is no way of telling why John was killed. But knowing the way he lived, he likely had a lot of enemies."

Cho turned away from the letter and looked directly at Burke. "But how did he know Sarah had the book?"

"I think we can safely assume that Joseph Cross was a member of the Custodis Joseph Lacuna. When President Lincoln found out the scroll was missing, he probably told his son. Based on what we can pull from these notes, Custodis Joseph Lacuna had likely been searching for the book for years. We have no idea how the members of that organization were chosen, but somehow it seems Robert Todd Lincoln met and worked with Dr. Cross."

"If Cross had the scroll," Cho said, "he must have bought it from Sarah. He as much as admitted that in this letter. So where is it now?"

Burke shrugged. "It's not here, and it's not in his stored files at the university archives. There's no place else to look. Except . . . on the map! But there are no reference points. There's not a single name on this map."

"What about the man whose name is on the envelope?" Cho suggested. "He was being sent these papers. He had to be in on it. Maybe he got the scroll after Cross died."

She picked up the envelope and, when she did, a small piece of paper fell out. They watched as it drifted to the floor, then they both reached for it. Cho was quicker. She read the short paragraph:

Jacob,

Plans have changed. Krueger knows I have it and he is in the States. Can't meet you in San Francisco. Let's meet at the camp. You probably remember how to get there, but I have included a map that pinpoints where I will be. After all it has been several years since our hunting trip. I don't think the snow will be too bad.

Meet me on January 17th. And take care you aren't followed.

Frank

"That's a game changer," Burke whispered. "We have to find Sonnenberg."

"But he'll be dead," she argued.

"Yeah, but if he had children, we have another link in the chain. Still, there is something that bothers me."

"What's that, Jeff?"

"Why didn't he mail the envelope?"

"I think I know," Cho said. "And it ties in to what I learned as a kid from my father as we restored cars together. But I don't want to let you in on my theory just yet. If we find someone in the Sonnenberg family and they have a story, I'll give you my thoughts on the unmailed envelope."

LUST FOR POWER

Bruno Krueger felt like a tiger in a small town zoo. His penthouse had become a cage—a luxurious cage, but a cage nevertheless. But as long as he was getting information, he had nothing to complain about. The mole was keeping him informed.

Getting up from his desk, Krueger strolled over to the window. Every city has a unique skyline. Chicago was different from Berlin and Berlin was different from Paris and Paris was different from Rio. But at this moment, they all looked the same. Everything was in black and white. There was no excitement. No life. Just waiting. And when you wanted something as much as he did, waiting was hell. But the only one who had any chips to toss on the table and get the game going again was Burke. Nothing could start until Burke made a move, and for the moment, his sources assured him, the professor was holed up in an ancient two-story house a hundred miles to the south. So that meant more waiting.

He glanced toward the TV mounted in the wall above the bar. Even though the volume was down, he knew the substance of the report that had dominated the news all day. A Taliban raid had killed a dozen UN troops. He'd financed that assault. His money was also behind a suicide bombing in Jerusalem that took the life of a general in the Israeli Army. Yet all of that was minor league compared to what he had planned for a few months down the road.

When he had the book and the team was trained, a Gulf of Mexico oil platform would explode. Unlike the BP disaster of 2010, this time the government would be prepared for tens of thousands of gallons of oil pouring into the Gulf. Paid crews would be on the scene within hours to mop up the mess. The best technology to separate the oil from the water had been developed by none other than Krueger International. His men would lead the cleanup effort. One of those teams, assigned to the Louisiana coastline, would make its way onshore and disappear into New Orleans. Within hours, several major refineries would be destroyed. Production of gasoline in the United States would shrink by more than 30 percent in one day.

After the attack, a Middle Eastern group he funded would step forward and take credit. In their statement they would point to the US support of Israel as the reason for the series of blasts. And the war on terror, which had already had a decade-long devastating effect on the US economy and national debt, would be forced to expand and siphon off even more of the weary country's resources.

In the new and expanded war, Krueger's company would get a majority of the contracts to equip this latest round of American freedom fighters as well as to rebuild the refineries and clean up the Gulf. And no one would be any the wiser.

With the scroll in his possession—and if it said what his grandfather was convinced it said—he would have a bargaining chip to complete the mission Hitler himself had conceived. In a private meeting, Krueger would use the scroll and Joseph's words as leverage when telling the Vatican and other powerful Christian leaders to support his plan. He would force the Christian church not only to support certain proposals that would favor his positions but also to convince their followers that these actions where aligned with biblical truth.

Israel and its lobbies would lose power in Washington and Europe. He already had pawns in the media spilling out opinions that terrorists hit the US because of the nation's support of Israel. Eventually, his plan would pave the way for the fall of the state of Israel. Krueger thought of his grandfather and the way he was forced by the Jewish intelligence to spend the last third of his life hiding and on the run. It was time for payback. Retribution.

And if Christian leaders refused his terms, then Krueger would simply print and release the *Book of Joseph*. The fallout would be enormous. He took great satisfaction in the idea of planting seeds of doubt. As they spread and bore fruit, he could see Christians throughout the world questioning the actual divinity of Christ.

Evangelism would become incredibly difficult. Contributions to the organized church would surely diminish. Struggling churches would close. For some, Christianity might become nothing more than a philosophical movement, such as following the wisdom of Confucius.

Ultimately, the power and moral influence of the church in the United States and the world would diminish, and with moral authority shifted in a new direction, the world would become a much different place. He was sure he could take advantage of that in many ways.

But that all depended on Burke uncovering the final clues to where the scroll was hidden.

There was a knock on the door, almost a hesitant tapping. It was only after the third soft rapping that Krueger finally barked, "Come in." It was more a command than an invitation.

"Excuse me, sir."

"What do you want, Duncan?"

"I don't know if this is important," the man whispered apologetically.

"What do you have?"

"Burke, Cho, and Mason are on the move again."

"Where to now?"

"West, a charter flight. Flight plan indicates they're going to San Francisco."

"How did you get the information?"

"From our people on the ground in Royal."

"Ah, good. The game's afoot," he whispered.

"What, sir?"

Almost ignoring that Duncan was in the room, Krueger said, "Without God there is no faith, and without faith there is no hope."

"Yes, sir," Duncan replied.

"Not my words," Krueger said. "I'm quoting America's most respected evangelist. And for the very first time, I hope he's right."

THE CRASH

Dr. Jacob Sonnenberg was an easy man to find. Well, at least he was a person who was easy to trace. He'd been an instructor at Stanford more than forty years. His expertise was ancient languages, but his doctorate was in mathematics. During World War II he'd combined his two gifts to become a code breaker. After the war he'd returned to Stanford, where he taught calculus until his death of a heart attack in 1974.

Sonnenberg's daughter, Rachel, still lived in the family home. Now in her seventies, the woman had made millions in the cosmetic business. Since selling her company, she spent much of her time traveling the world. Energetic and outgoing, she was very active in San Francisco's social set and still played a daily game of tennis.

Sonnenberg answered the door wearing a tailored navy suit and low-heeled pumps. Her makeup was perfect, her complexion flawless, and her dark hair was swept up in a bun.

"Welcome," she said as she swung open the twelve-foot-high entry door.

"Thank you," Cho said, answering for the group.

As she waved them inside, Sonnenberg said, "My secretary informed me you had a few questions about my father."

"We do," Cho replied.

"Then come into my den. We'll be comfortable there, and I have coffee and tea ready. I just love to talk about Daddy. He was such a gentleman! By the way Miss . . . is it miss?

Cho nodded.

"You have incredible skin and wonderful cheekbones. I could have used you as a makeup model. And I have something that will cover that—" Realizing she might be treading on unstable ground, the woman stopped in midsentence.

"Thank you," Cho replied, trying to defuse the suddenly awkward moment.

"Well, this is my humble abode," Sonnenberg announced as she led them through her home to the den.

Impressive was not the word. The home could have been the main feature story on any of the cable decorating networks. Though the rooms were large, they were crowded with antiques from all over the globe. They passed a library that echoed early American furnishings. The formal dining room was definitely Louis XIV. A music room reflected Bavarian Germany, and a small porch seemed to pay tribute to Japan. What Sonnenberg called the parlor would have easily fit in at Buckingham Palace.

After the team had been seated in Elizabethan chairs and served a choice of coffee or tea, Sonnenberg took over. Like a one-woman Broadway show, she controlled the first twenty minutes, sharing vivid details from both her father's work and her own life. She also showed them more than a half dozen photos of the man she called "Daddy." She talked so fast and moved from one subject to the next so seamlessly that no one could turn the conversation in a new direction until she finally took a sip of her tea. At that point, sensing it might be his last chance, Burke jumped in.

"Did your father ever speak of a man named Joseph Franklin Cross?"

For the first time, the woman seemed to be caught off guard. She tilted her head to one side, took a deep breath, and eased into a chair. She kept her back ramrod straight as she crossed her thin fingers over her lap.

"That's a name I haven't heard in a long time." Her voice grew soft and her words suddenly were more carefully chosen. "I recall Cross from a story Daddy told me. It was something he told me just a few years before he died. We were watching a late-night movie called *Nothing Sacred*. After it finished playing, Daddy brought up how the star of that film, Carole Lombard, had died in a plane crash. He then told me that a friend of his, a Dr. Franklin Cross, had also been on that plane."

Burke glanced toward Cho as he asked, "Did he, your father, that is, mention anything else about Dr. Cross?"

"Yes, he talked a lot that night. Might have been the brandy or maybe just something that had to come out. Dr. Cross was evidently an old friend. I think Daddy had once been his student. He told me they were working on something together. Anyway, as I remember it, he was bringing some kind of old text to Daddy for him to translate."

Sonnenberg rose from her chair and walked over to a cabinet. Opening the glass doors, she pulled out a framed eight-by-ten black and white photo. Returning to her guests, she handed the picture to Burke, then continued her story.

"Daddy flew to Las Vegas the minute he got news of the crash. He went up the mountain with the rescue crews. That picture shows him at the crash site."

Burke studied the image. A large motor with bent and broken propellers could be seen to the man's left. Large chunks of burned items, perhaps clothing, were behind him. His foot was propped on a tire. He appeared sad and worn out.

As the photo was passed from one person to the next, no one said a word. If the scroll was in that crash, then its fate seemed sealed.

The search was over.

MOVE

It was an energized Bruno Krueger who whipped out his cell and made a call to Dumont Overton. "That Dirty Pilot," as Krueger often called his special missions flyer, answered on the fifth ring.

"Yes, sir?"

"Are you sober?" the billionaire demanded.

"As a judge."

"Get to Chicago, get the new Lear ready. We're heading West with three of my best people."

"Business or—"

"This is war!" Krueger said.

"I understand," Overton replied.

"How long until you can be here and ready to fly?"

"Five hours," the pilot answered. "I'm in Atlanta."

"Make it four. I want to be headed to San Francisco by eight this evening."

Krueger didn't wait for a reply before ending the call and tapping in another number.

He now had a plan. It had "success" written all over it. Therefore he needed a very special man—someone who had no conscience and no fear. When a gruff voice answered with just one word, "Yes," he was sure that man was on the line.

"Schminsky. It's Krueger. I need you and one of our best for a very special job."

"When?" came a reply as cold as an arctic wind.

"We leave from my hangar at eight tonight."

"What's needed?" Schminsky's voice was robotic in its cadence, and a robot was exactly what Krueger needed for this job.

"I have a few items that need to be disposed of," Krueger explained. "It seems their expiration date might arrive soon."

"Spoiled goods?" the man asked.

"Come prepared for anything."

"I will."

Eight words, Krueger thought. That was all it took. In eight words Schminsky had agreed to eliminate an issue. Schminsky didn't ask the target or location. Krueger needed more men like this killing machine.

Now there was only one thing left to do. In the next four hours, he had to find out where the adventurers were going. It was time to bring Duncan back into the game. He pushed a button on his desk. Exactly three minutes later, the big spineless man was in his presence.

"Duncan, do you know where Burke is?"

"Not at this time. Our men couldn't jump on the charter with them."

"Okay," Krueger replied, his voice edgy but still under control. "That's understandable. But I have to know their location in the next hour. I also have to know what they know and where they're going."

"I can't find that out, sir," Duncan replied in a voice so soft Krueger just barely heard the reply. "We didn't place any tags on them. You wanted us too far back so our men wouldn't be spotted."

"Never mind what I said then. Do you know the mole?"

"Not who he is," he answered.

"But you have a way to get in touch with him?"

Duncan nodded.

"Good. Do it now. The message is short. Where are Mason and Cho? If we know where they are, we'll find Burke."

"I'll get on it," Duncan replied.

As he turned to leave the room, his boss issued a stern warning: "You have fifteen minutes. If you fail to get me what I need, you'll be joining Dr. Fogleman. And she's not in a pleasant place. Do you understand?"

"Yes, sir," Duncan answered and bolted from the room.

Walking over to his window, Krueger looked at the skyline again. Pushing his hand through his hair, he frowned. Burke wouldn't have gone West unless he had found something. Now it was just a matter of following the man until he uncovered the scroll. And though it would be much smarter to assign the mission to the team and wait in the Windy City, he had to be there this time. And, when the scroll was in his hands, he would break a personal rule and pull the trigger himself. There would be no slipups, no one left behind to talk.

The ringing of his desk phone brought the billionaire back into the moment. Three long strides took him to his desk. He grabbed the receiver.

"You got the information?" Krueger paused and listened. "You just earned yourself a raise, Duncan."

They were still in San Francisco.

FAITH

Historical research was often littered with dead ends. Over the years, Burke had run into more than he could count. Some of those had been in the middle of jungles and others in the basements of old libraries. But no dead end had ever been as dead as this one. A plane, remembered now only for having taken the life of a famous Hollywood icon, might have taken something of far greater value.

But maybe that was what needed to happen. Maybe not having those words become public was actually the best thing. Maybe that is the way fate worked. And what was fate? Wasn't that just an atheist's term for God? Yes, everyone had to believe in something. Now even he had to admit that.

On this mission, the people he'd come to respect the most were those who embraced faith. Briggs, Brother Abel, and even Sister Glory. They seemed to have a depth he hadn't seen in others. Was that depth due to their faith? And Cho, who outwardly didn't display any religious passion, still seemed to believe that her brother's life was saved by a miracle. And that thought gave her a great deal of peace.

Now, here he was, at the end of a mission that had brought him nothing but pain, suffering, and heartache, and he was still looking for clues. What was driving him on? Perhaps it was his natural curiosity. After all, it had gotten him in so much trouble in the past. Or was it something deeper, something he couldn't write off logically? Was faith pushing him now?

Columbo had come to him for answers. The little man from the Vatican probably knew Cross was the key and that Cross had once held the position of Lord Baltore. Cho had been assigned to the case, and it was her brother's blood spilled in a faraway monastery. Their lives had been saved by the man who should have died in a fall off a cliff. When their only way out was by using an antique airplane, Cho could fly it. And the car that held one of the keys was in Burke's own barn. And then there was Freedman and his connection to Meadows. Could fate have put all this together? Or was it chance? What were the odds? Maybe there was a greater power at work here. But if that was true, why bring them all to this point and then smash all their hopes? What was the purpose in that?

As he sat in his hotel room, an exhausted Burke glanced back at the items Mason had found in his search of the archives at the University of Illinois. Some of the pages actually filled in some holes in the story of Joseph Franklin Cross. The papers proved he knew Robert Todd Lincoln well, and the president's son had come to speak to the history professor's classes. The subject he covered always dealt with British-American affairs. That made sense, as Lincoln had once been an ambassador to Great Britain. But there was nothing pointing to a lost Bible book or a secret organization. So, just as Sonnenberg feared, the scroll must have gone down with the professor in the plane crash. It was the only obvious answer.

Burke looked across the room toward Cho. Just a few minutes before, she'd been studying the Bay Area views. Now she was sitting on the side of the bed glancing through Cross's date book.

"I'll give him this," Cho said, looking up from her research and pulling Burke out of his personal theological debate. Only when their eyes met did the woman continue. "Cross was a detailed type of guy. He even lists the flight number, time of departure, and type of plane he booked on his trip West. It seems he reserved a seat on TWA Flight 3 out of Indianapolis. It was due to leave on January 16 and arrive in Los Angeles later than night. He booked that flight on January 8."

"It fits," Burke replied. "That was the flight Lombard was on. I checked out the history of that flight online about an hour ago. It made several stops, including Albuquerque and Winslow before that final landing in Las Vegas to take on fuel. It crashed less than thirty minutes after that. Flew right into a mountain. No one has ever figured out exactly what went wrong."

"Nice information," Cho said, "but I'm not sure it fits with what we need to know."

"How so?" Burke said. "The plane crashed, Cross was on the flight, and he had the book. Sonnenberg looked at the crash site and didn't find it. That pretty much paints the whole picture."

Cho nodded. "If things had gone the way they had originally been intended, you are right. But the letter we found in Royal under the car seat was never mailed."

"Yes," Burke replied. "I know that. What does that have to do with anything?"

"I promised I would give you my theory on why the letter was still in the car. It seems our detail-oriented professor missed one small detail."

"What do you mean?" Burke asked. "What detail?"

Cho put Cross's old date book on the bed. She twisted her face in a quirky kind of expression Burke had never seen before. For an instant, she seemed like a little girl with a big secret.

"In a Special Forces mission or an FBI operation, everyone has to be on the same page," she explained. "Everyone has to have all the information. If one person is not aware of just one seemingly minor detail, then the whole mission might fail. Thus we go over things again and again and again."

"I still don't see what that has to do with Cross," Burke cut in.

"I'm getting to it," she assured him. "Cross was that kind of person. His class notes, his plans, even his reservations were done in great detail. Remember the map? He drew a map for Sonnenberg even though the man had been to the meeting point before. Cross left nothing to chance. But, when he found out that the elder Krueger was on his tail, he must have panicked."

Cho paused, pushed a strand of hair from in front of her left eye, then continued. "Cross and Sonnenberg were communicating by mail. Cross wrote a letter to Sonnenberg telling him of a change in plans. You read it, but for some reason, Cross didn't mail it. Sonnenberg never got the letter."

"Maybe," Burke suggested, "Cross decided not to change from the original meeting time and place."

"No," Cho argued, "if that were the case, he would have torn up those papers and thrown them away. I think something spooked him enough he thought he'd mailed the letter and he hadn't. Remember it had stamps on it? So maybe he actually believed he'd mailed it with other stuff and never realized it had fallen through the car seat."

"You think?" Burke asked.

"Sure," she replied. "I once had a whole batch of Christmas cards fall through my seat and didn't find them for months, and that was in a car where you could see under the seat. The back of the Packard's front seat went clear to the floor. Once you lost something under that seat, it stayed lost until you removed the cushion. Imagine this scene. You are sure Krueger is on your tail. You can't just leave the letter to Sonnenberg in plain sight before you mail it. So you slip it in with the other mail, between something you are carrying—like some books. The weight of the books pushes the seat cushion down. Maybe when he moved to get the stuff to mail, the envelope fell between the cushions. If he had been mailing several manila envelopes at the time, which wouldn't have been unusual for a professor, he would have never noticed."

"But the letter to the district attorney?" Burke said. "It was in there too."

"Yes," Cho said. "Cross was scared of Krueger. He was sure the man was watching him. He had no doubt Krueger might kill him. Cross trusted Sonnenberg. So, if he was murdered, the letter to Philadelphia would be mailed by his friend after his death, and Sarah Meadows' murder would be solved. That was the only way Cross could make sure that happened. And, if he and Sonnenberg did meet, then Cross could just take the letter to the DA back to Illinois with him. But he messed up. He didn't realize he hadn't mailed the envelope."

Burke rubbed his chin. The more he thought about the theory, the more it made sense. "If that was the case, Sonnenberg didn't know of the meeting change."

"And that means everything," Cho explained. "This goes back to what I was talking about—one element of a detailed plan messing up everything else. Sonnenberg knew Cross was going to be on that plane. So he raced to help in the search. He would've already known that everyone was dead. He was there to try to find the book. But he struck out. And the fact that he didn't get that letter is why."

"I'm not following you," Burke replied.

"As I said," Cho continued, "Cross booked the flight ahead of time, but according to his notes in this date book, he changed the reservation on January 12. He was on the flight when it left Indianapolis, but his new reservation didn't include Los Angeles. He also killed his connecting flight to San Francisco."

"What?" Burke was more confused than ever.

"His new reservation ended in Vegas," Cho explained. "That's where Cross got off."

"You're kidding."

"No," she said, "that's what it says here. The scroll would have left the plane when Cross deplaned in Vegas. So there was no *Book of Joseph* for Sonnenberg to find in the wreckage."

Burke jumped from the chair and grabbed his briefcase. He studied an old yellowing piece of newspaper that Cho had put with Cross's archival papers. There was a bold headline: "ILLINOIS PROFESSOR DIES IN NEVADA PLANE CRASH!"

The story continued for several paragraphs. Then came an interesting detail that Burke hadn't noticed when he'd first read the story.

> There will be a university memorial service for Dr. J. Franklin Cross but no burial, as his body was not recovered at the crash site. While some cling to hope that he might have somehow survived, witnesses saw Dr. Cross on the flight as it left Indianapolis. With such extensive damage and the fire that followed, it was assumed the body was completely consumed.

"You're on to something," Burke said. "No body recovered at the site was identified as being Cross."

He pulled another piece of paper from his materials and hurried back to Cho's side, joining her on the bed. His words shot out like fireworks on Independence Day. "Here's the map. We might be able to actually figure this thing out now. We have a location! This is where he was when the plane went down."

She glanced at the crude drawing and shook her head. "We could study that thing for months and not make anything of it, but I'm betting our people can."

"We're going to Vegas," Burke said.

She grinned. Her look was intoxicating, maybe even lethal. For a moment he almost forgot everything. But just for a moment. She had put legs once more to their quest. She had given him — dare he think it? — a dose of faith! Maybe everything in life did happen for a reason. Maybe every person who came into his life was also there for a reason.

POTOSI

Burke called Mason to his room. Not wanting to wait until morning, the team hurried to the FBI's San Francisco headquarters, where they presented the map to lab tech Mitchell Vire.

Vire appeared to be in his early thirties, but his hair was silver and matched his mustache. So he was either older than he looked or the world of technology had caused gray to creep in much sooner than it should have. Wire glasses rested on his long, thin nose, and his pale skin assured Burke that the man rarely roamed very far from his lab. Vampires had more color than Vire.

"Okay," Vire said as he scanned the document into his computer, "you're thinking this hand-drawn map was of something in the mountains outside of Las Vegas."

"That's our best guess," Cho answered.

"And the year?" Vire asked.

"January 1942."

Vire put his software to work. Thousands of images flew across the screen in the next five minutes, but there were no matches. The lab tech must have noted the worry on Burke's face. "This might take a while."

"If you find anything," Burke replied.

"Oh, we'll find something," Vire assured him. "What I'm concerned about is finding too many places this map might fit. We have no scale and no numbers or letters. So we'll have difficulty narrowing it down."

It took twenty-one minutes and thirty-two seconds for the search to end. Burke knew the exact time by the counter in the corner of the sixty-inch monitor that was affixed to the far wall. As the results flashed up, Burke also realized Vire's fears had been realized. The computer the lab tech called Betsy had given him five possible matches. The distance from one to another was in one case more than two hundred miles. It would take weeks or even months to search that much terrain.

"You said 1942," Vire said, glancing at the five possible locations. "What I'm going to do now is import maps from that time frame. That will give us roads that were in existence during that year."

They watched as the geek performed his magic. Thanks to the new information, within minutes the five locations had melted down to two.

"So," Burke said, "it's likely one of these two?"

"There is no guarantee of that," Vire replied, "but I feel pretty sure the location you're looking for is on one of these two mountains."

"Well," Cho replied, "it might be a needle, but now there are only two haystacks."

"I know both of those areas," a voice behind them said. "In fact I know them as well as Lisa Marie knows the back streets of Galesburg."

Cho turned toward the door and smiled. "Saunders, what brings you to the West Coast?"

The five-foot-nine-inch man laughed as he reached for Cho's hand. She didn't shake. Instead she opened her arms and hugged him. He smiled, patting her on the back before explaining, "Agency business. Following a lead on a human-trafficking case."

"So you're working both coasts now!" Mason said while reaching out to grab the agent's hand.

"It appears so," Saunders replied. "I just flew in. When they told me you were here, I wanted to come by and see you. It's been a while since you've been back to the DC office. This murder case in Illinois must be keeping you busy."

"Yeah," Cho replied, "it has been. Nothing like life back in our New York days. Much simpler then."

It was obvious that Cho and Saunders had a history. Burke couldn't help wondering what had happened during those New York days that caused her to hug the man rather than just shake his hand. That seemed so unlike her.

"You say you know this area?" Vire asked.

Mason jumped in before Saunders could answer. "This is one of the West Coast's best geeks, Mitchell Vire."

The two men nodded to each other as Saunders said, "Nice meeting you, and yes I do know this area. Grew up hiking in those mountains. What are you looking for?"

"A location for some missing merchandise," Mason said.

"I see," Saunders replied. "Then you probably need to search the spot on the left. That's Mummy Mountain. Much easier to get to. If you're going to hide something, makes sense to put it where you won't have to work too hard to retrieve it."

Cho and Vire studied the location as the latter began loading information to plot a course to the spot.

Mason looked over their shoulders. "Probably the place we need to start then. Thanks. Good seeing you. I'm sure you have to be going. The case. What did you say it was?"

"Ah ... human-trafficking," Saunders answered. "Good to see you. And you're right, Clark, I need to go meet an informant. Want to get there early and check out the surroundings. You can never be too careful."

"No, you can't," Mason replied. "Thanks, Greg."

Burke was a bit surprised by Mason's tone. He seemed abrupt. Dismissive. Yet as the other agent didn't react, Burke passed it off as his imagination.

Saunders, a smile filling his face, said, "Lisa, we must get together soon for dinner."

"I'd love to," she replied.

Burke frowned. There *was* a history here, and it involved more than just working on a case.

Saunders looked toward Burke. "Nice meeting you, Dr. Burke."

"And you," Burke answered. After Saunders left the room, Burke said, "Nice guy. Lucky he walked in."

"Real lucky," Mason quipped as he turned back to the screen. "Vire, tell me about the site on the right."

"Well, it's a rugged spot on Mt. Potosi. Not much up there. The reason it showed up was because there was a rough road up this side of the mountain back in 1942, but that's gone now."

"Can you look up some history on the site?" Mason asked.

Vire punched in a few quick instructions, and Besty went back to work. Within seconds the tech was reading the information to his guests.

"Interesting. I can't give you details on where the map leads, but I can tell you a famous plane crash took place on the other side of this peak."

"Carole Lombard," Cho noted.

"You're good," Vire replied.

"Anything else?" Mason asked.

"Well, except for those interested in seeing the crash site, not much goes on there. Evidently several old mine shafts are still around there. This article warns hikers to stay away from them as they are dangerous. The summit is about 8,500 feet high."

"Mining," Burke said. "The other Cross brother headed up the family's mining interests. At least that's what Major Cho told me. So Dr. Cross must have used one of his brother's places as a retreat."

"Doubt it," Mason cut in. "Whatever's on Potosi is not important. Vire, print out the information on Mummy Mountain. Saunders probably has it right. He knows the area. We'll start there."

Burke began to protest, but Mason cut him off with a quick wave of the hand. "Mummy is the word," the agent added. If it was meant as a pun, it wasn't funny.

Five minutes later, when they were back in the car, Burke finally got to issue his protest. "We need to go to Potosi."

Mason ignored him, instead shooting an order to Cho. "Turn right at the next corner and pull over to the curb. There's a place we need to try there. They have the best steaks in town."

As Cho pulled into an open parking space, Mason put his finger to his lips. Only after Burke had seen and acknowledged his action did Mason say, in a louder than normal tone, as if he was excited about the place, "You have to try the food here. I recommend the sirloin. But the ribs are good too."

Burke was confused. None of this made any sense. What was Mason up to?

Wordlessly Mason led them away from the car and into the diner. It defined the term "greasy spoon." It hardly looked like a place that could produce good burgers much less great steak.

"I should've worn my best gown," Cho muttered, obviously as unimpressed as Burke.

As this was a "seat yourself" kind of place, Mason picked a booth in the back. Except for one elderly man sipping a cup of coffee, they were alone.

After they were seated Mason, this time his voice barely audible, looked to Cho. "Did you notice Saunders called Burke by name as he left?"

"Yeah," she replied, "you introduced him when he came in. What's strange about that?"

"I only introduced Vire," Mason corrected his partner.

"Are you sure?" She seemed shocked.

"Yes. I made sure I only introduced the tech."

"Well," Cho replied, "he knew we were working on Jeff's case. He recognized him from photos." She didn't sound nearly as confident as she should have.

"Maybe, but why would he assume Jeff would be with us? We don't take civilians along on missions."

Cho started to answer, but her words seemed to catch in her thoat.

Mason nodded. "You may not like it, and he may be your friend, and in the past he may have meant even more to you, but—and I'll use one of your sayings—dollars to donuts, Saunders is the mole we've been looking for. And that means Krueger knows we're here."

She looked to Mason. "You think the car is bugged?"

"Yes," he replied. "Bet it also has a GPS tracker. He's following our every move."

Burke watched as the color quickly faded from Cho's face.

"Suggestions?" she whispered.

"We grab a bite to eat," Mason said. "They think we're going to Mummy. Saunders will tell Krueger that. That buys us some time."

"Okay, who can we trust to not blow our cover?"

"Now that we know who the mole is," Mason replied, "everyone else."

"You were assigned to this coast for a while," Cho shot back. "Call someone you trust and have them come and pick up the car. Tell them to drive it to San Diego, and don't let anyone know what they're doing."

Mason laughed. "Will do. That will keep Krueger hopping for a while."

"Let's hope," Cho replied. "Now we'll have to toss our cell phones." She grinned. "No, better than ditch them, let's drop them in the mail. Send them to three different locations."

"Won't fool them for long," Mason said, "but it's something. We can't use any credit cards, and I doubt if any of us has any cash."

"We have to have some money," Cho noted. "We need a plane, and when we get to Vegas we'll need equipment as well as a car there."

"Let me call Nicole Eady at the office," Mason said. "I think I know how to score some cash."

Mason hurried over to the phone booth and dropped in a few coins.

Burke should have been quaking in his boots. Yet for some reason he wasn't. The odds of his staying alive might be even slimmer now than the odds of finding the book. Yet as this played out, he began to wonder if he wasn't meant to be the keeper of the book. Maybe fate or Providence or even God had deemed that he was his generation's Lord Baltore.

Mason was grinning when he came back to the table. "Nicole's set. She'll pick up the car in thirty minutes. I got a place to leave the keys for it."

"What about the money?" Cho asked.

"Ah, this is really sweet. Just as I figured, there's a suitcase full of cash in the back of the vehicle Saunders checked out tonight. He's supposed to use it to pay off the informant. It's just up the street."

"Won't he see you?" Burke noted.

"No, he's across town with the informant scouting out the place where the raid will take place later tonight. Agent Ruford is at the car. And Nicole just gave him orders to give the money to me. Ruford thinks I'm taking it to Saunders at a new pickup spot. After we meet, Ruford gets the night off. Wish I could see Saunders' face when he gets back."

"Better yet," Cho added, "I'd like to see how he's going to explain this to the informant."

Mason was all smiles. "Let's eat and then hit our friendly ATM machine."

DOUBTS

The clock was ticking and Cho was worried. They may have momentarily thrown Krueger off their trail by ditching their car and cell phones and giving Saunders false information, but it wouldn't be long before he would no doubt find them.

As Burke sat on a bench in a small city park, Cho made a call on her just purchased disposable cell phone. One call was all it took to give her the location she needed.

"Clark," she said as she slipped the phone into her jacket pocket, "go get the money, then grab our stuff from the motel."

"Make sure you get my bag," Burke added.

"Get everything," Cho said. "Then meet us at the small airport just outside Oakland called Ried Port."

"Got it. See you all in a couple hours."

Cho's eyes followed her partner as he jogged down the street to the meeting Agent Eady had arranged with Saunders' partner. They would soon have the cash they would need in Vegas. Now it was time for her to make sure they could get there quickly.

As worries crowded her mind, she turned toward Burke and was surprised that he seemed as happy as a husband who has just found the perfect Christmas gift for his wife. His life was on the line, yet he was all but laughing. He was still smiling when he flagged down a cab and slid in beside her in the back seat.

"What's stoking your fire?"

He grinned. "I've got a card up my sleeve."

"Whatever," she shot back.

She gave the cabbie the address, leaned back, and closed her eyes. Sleep would be at a premium for a while. Had to grab it when she could.

OLD FRIENDS

From the looks of it, the airstrip was only used by individuals and perhaps a few small companies. It was obvious no commercial flights ever called Ried Port home. A call to her father had assured her that this was the place she could obtain a plane without drawing attention from anyone. It likely wouldn't be anything fancy. And that was fine. All they needed was something to get them safely from point A to point B. Yet it was the second point that gave the agent an unsettled feeling.

As the cab pulled up next to a small portable building, Cho turned her eyes to the six hangars on the other side of the concrete.

Burke must have noticed her gaze because he smiled and popped a question. It was hardly one she wanted to hear. "Are we safe?"

She shrugged.

"My gut tells me we are," he assured her, "but my mind tells something far different."

For the moment, the book meant nothing to her. Yet he did. He meant a great deal to her and that was the problem. Because of that creeping cancer called love, she couldn't stay focused, Yet she needed to focus. Lives depended upon her! It was time to go to work. Time to stop being concerned about matters of the heart. The long ride, her head resting on his shoulder, had stolen her focus. How could she get it back?

Pulling herself from the car, she paid the driver and, after the cab left, trudged into a cheap metal building. The office looked smaller on the inside than on the outside. The metal building looked like a purchase at a Lowe's or Home Depot that was assembled on-site. It was ten feet by twelve feet and contained three items: a desk, a file cabinet, and a small refrigerator. It was like nowhere she'd ever been or wanted to be again. Worse yet, the man who ran the place had likely obtained his pilot's license during the Truman administration.

"My dad called you about a plane," Cho announced as they entered.

The manager's smile, which was quick and easy, revealed chipped, yellowing, tobacco-stained teeth. Cho couldn't tell if there was much hair under the San Francisco Giant's cap, but he did sport a busy silver mustache.

His answer was as quick as it was friendly. "Got one for you, and it's a beauty. Major Cho said you'd love it." His accent seemed to indicate Midwestern roots — maybe Kansas or Nebraska.

"Can it hold four?" she asked.

"Lots more than that," he bragged. "It's a DC-3. Built during World War II. Fine bird it is!"

"A seventy-year-old plane is all you have?" Cho asked.

The man nodded. "Not all I got, but it's the one your father told me to give you. It's a good plane," he assured her. "I bought it from some drug runners. They did excellent maintenance on the old gal."

"You actually bought if off drug smugglers?" Cho shot back, her voice registering disbelief.

"Not actually," he admitted, his blue eyes laughing as he spoke. "I bought it at a government auction. But they seized it from drug runners. You need to check out the instrumentation. They added the latest of everything. The engines probably don't have two hundred hours on them. I thought it'd look cool here at the airport, so I actually put the seats and stuff back in the main cabin to return it to its passenger service days' appearance. It reminds me of the movie *Casablanca*. I can picture it taking off in the fog with Ingrid Bergman looking back at Bogie."

Burke glanced at Cho. She shrugged and said, "Let me check it out. Dollars to donuts, it has to be at least as good as our last ride."

"I haven't heard that one in a long time," the man said with a grin. "Your grandfather said it all the time. The plane's in the blue hangar. The side door's open. And because your grandfather and I served together, there is no charge. I owe him my life."

"Really?" Cho asked.

"Yep. And last time I saw you, you were about two feet high. Your pop is sure proud of you."

"Thanks," Cho said, a barely perceptible smile framing her lips. "I've got another guy coming in a few minutes. Send him over when he gets here. And thanks."

OUT OF THE NIGHT

It was cool and slightly cloudy, pretty much like every other San Francisco evening, but the steady breeze and the unforgiving dampness penetrated Cho's skin and pushed down through hard muscle to her bones. It was funny that she'd never really been cold in Afghanistan and now was shivering in California. But the haunting feeling she had was not caused by the cold. As Cho walked with Burke across the tarmac, she felt eyes on her. A quick glance proved there was no one with them, but the thought of being observed hung on like a bad dream, causing her to pick up her pace while crossing the two hundred feet of concrete.

As promised, the hangar's side door was open and a flip of a light switch revealed a relic from a much different age. And as they were on a wild trek to find an ancient scroll, maybe it was appropriate they kept getting rides in vintage aircraft.

A quick survey indicated the plane lived up to promises. It was painted with TWA logos and shined like it must have when it came out of the factory. Not only were the instruments updated but so were the engines. So in a sense, while it might have seemed vintage, under the skin, this was almost a brand-new plane. She was impressed!

"So it'll work?" Burke asked.

She'd forgotten he was with her; his words startled her just a bit. Yet not enough for her to take her eyes from the plane and fix them on the professor. "No doubt," she replied confidently. "Why don't you check if Mason is here while I do my checkup."

As Burke jogged back to the office, Cho reentered the old bird and sat down in the captain's chair. She smiled as her hands touched the wheel. A few days before, she'd gotten to fly this plane's older sister, and now she had been given the opportunity to take the helm of perhaps the most legendary model in aviation history. Suddenly life was good!

A quick ten-minute inspection proved the plane was everything promised. Seeing no reason to simply sit and wait for the other two to join her, she pushed the hangar's sliding doors open to ready for their departure. They were so well oiled, they made no noise as they rolled. As the night air rushed in, another chill hit her spine. Something else hit her as well. It was something she couldn't put her finger on. Once more the night seemed haunted, and she had the sense that something was wrong.

She had taken two short steps out into the darkness when she saw Mason. He must have just arrived. He looked like their Afghan pack mule. He was carrying three suitcases with a couple of backpacks slung over his shoulders. She started to call out, but stopped before a sound left her throat. He wasn't alone. Two men were walking in step with him. One on one side and the other a full two paces behind. Though she couldn't see their faces, the escorts were holding guns. Not friendly. It was more of us versus them. So much for thinking life was good.

She waited in the darkness for the trio to pass and then silently fell in about thirty feet behind them. Moving like a shadow, she quickly made up ground. At this rate she'd be up on them when they were fifty feet from the office. That would put them in an area where planes were fueled. Gunplay might ignite a fire, so it was important to be quick and efficient when she made her move.

On silent feet, she took two strides to the trio's one. Thirty seconds later, she placed one hand over the trailing man's mouth and the other around his neck. Her actions were smooth and sure. The man crumpled without so much as a moan escaping his lips. Mason and the other man noticed nothing.

Her eyes never leaving the other two, Cho carefully lowered the man to the ground, grabbed the fallen foe's gun, and hurried to catch up. When she was two paces behind the pair, she slowed to a walk. Falling into the position the previous hood had recently occupied, she strolled in step with Mason and his captor.

No reason to hurry. She was in complete control. She could cleanly kill the man at any moment. It was something she'd done before as a Ranger, and this would be much easier. She even had the luxury of choosing an option. She could deliver a round into the back of his head or just break his neck. As she weighed those options, another thought crept into head. Who was this man? Was he another of Krueger's henchmen? What was his story and why had he volunteered for the mission? Or had he volunteered? Maybe he was ordered or drafted. What were his motives?

These questions suddenly bothered Cho. On the battlefield and even as an agent, she'd never thought about them until viewing the body. But now she couldn't help thinking about her potential victim. Was he married? Did he have children? Would there be a mother left to mourn him?

Focus on the objective, not on the fact the enemy has personal hopes and dreams. That had been drilled into her head over and over again for years. That kind of thinking made the enemy no more than a rock to knock aside. But now she realized that was never the case. This man, as well as the one she'd dropped a few moments before, were people. They had hopes and dreams like she did. Maybe they were even falling in love like she was.

They were thirty feet past the fueling station and less than twenty feet from the office when it became apparent she had to make her move. Death or life? It was in her hands. What was the man's fate? She suddenly wished it were someone else having to answer that question.

Silently doubling her steps, she pushed the pistol against the man's head. As cold metal struck his skull she barked, "Drop the gun or die."

She didn't have a chance to pull the trigger and the man didn't have an opportunity to react. Mason spun, knocking the weapon out of his captor's hand as he brought a right cross to the chin. Four more quick blows followed, leaving the man lying in a messy heap on the concrete, out cold.

"Thanks, Cho." Mason bent to pick up the man's gun. "Take a look. It is our friend Saunders. I found one GPS bug in the suitcase. Must have been another. He got here just after I did and got the drop on me."

Cho glanced down at a man she once thought of as much more than a colleague. Emotions cloud judgment, but in Saunders' case, it must have blinded her.

"What about the other guy?" Mason asked.

"He needs a medic, not an undertaker," she explained.

"Great," he said, his eyes never leaving the form on the ground. "We'll tie these guys up and have some of our guys take them to some nice accommodations. Don't know about the other guy, but Saunders is not going to be smelling fresh air for a long time."

A door slammed. Cho automatically pushed her weapon toward the noise. It was only Burke.

"Hey, guys," he shouted from just beyond the office door, "you have any problems?"

Mason waved. "Nothing a quick call to headquarters can't take care of."

"You make the call," Cho replied, "and Jeff and I will drag these two over to the hangar. Oh, and tell the manager where we are stowing the trash. He can be trusted. He's an old family friend."

Mason glanced through the doors into the lighted building. "Is that our plane?"

"Sure is. Let's get this taken care of and fly out of here."

Cho and Burke dragged the unconscious men across the pavement and, using duct tape, secured them in the corner of the DC-3 hangar. She was glad they were alive. At least she thought she was. And that was the problem. Her once-decisive mind was now filled with questions, and she was no longer sure how she felt about anything.

"What was that all about?" Burke asked as he fell into stride behind her.

She offered nothing more until the two were sitting in the cockpit. As she waited for Mason, she turned to Burke and asked a strange question: "Do you follow auto racing?"

"Not really," he replied.

She could feel his eyes on her as she began her story. Why was she telling it? She didn't know. Maybe it was just an attempt to get a handle on her suddenly very raw emotions.

"My dad used to talk about a man named Jackie Stewart. He was one of the best drivers in the world. He won so often because he raced on the edge—meaning he pushed the car and himself beyond what other drivers would. One day he was going a couple hundred miles an hour on the oval track, cars were all around him—it was just another day of racing—when he suddenly realized that what he was doing was crazy. He was tempting fate and doing it willingly. He parked the car and quit. He never went back to racing."

"Good story," Burke said. "Takes a wise man to know when to quit. But what's the point?"

He was not applying the story to her situation. As much as she wanted him to, he couldn't connect the dots.

"Let me explain it another way," Cho said. Turning her face to a point where their eyes locked, she measured her words carefully. "There was once a great boxer. He was unbeatable until his punches killed another man in the ring." She let the reality of that picture hover in the air for a few seconds. "Before that moment, every opponent had been nothing more than a soulless dummy. After that fight, where he beat a man to death, he no longer saw a human punching bag in front of him, he saw someone with family. He saw someone with hopes and dreams. He saw himself."

Burke was obviously still confused. She needed to quit using analogies and move directly to matters of the heart. This was not something she was good at.

"Jeff," she began, struggling to find the words, "you know I like ..."

That was lame. Why couldn't she just say it?

"Jeff," she whispered, her voice now a bit shaky, "I'm that race-car driver. I'm suddenly scared of everything that has to do with my job. I'm the boxer. I no longer see the enemy as a shapeless, inhuman form."

"O-kay," he replied, "but—"

"No," she said, cutting him off in mid-thought by placing her index finger gently on his lips. "I don't think I can be an agent any-more. I don't think I have the nerve or the stomach for it. And I think you're the reason."

"Me?"

He still didn't get it. And the words that would spell it out clearly were words that were far too hard to say. There was only one thing to do and, as the clock was ticking, it had to be done now. Her lips quickly found his. She felt his arms move around her. For a moment there was no *Book of Joseph*, no wars, no terrorists, no other people.

Then she heard a noise. This time she knew there was no cause for alarm. Mason was pushing the bags into the plane.

Pulling back, away from Jeff, she quickly turned to stare out the windshield. She couldn't look at him. She couldn't let him see what was clearly written in her eyes.

A few seconds later, Mason was onboard and the door was closed. It was time to fire up the engines and head for Las Vegas. But the pilot who'd be taking them there was no longer a gambler. She'd found something that pushed her to cherish life—not just her own, but all life. And she wondered what she'd do now, if faced with another moment when she had to pull the trigger in order to save herself or a friend or someone who might be even more. Could she do it? She prayed she would never have to answer that question again.

END OF THE CLIMB

The flight was uneventful. The DC-3 ran like it did when new, maybe better. Their landing had been as perfect as their take-off. Just as promised by the plane's owner, the small desert field was deserted and a large empty hangar was waiting for them. After pulling into the vintage World War II building, the trio spent the rest of the night sleeping in the DC-3. At eight they called a cab and rode into the gambling capital of the world, where they used a bit of the cash Mason had "borrowed" and bought a solid 1988 Buick off a used-car lot. A quick trip to a sporting-goods store supplied them with climbing gear. A final stop secured some food. By noon they were on the mountain and working their way up what had once been an old mining road.

The country was rugged but beautiful. Small shrubs peeked out from a dusting of snow. Even a bit of green grass could still be seen. But the plant life wasn't what took Burke's breath away. The views were amazing! On one side were mountain vistas and on the other the flat desert. It was a panorama of contrast, and if they hadn't been trying to get to an old abandoned cabin before Bruno Krueger, Burke would have labeled this one of the most incredible visual experiences of his life. If he managed to live through this adventure or even this day, he vowed to come back as a simple climber. And he hoped he wouldn't be coming alone.

The trek was not difficult, but because of the steep grade and thin air, it was hard work that demanded they stop often to rest. During each of those breaks, Burke's eyes wandered over to Cho. Finally, just after three, she caught him looking and asked, "What do you expect to find?"

Quickly moving his gaze to Mount Potosi, Burke shrugged. He was glad the first words she had said since their kiss were about the mission. Those answers were easy. Those thoughts spewed out rather than catching in his throat.

"I don't know," he admitted, not allowing himself to look back toward the woman. "I'm hoping for clues. And if this was the last place Cross was before he died, if he had the document with him during that trip, then we might find even more. But I'm afraid the mining office we're going to has been stripped clean. Even though this is rugged country, it's likely that several hundred people have visited where we're going since that day so many years ago. This might be the end of the road. Our mystery might never be solved."

"And if that is the case, do you move on?"

"What do you think?" he replied. It was a question he wished he'd answered differently because there was nothing in his words that even hinted at his being involved with her in the future. And that was the problem. He thought selfishly like a man who had room for no one else in his life.

Her answer put that rigid view into words. "You will keep looking for it until the day you die."

She quickly stepped past him and continued up the trail. His eyes followed her until she'd slipped around a rock wall. She was right. Even though he might say it was over, it would never be over as long as he had breath in his body. The scroll would haunt and drive him as it had Columbo. It was in complete control of not just this moment but of his entire future. If that was true, then there would be no room in his life for anyone else. Not even Lisa Marie Cho.

As they silently worked their way farther up the mountain, Burke continued to beat himself up. He was a fool. Cho had given him an opening. She wanted to know if the kiss had meant anything, and he'd acted as though the only thing on his mind was the mission. And worst of all, he knew himself well enough to realize she was right. His curiosity was both a gift and a cancer. It left no room for anything else.

Burke was immeasurably grateful when he rounded a bend and

came upon a flat spot on the mountain. There in front of him, at just over 6,000 feet, was the old mining camp. Now he had something else to focus on rather than his own compulsive behavior and his convoluted emotions.

As he studied the scene in front of him, he thought of the story of the three little pigs. The only thing left standing at the ancient site was the office. The other buildings, quickly constructed, had been beaten to the ground by mountain winds decades before. Now, except for a few piles of lumber, they were gone. Yet the office had been built of rock. So while a small part of its tin roof was on the ground about fifty feet to the west, the building was still standing.

Scores of climbers had left names and dates scratched on the walls of the office. "Bob 1974" could be read, as could "Jim and Sue 1983." The most recent bit of graffiti had been scrawled by someone named "Jason" in 2007. Each of them had been here and left their mark. But what had they taken with them?

No one said anything as Burke tracked across a couple of inches of ice-crusted snow to the partially open front door. Stepping into the old building proved that his worst fears had been realized. There was a desk, a couple of overturned chairs, some candles, and a few empty shelves, but nothing else.

Moving by the fireplace, he opened a door into a small room. There was a bed, another chair, a broken nightstand, and an empty closet. Hearing footsteps behind him, he turned.

"About what you expected?" Cho asked.

Her question didn't need to be answered. It was exactly what he figured he'd find. Yet having his expectations realized didn't soften the blow.

He dropped his backpack by the door and walked back out into the open air. Shielding his eyes from the snow's glare, he glanced up toward the peak. A mineshaft was up there. An old map he'd studied online had shown its location. Now it was a matter of finding it and hoping it hadn't fallen in on itself.

He led the way as they trekked up an old trail toward where they knew the mineshaft had to be. It was now their only shot. If they struck out, the quest would be over. There were no other options. But he knew that if their search failed, the scroll would continue to haunt him. In fact, Lisa was right, he'd never quit looking.

The trail to the shaft was little more than a semi-smooth spot in the grade. Evidence that it had seen human traffic included a few empty bottles and some crumpled and faded food wrappers.

"Look at this," Mason said as he bent and picked up an old horseshoe.

"Pack animal," Burke explained as he continued moving forward and upward. "Likely came from the old mining days. Hope it means we're in for some luck."

Twenty minutes later, he stopped and stared at some brush growing beside a wall. Pulling out a copy of Cross's old map, he studied the professor's drawing. At the end of a line, right where the old history professor had placed a cross, was a slight hook. Initially Burke figured it was simply a hurried man picking up a pencil and leaving a mark that meant nothing. Now, as he studied the terrain in front of him, he sensed that Cross meant what he drew.

"Is that the shaft?" Mason asked.

"Yeah," Burke replied as he walked over to the shrubs. Yet rather than stop and look behind the bushes for the opening he knew was there, he continued around the edge of the rock face and to the right. Another twenty steps brought him to a place where the rock wall had a natural split about five feet wide and perhaps thirty feet deep. As it had no roof, it was not a cave, and it offered no shelter from the elements, so most climbers would have walked right by it.

To confirm his theory, Burke looked again at Cross's map, then stepped into the gap and walked to the back wall. To his left there was an eight-foot-tall bush. Peeking out from behind it was a wooden door that probably covered a mineshaft not on the survey maps. This had to be where Cross was directing Sonnenberg. This was the meeting place! What was still here?

It was quickly apparent that Burke was not the first to find the old shaft. At some time in the past, two climbers had left their names scrawled over the door, but it appeared no one had entered. The solidly built wooden covering looked to be undisturbed. Maybe they had caught a break. Concentrating so hard on his discovery, Burke didn't notice the other two join him.

"So how did you find this?"

Cho's voice caused his heart to momentarily leap into his throat. Once the hairs on the back of his neck laid down, he replied, "The map. I think this is where they were supposed to meet. We assumed the office or the shaft, but Cross was a precise person. The final crook in the path leading to the place where he drew the cross wouldn't have been a mistake. There was no final curve leading to the main shaft. So I moved on around the wall."

"Interesting," Mason said. "You seem to be getting pretty good at profiling. By getting inside Cross's head, by knowing his habits and tendencies, you went past the obvious to the real objective. Jeff, there might be a place for you in the FBI."

"Maybe," Burke replied, "but not likely. Remember, none of what I think has been proven. And it won't be until we open this door."

"That won't be hard," Mason replied. "It might fall over if we just blow on it."

It was more stubborn than that, but not by much. A few well-placed blows from a pickax separated the hinges from the wood. Then it was just a matter of cutting enough brush to pull the door away from the mine shaft.

As Cho and Mason pushed the old barricade to one side, Burke peered in. The sunshine penetrated only about four feet into the opening. He saw nothing of interest.

"Going to need some light," Burke announced.

"I've got a couple of Maglites," Mason replied, reaching in his backpack. Cho also pulled one from hers.

"Look at this," Cho said, pointing to the back of the door they had just removed. "This thing was locked on the inside. See the old padlock that is still attached to the wall. It came off the door when we moved it. If it was locked from the inside, there must be another entrance somewhere. We have to be coming in the back door."

As Cho continued to examine the clasp and lock, Burke studied what he could see of the shaft. He could make out little until Mason directed his beam into the man-made chamber. A cursory inspection revealed that nothing had collapsed, the framing appeared solid, and there were even a few oil lanterns left on the floor. Best of all, it was untouched by time or the explorers that had made the trek up the mountain.

"Looks solid," Mason noted. Yet he didn't appear eager to prove that assessment. For several seconds, no one moved. Finally Mason stepped in and worked his way forward. The others followed in single file, with Burke second and Cho last. Thirty feet into the man-made chamber, the shaft ended. To their right was a door. The trio gathered around the entry and studied the knob, then glanced toward each other. With no one seeming to be ready to make the next move, Burke reached down and gave the knob a twist. The door latch released. The hinges screamed as the old door swung open. Again he was greeted by darkness.

As Burke stood in the doorway, Mason and Cho swung their lights into the small room. The beams caught three chairs, a table, a shelf with a few ancient cans of beans, some dusty plates and cups, and three books. Fishing equipment and a .22 rifle were leaning up against a wall. To see more, Burke was forced to step in.

To his right was a bed. It was not empty. A man was lying there. Actually it was not a man, but rather a still-dressed mummified body. He was even wearing his shoes.

As the flashlights played on the long-dead form, Cho calmly walked over to it. Carefully she reached into the coat pocket and retrieved a leather wallet. She held it in the beam of Mason's flashlight.

"See if that lantern will light," she said. "It'll do a better job tossing light all over the room than this flashlight."

Mason moved to the oil lamp, picked it up off the ground, and placed it on a table. Burke could hear liquid sloshing. The flashlight revealed a good wick. Dropping his pack off his shoulders and to the floor, the agent fished out a lighter, and a few seconds later a small flame appeared on the lamp. The light was low and unsteady until Mason adjusted the wick height. While not bright, with the glass globe in place, the lantern provided dim illumination for the entire room. When two more lamps were lit, the team cut the power on their flashlights. Flickering flames danced behind the glass globes. Their trek back in time now seemed complete.

Pulling up a chair, Cho opened the dry well-worn leather wallet. She pulled out several bills, including a half dozen ones printed in 1934, the last year for a couple of decades that the dollar bill was designated as a silver certificate. Along with the money came a few pieces of paper with notes on them. There was a driver's license. She checked the date. It had expired.

"This is Joseph Franklin Cross," she announced. "He evidently died right here, in this bed."

Burke's eyes fell back to the man. His skin was dark and leathery. He looked more like a movie prop than a history professor. Yet there was something that remained evident — even in death there was a sense of refinement in his bearing. He might have been in an old mine shaft, but he was wearing a suit and tie. There was a timepiece partially exposed in his vest pocket. A fountain pen was clipped to the inside pocket of his suitcoat.

Burke looked at Cross's right hand. His boney fingers were clutching a leather attaché case that was resting on the room's stone floor.

THE CODE

Cross didn't give up the attaché case easily. Burke had to pry it from his hand. And there was no time to be dainty. Parts of two fingers fell to the floor when the bag finally came loose. Burke doubted that Cross would have cared.

Moving to the table, Burke fiddled with the latch and then unzipped the top. Inside was one compartment divided into three sections. There was nothing in the first two. The final one contained a book.

Burke pulled it out and placed it on the table. It was about the size of a mass-market hardcover novel, but much thinner. There was no title on the black leather cover. Inside was carefully done handwriting. Because of the unmailed envelope and the boxes of classroom records, Burke had seen enough of Cross's penmanship to know it was his.

"It's a journal," Burke explained to Cho and Mason, who were eagerly looking over his shoulder. As he scanned through the pages he added, "There are only a few entries. I'll read them."

January 15, 1942
    I had the strong feeling I was followed to Indianapolis. Yet I could never see anyone behind. It might well be my apprehension that is causing my nerves to see things where there is nothing.

January 16, 1942
    Flying would be so much better if we did not stop at every airport. Nevertheless, I saw no one on this plane that appears to be paying any attention to me. All eyes were on

Carole Lombard. I thought she looked tired. But she was still beautiful and gracious. I didn't ask for an autograph, but everyone else did. I felt much better when I got off the plane and hired a driver to take me to the old mining camp. As the vein played out years ago, I knew there would be no one here.

January 17, 1942

I spent the night in the office. I got up early and opted to take a walk. It was a mistake. Someone shot at me. I raced back to the office to grab the rifle my brother had left there. I was just getting the gun loaded when he forced the door. I managed to get off a shot that must have hit the man. He rolled backwards out the door. When I followed he grabbed me. I can't describe the fight. I don't remember much except that we rolled all over the ground. I felt a pain in my side at one point. Breaking away, I found a rock and as he rushed at me, I hit him. He staggered for a moment, then fell over the cliff. I should have felt remorse, but I didn't. It was only when I returned to the office I discovered the extent of my injuries. I'd been stabbed and was bleeding badly.

January 18, 1942

I'm dying. I am sure of that. As you were to meet me in the old short shaft, I have moved to it. I hope you get here before I die. Otherwise I won't be able to let you in. With Krueger on my trail, I can't take a chance on his finding the Book of Joseph. Sonnenberg, you are Lord Baltore now. I am holding out hope you can retrieve the document from its hiding place. If you don't, I have failed.

The Trinity, Creation, the Right Hand of God, and the fires of Hell can be found where the elder once made his decisions.

That was the last entry. Burke quickly studied the room. There was nothing that fit the instructions here. Grabbing a lantern, he pushed his chair back and walked out to the main shaft. Nothing there either.

Mason followed Burke into the main chamber. "What about the scroll?"

"It's not here," he replied.

"So someone got it?" Mason asked.

"Couldn't have," Cho said as she emerged from the room. "The door was still locked from the inside."

Burke once more studied the journal he was holding in his left hand. He again read the last entry. What did it mean?

Suddenly he knew.

He didn't wait for the others. Racing out of the shaft, he sprinted through the gap and out to the trail. With the two FBI agents about twenty yards behind, Burke's long strides quickly carried him back to the camp. He didn't slow up until he charged into the office. Holding the book at eye level, he looked at the far wall. This was it!

Cho was the next one inside. Her breathing was ragged as she stood there watching him.

He moved across the room and to the right side of the old stone fireplace. He began to count. "One, two, three." Holding his hand on the third stone from the edge of the structure, he counted from the ceiling. "One, two, three, four, five, six, seven."

"What did you find?" Cho asked.

"It was a code," Burke explained. "It was something a theologian or historian would understand. If Krueger found this journal, Cross figured he wouldn't get it."

"I don't either," Mason added.

"Do you have a knife?" Burke asked.

"I've got a pickax," Cho replied.

"Give it to me."

"It's back at the shaft in my pack," she said.

"Never mind," Burke said. Grabbing an old poker from the fireplace, he went to work on the mortar around the rock that was three stones from the side and seven stones from the top. As he expected, it took only a few seconds to chip away the thin layer of mortar. Locking his fingers on the top and sides of the six-by-nine-inch rock, he gave a yank. It came loose easily. He set it on the floor.

"I need a flashlight."

Mason handed him a light, and Burke shined the beam into the cavity. The hollow space was about eighteen inches deep. There was something toward the back. Reaching way in, he retrieved a roll of papers.

Moving to the table, Burke set the papers down and slowly unrolled the old documents.

Mason groaned. "They're stock certificates."

Burke had found about twenty certificates for the Cross Mining Company. The only mention of Joseph was the owner's name on each certificate—Joseph Franklin Cross.

Though he knew it was futile, Burke returned to the exposed chamber. There was nothing else there. Leaning against the wall, he contemplated his failure. He had figured out the code, but the treasure wasn't there. Who'd beaten him to the punch? It wasn't Krueger, or his grandson wouldn't still be looking. It wasn't Sonnenberg. He'd never gotten here. So who was it? Who had taken the scroll and did they have a clue as to what they'd found?

"How did you know to look behind that particular stone?" Cho asked.

Burke felt every bit a failure. "The journal. The final entry ended with the code."

He handed her the old book. Mason looked over Cho's shoulder as she turned to the final entry, which ended with: "The Trinity, Creation, the Right Hand of God, and the fires of Hell can be found where the elder once made his decisions."

"The Trinity represents Christ to most of those who would read the words," Burke explained. "Creation would also likely bring most minds to thinking about the act of creating the world. The Right Hand of God is where Jesus would sit. So it really sounds very much like a prayer or a formal closing, such as 'God bless you.' But then come the interesting words that tie it all together. Read them."

Cho read, "The fires of Hell can be found where the elder once made his decisions." She looked back at Burke. "What does that mean?"

"Look at that passage as a map in code form," Burke said as he walked toward the two agents. "That was what Cross figured Sonnenberg would do. After all, he was an expert in cracking codes that were much tougher than this one. The Trinity becomes the number three. Creation becomes seven as in the number of days God took to make the world and his day of rest. The Right Hand becomes a direction. In this case, the fires of Hell are nothing more than the fireplace. The man who ran this camp was Cross's older brother, or the elder. He would have made decisions in the office. Hence the hiding place was three rows from the right side of the fireplace stones and as God looked down from heaven, the seven would be counted from the top. That's all there is to it. But the book was not here."

"Good deductive work," Mason said, "but the stock certificates don't do us much good. Unless ... maybe they contain another riddle."

"Maybe that's it," Burke said as he set one of the room's chairs upright. He was tired and discouraged. He didn't want to have to think anymore. He didn't want to have to try to figure out anything else.

"You two stay here," Mason said. "I'll go get our stuff in the shaft."

Burke let his eyes wander over a section of the floor. Cho walked back toward the fireplace. She gathered a few ancient pieces of wood and stacked them in the hearth. "It's cold in here. And it's getting dark. We're going to have to spend the night in this drafty old building. We'll need a fire."

The dry wood immediately caught the lighter's flame. As fire spread across the very dry hunks of firewood, Cho walked into the second room and brought back an end table. Using the poker, she knocked it apart and put the pieces on top of the burning wood. Satisfied the old chimney was drafting properly, she stepped back and studied the wall. As Burke watched, she began using the poker much as he had earlier, but this time she went to work on the left side of the fireplace.

"Strange," she said. "There's no mortar here. The stone was just slid into place."

"You're not going to find anything." He sighed. "There's only one way the code can be interpreted—three, seven, and from the right."

Cho focused not on his dispiriting words but rather on an eight-by-ten-inch stone. She leaned the poker to one side against the wall, then pulled the rock, which was three inches deep, from the wall. She placed it on the floor and walked back to the table to retrieve her flashlight.

"What are you doing?" Burke asked.

With her fingers wrapped around the light, she smiled and declared, "You're not nearly as bright as you think you are."

"What do mean by that?" he asked.

She didn't answer. Instead she turned and walked back to the left side of the fireplace. Shining the light into the hole she'd just created, she reached in with her left hand and brought out a leather pouch. It was at least a foot wide.

Burke's mouth dropped open as Cho walked back to the table and set the object in front of him. "Jeff, the right hand of God would be to his right side. He would be facing us. Therefore, it would be on our left."

"Of course," he whispered. His eyes were locked on the leather pouch.

"Lisa, do you still have the metal tube? The one that had Sarah's ashes?"

"In my pack."

"Could you get it for me? It'll protect the scroll much better than this old leather pouch."

Cho nodded and went outside. When she returned, she had the tube in one hand, her pack in the other. Mason was with her, loaded down with the rest of the gear.

"You found it?" Mason asked.

"Actually," Burke said, "it was Lisa who found it. My code work left a bit to be desired. And I must emphasize the direction *left*."

"It's in amazing shape," Cho said, moving closer to look at the scroll. "What's it say?"

"I have no idea," he replied. "I barely opened it. I can tell it's Aramaic. I know nothing about that language, but Joseph would have written his book in Aramaic, so it fits. Give me the tube. We'll keep it safe in there and take it back to Dr. Briggs. He can figure out if what we've found is the real thing."

Cho and Mason were completely lost in the moment. They stood mesmerized as Burke carefully slid the document into the metal container that had held the scroll for so many years. It was home!

Burke had finally beaten Krueger to something.

STANDOFF

I suddenly find myself so glad you lived!"

Burke looked past Mason and Cho to the open door.

"Bruno." Burke's voice showed no hint of shock. It was as if the guest had arrived right on time. "I expected to see you on our way down the mountain tomorrow. If I'd have known you were going to get here this early, I would've already put dinner on the stove."

"None of you move," Krueger barked. As he did, three men clad in dark clothing entered the tiny stone building. "Get their guns," the billionaire orderered, a smile playing on his lips.

Burke watched as two of the men pushed Mason up against the wall. The third came toward Cho. She didn't move as he pulled the pistol from her belt. She continued to remain still as he roughly ran his hands over the rest of her body. Satisfied she was now unarmed, he turned back to Krueger for more instructions. As he did, Cho reached down and pulled a knife from her boot. The man standing in front of her never saw what happened. One minute he was looking toward his boss, the next he was gasping for air. Just as quickly, the gun that had been in his hand was in Cho's and she had it pointed right at Krueger's face.

"Now," she ordered, "it's your turn not to move."

If he felt fear, Krueger didn't show it. Lowering his weapon, he smiled and said, "My men have your two friends in their sights. I believe this is called a Mexican standoff."

Cho's eyes never left Krueger's as she calmly extracted her knife and let the man fall to the floor. As he struggled to find another lungful of air, Cho added, "It's not really a standoff. In a standoff we would both be assured of dying. I like my odds. Yours don't look too good.

Since this is so close to Vegas, I'll use a local expression: I'm holding all the cards."

"But your friends?" he argued.

"When I was in Special Forces, we called it collateral damage," she said. "You're the primary objective. If I take you out, then my mission has been successful. Odds are pretty good I can pick off one of your friends before they can kill me, and Clark can get the other. I'll admit that if your goons get Clark first, that's not a good thing for our side. But even if they get lucky and that happens, the victory still goes to the good guys. That would be the side I'm on."

Burke looked from Cho to Krueger. Neither showed any hint of backing down. When he considered who would blink first, he strongly doubted it would be the woman.

"No one has to die," Krueger finally acknowledged. "All I want is what Burke put in that tube. Give me that, and everyone lives."

"For the moment, that might be true," Cho replied, her gun still locked on the intruder, "but once you have the scroll, that likely means millions more will die. I can't let that happen. Besides, the scroll is not going to do you any good if you're dead, and I'd like you much better that way."

Neither was going to give up until a trigger had been squeezed. With their backs against the wall, the other hired guns were looking to Krueger to give an order. Their weapons were pointed at Burke and Mason.

Slowly raising the tube above his head, Burke said, "I seem to be the only one here who doesn't have a gun. As I'm not a threat to anyone, I'm going to carefully get out of this chair and go over to the fireplace."

Burke stepped away from the table and moved to a point to the right of the now roaring fire. When he felt the stone wall against his back, he slowly slid down to a crouching position. Lowering the tube, he popped the lid and looked back at the others.

"This is what this is all about, the *Book of Joseph*," Burke said, carefully sliding the ancient scroll out. Grasping the scroll in his right hand, he dropped the metal tube. It clanged as it landed on the old wooden planks and rolled a few feet over toward the table.

Krueger's blue eyes lit up like a homecoming bond fire. "Give it to me and you live."

"Yes." Burke smiled. "That's not what you said at the monastery. And that was just for the treasure. No, as long as the *Book of Joseph* is around, my life is pretty much worthless."

His tone suddenly much more gracious, Krueger said, "We'll work something out."

"Don't think so," Burke answered. "But we do need to talk. So have your men drop their guns. If they do, I assure you that Cho will also lower hers."

Burke looked to Krueger and then to the others to see if anyone was interested in his proposition. With no one apparently ready to make the first move, he offered an alternative.

"Fine. Then I'm going to burn it."

As he moved his hand toward the fire, Krueger barked, "Schminsky, you and Barker lower your guns."

The two hired guns immediately complied, moving three steps away from Mason. Cho remained rigid, her gun still fixed on Krueger. Burke was not surprised.

"Burke," Krueger barked, "call off the woman."

Moving the scroll away from the fire, the professor shook his head. "Not sure I can."

"We had an agreement," the billionaire said.

"Actually," Burke replied, "it was really more of a suggestion. Why don't you move to the table and take a seat in the chair. I'm going to stay where it's a bit warmer."

Krueger almost tiptoed to the table and eased himself down onto a chair. As he did, Cho, her gun still locked on its target, backed up to the wall on the other side of the fireplace. She seemed more than ready to start the fireworks.

Burke glanced up through the hole in the roof. It was almost dark. No one was going anywhere now. This might well be the longest night of his life. So, rather than spend hours silently staring at each other, he figured kicking up some conversation might help time pass.

"How'd you find us, Bruno?"

"Didn't," came the cold reply. "When Saunders saw your map,

he figured the document had to be hidden here. He assured me he'd steered you to the other peak."

"He won't be steering anyone for a while," Mason quipped. "Your mole is above the ground now."

Krueger glared at Mason.

Burke rolled the scroll in his hands, then looked at Krueger. "This scroll has caused a lot of problems." He looked down at the old document. "I'm beginning to wonder if it's worth it."

Burke was shocked when Mason was the first to jump into the debate. "Of course it is. It needs to be published. The truth needs to come out."

"You believe that?" Burke asked the agent. "I'm thinking it could upset the whole structure of faith. Consider its potential damage to the organized church. In fact, to all of Christianity."

"I know what you think it can do," Mason explained, "but in my line of work, the truth never hurt anyone who was honest."

Mason's smile appeared to cut Krueger like a sharp knife.

Unexpectedly, another opinion was added to the debate.

"It doesn't need to be published," Cho argued. "People need something to hang on to. If you take away one of the key elements of faith, that Jesus is the Son of God, then you might destroy the hope for eternal life for millions. I've seen people without hope. You look into their eyes, and there is no spark of life. When you give up faith, you lose hope, the will to fight."

Almost forgetting their dangerous situation and completely into his comfortable role as a teacher, Burke said, "Even if it means the divine birth of Christ is a lie, you don't want to reveal that information to the world for fear of the harm the truth might cause."

"Yes," Cho answered.

"What about you two guys?" Burke asked Krueger's henchmen. Neither changed expression or spoke. "Must be mutes."

Burke looked back at Krueger in an attempt to draw another voice into the mix. "The words of the father," Burke whispered, "and the secret of the lost scroll."

"Your whole life is all about history," Krueger said. "You know that what's in the scroll has to be published."

Burke shrugged. "Normally, I'd agree with you. But ... is it really important that we know every detail of every historical figure's life? Does my understanding of Kennedy and his presidency become greater if I know the details of each of his affairs? Does it matter how well he and Marilyn Monroe knew each other?"

"That isn't the same thing," Krueger argued. "The book billions believe in is a fable. Historians search for truth and expose lies."

Burke held up the scroll. "You're pretty sure of what's written here."

"Aren't you?" Krueger asked.

Burke held the scroll with both hands, rolling it casually back and forth. "I'm a historian. I never guess; I read. And as this is in a language I can't read, I have no answers now. And I'm not going to guess. But I am hungry. Mason has some food in his backpack. I think it's time for supper."

The professor studied Krueger as he sat at the table.

Mason walked across the room to where he had dropped his backpack. As he did, the two henchmen tensed their shoulders. Too late, Burke realized that supper was a bad idea. Yet the script had already been written, the plot was in motion, and it was too late to say anything.

Playing the hero, as Burke should have known he would, Mason yanked a Luger from his pack. It was one of the guns he had taken from the men at the Oakland airport. He got off two shots before the Krueger's hoods countered. In the blink of an eye, a half dozen rounds tore through the cabin. One of Krueger's men caught a round to the head. The other scored two hits to the FBI agent before racing through the door and out into the darkness. Both of Mason's shots missed their targets. It was Cho's gun that dropped the first thug and chased the other from the office.

Sensing a moment when a gun was no longer aimed in his direction, Krueger overturned the table and leaped toward Burke. The professor, his eyes still firmly locked on a crumpled Mason, was not prepared. The billionaire hit him like a linebacker tackling a wide receiver. Both men crashed into the stone wall, then slid to the floor. Stunned, Burke rolled over and dropped the scroll. Krueger reached for the scroll. His fingers were only an inch away when a bullet tore through his hand.

The billionaire looked up as Cho bore down on him. Four quick steps placed her in front of the kneeling and wounded Krueger. A kick to the chin sent him flying backward. She stood over his fallen form. When he didn't move, she whirled back to her partner.

Mason was bleeding from two wounds to the chest, but he was still conscious.

"Hate to die on a mountain," he whispered. "I'm more of a beach guy."

"You're not going to die," Burke said as he tore open the man's shirt looking for the entry wounds.

"I've got a really warm feeling." Mason sighed. "Don't think that's a good thing."

Burke didn't answer. His eyes were focused on the source of that sudden warmth. Blood was gushing from two holes in Mason's chest about an inch apart. The bullets must have torn through a lung and maybe even hit the heart. Tearing off his coat, Burke pushed it against the wounds.

"Lisa," Mason moaned.

"Don't talk," she begged him.

Burke pushed harder on the wounded man's chest. Blood soaked his coat and seeped between his fingers. Mason coughed and blood seeped from his mouth. Then his eyes became two pools of nothing. Clark Mason would never see anything again.

"Jeff." He heard Cho's voice, but he couldn't respond. Pulling his blood-soaked hands from Mason's chest, he held them out toward the woman, as if pleading with her.

She nodded. "Jeff," she said again, her voice strong and steady, "I'm going to check on the other guy. I know I caught him with at least one round. He can't get very far. You stay here while I clean up what's left."

Burke turned back to Mason. His unseeing eyes were still open. The agent had come back from a fall over a cliff, but this time he wouldn't return.

Burke stood up and saw the scroll still resting on the floor. He looked across the room at the billionaire. Krueger was just coming to. Showing amazing resiliency, the man pushed himself to his knees with his injured hand and shifted his body as if intending to close the distance between himself and the *Book of Joseph*. He didn't get far. Burke's bloody right hand caught Krueger on the left cheek. Both fell to the floor. Bone on bone may have caused both men to wince, but neither was ready to stop the battle. As they pushed to their feet, their arms found each other. Pulling and prodding, they bounced across the room, each digging blows into the other's kidneys. For a few moments the battle seemed even, but Burke finally broke free from Krueger's arms, stepped back, and unleashed a right hook that caught the billionaire on the temple. The blow knocked the bigger man out the door.

Krueger didn't try to reenter. Instead he pulled himself to his feet and stood there, waiting for Burke outside. The professor was more than willing to accept the invitation. A mad lunge caught the billionaire around the waist and slammed both men to the rocky ground. Locked together, each trying unsuccessfully to land more blows, they rolled down the steep grade toward the old mining road. A boulder finally separated them enough for Krueger to break free and retreat. Burke wasn't going to let him escape.

Pushed by a need for revenge, fueled by passion and hate deeper and hotter than the depths of hell, he got up and raced into the darkness. The professor caught up with Krueger about sixty feet down the trail. Though the night was now almost too black to make out his opponent's face, Burke managed to land two more blows. One caught the jaw, the other landed on the right ear. Krueger staggered backwards. He seemed to recover his balance for a moment, but as he turned, he stumbled. For a second, a bit of moonlight caught the billionaire's eyes. Burke saw dark empty pools. There was no more hope.

Like a tightrope walker, Krueger balanced on the edge of the trail for a few seconds, his body swaying back and forth. He almost pulled himself to safety, grabbing at a tree branch. Then, just as he seemed to gain his equilibrium, his left foot slipped over the edge. He screamed, a bloodcurdling shriek that echoed off the mountain walls behind Burke. Then Krueger was gone and the night was again silent.

Burke staggered over to where Krueger disappeared. He couldn't see where he had landed, but even in the darkness, the professor could tell it was a long way down.

He didn't know how long he had been standing there, staring down into the void, when he heard three shots fired in rapid succession.

ASHES TO ASHES

Burke stumbled back up the trail to the mining camp office. He counted three dead bodies. Cho had not returned. Was she out there bleeding to death? Or maybe she was dead!

Retrieving the Luger from the floor, Burke turned. He was determined to find her. It might be the last thing he did, but he was going to be with the woman he loved. He never got the chance to prove himself a hero.

"You've got no business with that gun," Cho said as she stepped through the door.

"You're okay!" His words were not framed as much in a question at they were by a sense of gratitude and relief.

"He didn't have a chance. Just found out I was not quite ready to quit racing or boxing yet." Her eyes locked on Mason's body. "But what difference does it make now?"

Cho looked around the room, then back at Burke. "Where's Krueger?"

"Visiting his grandfather," he replied. "He took a short step off a very steep cliff."

"So that's what I heard. I kind of wonder if real evil ever dies." She sighed. "And I have no doubt that Krueger defined evil in almost biblical terms."

Burke was exhausted and merely looked on as the small woman dragged the two dead thugs outside. Then she covered Mason's body with a blanket. After breaking up a chair and tossing the wood on the fire, she fell to her knees.

As she stared into the fire, Cho suddenly seemed very fragile. It was as if she wanted to cry but wasn't going to allow herself to break down. Once more Burke felt protective toward this woman who had come to mean so much. Except this time it wasn't about giving his life for her, it was more about giving his heart.

"You okay?" he asked. It was a stupid question. No one in this adventure was okay anymore. He and Cho might have lived through the carnage, but they were both damaged goods. They would never be the same.

She looked up at him and slowly shook her head. Her expression was drawn, her eyes moist. Barely opening her lips she whispered, "No, I'm not all right."

"Guess none of us are," he replied. "But at least it's over."

"It's not over," she said as her eyes locked on the scroll. "Not yet. What we've seen so far might just be the beginning. Imagine millions with no hope, no light, no reason to believe. Imagine a world where dying means nothing but a cold black grave. Imagine Christianity as a philosophy rather than a faith."

He was far too pragmatic and too tired to consider the future ramifications of what had transpired in this remote place, but she was spot on about tonight. Like all major wars, this battle here tonight had been waged over possessions, territory, and power. Yet even more than that, it had been a battle between good and evil. And when the smoke had settled and the bodies had been counted, the victory rang hollow.

Cho moved from the fireplace to where he sat. Falling to her knees, she rested her hands on his legs. "Jeff, I need for you to hear this and really consider it."

She paused, but only for a moment. Looking up into his green eyes, she said, "I love you." She took a deep breath. "That's not easy for me to say. In fact, I've never said those three words to anyone in my adult life. But I know as I am alive, I love you. Please believe that. And I would do almost anything for you."

Burke opened his mouth, but her finger, placed on his lips, stopped him just like it had the previous night.

Rising to her feet, she brought her face to his and looked into his eyes. Her grim, resolute expression was suddenly not that of a woman in love but of someone she hadn't been in more than a decade—a soldier. She whispered, "I can't be anything other than the way I am. I don't expect you to understand that. But at least accept it."

Without a word, she scooped up the scroll, and with four stiff and purposeful steps, walked to the fireplace. Burke never had time to react, much less act. Cho tossed the document into the fire. As the flames consumed it, tears ran down her face. It was as if when that document turned to ashes, so had she.

Burke deliberately pulled himself from the chair and moved behind the woman. He stared over her shoulder into the fire. They both watched until the last piece of the scroll was nothing but hot ash.

"If it took that act for you to tell me you loved me," he whispered, "we'll let it burn."

She turned to look into his eyes. She was no longer a soldier or an FBI agent. Now she was a woman, a woman he knew he loved and could never forget. He knew he could never let her go again.

LOSS

There were two twelve-hour days of debriefing that followed. By the time Burke finished, Agent Greg Saunders was languishing in a jail cell and Burke was grieving for a man he hadn't gotten to know well enough. He looked out a tenth-story window. It was morning in Las Vegas. Though not as busy as it had been at midnight, when he'd shut the shades and gone to bed, there were still people everywhere outside. Thousands thought they were risking it all, but they weren't. Burke was now very aware of what risking it all meant. There was nothing entertaining about the gambling he'd done. The stakes were too high and the losses too great.

Taking a sip of a Coke, his thoughts turned away from an adventure finished to contemplate another that had not really started. He hadn't seen Cho for two days. They hadn't even ridden in the same FBI car for debriefings. He didn't know where she was and had no way of connecting with her. It seemed she'd vanished from his life as quickly as she had entered it. He was as alone as he had been in the days before Columbo walked into the library. The only difference was that the loneliness now hurt worse than anything he'd ever known. He'd finally beaten Krueger, and there was nothing to celebrate.

As he leaned against the wall, a solitary thought crept into the deepest recesses of his mind. Once more he'd been done in by his uncontrollable curiosity. And while it hadn't killed him, it might as well have. His insatiable need to know had been fueled by an ancient piece of parchment. There had been so much death over a document few had read.

In the past, rationalizing had worked to clear his conscience. That scapegoat was still at work this morning. It was telling him it was all

Baltore's fault. The priest should have destroyed the book as ordered. If he had, Columbo and Mason would still be alive and Burke would be teaching a class this morning instead of pacing a hotel room eaten up with the greatest sense of loss he'd ever known. Yet in truth, it wasn't Baltore's fault or Columbo's or even his. It was just fate! Or was it something greater than that?

A knock on the door ended his contemplation of questions that had no answers. As the only ones who knocked were the FBI's finest and they all had keys, Burke didn't cross the room. He simply turned to see who would be walking through the door this time.

"I've come to tell you a couple of things," Agent Justin Smythe announced in a flat tone.

"Good news or bad?" the professor asked.

"Some really good news," Smythe replied. "And then some better news."

"Shoot."

"Okay. And this one sounds stranger than it is. The search team found Krueger's body. The fall didn't kill him. He crawled about a hundred feet down the trail. Probably took him more than six hours to make it that far. His back was broken. One tough bird."

Burke shook his head. "Just so he's dead. Wonder who will take over his business empire."

"He has a son," Smythe said.

Another generation, Burke thought. Would it be as evil as the others, as filled with anger and rage?

"The other good news is that we're all finished with you. You can leave anytime you want. And the old Buick is yours."

The agent smiled, as if the car transfer was funny. He tossed the car keys on a table and walked to the door. As he was turning the knob, he looked back at Burke. "One more thing, Dr. Burke. Lisa Marie Cho has two weeks' leave. She's packed and in the lobby."

The door closed and Burke rolled the agent's last line over in his head. The ball was in his court.

Burke quickly picked up the few things he had and stuffed them in a bag. It was time to discover his future. And, if all worked out the way he hoped, it would also be time to tell Cho the truth.

FATE

Cho was sitting in a chair that faced the Strip when Burke emerged from the elevator. She was dressed in jeans, running shoes, and a bright red T-shirt. Her hair was pulled back, held in place with a St. Louis Cardinals baseball cap. She'd applied just enough makeup so that her dark eyes seemed to jump out at him.

"Where you heading?" she asked as he approached. Her tone seemed casual, but it had a hint of insecurity.

"I'm getting out of here," he said, his eyes still locked on hers.

"Got room for one more?" Her voice was a bit unsteady, unsure.

He didn't answer — not with his voice. He just hoped his face told her all she needed to know. He leaned over and kissed her, then wordlessly picked up her two bags and headed toward the door. She followed.

"Where we going?" Cho asked.

"Wherever Fate guides us," Burke answered, tossing the bags in the trunk. He opened the driver's door and stepped back. Cho slid across the front bench seat and Burke got in. As he started the car, it felt as though his life was restarting as well. They headed northwest. He reached down and turned on the radio, spinning the dial until he locked onto a classic country station that was playing "Happy Trails to You."

Eight more songs followed — Shania Twain, Alan Jackson, Elvis Presley, Martina McBride, Diamond Rio, Taylor Swift, Reba McEntire, and Barbara Mandrell — and neither one said a word. Cho had fired up her iPad, but then put it away. Only after they'd left the city far behind did she break the silence.

"Why Fate?"

"What?" His eyes left the black surface of the lonely two-lane state highway to glance at his passenger.

"You said Fate," she said with a smile that grabbed his heart. "According to the Google search on my iPad, Fate's about an hour from here on a road that no one travels anymore. Seems a US highway bypassed it by miles decades ago."

"You're serious!" Burke laughed, turning back to the asphalt ahead. "There really is a Fate, Nevada? I was talking about the car. I named the old Buick—the car—'Fate.'"

She laughed. "Well, if you and I are beginning a life together, then let's do it right. Let's take Fate to Fate and see what it has for us. We can get there by making a right at the next intersection."

MICKEY'S

In their first thirty minutes on the highway they only saw one truck, and it was headed in the other direction. Finally about twenty miles from their planned destination, Cho saw the first signs that Fate might actually be a real place and not just a word on a map.

"Look."

Burke glanced to the right side of the road. There was a faded four-by-six-foot sign promising good food, good times, and good memories at Mickey's Roadhouse and Museum.

"I'm hungry. Let's hope it's still open."

A series of signs, all in the same state of neglect, warned travelers they were getting closer to Mickey's. Each one also promised great things if travelers made the stop. Ten miles after the first sign begged them to pull over at Mickey's, they finally saw Fate on the horizon. It looked small from a distance and appeared even smaller as they passed the well-worn city limit sign. The whole community consisted of seven weatherered clapboard houses — all in need of repair — a couple of deserted stores, and the roadhouse. They weren't surprised to see that its paint was peeling and there were no cars in the parking lot. Still, Mickey's appeared to be open.

Two gas pumps were out front, along with a Coke machine and a newspaper rack by the main door. A man in a ladder-back chair sat beside a vending machine. He looked as dusty as everything else at Mickey's.

"Still want to stop?" Burke asked.

"You said you were hungry." Cho's reply hinted at a determination to test the promises she'd read on the road signs. After taking a deep breath, she added, "Unless you are up to killing something and cooking it over a fire, I don't see you have much choice."

Cho was right. In this part of the desert, there might not be anything else for an hour or even more.

Still not sure what Fate had in store for them, Burke pulled up to the gas pumps, shut the car off, and got out. As he considered what the desert must be like in the summer, he was suddenly glad it wasn't August. Really glad.

"Howdy folks," the fifty-something man said as he slowly worked himself off the chair. "You lost?"

"What makes you think that?" Burke asked.

"Because strangers don't come here 'cept when they're lost," the man replied.

The professor grinned. "No, we just had an urge to take the road less traveled."

As Cho got out, the proprietor laughed. "Well, you two chose the right one. What's you need?"

"You still feed folks here?" Cho asked.

"Sure do," he replied. "My wife's a great cook if you keep it simple."

"Then we'll fill up the Buick and fill ourselves up too," Burke said.

"You go on in. I'll take care of the car. When I finish, I'll join you. Just tell Suzy what you want and have a seat anywhere."

Burke opened the door and glanced around the inside of the diner. It was apparent that Mickey's was stuck in the past. It reminded the professor of the place Humphrey Bogart and Bette Davis had frequented in a movie called *The Petrified Forest*. The signs on the wall, the old green booths, the neon Dr Pepper clock, and the cash register were all from the 1940s or before. Even the unmatched salt and pepper shakers looked vintage. The old wooden floor was so worn by thousands of feet that had come in and gone out that it bowed in by the counter. To his left was a small stage that he could imagine had hosted bands.

"What can I get you?"

Burke saw a jovial, heavyset blonde coming through a swinging door behind the counter. "Suzy" was embroidered on her stained apron. She was probably fifty, but her weathered skin made her appear older. Still the lilt in her voice and the beaming smile indicated she was not just resolved with her lot in life, but enjoying her life.

"What do you suggest?" Cho asked.

"A steak sandwich on wheat with fries."

"Make it two with a couple of Cokes," Cho answered as she headed to a booth against the back wall. After looking at the choices on the jukebox, Burke slid in beside her.

"So this is Fate," he said, not expecting an answer.

"Used to be called Faith," Suzy announced as she approached with their drinks. "Then, when the new highway gave folks a shorter way to go to Vegas—that was about 1963—Mickey changed the name to Fate."

"Mickey?" Burke asked, looking out the window at the man servicing their car. "Boy, he sure doesn't look old enough to be making decisions like that in 1963."

"Oh, no, not John." She laughed and set the glasses down in front of them. "His grandfather's name was Mickey. He started this place. And then Jake, his son, John's father, took it over. John and I've been running it for almost thirty years. Don't make anything now, but there was a time this was a happening place. I've got pictures that show this diner packed. And it always was until the traffic went farther north. Things have gotten slower every year since then. About the only folks who come in now are those few locals who buy their gas and groceries. We stay open for them and because we like it here. The desert's our home and this place is paid for."

"What about the museum?" Cho asked.

"That hasn't been open since the sixties," she explained. "John's been trying to sell the displays for decades. Nobody's much interested in owning stuffed critters and pieces of fool's gold. He still keeps it clean, hoping to find a buyer for the junk. You ought to get him to show it to you while I rustle up your grub. It's kind of fun, if you're into stuff from another age."

"I think we'll pass." Burke smiled.

"Suit yourself," Suzy replied as she headed back toward the kitchen. The woman had just disappeared behind the swinging door when her husband walked in.

"Suzy get your order?" he asked.

Burke nodded.

"Where you from?"

"Midwest," Burke replied.

"Come to Vegas to gamble?"

"Well," Cho answered, "we kind of did, but not in the casinos. Up on a mountain."

"Climbers? My grandfather was a climber. He loved it. Got to be in good shape to do that." John slid into the other side of the booth. "Hope you don't mind. Don't get to talk to strangers much. Can I ask what you all do for a living?"

"I teach history," Burke explained. "I'm a professor at the University of Illinois."

A huge smile crossed the owner's face. "I got something to show you then. My grandfather built this place, and he collected everything. He was always on the lookout for more stuff. He'd buy anything. He went to ghost towns, closed-up gas stations, and even bought equipment out of shutdown mines. He came up with some interesting stuff in his museum. We got a few minutes, why don't you come look. As a teacher, I think you'd enjoy it. It's like American history come to life. Besides, I just cleaned the place up yesterday and need to show it off."

"Well," Burke replied, "We—"

Cho cut him off. "Think it might be fun."

"I'll get the key," John said. With the speed of a track star, he got out of the booth, rushed across the diner, and disappeared into the kitchen.

"Why did you do that?" Burke asked.

"It means something to him," Cho replied, "and we're not in any hurry anyway. Let's tempt fate."

"Your puns are getting weaker," Burke said. Yet it wasn't the play on words that bugged him. He had little use for real museums, much less roadside attractions. If he wanted to view history, he found what he needed on digs or in books. Yet if Cho yearned to take a gander, as the locals would say, then he would take a look.

They met John at the front door. He guided them across the gravel parking lot to an old stone building. It looked to be about four thousand square feet. The front window displayed a stuffed mountain lion, a miner's hat, a prospector's pan, and an ancient Magnolia Oil sign. As John turned the lock, a bell, still attached to the door on the inside, rang. Then with a single flip of a light switch, Mickey's Roadside Museum was once more open for business.

Like the inside of the diner, it seemed to be caught in another time. As Burke made a quick study of one man's treasure, John began his well-rehearsed lecture.

"In this display case, you will see some artifacts from local Indian tribes. Some of those pots are more than five hundred years old. Note the arrowheads. We have over five hundred. The next case is filled with guns that won the West. Study that Remington. I'm betting that it killed a lot of buffalo a hundred and thirty years ago."

Cho peered through the case at the antique firearms. Burke moved over to a display on a large oak table across the room. Behind the table was a large bookshelf, and above the shelf was a poster-sized framed portrait of Carole Lombard. In one of the bookshelves was another photo, this one of a distraught-appearing Clark Gable. Burke's recent study had familiarized him with the events, but John was more than ready to fill in any details the professor might have missed.

"That photo of Gable was taken after the plane crash that killed his movie actress wife," John explained. "He came to the mountain as quickly as he could after receiving the news. He was at the base of Mt. Potosi, but I don't think they let him go to the crash site. My grandfather was there too. He was on the search team. The stuff on that table came from the plane. The big piece is a part of one of the props. That whole section over there is what my grandfather called his Mt. Potosi display."

Burke glanced through a few plane parts, a partially charred book, and a TWA pilot's hat. There also were four yellowed newspapers detailing the events of the tragedy. Just beyond those framed newspapers were displays probably taken from the Cross Mining Camp. The items included lanterns, picks, samples of ore, and even a few photos of the camp when it was in full operation.

"When did he get this stuff?" Burke asked, pointing to the mining paraphernalia.

"My grandfather kept going back to the mountain for months after the plane crash," John explained. "When he got all the things he could from the crash, he made his way over to the camp. The place had been closed down for only a couple of years. So a lot of stuff was still there. There was one really strange thing he found at the Cross camp. Never did know what to make of it. So he just dumped it in a case with some old maps and stuff. It had some kind of weird writing on it."

"Do you know where he found it?" Burke asked, suddenly much more interested in the museum and its wares.

"Because of how weird it was, I asked him that very question," John said. He leaned up against the gun case and folded his arms. "Grandpa made up a lot of stories. He had a great imagination. You never knew if what he was saying was real or not. So you might take this with a grain of salt. He told me he found it behind a stone in the wall at the mining office. One of them stones was loose. So he pulled it out and there it was. Couldn't read it, of course."

"We were just at that same mining camp," Burke said.

"Oh, I haven't been there in years. What's the camp look like now?" John asked.

"Not much left," Burke replied. "The only building still standing is the office where your grandfather found the paper with the weird writing on it."

"Well, Grandpa took the thing, but got worried that the company might want it back. So a few weeks later, he went back up there and put the leather case back in the hole and sealed it up again. But he just couldn't part with the scroll. Still, he was so scared he'd get nabbed for a theft, he didn't display the thing for more than twenty years. By the time he felt it was safe to put it out for visitors to see, the highway had bypassed this place and no one came to the museum anymore.

So he tossed it in the map pile and pretty much forgot about it. Told me once he thought it was some kind of Indian legend or something."

"John," Burke said, "could you show it to me?"

"Sure."

The small man walked to a far wall and opened an old rolltop desk. He moved several maps aside until he found what he was looking for. Picking it up, he walked back over to Burke. "Sure love to know what this says. I've never seen anything like it, but I've heard some Indians had their own language and stuff. Maybe it's Mayan."

"Let me take a look at it."

The professor carefully unrolled a small portion of the scroll. One quick glance at the writing on the thin leather document told him all he needed to know.

"Can you read it?" John asked.

"No," Burke admitted as he carefully rerolled the document. "But I do know a man who can. Would you be interested in selling it?"

"Not by itself," John replied. "Haven't sold any single item out of this place. I have one man who wants that old Elvis sign advertising his first appearance in Vegas. I wouldn't sell that either. Sorry, but nothing goes out by itself. It might sound strange, but I know Grandpa wouldn't have wanted the stuff separated. But I'll sell you the whole lot. And whoever buys it has to move the whole shebang out of the building. You see, I'd kind of like to turn this place into a real home for me and Suzy. We've always lived in the back of the diner. She works hard. She deserves a place of her own. Away from where we work."

Burke glanced around at the mishmash of junk that surrounded him. "How much for the lot?" Burke asked.

"Price is $40,000."

"How about $20,000?" Burke countered.

Cho was still studying a display on the other side of the museum. She had no idea a deal was going down.

"Low as I'll go is $30,000."

"Okay," Burke replied. "Is there a bank around here?"

"The bank's about forty miles up the road," John said.

"I'll have the money for you in about three hours."

"If you've got the money," John assured him, "it's a deal."

Cho walked over just as the two men were shaking hands. "What just happened?"

"Your man just bought all this stuff," John explained.

"What!"

Burke smiled. "I'll explain after lunch."

THE TRUMP CARD

The eighty-mile round trip and the time spent in a branch of Wells Fargo took three hours and forty minutes. To Burke it seemed much longer. It then took another fifteen minutes for the owner of Mickey's to create a proper bill of sale. When the deal was finally done, both men looked happy.

"John," Burke said as they once more toured the museum, "I'll take this document with me and send for the rest."

"Whatever you say. The stuff is yours now. Just remember to have it all picked up within the sixty days."

They were five miles down the road before Cho posed her question. "I know you have lots of money and you like history, but why did you do that?"

"You mean buy the museum stuff?"

"What else would I be talking about?"

"To get the scroll Mickey took from the mine office," Burke said.

"I burned the scroll," Cho said. "I burned the only copy of the *Book of Joseph*."

Burke smiled. "Actually, you didn't. What you burned was a document that looked like an old biblical scroll. Briggs used it as a prop in his lectures. I once borrowed it and never gave it back to him. I brought it on the trip in case Krueger and I got into another game of poker. I was going to use it to run a bluff."

"But the leather case I found. What was in it?"

"Nothing," Burke said. "It was empty, just the way it was when

Mickey put it back in the wall after he had taken the scroll out. I put the scroll from Briggs in it when you went to get the tube."

"Why didn't you tell me?" Her voice reflected a mixture of anger and pain.

"Too dangerous," Burke said. "Krueger wasn't going to stop hounding us until he thought the *Book of Joseph* was destroyed. So I was going to burn the scroll I'd brought as a decoy. I was going to make a big deal out of doing it, make sure he believed it was destroyed. I had to make it look like it was the hardest decision of my life. So I had to take my time. If I didn't, he wouldn't believe the scroll was actually gone. Tragically, Mason went for the gun."

"But even after Krueger went over the cliff," she said, sounding both hurt and angry, "you let me believe that what I threw into the fire was the real scroll."

"I had to. If anyone knew that the scroll had not been destroyed, that the search would continue, the FBI would still be all over it. I couldn't let that happen. Way too many had already died for this relic. It had to stop. And I don't want you getting the FBI involved now either."

"Would you have kept looking?"

Her question was really much deeper than it sounded. In fact, their whole relationship now hinged on his answer. So it was time to be bluntly honest.

"When you told me you loved me, and you burned what you thought was the scroll in spite of your feelings for me, you put your principles above your own desires. I was going to follow your example. My search was over. I mean that. If the town of Fate hadn't stepped in ... Isn't it strange that when I gave up on my quest to find the *Book of Joseph*, I found it. And when I gave up on love, I fell in love."

He let her chew on those words. "I don't know how good you are at reading between the lines, but I just told you I love you."

THE WORDS

It was after nine the next morning when the exhausted couple walked into the office of Dr. Alexander Briggs at the University of Illinois. Thanks to a call made the night before, he was expecting them. It was obvious the older man had not slept.

"Hard to believe you found it," the religion professor said as he looked at the metal tube Burke was holding in his hands. A nervous Briggs added, "I'm guessing it's in there?"

"And," Burke replied with a smile, "it is in remarkable shape. It was written on some kind of leather. It has withstood the passage of time very well."

In a whisper, Briggs said, "Let's take a look."

Burke handed the man the tube that had been passed from one Lord Baltore to another until the time it was used to hold Sarah Meadows' ashes. Sitting at his mahogany desk, one that had once been in the office of Joseph Franklin Cross, Briggs lovingly ran the fingers of his right hand over the tube's side. He then carefully pulled the top away from the body and set it on the desktop. Peering in, he got his first look at the words of the father. Moving the tube to one side, he retrieved gloves from his desk. Only after pulling them on did he gently remove the scroll.

His brown eyes afire with curiosity, Briggs unrolled the document. His eyebrows shot upward as he studied the first few words. Then he nodded and said, " 'These are my words and he was my son.' That's how it begins."

Briggs said nothing more. Instead he turned his full attention to the text.

Sensing nothing further would be coming for a while, Burke sat down in a chair in front of the old desk and picked up a copy of *Theology Today*. Cho stood behind him, her hands on his shoulders. Neither said a word as the religion professor carefully went through the document, occasionally pausing to scribble notes on a legal pad. The old eight-day clock on the bookshelf behind the desk ticked away the seconds. Though the hands proved only twenty minutes had passed since Briggs had last spoken, it seemed much, much longer.

The clock tolled the hour of ten. Briggs leaned back in his chair and rubbed his eyes. For another sixty seconds he seemed lost in thought. Finally he turned his attention back to his guests. The mystery that had begun almost twenty centuries earlier was going to be revealed.

"If this is real, and carbon dating and a myriad of other tests will be required to prove that fact," Briggs began, his tone serious and reserved, "this book would be one of the shortest in the Bible. It is probably only a bit longer than Jude. Because it is so personal, because the words in this text might have been written by the man who raised Jesus ... if proven true ... it is one of the most powerful things I have ever read."

"Alex," Burke asked, "what did Joseph write that made the church leaders decide the book had to be destroyed? Was he the biological father of Jesus?"

"No, the writer makes no such claim. In fact he states very clearly he was not the biological father of Jesus. Mary was with child when they were married. This book refutes nothing that is found in the Bible. It is more about Joseph's own feelings of inadequacy than anything else."

"Inadequacy?" Cho asked. "What do you mean by that?"

"It's not what I mean," Briggs explained, "but what Joseph felt. He had all kinds of doubts as to his role in this grand plan. He admitted in his words, written by his hand in the short book, especially early on, that he couldn't fully believe that Jesus was God's Son. Yet he was so devoted to Mary, he put his faith in what she told him. And in that way, it is a book about the ups and downs of faith. In a sense, it is very modern. It expresses some of the same doubts I find in my own life and raises some of my own questions."

"Interesting," Burke said, "but there has to be more." His response was more of a hopeful man than a scholar.

Briggs nodded and pointed to the scroll. "The rest of the words on this document tell us that while he loved his adopted son, he never felt he measured up as a father. There are two stories from the boy's childhood we haven't heard before and a new miracle of healing from early in Jesus' ministry. But over half of the short book dwells on the crucifixion. That is what is so moving and so riveting. When Joseph watched Jesus being nailed to the cross, when he saw his wife's incredible grief and anguish, he thought he was somehow to blame. He felt he had done something wrong. In other words, he was all but destroyed by his inability to change a thing. I think we can imagine that feeling, but until you read about these events through a father's eyes, I'm not sure you can fully appreciate it. The pain he felt was beyond what I can fathom."

Briggs wiped tears from his eyes. He looked back at the scroll and tapped his fingers on the desk. It was as if he'd been transported back two thousand years and was at the cross.

He finally said, "If this is a forgery, then the person who wrote it must have been very close to Joseph. I pray testing will prove these are the real words of the carpenter who raised Jesus."

Burke felt Cho's fingers dig into his shoulders. He thought she too was trying to picture Joseph at Calvary. For her, Joseph's writing about his helplessness at not being able to stop his son's death was perhaps a reminder of her own feelings in the mining camp office, when she couldn't stop the the man who shot Mason. Cho likely believed she'd let Mason down.

"Naturally," Briggs continued, "the early church leaders would not have wanted Joseph to show any doubts. In the Gospels, he was framed by the writers of the time as a man who gladly accepted his task and then faded into the background. Only through his own words do we see the truth. He would have taken Jesus' place if he could have. Not understanding what was happening and what was to come, he would have prevented the execution that launched the Christian faith. A true father's love."

Briggs looked down at his notes, reviewing what he had written.

He looked up. "Today we would understand what this man felt, but back then they didn't. So if not for Baltore, we would not have this fascinating look at a very human father wrestling with events concerning the Son of God that were far beyond his understanding or control."

"Does it mention the resurrection?" Cho asked.

"No," Briggs said. "This was written the night Jesus died on the cross. Nothing was added later."

"So this story will not do what Krueger wanted. It won't create a wedge in church doctrine," Burke said.

Briggs shook his head. "In fact, the secrets found in this scroll might bring an even deeper understanding of the way faith works for all of us. Like Joseph, we must accept what we can't see and pray that what we accept is the truth."

"Krueger would have been so disappointed, so angry," Burke noted. "This time, he really did lose."

Briggs carefully rolled up the scroll and placed it in the metal tube. He handed it back to Burke.

After the couple left his office, the older man sat down to think about what he'd just read. He was soon lost in thought.

Holding hands, the two walked out of the building and into the fall sunshine. For Lisa Marie Cho and Jeff Burke, one quest had ended, but another adventure was just beginning.

Farraday Road

Ace Collins, Bestselling Author

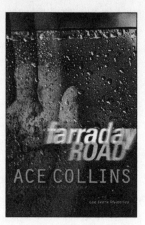

A quiet evening ends in murder on a muddy mountain road.

Local attorney Lije Evans and his beautiful wife, Kaitlyn, are gunned down. But the killers don't expect one of their victims to live. After burying Kaitlyn, Lije is on a mission to find her killer — and solve a mystery that has more twists and turns than an Ozark-mountain back road.

When the trail of evidence goes cold, complicated by the disappearance of the deputy who found Kaitlyn's body at the scene of the crime, Lije is driven to find out why he and his wife were hunted down and left for dead along Farraday Road. He begins his dangerous investigation with no clues and little help from the police. As he struggles to uncover evidence, will he learn the truth before the killers strike again?

Swope's Ridge

Ace Collins, Bestselling Author

September 12, 2001. Four members of the Klasser family are found dead outside Dallas, Texas. In the wake of 9/11, the Klassers' neighbor, Omar Jones—an American citizen of Arab descent—is convicted of their murder.

A month before Jones' execution, attorney Lije Evans searches for evidence that will prove the man innocent. But Evans' quest goes deeper than solving one crime. He is determined to find the secret behind the dark history of sleepy Swope's Ridge—and how it ties into his wife's murder.

Interlocking mysteries lead Evans and his team to the battlegrounds of former Nazi Germany, the dirt roads of Kansas, and a rusty cargo ship in the Gulf of Mexico. Along the way, they discover a secret that offers the promise of great power—and the greatest temptation they've ever faced.

In the second book of the Lije Evans Mysteries series, bestselling author Ace Collins immerses readers in an intricate and deadly international plot. Racism, betrayal, and death-defying escapes compound an adventure that knows no bounds in this harrowing novel for suspense lovers everywhere.

Available in stores and online!

Turn Your Radio On

The Stories behind Gospel Music's All-Time Greatest Songs

Ace Collins, Bestselling Author

Turn Your Radio On tells the fascinating stories behind gospel music's most unforgettable songs, including "Amazing Grace," "The Battle Hymn of the Republic," "He Touched Me," "I'll Fly Away," "Were You There?" and many more. These are the songs that have shaped our faith and brought us joy. You'll find out:

- What famous song traces back to a sailor's desperate prayer.
- What Bill Gaither tune was recorded by Elvis Presley in 1969—and won a Grammy.
- What song was born during a carriage ride through Washington, D.C., at the onset of the Civil War.

Turn Your Radio On is an inspiring journey through the songs that are part of the roots of our faith today.

Available in stores and online!